Pillars

By Claire Theriot Mestepey

© 2022 v4

Dedicated to my muse and my love, Bob

And Donna and Pat for your continuous support and pretending to love it...

Chapter 1

Madeline Jourdain has recently moved from her hometown, Houston, Texas, to New Orleans, Louisiana, for a paid Internship at a new art gallery. Not in her wildest dreams could she have imagined starting such a fantastic position at the young age of 22, a week after graduating with a liberal arts degree.

The last few weeks are a blur. Madeline, of course, received a standing ovation at graduation. She felt beet red, humiliated. In a wheelchair, you receive applauds for the dumbest stuff. The only way she got through it was to lock eyes with Jane Summers, who was sitting behind her parents, as instructed. This gave Madeline the courage to smile at the well-meaning but patronizing crowd. Her parents received her beaming smile as a sign of excitement. No one ever suspected that the reason she looked so giggly was that Jane was standing up behind her parents, rolling her eyes, doing a mock golf clap. No one on earth will ever understand Madeline Jourdain better as she winked at Jane, and their eyes kissed.

Madeline Jourdain knew she should be more gracious about these things. It had been a long road getting here from being an abandoned baby found in the back parking lot in a church in a tiny town in Louisiana. The small parish priest, Peter's oldest and dearest friend, asked if he and his wife would foster this abandoned baby. That was that. Her adopted father, Peter, although she never thought of him that way, says she was their serendipitous angel. And even if she was born on the other side of the world, they would have found their daughter. Madeline has never considered searching for her birth parents. Not even for a second, Linda Vu Jourdain, adopted mother sent from heaven, was her mama.

Linda was a very loving but stern mother. Yet, she had a dry wit that could send Madeline into hysterical laughter. She was fiercely protective, never allowing Madeline to be treated differently, even though her daughter was in a wheelchair. And to Peter's dismay, Linda and Madeline bonded over food and shopping, as often as schedules would allow. These Mother and daughter dates fizzled out during the high school years. Still, they made a strong comeback during Madeline's college career.

Bed, Bath, and Beyond, kind of their jam. Linda has taken her on a shopping spree for the last four years before moving Madeline into her dorms. The move to New Orleans should have felt routine, but somehow this felt bigger, not just because college was downtown and her Internship was in a different state. Something was pulling Madeline East.

Luckily the Internship came with a furnished apartment. Caravanning two cars from Houston to New Orleans was a simple move. Mostly clothes, kitchen stuff, and art supplies. And no one ever knew that Madeline played sad songs for the entire drive down I-10, sobbing. Knowing that this moved ended a chapter that did not have a happily ever after.

The apartment was a smudge bigger than her dorm room but felt like a palace to Madeline. It had three rooms counting the kitchen and the bathroom/closet combo. The main area was about 700 square feet, cute rugs defined the kitchen and living area. A futon faced a tiny tv that looked 15 years old. Linda made Madeline promise to make her bed every night, including fresh linen. Peter smirked, knowing this was unlikely, but a mother could dream. The broken brick walls made the tiny, very ordinary efficiency apartment feel magical. The front door opened into a small courtyard.

For a second, Madeline dreaded trying to get into the bathroom in her wheelchair, even though her employer guaranteed everything she needed would be accessible. Because it did help on at least a spiritual level, Madeline held her breath as she rolled into the small but oddly large bathroom. Somehow her wheels did not even come close to touching the doorframe.

Peter inspected every inch of the apartment, frowning at the number of deadbolts on the door, knowing his daughter would lose interest after one or two clicks. He immediately researched getting an alarm. Madeline smiled and nodded, knowing this was one battle she should not even express an opinion on.

Madeline twirled in her new apartment, giggling like she was drunk the second Peter and Linda left. Of course, her folks wanted to stay longer, to help her really settle in. She somehow convinced them to return in a month when they all could enjoy the city. Madeline said she had to get to work immediately, and on their next visit, her mom could take her shopping for bathroom stuff. This seemed to appeased mom, a little more than it should have.

To ease the guilt of sending her parents home early, Madeline would go into the gallery in the morning for a few hours just to soak in the vibe. Then she sort of had a week off, and Jane and Steven were coming up for a few days the minute Peter and Linda headed back to Houston. Madeline was just glad she was not stuck in a 6-hour car ride with neither the departing nor the arriving visitors. Even though they were her four most favorite people in the universe, they were most enjoyable when separated.

Madeline Claire Jourdain is 22 years old. Her birthday is celebrated on October 22nd. The priest found her when she was a few days old, and since she was four, Madeline has persuaded her dad, Peter, into celebrating her birth week, in case they were off by a few days.

Peter and Linda headed to Louisiana the day after Father Michael called to pick up their baby girl. It was truly textbook, love at first sight. Father Michael had warned that the baby looked to have special needs. And for the past 24 hours, that is all the couple could talk about. Could they love and support a child with a disability? Would that be all that they saw when they looked at the baby?

The second that Father Michael put baby Madeline in Linda's arms, their world changed. Linda could not stop smiling, and Peter kissed her tiny fingers a hundred times. And that was that.

For the next 5 years, Peter, Linda, and Madeline visited 20 doctors and specialists in four countries. They also visited different historic churches and supposedly sacred places where miracles had taken place. Somewhere in a dusty album, there is a picture of young Madeline in a wheelchair at the Marian shrine of Our Lady of Lourdes in France. In front of a row of crutches, the cured had left. This was the only family picture ever taken that made Madeline extremely sad.

Doctors spoke in different accents and speeds. Some expressed empathy, too many were blunt and dismissive. One even suggested Madeline was just extremely lazy and stubborn. Well, ok, he was half right...

Overall, the consensus was the same; besides being paralyzed from the waist down, Madeline was one of the healthiest kids they had ever seen. But even with the hundreds of scans, MRI's, blood tests, and x-rays from a million different positions, no one could explain why she could not walk.

On Madeline's 7th birthday, she received the best gift ever. Her parents promised her that aside from wellness checkups, they were done. She was their perfect miracle, as is, no questions asked. And for a very long time, this fairy tale kept away her demons late at night.

*

There was a knock on the door early the next morning; luckily, Madeline had been awake for hours. She did not sleep well on her first night in her new apartment in her new city. Her lack of rem sleep was a mixture of nervousness, really weird dreams, and maybe she missed her mom, oh the horrors!

"Hey Madeline," The light knocked at the door came with a familiar voice. "It's Danny Boudreaux, from NL Foundation." She rushed to the door, cursing the 4 locked deadbolts that her father stood outside, impatiently waiting to hear the clicks before they headed back to Houston the night before.

"Finally, we meet in person." Madeline opened the door and was pleasantly surprised. She had been talking to Danny almost every day for the last few months. He oversaw the foundation that hired her to open the new art gallery. He was instrumental in finding her apartment and mentioned he looked forward to having a new neighbor. She knew he was also part owner in a hole-in-the-wall restaurant across the street from her new home. He, however, neglected to mention how gorgeous he was. Looking back, this may have been a very good thing.

"Umm, you knew I was in a wheelchair, right?" Madeline suddenly felt self-conscious. Why was this man staring at her? Like almost stalker-like?

At least most of her boxes were still packed. Steven and Jane could help her make a quick exit back to Houston if needed.

"No," Danny started backtracking, which restored the cuteness and safety factor.

Madeline grinned again. He was leaning against the tiny bar that separated the kitchen from the living area. Although she didn't focus on his voice during the hundreds of phone calls over the last month, Madeline quickly found a new appreciation for it. His voice was deep but friendly. Which kind of matched his three-piece suit. She really didn't know what to expect.

It made sense that he was wearing a suit since Danny was an attorney and board member of the NL Foundation that hired her. He just sounded less business-like on the phone. He stood about 5'11. It was a strange knack that Madeline had; she was very accurate in telling people's height. Probably because she had always felt short in her wheelchair.

Danny Boudreaux had salt and peppered hair, a little premature for his age, maybe late twenties, but it fit him. His eyes were hazel, and his skin more olive than white. He probably went to the gym as an obligation, not as a fun outing. He was just very attractive physically, and his warm personality added to his charm.

"No. Yes... What I meant was," Danny grinned from embarrassment. "Did I mention I'm an eloquent speaker in court? I apologize; yes, I knew you were in a wheelchair. You are not what I envisioned during our conversations, you're stunning. I'm sorry. I don't know why I blurted that out."

"Coffee?" Madeline offered, breaking the awkward silence, feeling herself blush. Luckily the coffee maker was the only thing unpacked and ready for duty.

"Coffee." And except for one more very unexpected moment later that week, they immediately talked like they knew each other all their lives. There was something about him that felt like home.

Danny finished his 2nd cup of coffee, apologizing for the 4th time that he had to be in court most of the day, ruining his "Welcome to New Orleans tour extravaganza." But he did offer to be Madeline's personal tour guide that weekend. Madeline debated sharing him with Jane but figured she owed her after what Jane is currently doing and figured it might make her less grumpy. Danny seemed pleased that there would be a group and promised a good time would be had by all. Madeline was less certain, but stranger things have happened.

On a piece of paper, Danny jotted down directions to the art gallery, which was only three blocks away, and the alarm code. And handed her a set of keys. They laughed as they felt a spark. Madeline usually hated static electricity sparks…

She tried to hide how pleased she was as she closed the apartment door behind her. The two left the quaint courtyard together but parted ways at the main street. Danny now rushing, not realizing where the morning had gone.

Madeline didn't remember anything about her swift roll from her apartment to the gallery, but she will always remember every detail of the new art space. The building itself was an old house, outside kept to the original structure as much as possible. Three sides of the house untouched except for replacement bricks. The fourth updated to look more like a modern business. The front had two huge windows on each side, double doors in the middle, made from cypress wood, with colored broken mosaic stain glass as panels. Three steps led up to the door, and a side ramp lined with flowers led to the same entrance.

Madeline didn't think she had been in front of the store that long, but when the 4th stranger walking by asked if she needed help, Madeline forced herself to go in. The lock felt a little stuck, but as Madeline turned the key, both doors swung open, as if a light breeze pushed them.

Besides the somewhat accessible path, this looked like a scene from extreme hoarders. The peaks of the stacks of treasures, trash, and junk towered over Madeline's head, And for the first time, she wondered if she should have asked for hazardous pay. She looked around and started playing eye spy. Just off the top of her head, she spotted two bikes, four

TVs, stoves, broken furniture, books, paintings, some in one piece, others not so much, clothes, jewelry, and boxes and boxes of general crap.

"Hey Danny," Madeline left a message, knowing he was doing lawyerly things, trying to sound firm. "The outside looks spectacular, but unless our first exhibit is '1960s junkyard', I really don't see a finish line within our three-month target date. Please call me asap. Hope you're having a good day." She smiled at the phone as if he could see her.

"Hope you're having a good day?" Madeline mumbled to herself, what the hell? That kind of nulls and voids the urgency of the message, dummy.

Madeline felt completely turned around, somewhere towards the back, mentally sifting through another mountain of stuff when she heard an alarm beep announcing that someone had come in.

"Hello," She began her introduction speech she had been rehearsing in her head for a week. " Welcome to the Phyllis L Art Gallery. Please excuse the mess..." her voice trailed off.

"Hi." He said softly as if asking for permission. He was an athletic-looking guy in khaki shorts and a purple polo shirt, in his mid-twenties. Too pretty and cocky for boyfriend material, unless you were into that. Madeline certainly wasn't, anymore.

"Hi," Madeline whispered, with sadness in her voice; her heart was a different matter. He bent to his knees to kiss her. Madeline tried to resist but giggled as she gave in. "Jane is going to kill me, but I did find her a new distraction," Steven laughed and kissed her forehead as he stood up, now looking at the space in disbelief.

"Muffaletta. Let the food fetish weekend begin." Jane suddenly appeared, as if magically. Madeline didn't hear the door open. Steven jumped away from Madeline as if he was a 5-year-old who got caught putting gum in the hair of the girl he loves. "Oh damnit, Madds. You promised."

"He was just saying hello." Madeline was trying not to grin because Jane seemed genuinely irritated, and Madeline really wanted a Muffaletta. "I promised that he wouldn't get to third base. Besides, what is the proper way to greet your ex-boyfriend?"

"I'm pretty sure Emily Post would strongly suggest… No. Tongue." Jane was hiding her smirk behind the big bag of food she was laying out over a picnic tablecloth on the floor in one of the clearings.

"Do I get a vote…" Steven asked, knowing what the answer was.

"Nope." The girls sang in sync. Madeline laughed until Jane joined in. Finally greeting her best friend with a kiss on the cheek.

Jane was Madeline's most favorite person on earth. They met freshman year on the first day of orientation and have not gone 48 hours without talking since. They met Steven on the 2nd day of orientation, so of course, they still tease after 5 years that Steven was the third wheel. And to some extent, it was true.

Jane Summers was a gorgeous girl. A little too gorgeous for Madeline's taste, but we all have our own cross to bear. To Jane's absolute disgust, Madeline frequently referred to her as a Greek goddess. With perfect cream skin, green eyes, graceful, and long spirally red hair, how else would anyone describe her besides the Greek goddess? To add insult to injury, she was very smart. A month ago, Jane finished culinary school after getting her B.A. in three years. They really should not be friends at all.

"Can we just have a really fun weekend?" Madeline asked, raising a can of soda. Trying to shake the feeling that this would be the last weekend the threesome could be together, pretending they were sophomores when things were still pure.

"Cheers." Jane winked at Madeline and leaned into Steven's arm.

"Cheers," Steven added. "Hey, Madds said she found you a shining new plaything."

"Ooh, do tell." Jane smiled. "Is he cute?"

"Oh my god, I'd definitely tap that," Madeline admitted.

"Hey!?!?" Steven screamed, almost choking on his sandwich.

"He is gorgeous." Madeline continued, ignoring Steven's outburst. "And he owns a restaurant. You may flirt with him, but no hokey pokey until I'm hired permanently, then you have my blessings."

"Hey!?!?" Steven screamed again, this time louder and with more feelings. Madeline and Jane burst into uncontrollable laughter.

The quick lunch lasted far into the night. They did discuss Danny a little more, but it was just nice to have a long, flowing conversation like they used to, before things got complicated, before words broke hearts. They talked about almost everything from Steven starting his Master's Program in the fall in Atlanta to Jane's plans now that she just finished culinary school. They mostly enjoyed watching Madeline trying to roll around the gallery, pointing out her ideas for projects she could not wait to start.

The next morning, Danny appeared at Madeline's door with coffee and fresh beignets.

"Hey, you must be Danny. " Jane opened the door and invited him in. "Have you met Steven? Madeline's boyfriend?" She giggled, her signal to Madeline that Danny would do just fine.

"I'm so getting to third base; your bodyguard just approved," Steven whispered in Madeline's ear before getting up from a sleeping bag to shake Danny's hand. Madeline felt embarrassed, but she wasn't sure about whom or why.

And so began a wonderful weekend. A little warm for late June, but the low clouds tamed the sun to a pleasant temperature. It was interesting to Madeline that even though her dad was born in a small town west of New Orleans, they rarely visited this amazing city. Everything Danny introduced them to was fresh and wonderful.

Of course, the three were obsessed with the food equally as the next meal seemed better than the last fabulous one. For lunch, they ate at Oceana. Danny called it a local favorite; no one argued. Everyone ordered a different entrée and shared bites. The winner with an overwhelming clean plate was the blackened duck stuffed with crawfish.

After the amazing lunch, the foursome wandered around the French Quarter, just enjoying the relaxing day. Steven loved the architecture, Jane stopped to read every menu, and Madeline had to stare into the window of every gallery, making mental notes of what she needed.

But indisputably, the favorite outing Saturday was Preservation Hall. In all the churches in the world that Madeline had visited, she had never felt a stronger presence of a higher being than here.

Preservation Hall was a small space. Maybe held 150 people, most of them sitting on the floor. Danny had gotten them a VIP table, but Madeline would have been just as happy on the floor. The hall featured local old school jazz bands. The youngest musician in the band they saw was 75 years young.

Maybe it was the candles or the old brick building that looked like it had survived hundreds of fads and was still standing, almost as is after decades of change. Opened in 1961, the music venue features acoustic concerts featuring over 100 local master jazz musicians.

Madeline was surprised as tears ran down her cheek when the crowd was brought to their feet as the band played "When The Saints Go Marching In." She looked around her, finding unexpected comfort that the other three had tears too.

Madeline promised herself that she would return to Preservation Hall as much as she could. A tiny part of her worried it would get old. But in all the years she would live in the city, she went at least once a month, Usually for their Sunday brunch. And never once did it feel old.

After this spiritual event, the four agreed the only way to end the night was drinking and dancing, celebrating the true essence of the French Quarters. And that they did.

"Oh, damn," Danny mumbled as the four stepped out of the third bar of the night. "I didn't see this text. My grandfather is short-staffed tonight. I should go help close up. Will y'all join me for brunch there tomorrow? I saved the best for last."

"That sounds fantastic." Madeline nodded as Steven shook his hand, thanking him for the day.

"Can I tag along?" Jane offered, dying to see the restaurant Danny had been telling her about. Madeline giggled, wondering what Jane was more excited about, getting her hands on a kitchen or Danny. The group said their goodbyes, and Jane and Danny disappeared into the crowd on Bourbon Street.

"We should go get coffee and Beignets," Steven suggested. Madeline suddenly felt nervous. They once bonded over coffee. They decided they were best friends over coffee. Steven confessed he was madly in love with her over coffee. And two years later, Steven confessed something else, again over coffee.

"Stupid coffee," Madeline muttered under her breath as they were seated at Café Du Monde. She had been here a few times on family trips, but the night had a different feel to the airy restaurant, tables, and people packed in like sardines, even after midnight.

They ordered six Beignets, square-looking doughnuts that tasted better than any pastry should.

"So." Steven started. Madeline bribed herself. If she could get through this conversation without either bursting into tears or stabbing him, preferably in the penis. Then, she could buy an insanely expensive brush Monday.

"So..." Madeline's devilish grin hid the tears she felt swelling.

"Excuse me," Their moment was interrupted by two ladies. "We hate to bother you, but we'd be so honored if you could say a blessing; my mother just got into a car accident. And she would be in awe if she was blessed by a direct descendant."

"I'm..." Madeline didn't see this conversation. "I'm sorry, I'm from Houston, but I certainly will keep her in my prayers." The words just came out. Madeline didn't want to sound mean, but this was bizarre.

"We are so sorry; please accept our apologies. Have a good evening." The other lady said, now kind of bowing. They both insisted on shaking Madeline's hand. This was beyond weird as the last one cuffed her hand for what felt like an eternity. The two backed away and disappeared into the crowd.

"Ok, they did drink too many Hurricanes." Madeline tried to laugh it off, feeling very uneasy. Now very annoyed that Steven seemed glued to a card that one of the ladies must have left on the table. "Steven!" Madeline hissed. Holding the card up so she could see it, he looked directly at her with a very strange expression.

It was a laminated card, 2x3. On the front, one of those old-timey portraits, the back, a paragraph. It looked like a Saint's card from the Catholic Church.

"You have her cheeks." He continued to study the picture. "And her eyes. Look, Madeline."

"And we are extremely drunk." Madeline flat out lied. Madeline had maybe a total of half a drink the entire day. Between her new co-worker and her ex-boyfriend, she wanted to keep a clear head. Steven did have a drink or two but wasn't even tipsy. Madeline took the card from Steven, ignoring the picture and the shiver that ran up her spine the second she touched the paper.

"Listen to this crap." Madeline read the back of the card. "I seek protection and sound my alarm, my body, mind, and spirit be safe from harm. My aura a shield to help me stay strong. I block negativity and all that is wrong. Blah blah blah. WHAT!?!?"

"That paragraph is written in French." Steven leaning towards Madeline, angrily whispered. "You do not speak French! You speak English, Vietnamese, and a little bit of Spanish. NOT French! How the hell are you reading this?"

"This is NOT in French." Madeline tried not to raise her voice. How in the world was this turning into a fight? Madeline wondered as she felt her blood boiling. Worse playful fight and excuse for makeup sex ever!

"Come on." Steven said forcefully, "I texted Jane. She's going to meet us back at the apartment." He got up and left, hoping Madeline would follow. He knew her. She would have stubbornly sat at that table at Café Du Monde until she could prove she was right, or at least less wrong than

Steven. Madeline followed against her better judgment. At least Jane would bitch Steven out for the strange game he was playing, And Madeline would win. And everything would be fine.

Chapter 2

"Go into the apartment." Jane forcefully told Steven. She was waiting for them in the courtyard, sipping on a coffee. "We will be there in a second." Steven knew arguing with these two was futile. He took Jane's coffee as a sign of protest and disappeared into the apartment.

"He... and they... and freaky picture... but now that I've had time to reflect, I think someone drugged us." Madeline blurted out. And for a split second, she smiled. All her life, she had been accused of following her heart and making decisions based on emotions. But this was a rational, logical argument. "So ha, dumb boy." She said, now losing conviction.

"Focus." Jane clapped. Trying to keep Madeline from spiraling. "I have to tell you two really important things that happened to me tonight. Then we'll figure out if you were drugged." Jane said, sounding a little patronizing, but at this point, Madeline didn't care.

"One..." Jane continued. "I think I got a serious job offer, so we might be neighbors." Madeline squealed so loud Jane tried to cover her mouth, thinking they probably should not wake up the whole complex on Madeline's second night there. Jane quickly spoke in fragmented statements. So excited to share the news but wanted to get to the strange story that Steven seemed weirded out about.

Steven never ever freaked out, and his text to her looked urgent. But first, Jane's news. Danny's grandfather did indeed owned a restaurant, and talked to Jane for the last two hours. Long story short, he's looking for help. Offered a week's training, and if he felt like they were a good match, he would offer her a permanent position. This time Jane anticipated Madeline's reaction and pressed two fingers to her lips as Madeline tried to scream.

Because no one was watching, they hoped, Jane did allow a 25 seconds silent happy dance. Two best friends, both starting dream jobs, in the same town. The fates were smiling on them.

"So, what's the other news?" Madeline asked as she reached to open her apartment door.

"It's awful. Danny seems to be yet another Madeline worshipper." Jane pretended to be annoyed, and Madeline pretended not to care.

Entering the apartment, Steven was crouched over his laptop at the small kitchen table. The feeling of sheer happiness Madeline had felt a moment ago as she danced with her best friend was completely gone, replaced by dread. The girls sat at opposite ends of the table. Jane reached for the prayer card, trying to ignore Madeline's eyes, begging her not to.

"Is the prayer on the back in French, Jane?" Steven quietly asked, now closing his laptop. She ever so slightly nodded, not wanting to betray Madeline. Now Jane, reaching for her phone, fingering it, as if internally struggling with something.

Jane slid the phone across the table to Madeline; it was open to photos. "I can't play this game now. I won't." The three sat in silence, knowing eventually curiosity would get the better of her.

It was a thing they did. Freshmen year at some bar, a group of frat guys kept staring at Madeline. This angered Jane beyond belief, whereas Madeline was used to it. Jane, who had bigger balls than most men, walked right up to them and asked to take their picture. And because Jane was hot, they agreed. And so the wall of stares was born. Jane usually did this in secret and showed Madeline whenever they needed a good laugh. It wasn't a daily nor even a weekly thing; just every few months, Jane would catch a wheelchair gawker.

Madeline finally glanced at the phone. Nine pictures, all from today. Some were even pointing at Madeline. Usually, they never point. Two were kids, which was normal. But most were older folks, and three were owners of a voodoo shop that they looked around in.

"These stares were different, Madds," Jane said. "The three older ladies almost cried, but they were scared to approach you as if you were royalty."

"Omg, it just clicked, there was an old guy at the record shop that tried to pull out one of your hairs. I chased him away. You were lost in thought, looking at the records. He never touched you." Steven said, trying not to scream. "How the hell did I forget that? I was going to tell you as we left the store, but it was like a dream, and after a few minutes, it completely left my brain. Wow, this is the guy." Steven pointed at Jane's phone, now remembering everything clear as day.

Not meaning to, but in a moment of frustration and anger, Madeline through Jane's phone across the room. No one noticed that it was supposed to land on the hardwood floor but managed to travel an extra foot to fall softly on the futon.

"Best. Prank. Ever." Madeline said. Now in full pissed off denial. "It's not bad enough that the gallery looks like a scene from Hoarders or the love of my life, which by the way turned out to be a cheating bastard is leaving me, yet again in two days... You guys decided to call a truce to pull off this bizarre joke. So thank you for ruining my first weekend here." Madeline stormed into the bathroom and locked the door behind her. Steven and Jane were smart enough not to follow.

About 30 minutes later, Madeline quietly came out of the bathroom to darkness. Madeline saw Steven on the floor in a sleeping bag. She maneuvered around him, tempted to lay beside him. Instead, she pulled herself onto the futon where Jane had a space waiting for her, a blanket folded across half of the mattress, waiting to cover Madeline.

"The third bar reeked of the pot; maybe it was just a strange day. A few oddities and you're stressed and hell, maybe we are all high from second-hand smoke." Jane whispered, now rolling over to face Madeline. "Remember the old Mexican lady who tried to lay her hands on you with a crucifix in the middle of the grocery store?" They both giggled.

"Tell me three truths," Madeline asked. Another thing they did when one was spiraling.

"1..." Jane started. "My wonderful opportunity is real. If I get it, we will have such a great year."

"I'm going to assume you will get it." They knew they were grinning at each other, even in the darkness.

"2..." Jane continued. "The gallery space really does have great bones. Danny did say you could hire an assistant. And I know you, you wanted to watch every step of the renovation."

"But, so. Much. Junk…" Madeline said. "Guess I could hire a strong man to help remove everything," they both sighed in agreement.

Just then, the bed shook as Madeline screamed in laughter. Steven had squeezed himself onto the bed beside Madeline. She waited for Jane to scream obscenities and objections, but none came.

"3…" Jane started to finish, "Steven is a dick, but I see you guys difunctionally in each other's lives forever. God help me. I hate bitching, but I really got the grunt of it. The six months you weren't speaking to him, he called me every week to see if you were ok. But whatever… Anyways, go to sleep. We have to be charming tomorrow at brunch. I swear if I feel any thumping, I'll kill you both." Both Madeline and Steven giggled as they both tried to sleep, or at least be very still, knowing Jane was dead serious.

It had been about a year since they had broken up. And for six months, Madeline avoided him. Took different routes to classes. Didn't go to his favorite places unless she knew he was at work.

Then he showed up at her door about six months ago, soaked from a storm. Mourning the death of a mutual friend. She took him in and dried him off. They went to the funeral together. And it was as if time reset, before the year of dating.

He tried to explain himself a few times, but Madeline said she couldn't handle it. And if he ever loved her, he would never bring it up again. And Steven knew she meant it. Of course, she always wondered. Not knowing what explanation would be worse, that he never really was in love with her, or that he was, just not enough to keep it in his pants.

Jane had never told Madeline about his phone check-ins. Looking back, it was probably a good call. Emotionally drained, Madeline was the last to fall asleep, finally feeling a moment of safety, surrounded by love.

*

Madeline slowly blinked her eyes as the sunlight pushed through the shades. As she stretched her arms, she wondered where her bedmates were. She heard the shower running, one mystery solved. Her hand gravitated to a note on the pillow.

"Madds," Jane wrote. "I got up early and remembered Henry said he is usually at the farmer's market Sunday mornings. I'm going to see if I can find him and earn some brownie points. Do not go to the gallery, or you'll lose track of time, and you'll be late for brunch. Do NOT engage in any other activity that will make you late for brunch either. I took the condoms in Steven's wallet, just cuz."

"Witch…" Madeline babbled; she wanted to be offended, but…

"Love, Jane." Madeline continued reading. "P.S. I hate to add salt to the wound, but this note was written in French, however poorly. Don't freak out; after Steven leaves tomorrow, we will figure it out. Kiss."

"Damnit." Not sure what Madeline was more annoyed about as the list was growing longer by the second.

"What the hell?" Steven was pissed, now appearing in the bathroom doorway. Madeline tried really hard not to laugh, but there he was, in all of his glory, with red blotches all over.

"Did you use Jane's body soap?" Madeline asked, trying not to mentally connect the dots. He sadly nodded, now muttering cuss words in a low grumble. "Her stuff is not hypoallergenic, silly boy."

"I swear she is trying to kill me," Steven muttered, now wrapped in a towel, searching in his bag for a Benadryl.

"Oh, don't be so dramatic," Madeline sighed. "If she wanted you dead, you would know, without a doubt." He sarcastically laughed, then finished changing.

After Madeline got ready for the day, and Steven regained his sense of humor, they decided to walk to Jackson Square to enjoy the street musicians. As a history major, Steven was in his element. He told Madeline the interesting facts about Andrew Jackson and the Square.

The morning was so beautiful, and the conversation was flowing so well that Madeline unintentionally proposed something to Steven. And before she could even take it back, he accepted, offering a pinky swear before she realized what she had done.

"Just let me tell Jane, tonight… after a hurricane or two…" Madeline begged Steven, even kissing him on the cheek. He was already distracted, making lists, wondering if he could make it back in two days.

Jane would be fine, Madeline reassured herself. It was a practical, smart move. Jane will be thrilled.

*

Madeline showed up at the restaurant at exactly 11. The place was even more charming than Jane described. About 15 tables on the left half and a full bar along the right. Music from the twenties softly playing in the background. Even though the restaurant had just opened, two couples were ahead of her, waiting to be seated.

"Hey Madeline," Danny appeared in the swinging doors, waving her back to the kitchen, "Where's Steven?"

"Umm, his summer plans just changed drastically, and he decided to go back to Houston. But I do have a bit of business to talk to you about." Madeline tried to sound professional over the kitchen noises. Just then, she spotted Jane washing vegetables in the corner. They grinned at each other as Jane continued working.

"My grandfather strictly forbids business talk at Sunday Brunch. If it's urgent, we can speak afterward," Danny explained. Leading Madeline from the large kitchen through a narrow brick hallway. Madeline was a little nervous about scraping her knuckles while pushing her wheelchair down the narrow hallway. They never did.

"Madeline, this is my grandfather, Henry." The hallway led to a small room with a gorgeous wood dining table, probably too big for the room. Madeline had absolutely no idea how they got the furniture in the space, but it was amazing.

"Hello, sir," Madeline was relieved to be able to reach him as she shook his hand.

"You are just as charming and beautiful as Daniel and Jane described." Henry was so warm and welcoming that Madeline only slightly blushed. "I can assure you, I had no intention of putting Jane to work today, but I cannot seem to drag her out of the kitchen."

"I can promise you, she is in her happy place," Madeline reassured him, not exaggerating one bit.

"And, this is Charlie, my best friend, and your neighbor to the left." Danny patted the other person in the room.

"Hi," Madeline said shyly, trying not to stare at the large bearded woman in a beautiful tight-fitting dress. And even though Charlie was certainly a large bearded woman in a tight-fitting dress, it wasn't why Madeline felt drawn to stare at her. It was just a familiar feeling, like something Madeline didn't know she was missing, but now it fits.

"This one's going to break your heart." Charlie got up from the table and squeezed Madeline's shoulder as Danny gave her the dirtiest look. "I'll go round everyone up, so we can start the meal, Henry."

About eight more people joined them for brunch. Madeline playfully thanked Charlie for bullying Jane into joining them. Although she looked like a little kid, who was forced to join the adult table when Jane would rather be playing in the kitchen. This absolutely tickled Henry and cemented their adoration for each other.

Henry apologized that it was a small group. Usually, it averages about 25. This was, hands down, the best meal Madeline had ever had. Henry just called it a simple crawfish bisque and day-old garlic bread.

Madeline was grateful for the noisy room and the new friends who seemed to have perfect timing, always introducing themselves as Jane was just about to ask about Steven.

"Let us pray for the week before we leave each other's graces." Charlie stood up, still warm, but a sternness in her voice. Madeline was heartbroken to put the crème Brulé dish down even though the bowl looked like it had been washed.

"Dearest ancestors," Charlie began, as Madeline completed the circle by taking Jane's hand to her left and Danny's hand to the right. When Madeline realized she hadn't held another man's hand since Steven. She slowly pulled away, just leaving their pinkies to touch. Hoping he wouldn't notice. Madeline sadly remembered some article that said in some cultures holding hands was considered more intimate than kissing. "Please guide us through the week to make good choices, to be kind to one another, and to never allow us to turn our backs on our true callings..."

Madeline was embarrassed as her eyes saw Danny and Henry in a stare-off. Trying to look anywhere else, Charlie offered a safe place. That is until she mouthed "Big drama" to Madeline, making her bite her tongue to prevent herself from giggling.

"Bless it be." Charlie finished. As the guests bowed to her and said their goodbyes, and left the room one by one.

Jane insisted on staying for the lunch rush, and Danny said he had a few things to do before his hectic week, but they could have a breakfast meeting in the morning. Madeline agreed as she found herself alone in front of the restaurant as the rest of the group said their goodbyes.

Madeline mentally flipped a coin. Heads, go home, and unpack. She needed to make room for her unexpected guests. Tails, go to the gallery and figure out the best way to start clearing out the junk. Yeah, flipping a mental coin works better as a concept. In reality, not so helpful. Madeline decided to go home for an hour, work for two hours at the gallery, then take Jane out for dinner, a very public meal. Jane would resist strangling her in a nice restaurant.

"Well, hello, new neighbor," Charlie said as Madeline rounded the corner, entering the courtyard to the apartments. Charlie was sitting at one of the three patio tables surrounding a small dried-up fountain.

"What are ya up to? I'm trying to avoid a food coma and have a productive Sunday, but I think it's a losing battle." Madeline admitted, now sitting close to her.

"Just relaxing until I sing tonight," Charlie said. "Danny mentioned you might need a manly man part-time at the gallery. I am throwing my hat in the ring. I perform six nights a week and only need two hours of sleep a night. So I'm usually bored. Please, dear God, use me. My nails are insured, but besides that, I'm ridiculously strong."

"Oh, Charlie," Madeline sighed. "Where were you yesterday? You could have saved me from making a big mistake that might have lifelong repercussions." As the hours passed, Madeline questioned more and more about the impulsive decision she had made with Steven. Usually a very guarded person with her feelings and fears, Madeline poured her heart out to Charlie for the next hour. And Charlie listened without judgment.

"I hired Steven for the summer." Madeline just blurted out very loudly as Jane appeared in the courtyard, looking ragged. She didn't mean to.

"Nope... Nap. Drinks. Then you'll call him to say you changed your mind." Jane said without really stopping her slow walk. She kissed Madeline on the cheek. Squeezed Charlie on the shoulder and disappeared into Madeline's apartment.

"Wow, that was harsh," Charlie commented.

"Harsh, hell, that went a hundred times better than how it played out in my head," Madeline said, truly feeling better. "Now that you are caught up on my life, please explain how a burly giant like yourself is prettier than me? It's really annoying," Charlie's eyes danced.

For the next hour, Madeline was memorized by Charlie and her stories. Although she only seemed a little older than Madeline, Madeline guesses Charlie was in her mid-thirties at the very oldest; what an interesting life Charlie had led. It was obvious Charlie hated to brag, so she was very careful when telling her story.

Charlie's true passion was singing. She said she had sung everywhere from street corners to sold-out stadiums, and as long as there was one person lost in the music, it really did not matter where she was. It was the feeling of connecting with humans.

"Connecting with humans?" Madeline thought this was an odd statement, but she had often heard that musicians thought of themselves on a different plain.

"I just mean when you work with big stars who only eat purple jelly beans..." Charlie explained herself, relaxing Madeline's thoughts again. Charlie went on to say she has traveled the world three times as a backup singer for various artists, but New Orleans was her home and where she felt most like herself. Madeline was dying to know who she had sung with. "Everyone you can imagine," Charlie finally confessed, giving in and showed Madeline a picture on her phone of her last tour.

"You are kidding?!?!" Madeline gasped, not caring if she sounded like a crazy teen stalker of a pop idol. After she regained composure, she noticed a sadness in Charlie's eyes. "So, if you're a backup singer for him..." Madeline tried not to squeal again, "You are obviously a badass; why aren't you a pop diva goddess?"

"It's just not my thing," Charlie said.

"Oh my god, I'm so sorry, I overstepped. I do things impulsively. I just learned to breathe around my ex-boyfriend again, so the very first thing I do is invite him to stay and work for me. If Jane kills me, it would probably be justified."

"Naw," Charlie said. "Danny's been after me for years to go solo. But it's probably because he wants to get away from here, and he expects that I'd take him with me as my lawyer and manager, which I totally would. I just don't feel comfortable in this body, but it's the best I can do."

"It must be hard." Madeline said, "May I ask, have you ever thought of... medical help? Like a permanent change? A friend of ours has just begun hormones," Charlie started laughing uncomfortably. Madeline really felt bad now, "I'm going to shut the hell up." Madeline touched Charlie on the arm to apologize. The most shocking thing happened, and they spent the next 5 minutes, screaming and pointing at each other.

"How did you do that? No one can do that by touching me, but... holy shit, is that you?" Charlie asked frantically, now in her natural state. First screaming in anger as if she had been violated, then shocked. The

Page | 25

possibility of this miracle in front of her, now crystal clear. How could Charlie not have seen it at the restaurant? One look directly in Madeline's eyes, and there was no doubt. Even so, Charlie couldn't seem to stop screaming, with tears of joy now streaming down her face.

"How did I do that? What the hell are you?" Madeline should have been horrified and scared, but it was the most beautiful sight she has ever seen. Now standing in front of her on the table was a six-inch pixie. Madeline was screaming now, although she wasn't sure why. It was a mixture of sheer confusion, a little fear, but not of the pixie yelling back at her, but the dreadful feeling of the unknown. Like she had forgotten something so important.

"Why are you guys screaming?" Jane appeared with a tray of paper cups, sodas, and a bottle of rum. Suddenly Charlie disappearing into thin air reappeared in the chair as burly Charlie. "it sounded like a bitch fight. She looks scrappy, but I'm pretty sure my girl could take you, Charlie. Please be fighting over Danny."

"Look at this picture." Madeline needed a huge distraction until she could regain her composure and figure out what the hell just happened. She wanted to write it off as a weird dream; maybe she dozed off in the afternoon heat. But Charlie was working too hard at trying not to make eye contact with Madeline, now showing Jane all of her pictures on her phone.

"Unbelievable," Jane exclaimed. She was a huge music lover, so it didn't take much before these two were lost in conversation. Madeline nodded and smiled ever so often, trying to appear like she was still interested in their chit chat. Madeline noticed that Charlie had moved her chair a bit back, no longer in arm's reach of her. This made Madeline extremely self-conscious.

"Are we?" Jane snapped her fingers about 2 inches from Madeline's face. "Charlie just invited us to her gig tonight. Let's go."

"Yes, no...." Madeline wavered. "I should really try to get settled, and we do need to talk about the elephant moving into my room."

"Please do come tonight," Charlie said sincerely, now staring at Madeline with quiet reassurances. "I would love it. I'm sure everything will work itself out. Danny said you're not even on the clock for a week. I bet we could find a little mischief to distract you till you start your brilliant career." Everyone agreed but nodded for different reasons; Charlie offered an air fist pump. Madeline grinned.

"That's beautiful," Jane said as the fountain that the three girls were sitting by suddenly came on. Charlie decided not to mention that despite having been looked at by every plumber in the greater New Orleans area, the fountain had not worked in 150 years.

*

Madeline tried her hardest to sneak out of the apartment as Jane finally moved from her dead sleep, now completely sprawled out on the futon they recently shared. Locking the door behind her, Madeline wondered why the sun was extra bright this morning.

Madeline's head was pounding, and her theory that getting fresh air would make her feel better now seemed overly optimistic. Madeline didn't think this was fair. She did not even order a single drink last night... She just shared two with Jane and three with Charlie. This pounding punishment against her head seemed way too severe for the crime of sipping.

Madeline grinned through the pain. Last night definitely would make it on Jane's and Madeline's top 5 dance evenings. Charlie describes her venue last night as the best dive biker bar in the Quarter. Madeline guessed that the sign in front of the bar that read "200 people capacity" had to have been a mere suggestion because the place was packed. And you could tell that 95% of the crowd was there to see Charlie. And after she sang the first 10 notes in her set, Madeline and Jane understood why and became instantly captivated.

Charlie had to get to the bar before Jane and Madeline but left instructions with the bouncer to seat them at her table. And to tell Madeline "To lose herself in the music and allow herself one night without the past or future weighing on her mind and heart." Jane thought this was a very odd thing to make a bouncer relay to a friend of eight hours. But for some reason, it soothed Madeline.

For two hours, Charlie's audience, especially the two girls, were enchanted. They danced to the fast songs, swayed to the slow ones, and sang along to every word when Charlie invited them.

Madeline twirled in her wheelchair on the dance floor like there was no tomorrow. When Madeline was younger, she hated dancing. She always felt like she was in the way. Jane set her straight the first time they went clubbing their freshmen year. Everything Madeline took as a negative from dancing waist height to everyone else, Jane turned into a positive. From guys tripping over her wheels to girls in their short dresses exposing their new undergarments or worse, not. Jane really didn't understand the downside of any of this. So they danced. And on rare occasions like tonight, Madeline felt free from the limitations of her wheelchair.

The rowdy audience could not get enough of the 6 foot 2 bearded guy in a pink sequence dress with the voice of an angel. But as the evening went on, occasionally when Madeline was entranced and stared at Charlie, she saw a beautiful female face underneath the bearded disguised.

Chapter 3

Although the sun still hurt her eyes, Madeline decided to get coffee and then go to the gallery. Steven had just texted her that he would be ready to work Thursday. So Madeline really did need to make a plan of attack to remove the junk in the gallery.

"Welcome home, Madeline Laveau." Madeline heard a soft voice speaking to her in the empty courtyard, but she did not see a person in sight. Just then, the fountain started again.

"Hello?" Madeline whispered and waited for a response, none came. She carefully inspected the courtyard and the apartments surrounding her. However, everything was eerily still, except for the water fountain; its water flowing sounded like a distant melody.

For some reason, Madeline decided to jot the name "Madeline Laveau" in a note on her phone and texted it to herself. She took one more look around the sleepy complex and headed towards the gallery.

Her folks were very concerned that the French Quarter's sidewalks may be unkind to Madeline's wheelchair. Still, for some reason, Madeline had never felt more graceful, rolling towards her new place of employment.

Madeline felt the same excited butterflies as she sat in front of the gallery's beautiful exterior and the exact sinking feeling as she opened the doors to a scene from extreme hoarders. She sighed as she pushed through the first mountain of junk, locking the doors behind her.

She explored the nooks and crannies as best as she could in the wheelchair. And started making notes on what she needed. Garbage bags, lots and lots of garbage bags, Danny was checking on renting a small dumpster for a few weeks. That would definitely help the process. Maybe she would ask Jane and Charlie to help a few days to speed up the job.

"Miss you. See you soon." The text startled Madeline as she was lost in thought. She responded with a thumbs-up emoji. Immediately wanting to take it back. Madeline wanted to analyze what the emoji truly meant, but then she remembered she would google something.

Madeline wondered why everything in the last week felt like a foggy memory. It used to drive Steven crazy that Madeline was a stickler for details and usually remembered everything. So it bugged Madeline that she seemingly had forgotten she had sent herself a text of a name to research.

There was a small table that Jane had cleared off when they had their picnic. Madeline rolled up to it and started up her laptop that she carried in her backpack.

"I'll just type in the name, nothing will show up, and I can get back to work," Madeline said sternly to herself. "How bizarre..." she exhaled as google showed the results.

"Hello..." Madeline must have been so lost googling that she didn't realize that a stranger had come into the gallery. He was standing over Madeline's laptop. Madeline slammed down the screen, a little harder than she intended to, feeling a little uneasy. He obviously didn't read the memo of the appropriate distance when greeting a person in a wheelchair. Madeline honestly thought she felt his breath on the top of her head. "I'm sorry if I startled you; the door was unlocked." He said, now backing up to Madeline's relief.

"No, it's no problem," Madeline said, trying to hide her doubts. She was almost positive she had locked the door. The only one scheduled to come by today was Danny. He had a key and was insistent that Madeline kept the doors locked until the gallery was opened for customers. And if she did, in fact, left the door unlocked, she should have heard a chirp from the alarm. "Please pardon our mess; we won't officially be open until late fall."

"My name is Louis Delcroix; I'm with the local paper. We are always looking to feature new businesses in the quarter." Louis said. He was a tall, lanky fellow wearing a page boy's hat. Madeline thought he looked like he stepped out of a Dick Tracy cartoon. "May I ask you a few questions while I'm here?"

"Of course..." Madeline tried to be warm and friendly, even though she felt extremely uncomfortable. She was trying to overcome her natural shyness around new people.

"So this will be the Phyllis L Art Gallery?" Louis asked, looking around.

"Hopefully with a lot of elbow grease."

"They really are a great family foundation, continuing the arts in New Orleans as they have done for generations. But they are a bit of a reclusive clan. Have you had the pleasure of meeting any of them yet?"

"No, I haven't, but I'm working closely with the foundation's lawyer, and he promises that the family will be very involved in the exhibits that will come through," Madeline said.

"Are you native to these parts?" Louis asked.

"I was raised in Houston." Madeline had decided that this was the simplest truthful answer.

"So no connections to Louisiana?" Louis seemed extremely curious.

"Not really." Madeline's guard went up, and there was no way in hell she was going to explain her family history.

"Hey Madeline?" she heard the door unlock, the alarm chirp, and Danny calling her. "Sorry I'm late; court was a nightmare; besides, Charlie thought you'd be unconscious today. Oh, I apologize." Danny said, now seeing that the gallery had a guest.

"No, not at all," Louis said, now backing up towards the door. "It was a pleasure to meet you, and I'll be in touch." He did not make eye contact with Danny and was gone before either could respond.

"I'm sorry I was late." Danny apologized after he was sure that Mr. Delcroix had left.

"No, don't be silly. We never really even set a time." Madeline smiled, feeling less defensive now that the reporter had left. "Hey, have you seen Louis before? Charlie mentioned you knew everyone in the greater New Orleans Area."

"No, which is a little odd because I do have several friends at the paper, and I'd certainly remember a Dick Tracy look alike in the building." Danny grinned, and Madeline laughed. "So what else did my dear friend say about me?"

"I will tell you what YOUR friend said about you if you tell me what MY dear friend has said about me." Madeline felt her cheeks blush the moment the words left her mouth. Damnit, she thought.

After a few minutes of shy flirting, Madeline knew she had to get the conversation back on track, whether her heart wanted to or not. She told Danny that she had hired Steven for the summer and was just a tiny bit disappointed that he approved. Everything could be fixed if he didn't approve Steven in the budget.

But after Danny did, Madeline felt obligated to point out that Steven was a history major, so it was a good fit. She hoped the quick hire sounded like a smart business decision, not a romantic one. Danny and Madeline talked a bit more about business. The dumpster would be delivered by the end of the week, and he liked the idea of hiring Jane and Charlie for a few days. And promised he would help out as much as he could.

Madeline tried to hide her disappointment when Danny said he had to get back to the office and insisted Madeline leave the gallery. Stubbornly she agreed. Madeline really could not do much until all the junk was removed. They parted ways at the sidewalk, and Madeline grinned all the way back to the apartments, sensing he watched her roll away.

The courtyard to the apartments seemed more alive as Madeline turned the corner.

"Howdy neighbor," Jane waved at Madeline from the second floor. It was something they had discussed last night. One of Charlie's many hats was the apartment manager. She had one more vacancy, which was almost unheard of. The tenant had suddenly moved out despite being paid up until the end of the month. Since they left with a handshake but without a legal termination of a contract, Charlie could not advertise the apartment for rent for 15 days. She suggested Jane stay there until Henry decided whether or not he would hire her permanently. Everyone but Jane was 100% certain of the answer.

"Come to the restaurant tonight. Henry said he feeds all of the favorite single children every night at nine-ish, and you made the cut!" Jane blew Madeline a kiss and disappeared into her new digs.

Madeline was still feeling all warm and fuzzy when she noticed an Amazon box by her door. She almost squealed with joy. She bet it was either something practical from her mom. or something silly from her dad. As Madeline closed the door behind her, she noticed that she was wrong on both counts.

Sitting on the futon, Madeline set the surprise delivery on her lap, not noticing that the last name wasn't hers. She carefully opened the box then flung the empty package towards the kitchen trash, of course missing by a mile. But she was too distracted by the bubble wrap to care. After playing with the plastic and giggling at the satisfying pops, Madeline unwrapped the gift.

Definitely from dad, Madeline thought. It was a beautiful, leather-bound journal, long laces decorating the spine. The tethered key was beautiful, engraved with hearts and floral vines. She gently pressed the key into the lock. With a soft click, the leather strap unlatched itself and unfolded to the side.

Madeline slowly opened the cover and felt a mixture of confusion and curiosity. There was a single, beautifully written word on the first page, in a language Madeline guessed was French... Madeline traced the foreign letters, admiring each precise curve. Reaching the last circle, with quiet confidence, she whispered, "Read."

The book graciously turned itself to the next page. The blank page slowly revealed its secrets line by line. "Welcome back, Madeline Laveau; you just learned the most basic part of a spell, yet again."

*

"Madeline, Open up, ya weirdo." Jane banged on the door about 11 that evening.

"Oh, shoot." Madeline barely opened the door, leaning forward so that her head looked like it was stuck. "hi."

"I made you an omelet with crawfish. Worship me." Jane tried to push the door open, Madeline's wheels did not budge. "Hey, let me in."

"I'm sorry," Madeline said. "I just don't feel good, so I took a nap, which lasted longer than I was planning on. And now I'm groggy, and I just wanna go back to sleep. I'll be back to my warm perky self tomorrow."

"Swear you're not doing something weird with Steven."

"Not with Steven." Madeline accidentally blurted out and felt Jane smile.

"Do you want your food?" Jane asked.

"Oh, hell, yes." Madeline reached her arm as far out from the door crack as she could, signaling Jane to hand her the food. "Thanks. Love you, bye." Slamming the door after the doggy bag was safely inside. She didn't know how to explain her interesting evening.

Jane walked away, a little worried when she heard two deadbolts click. To ease her consciousness, she peaked at the parking lot across the way: Nope, no Steven's car. Madeline may live.

"Oh, god, I'm sorry." Danny ran into Jane as she slowly lingered in the courtyard. "Have a good night." He quickly left the apartments with an Amazon box under his left arm. He seemed very upset. Jane thought about following him, but she worried that she would cross the brand new friendship line. So Jane decided to call it a night.

"Henry?" Danny called out as he let himself into the dark restaurant. "Grandfather! Are you here?!?" Danny sounded more and more frustrated, now stealing a handful of grapes from the kitchen's main island.

"I know you can hear me, grandfather." Danny left the kitchen, now going down the narrow hallway, turning left into Henry's office. The old man was sipping on bourbon behind a large desk with a marble top.

"Your mother loved this picture of you two," Henry said, not bothering to look up from the large dusty album he was enjoying.

"Mom was so beautiful." Danny knew this was a trap, but he just couldn't continue his harsh tone. He sat down in front of Henry, taking a sip of his grandfather's drink.

"So, what can I do for you?"

"You can take this back." Danny pleaded.

"An Amazon Box? I don't understand." Of all the things Henry was and was not, Danny had never known him to be a liar.

"Please, Grandfather, please." Danny did not realize how upset he was until this moment, his voice weakening.

"I have no say in the matter, son." Except he did, and they both knew it.

"The community is talking." Danny barely got the words out. "Books are being sent out. I do not want one. Tell them."

"The community? The community you have turned your back on? The community that needs you now? You mean THAT community." Henry stood up, pounding his fist on the table. Spilling a little bourbon from its glass from the vibrations. Henry no longer looked like a fragile old man.

"The community that watched my sister die..." Danny laughed a little through a stray tear, set the box down, and left the restaurant. As a grandfather, Henry wanted to run after his heartbroken grandson; as an elder, he knew he could not.

Danny walked back to his apartment; as he closed the door behind him, he sensed a presence. In her natural state, Charlie was standing on the kitchen table as a pixle, next to the Amazon box. The same box that Danny had just left in Henry's office. Beside the box was the only copy of his mother and Danny's favorite picture that Henry never let out of his office.

"What are you going to do?" Charlie asked as carefully as she could.

"Damn if I know," Danny said.

*

Almost nothing could have distracted Madeline from the mysterious leather journal, except for maybe Jane's omelet. Madeline had no idea how many hours had passed but judging by the way she inhaled her dinner, it must have been quite a few. After scraping the fork across every inch of the plate, Madeline set the dinner down on the end table. She immediately reached for the leather journal, which slowly revealed a new spell on the next page. It included the correct pronunciation and very specific diagrams showing what motions your hands should be doing when reading the spells.

Because Madeline was so quick to unlock the journal, she assumed her first spell would be simple too. She was mistaken. Madeline carefully and slowly traced the foreign letters, closed her eyes, and tried to pronounce the spell in French as well as she could, waiting for something amazing to happen.

Spell one - "la lumière de la bougie," Madeline said as boldly as she could, sighing loudly in frustration when nothing happened. She tried about 20 times in different accents and tones. Suddenly an animated finger drawing popped out of the book. The finger rudely thumped Madeline on her forehead and pointed at each word. It silently but obnoxiously forced Madeline to repeat them over and over until she got the pronunciation correct.

Then the finger drew a diagram of a candle. Luckily Madeline had two of them on the counter. She followed the directions to a T, or at least she thought so. Breathe, point, words, twirl, ignite... nothing.

"The Finger," as Madeline lovingly or not so lovingly soon referred to as her animated teacher, kept pointing out her missteps. First, Madeline breathed too creepily. Then Madeline pointed with too much indecisiveness. Then Madeline pointed too forcefully. And then there was the twirl, omg, the finger twirl was too girly... The finger did not appreciate Madeline's hand twirls at all.

Madeline finally successfully completed her first spell just as the sun was coming up. Before she could congratulate herself, there was a loud patterned knock on her door. Madeline grinned in disbelief, carefully hid the leather spellbook under the pillow on the futon. She opened the door without looking through the peephole.

"I couldn't sleep, and everything was already loaded in the car." He smiled, offering coffee. Madeline grinned and invited Steven in.

For the next few days and with a final blessing from Henry about Jane's job, she, Madeline, and Steven settled into their summer living arrangements. Since Jane had a two-bedroom upstairs, she proposed that Steven stay with her. To everyone surprise, Madeline loved this idea. Jane assumed it was because she liked Danny more than she admitted. Steven assumed Madeline was trying to keep boundaries, which he hated but respected. Only Madeline knew the truth; her nights would be occupied by a journal.

The next week, Steven and Madeline were knee-deep in sorting the mostly trash but occasional treasure at the gallery. Though they never specifically made a plan, Steven and Madeline had always been able to work together very well. Steven first threw out all the broken furniture and the rusted appliances. Madeline sorted through all the boxes that were mostly newspapers, empty containers, and clothes. On rare occasions, she found a hidden gem, like an old book, a record in perfect condition, or a black and white picture of a story never told.

Madeline teased that the gallery was like a clown car. Even after filling up the dumpster twice, the room still looked like a natural disaster.

"I hunger," Steven yelled, coming from a corner holding a broken chair above his head. "I shall go seek food. Burger and fries?"

"Yes, Please," Madeline shouted shortly before the door closed behind Steven.

Madeline sighed, feeling like she had not made a bit of progress all morning. Out of the blue, something in the back corner caught her eye. It looked to be a faced down picture stuck in between the wall and baseboard. Madeline rolled towards and reached for it, and the most bizarre thing happened, Madeline fell out of her chair, making a loud thump.

Madeline has been in a wheelchair since she was three; she can count the times she has fallen out of them. Once when she was 11, wrestling with her cousins. And once last year on the night she broke up with Steven.

Madeline had much too much to drink. Jane swears that she just gracefully slid out of the chair like a cartoon character and then hurled all over Jane's shoes. Jane still believes Steven owes her new shoes.

So falling out of the chair was very particular, indeed. If she thought about it, the fall might have freaked Madeline out, but she was too fixated on getting the picture. On her butt, Madeline wiggled the picture loose and gasped when she saw what the photo was.

"I got fries, curly fries, and sweet potato fries," Steven announced as Madeline rushed to sit back up. Sticking the picture between her seat pad.

"I forgot some paperwork at the apartment, and I might have to take them downtown, some licensing stuff; I'll be back in a few hours." Madeline nervously lied, hoping Steven wouldn't offer to go. Luckily he was lost in fries.

Madeline stood at the door for a minute then forced herself to knock. "Come on in." the voice invited.

"Hi." Madeline rolled in. "I'm sorry, I didn't know you'd be here too."

"No, it's great to see you." Danny and Madeline grinned. Charlie rolled her eyes. "I'm sorry I have not been around; work and family have just been intense lately. Are you still doing the workday, Saturday?"

"Yup." Madeline nodded.

"I'll be there with bells on." Danny said, "Will you let me know if you hear anything, Charlie?"

"I will, indeed," Charlie reassured him as Danny gave her a weird look, smiled at Madeline, and left, closing the door behind him.

"Hi…" Charlie said. Reminding herself that she had a promise to keep and had to let Madeline direct the conversation. "How are you?"

"You are going to think this is the craziest question you have ever heard, probably in your life." Madeline nervously laughed.

"Probably not even the craziest I heard this morning," Charlie confessed unexpectedly, then remembered she probably should not have. "I get weird questions all the time, mostly about my legs." She laughed, mentally patting herself on the back. Clever save.

"Ummm," Madeline stumbled on her words. "Charlie, I have to just spit it out and ask... is... is this, a picture of... us?"

"Let me see," Charlie's head was spinning, but she really wanted to stay cool. Cool Charlie is what they call her. Actually, no one called her that, but maybe she would run it by Danny. Focus Charlie focus. Stay in human form, and don't squeal because you've been looking for that damn picture for a century. "Nope."

"Nope?" Madeline prepared herself for a long dissertation but was not ready for a simple, nope. "Don't you think that looks like me?" Charlie nodded. "And that looks like you when you sing."

"What's my name?" Charlie suddenly popped into a pixle and just flew out of Madeline's arms reach.

"What?!?" Madeline was so confused, a little aggravated, and more entertained than she should have been.

"I cannot tell you anymore until you say my full name," Charlie yelled quickly, now floating at eyesight level with Madeline.

"That's ridiculous." Madeline sighed in frustration. "Who told you to do that?"

"You did, dummy." Charlie landed in Madeline's lap. "I told you it was a bad plan, but you insisted. Now, not only do you have to say my name, but you also have to admit you were wrong. Damn, it's a good day."

"So, do we know each other?" Madeline pressed on.

"Yup," Charlie nodded.

"Are we..." Madeline asked

"No. and EWW!" Charlie added. "And your next question is. Double eww, hell no. Danny's like a very annoying little brother. Eww."

"Omg, can you read my mind?" Madeline covered her ears, although she didn't know why.

"It was, I mean… it's our thing." Charlie stretched out her arms and bowed, waiting for applause. Madeline rolled her eyes.

"So you know everything about me?" Madeline questioned.

"Pretty much." Charlie grinned.

"How is that fair?" Madeline asked.

"Once again, my long lost friend, not my fault,… this time. Sure I've made many questionable choices. Ooo, that you don't know about, but this is all on you." Charlie said, giggling.

"So, I really did put a spell on myself?" Madeline asked. Charlie sighed and rolled her eyes. Charlie wondered if Madeline had lost some of her quick wit; she hoped not. That would be annoying. "So, if I put a spell on myself, maybe I… added some conditions… like, you have to… answer all direct questions."

"You're you. Not more stupid. Yay…" So excited, Charlie almost choked Madeline as she hugged her neck. "Although we do have to talk about the Steven thing."

"Are you really a pixie?" Madeline asked. Charlie nodded and gave Madeline the short version with demonstrations. In Pixie form, Charlie stood six inches tall. Standing in front of Madeline, Charlie allowed her to soak her greatness in. Charlie was incredibly gorgeous, with long blonde hair, with the bluest eyes Madeline had ever seen. Madeline grinned as Charlie graciously spread her wings. Charlie admitted she enjoyed flying much more than doing spells, but she was decent in a pinch.

Charlie confessed she has only been performing as a drag queen for about 25 years. She enjoys singing, and it was a way to fit into the community.

"Ok, I have to get to a gig." Charlie popped into her drag queen form. "Do you want me to help you learn spells?"

"See you tonight, Charlie A…" Madeline mumbled a last name starting with an A, nodded, and grin.

"Nice try…" Charlie said. "But who says my name is even in English. But for what it's worth, I have missed you with every fiber of my being."

While Charlie was talking, she had gotten something from her closet. She carefully put the newly found picture in the perfectly sized frame. Everyone who would see it would see a picture of drag queen Charlie towering over Madeline at a recent gig. Only Madeline and Charlie saw a black and white picture of themselves in another time. Madeline sitting in a chair, Charlie standing on Madeline's shoulder as a pixle, both looking like they were going to burst into laughter.

*

Madeline could not help but grin at all the people who showed up to help her Saturday morning. She had three piles outside, save, donate, and trash, and told everyone just to use their best judgment. Madeline knew almost everyone who was helping. Jane did bring a gorgeous boy-toy but winked and said Madeline didn't need to learn his name. Danny and Charlie brought a girl she had seen a few times in passing but had never been introduced to.

"Madeline, this is our friend, Treeva." Danny introduced her to Madeline. "She runs errands for me at the office and will do almost anything for a pineapple pepperoni pizza." Treeva shyly smiled, then got back to work. Treeva appeared to be a cute teenage girl, maybe a few years too young to have a full-time summer job, but she seemed to be working well with Danny. And Madeline was thankful for the extra hands.

"Psst," Charlie whispered rather loudly at Madeline, who was alone in the storage room looking for packing tape. "Pop quiz, try your sight spell on Treeva." Before Madeline could question her, Charlie disappeared back to the front room.

For the next hour, Charlie taunted Madeline as Madeline tried to ignore her dare by continuing working. But as Charlie knew it would, curiosity finally got the better of her.

Madeline found an out-of-the-way spot where no one would notice her creepily staring at this young kid, except for Charlie, who could barely keep a straight face. Madeline finally gave in, stretched her wrist five times as if she was warming up. Pointing her finger at Treeva, who was across the room, then spoke the magical words she had learned the night before. And. Just. Began. Screaming...

"Paper cut!" Charlie was right behind Madeline even before she started freaking out. "It seems our girl doesn't like paper cuts. I, on the other hand, enjoy just a little pain..." Charlie announced in her full drag queen singing voice. Everyone laughed and went back to work—everyone, that is, except for Madeline.

"Charlie, can you help me look for a bandage in the storage room?" Madeline asked, trying to sound normal.

"I have one," offered Steven.

"I have one too," Danny raised his voice.

"So do I..." Jane yelled just to entertain herself. She most certainly did not.

"Naw, I have one in my purse, and I just wanted Charlie to get it." Madeline grabbed Charlie's arm. "Is. That. A demon.?" Madeline hissed as soon as they reached the storage room.

"Demon is such a negative word," Charlie sighed. She explained that MOST demons get a really bad rap because they are ugly, really ugly. Charlie has known Treeva for decades, and except for cheating at every poker night, she's mostly harmless. And for some reason, she worships Danny, so she is usually on her best behavior around him.

"Does Danny know about Treeva?" Madeline asked, finally calming down. She was still totally freaked out about the demon in her gallery, but Charlie had a strangely calming effect on her. "Charlie!" she scolded as Charlie giggled.

"I keep meaning to tell him..." Charlie confessed. "But it's so damn funny because sometimes he gets on his high horse. You can see him so serious about trying to mentor this homeless teenage girl. All I can see is this four-foot demon with beetle eyes and ugly tangled horn staring at his butt as he walks away. Treeva's short, deformed claws trying to grab his package when he walks by her." Madeline tried not to grin.

The day was an amazing success. The crew got about 2/3rds of the stuff out of the gallery. Madeline finally saw the light at the end of the hoarding tunnel. It would take Steven and Madeline a few more weeks to completely clear out space, but with so much more room, the process would move much faster.

"My grandfather will have a catered dinner in the courtyard of my apartments at 7, y'all, please come. Henry always cooks enough for an army. Please bring a date and at least 2 friends and/or family members." At 5 o'clock Danny announced he had a surprise. Everyone clapped, knowing a meal from Henry was a gourmet experience. The group finished their work areas and left the gallery soon after, wanting to clean up for dinner.

*

Madeline had loved the courtyard at first sight. Still, when she opened the door from her apartment after a quick shower and change, the small outdoor area felt magical. Christmas lights flickered. The water from the fountain seemed to dance, reflecting a rainbow of colors. A three-piece band played a jazz piece that Madeline recognized but couldn't name. And the buffet table included a prime rib roast and a choice of seafood for an entrée.

"Believe it or not," Danny said, sneaking by Madeline as she was lost in amazement. "Henry decided to do this, this morning, just because the meat looked extra fresh at the market." They both laughed.

In a blink of an eye, the usually solitary courtyard was wall to wall with people. Madeline knew about a third. She was a little embarrassed to be seated at the only round table with a cloth. Still, She felt less guilty as Henry, Jane, Danny, Charlie, Steven, and Treeva joined her one by one.

Everyone ate, drank, danced, and sang until the early morning. Madeline felt obligated to dance with Henry when he so charmingly stretched out his arm. Then she was kind of stuck in dance mode because Steven asked even before Henry released her hand. Then Danny asked. Then Steven asked again. And Madeline was absolutely thrilled that both Charlie and Jane seemed so entertained by her suiters. Madeline swore she saw money being exchanged as if they were taking bets.

With the slightest bit of suggestion, Charlie was persuaded to sing with the band. Madeline stared at her, almost hypnotized by a melody she didn't think she had ever heard in her life. Yet, she knew every word, even mouthing them with the crowd as everyone began to sing along. The crowd was having such a good time, no one noticed the tiny droplets of water seemingly appearing from nowhere. There wasn't a single cloud in the sky.

The fully lit fountain in the center of the party now seemed to have taken over the full courtyard, growing water spouts sporadically, spitting water into the air in rhythm with the band. Although it was pretty as if the fountain was a music conductor and the water its musical notes. Madeline could not shake the feeling that something bad was coming.

Madeline noticed Henry staring at the fountain intensely, after closing his eyes for what seemed like forever. He looked like he was talking to the fountain or pleading with an invisible god.

Madeline tried to get Charlie's attention; she knew Charlie could explain what was going on. But Charlie, along with everyone else, was lost in song and dance.

Although many voices were singing, they all seemed to fade away as one voice became louder. There was an instant change in the mood, from a whimsical dance to a sober affair.

Charlie suddenly had stopped singing, the band followed suit, then the crowd lowered to anxious whispers. Yet, the mysterious voice kept getting uncomfortably louder. As if woken up from a bad dream, the crowd began looking around, trying to figure out where the strange voice was coming from.

Danny, who had just been at Madeline's side, was now by his grandfather's, whispering something in his ear. All the while, Henry did not take his eyes off of the fountain. The two seemed to be quietly arguing. Henry seemed to be pushing Danny to do something, and Danny sternly refusing.

Madeline finally spotted Charlie, who was looking down from the balcony. She swore she heard Charlie's voice in her head saying, "Just keep calm. This is like a dramatic emergency broadcast message system for magic users without those annoying beeps."

Ever since Charlie had helped Madeline with the first spell, Madeline felt a heightened sense of Charlie's feelings. Charlie felt happy when she was singing; she was very guarded the rest of the time. Even though Charlie was trying to make Madeline feel safe, Madeline noticed how intensely Charlie was staring at Danny.

It felt like the courtyard had surround sound even though there were no speakers to be seen. The ground vibrated in rhythm to the solo voice singing.

When the singing ended, all the lights in the courtyard and the bordering apartments went dark. The fountain's lights now seem so much brighter, almost blinding. The ground growled a little like a mini earthquake or at least an aftershock.

The fountain's lights reflected its waters now flowing with strange reddish dye, and the voice coming from the water's base said... "Danger is coming." The water in the fountain whirled around the basin and formed an outline of a being.

"Charlie," Madeline said and instinctually held out her arms in a defensive pose.

"What!?!" Charlie said. Madeline was so happy to see Charlie appear on her shoulder, she didn't see what was going on around her. Charlie noticed the fountain, and her whole demeanor changed. "Oh... Oh..." Charlie began sobbing. "Kisseis..."

"Hello, mom, my love," Kisseis said. Madeline was paralyzed with wonder and amazement.

"I thought you were dead." Charlie was still visibly shaken. "I would listen for you night after night, but you never came. And Madeline was… and I was so alone."

"Madeline was what!?!" Madeline finally was able to spit out a sentence.

"I cannot stay long. They don't know I am moving freely through the compound." Kisseis said.

"You can't go back." Charlie pleaded.

"I am needed there," Kisseis said. "My waters keep the weak alive. I didn't even want to come here tonight, but I had to warn Madeline, darkness you can only fight is trying to free itself from your ancestor's spell. You must return to the source and finish what they couldn't."

"Oh god, they are coming," Kisseis said, sounding suddenly distressed. "Madeline, I will try to find out more, but you need to talk to the five pillars of the community; each will teach you a spell you need. And together, you can finally defeat the darkness. Blessed waters be with you always."

Charlie quickly flew to where Kisseis was standing, but she melted into the fountain. Charlie screamed with grief. Madeline's first thought was to comfort Charlie, but before she could, Madeline noticed something. Everyone around her, except for Charlie, was frozen. No one moved; it was as if someone or something had pressed pause.

Instinctively and without knowing she was doing it, Madeline snapped her fingers. Suddenly the band started playing right where they left off. Everyone started dancing, singing, laughing, and drinking again. The lights came back on.

There was no sign of the beautiful water nymph. It was almost like the fountain with Kisseis never happened, except when Madeline spotted Charlie, she knew it was true. Charlie was human again, sitting on the ground beside the fountain, tears running down her face.

"You need to save her, Madeline," Charlie said. "She is my daughter."

*

Danny escorted a distraught Charlie back to her apartment. Jane and Steven offered to helped Henry pack up the buffet and dishes. Madeline insisted on sitting with Charlie after Danny gave her a glass of water and made Charlie lay down on her couch. Before they knew it, Charlie was snoring,

"I can't believe she fell asleep," Madeline said. She noticed Danny avoided eye contact, "What did you do?"

"I've known Charlie my whole life," Danny confessed. "She would have cried three more minutes, then oh my god ... she would have done something impulsive that might have ended really badly. Like death and destruction badly. So after she slugs me in about 20 minutes, she will forgive me."

"You drugged her?" Madeline asked.

"My family knows a little magic..." Danny shyly whispered. Madeline's brain was already spinning with questions, what's one more. "Did she tell you how she evolved into a drag queen?"

"No..." Madeline said. She needed to know about 20 things, but this, this moved to the front of the line.

"When I was five, I caught her in Henry's restaurant in Pixie form. I yelled, "Fairy," as any mischievous boy would do. It startled and pissed the shit out of her that a little boy saw through her powerful spell that she had spent years perfecting. I yelled "Fairy" so loud that a six-foot hairy drag queen was sitting at the bar when everyone turned to see. To break the awkward silence, Charlie started singing, And the rest, as they say, is history."

"That's hysterical." Madeline smiled. "Weren't you freaked out or scared?"

"Oh..." Danny hesitated, choosing his words carefully. "I had a very unique family. They believed in monsters under the bed and ghosts in the attic..."

"Damnit, Danny." Charlie's voiced screamed before her eyes fully opened. She sat straight up, ready to banter with Danny about her involuntary
Page | 47

nap. Then she remembered. She lovingly patted Danny's arm and then stared at Madeline.

"Charlie, who or what are the five pillars?" Madeline asked quietly. Charlie stared at Danny, knowing he should answer this.

"I honestly don't know who the five pillars are," Danny said.

"Well, that is a lawyer's answer if I ever heard one," Charlie said in sudden anger.

"Maybe I should go," Madeline said. This was the first time since she moved to New Orleans that she felt like an outsider.

"I actually think Danny should leave now," Charlie said sternly; she could not look at Danny.

"Henry..." Danny whispered as he opened the door. "If I had to guess, Henry would be one... I know he was a pillar at one point. But he stopped telling me stuff. And now I refuse to be drawn back in. I'm truly sorry, Charlie; I love you like a sister, but you know I can't. Please don't make me ask. I just can't." and Danny left.

Chapter 4

Danny drove 30 miles west, the last five in almost complete darkness. But it was as if the car followed the cement, then the gravel, then the dirt roads on autopilot. Danny closed the car door carefully, trying not to slam it. The full moon drew a pretty outline of the old house and lit the sidewalk leading to the back patio, overlooking the lake. The two-story house was dark except for the kitchen and the back porch. Danny decided to go around back instead of waking the sleepy house.

"You look tired." She said, staring at the water, not even turning around to greet Danny. On the patio table, there was a bowl of Shrimp and Grits, fresh from the stove. Danny knew arguing was futile. And it wasn't until that second he realized how hungry he was. He took a few bites in silence, then took her wine glass and drank a few sips. She grinned as she heard her son smack his lips in joy.

"Where's Father?" Danny asked, leaning over, giving his mother a kiss on the cheek.

"He is out of town," Ida confessed, now looking at Danny.

"Mom, you promised you would come to stay with me whenever he was gone," Danny said, very annoyed.

"He will only be gone a few weeks," Ida said. "Besides, you're busy courting ."

"I. Am. What!?!" Danny asked, now completely irritated. "You're ridiculous! Anyways..." Danny softened his tone. "She's still hung up on her ex. And worse, he seems like he completely adores her. Damnit, mom." Danny had no idea why he just said all that. Danny had no idea how Ida knew about Madeline and why she always had a meal waiting for him. Every meal was exactly what he craved, no matter the time of day. Even at 3 am, like tonight. He just laughed quietly out loud as if surrendering to a greater force, wiping an unexpected tear away.

"Can you ask father to help Charlie get Kisseis back?" Danny got up from the table and knelt by his mother's side, tucking his hands between hers.

"You know I cannot. But you probably can." Ida said, patting his hands, staring at the sky. "Do you remember how much your sister loved full moons? She would stay up all night on the docks, just staring at the moon and talking to the fireflies. Telling them all her secrets."

"I remember mama, I do." His anger disappeared. She could ask his father to help. Just as Danny could have helped Charlie. But it would open up wounds that still haven't healed in 10 years.

"Can you sit with me for a while?" Ida asked. "Maybe your sister will show up, and I can cook a ridiculously big breakfast for my two wonderful children."

"Yes, mama, I would love to sit with you for a while." Danny turned his head to hide his tears. His mother has moments, even hours or days of such clarity. And then a smell or a sight or a sound will remind her of Abigail, and it will send her mind to another time, where she waits for a daughter that will never come home.

*

"Please come and stay with me for the week." Danny pleaded as Ida set a bag of food in his trunk and closed it. "Henry would be over the moon, and Charlie might even forgive me if I brought her favorite person to see her."

"You know I like to stay close to home," Ida said, giving her son an extra squeeze as he rolled down the window to say his goodbyes. "I'm sorry you worry about me so. But here I still hear Abigail's laughter. Here I can still talk to her spirit. And I'm pretty sure your dad put a watch spell on the house, so I can't do anything too crazy." Neither laughed.

"Don't look so sad, my darling Daniel," Ida added. "Abigail worshipped you and would be so heartbroken if you turned your back on your destiny because you felt responsible for her death. Charlie already misses you so, go fix the things you can control. Maybe I'll come up next Sunday for brunch. Then we can walk through the farmer's market."

"Love you, mom. I'll try to come to dinner a few times this week." Danny said. He slowly drove away as Ida released her touch on his extended arm. He sighed when he looked in the review mirror, and saw his mom with her right arm out, as if holding a little girl's hand while walking back to her house.

Ida found comfort living in Danny and Abigail's childhood home. But it broke Danny each and every time he saw the old house. The house he used to think of as a magical mansion.

Danny wondered why happy memories always seemed to fade faster than tragic ones. He rationally knew he had a thousand happy memories of the house and the water and the dock. But all he could remember was the last time he saw Abigail in the kitchen.

Danny was his mom's favorite, just by a smidge. Abigail was dad's by a mile. The only difference was mom hid it; Father didn't.

Mom always teased that her marriage with their father was arranged. Looking back, Danny realized this was probably true. On their best days, they seemed like friendly co-workers. Danny could name the handful of times he saw them kissing.

Through the grapevine, the story was mom was on track to be one of the most powerful psychics in the magic world. And because one of dad's ancestors was a great warlock, they were destined to be Louisiana's power couple.

For a while, mom's powers did grow. But dad's never seemed to. The second that Abigail showed an interest in magic, dad saw it as a chance to redeem himself. If Eugene Boudreaux couldn't be the most powerful warlock in the world, or at least in the great state of Louisiana, he could be the father of the most powerful witch.

Danny enjoyed magic but never took the time to learn. This annoyed Eugene and slowly became the iceberg between them. Although 5 years younger than Danny, Abigail was smart as a whip. She saw her chance to win over dad, which seemed important because Danny was good at everything else.

"What are you doing in here, Abigail?" Danny replayed the last conversation he had with his little sister a million times. "Dad's going to have a meltdown."

"Ha! That's where you are wrong; Mr. Know It All." Abigail said, sticking her tongue at her brother, "Dad said now that I'm double digits, I can hang out in his library." Abigail sat straight up behind the overgrown desk that made her look even smaller than she was.

"Don't tell mom, but he said I'd get a buck for every spell that I learn this summer. And I thought if I wow him, maybe he will pay more." She tried to evilly laugh, which Danny found adorable. This only made her mad. Abigail punched him while putting a scrap of paper in her pocket, and skipped out of her father's office. "Better get out of here, brother! You don't have his blessing to be here." Danny chased Abigail all the way downstairs through the house to the kitchen.

"Settle down," Ida said, trying to hide her amusement. "Hey, I sense a storm is coming. Can y'all stay in the house today?"

"No can do, mother," Danny said. "I'm going fishing with Grandpa Henry today."

"If he doesn't have to, neither do I." and Abigail stomped out of the kitchen. That was the very last time Danny saw his sister.

On the morning that Abbigail died, Danny was gone for 3 hours and 27 minutes. He doesn't know why but the number stuck in his head. He would have been gone longer, but, as usual, Ida was right. There was a storm coming. Instead of going fishing, the two just grabbed lunch at Henry's, then Henry took Danny shopping to buy a video game.

Henry had sworn him to secrecy on this purchase because one, Eugene, hated video games, which encouraged Henry just a little. And two, Abigail wouldn't get her monthly surprise from Henry until a few days later. Danny teased that he would take this secret to the grave to avoid Abigail's whining that he got his surprise before hers... But neither feared a lecture from his dad about the video game because Eugene never went into Danny's room.

Before Danny even open the car door, he heard his mom screaming. Henry and Danny jumped out of the still-running vehicle to the back. Ida had collapsed just short of the docks. Eugene was standing at the edge of the water, hands above his head, muttering spells in French.

Henry jumped into the lake. For hours Ida screamed, what felt like one long agonizing breathless cry. For hours, Henry swam. And for hours Eugene muttered spells. As if tied down on a track, Danny was paralyzed, just watching the train in slow motion coming towards him.

Danny's father was the first to come in, "She's not gone; I'll just go find a spell. There surely must be a spell." Eugene said. And he disappeared into the house, not offering his grieving wife any support or acknowledgment.

Henry finally stops swimming when he realized Danny and Ida were now completely alone in the twilight. Henry silently hugged Danny, then scooped up a sobbing Ida and carried her into the dark house.

Danny knew he needed to follow but wanted just a minute. The fireflies were coming out. He allowed himself to walk around the lake's edge, stopping back at the docks that seemed eerily quiet now. Danny was trying to find the strength to go into the house.

A light wind blew, and he noticed a tiny piece of paper folded in a cute way that only girls could have the patience to fold, in the grass near the water's edge. He carefully opened the note as if it was the most precious thing in the world.

"Summon a beautiful mermaid for father and be his favorite forever." with a drawn happy face. It was in Abigail's handwriting. Danny slept on the deck that night, and many nights after that. Henry always covered him up with Abigail's favorite blanket on most nights. Ida tried to on her better days when Henry wasn't there.

Danny thought about giving the note to Ida or Eugene, but that seemed cruel. So he kept it in his wallet. And every new wallet since the tragic day.

*

"Hey, Danny." Jane greeted him as he came through the courtyard late Sunday morning; she and Steven were sharing a newspaper by the fountain, no longer running water. "I'm going to go help Henry set up for brunch in a few minutes."

"Can you tell him that I'm feeling a bit under the weather, but I'll help close tonight?" Danny asked.

"Madeline has a bug, too," Steven added. "We had a whole afternoon in the Garden District planned, but she said she needed a raincheck." Steven felt a bit like an ass, trying to establish his territory, but not big enough of an ass to take it back.

"Ok, well…" Danny did feel a little targeted by Steven but could not muster a clever banter. "Have a good Sunday." Danny slowly dragged himself up the stairs carrying a grocery bag of food that Ida had sent with him. He closed the door behind him, locked the chain, slid down the door's wall, and just cried.

"Let me in." Charlie banged on Danny's door 45 minutes later. "You don't have to talk to me, but I bet Ida sent me a Tupperware of yummy goodness, so cough it up, Boudreaux."

"Enter," Danny said, unlatching the chain lock. Charlie smiled when she saw a lunch setting for two, well, at least two plastic forks.

"How's Ida?" Charlie asked, taking a fried shrimp from the basket.

"Bat shit crazy," Danny said. Charlie was the only one with who he could be honest about Ida. Even after 10 years, Eugene really believed that she would just snap out of it at any moment. And even though Henry was the strongest, most logical person Danny had in his life, even Henry needed hope for his only granddaughter. Henry would absolutely light up when he hears Danny had a good visit with Ida. Danny eventually stopped telling him about the bad visits and never ever about the violent ones.

"How's Eugene?" Charlie asked, just to be cordial. Charlie hated Eugene as much as she loved Ida, and that was an awful lot.

"No idea," Danny said, surrendering. "Mom said he left a few days ago and that he would be gone a few weeks. With her sense of days, lord knows what that translates in real-time. I think he got an apartment on campus now that he's tenured. I wish he would just leave her. That would be the kindest thing he has ever done. But she looks good on his resume. Professor of History of Voodoo and magic married to an original Guidry…"

"Henry would love to set her up in the Quarter. We could all look out for her."

"She just refuses to leave the house; when was the last time she was in the city for longer than a meal? Or even a full show of yours? At least, up until I left for college, she made an effort to try to participate in my life. No matter how bad things got, she made me breakfast every morning, sometimes half-dressed with crazy hair, but she made that breakfast every morning, kissed me on the cheek, and told me that she loved me."

"And on the way home I would hope and pray that when I got to the house, she would still be with me, but she was lost in a fog more often than not. At least I had her in the mornings." Danny confessed. "But the moment I left for college, I guess she felt done. And she could finally let herself drown in grief."

"I'm really sorry about last night," Charlie confessed. "I was a bully. I should have known you needed time to think about it before you could help me find Kisseis."

"See this?" Danny angrily raised his voice, and pulled out a folded piece of paper from his wallet that Charlie had never seen nor known about. "Read it!" Danny pounded his fists to the table. Charlie was actually scared.

"Summon a beautiful mermaid for Father and be his favorite forever." Charlie read quietly.

"Louder," Danny screamed.

"Summon a beautiful mermaid for Father and be his favorite forever." Charlie started tearing up.

"Abigail wrote this five hours before she drowned." Danny was still screaming, but Charlie no longer felt threatened. "I know this because I saw her write it. And when I teased her about it, she drew a happy face, punched me, then ran to mom."

"I don't..." Charlie said, trying to understand.

"I was there, Charlie." Danny speaking matter-of-factly now. "For weeks, she had been going on and on about buying a boombox. Mom said if she did chores and saved half, mom would pay for the rest. I knew she was going to do something crazy..."

"You couldn't have..." Charlie tried to reason with Danny, but this only made him angrier.

"Yes." Danny was screaming again. "Don't you get it? I had my first premonition that day. I knew something bad was going to happen. My mom even asked us not to go out. But Henry said he was going to buy me a video game. So I figured, what's the worse that could happen? We get a flat tire? The stove dies? I lost everything that day. I lost my baby sister, mother, and father in one bad spell that I could have stopped. There's a reason why people think magic and voodoo are bad. Because they are, so I beg you, do not ask me to help you find Kisseis. I cannot. I killed my sister that day, and I have slowly killed my mother and Eugene every single day since."

"But..." Charlie pleaded.

"Get out, Charlie."

"You're just emotional from being with Ida." Charlie tried again.

"Leave before I hurt you, Charlie," Danny said in a voice Charlie didn't recognize. Danny's eyes turned cold, the lights in the apartments flickered, and the door opened. Charlie left in pixie form, crying. And Danny pointed, magically slamming his opened door.

*

Madeline slowly rolled out of her apartment. She locked the door, put on her sunglasses, the extra-large ones, and slowly left the courtyard, a little surprised that it was empty. Normally at least one or two of her neighbors would be sitting by the fountain, having a cup of coffee. She crossed the street to try to catch up with Jane.

"I'm sorry to bother you, Henry," Madeline said. "Jane wanted to borrow the car today." Madeline took out a set of keys as she moved closer to Henry, finding him sitting at a table at his closed restaurant.

"Please feel at home here." Henry smiled, now looking up from a stack of papers. "Jane ran to the butchers, but can I make you a quick breakfast?"

"Oh no..." Madeline said. "I really need to get going. I'm dragging this morning."

"Please, I am so hungry for an omelet, but Danny teases that I cannot cook anything for less than three people." Henry pleaded, and Madeline nodded with gratitude. Madeline could not remember if she ate anything since the party more than 48 hours ago.

"If you don't mind me saying, you look a little rough around the edges." Henry returned almost immediately with two huge fluffy omelets.

"I promise I am usually more put together on a Monday morning," Madeline said. Feeling like she ought to show her new co-worker's grandfather, possibly supervisor, that she was not nursing a hangover. Although it sure felt that way.

"I know those glazed eyes and little shakes," Henry said. "If you are half as diligent and committed as Danny goes on about you, I assume you haven't eaten or slept since meeting Kisseis. How many spells have you learned?"

"The book," Madeline didn't expect to be so blunt. Still, she had a feeling that trying to hide the truth or even watering it down would be completely wasted on Henry. "The whole book. Some spells better than others but yup, the whole book."

"Do you need another omelet?" Henry asked, in the complete delight of Madeline's eagerness to learn. Madeline grinned.

"Excuse me, Mr. Guidry." A man walked into the restaurant. Madeline thought he looked familiar. "By any chance, have you seen Charlie? She had a performance last night, but she called in sick. I just wanted to check on her. In the last ten years since I've been booking her, she has never missed a gig. She doesn't seem to be home either.."

"No, I actually thought it was strange that she missed brunch yesterday. I will check and let her know you stop by." Henry said. The man thanked him and left.

"Are you worried?" Madeline asked after the man was out of earshot...

"I'm not, not worried. I'll call Danny."

*

"Hey, Daniel." Henry had to leave a message. "You're probably in court. We were just wondering if you had seen Charlie lately? She missed a performance last night, and we were a little concerned. Anyways just tell her to check-in. Come to the restaurant tonight, and I'll cook us a late dinner. Love you."

Danny didn't bother listening to the message. As soon as he saw who was calling, Danny let it go straight to voice mail.

"Hey, I thought it was you." Danny's secretary, Anna, stuck her head in his office. "I thought you were taking Mondays off to work at the foundation."

"I wanted to catch up on some paperwork," Danny said. "Can you print out the weekly reports, pull Hernandez's file, order lunch, and hold all my calls."

"Even from Ida and Henry?" Anna asked.

"Especially from Ida and Henry..." Danny said, immediately feeling bad. "But do try to figure out if Ida needs something tangible," Anna nodded in an unspoken understanding and left his office, closing the door behind her.

This is where Danny was happiest, felt most in control. He liked organizing files and scheduling dates. To outsiders, his desk looked cluttered, but to Danny, it was comfort. Everything was in black and white; all the laws were written, people were either guilty or innocent. Danny knew with a shake of a hand and a direct look in the eye which his clients were.

Anna tried very hard to make him eat in the lunchroom, but her efforts fell on deaf ears, so she left him alone. He was still frantically typing an argument when she left at seven, two hours after the office closed.

"Good night. I'm probably going to make a dinner pick up." Anna said. "Can I tell Henry you're alive?"

"If you must." Danny grinned for the first time that day. "Thank you. Hey, can you tell him I'm in court all week and will probably stay at mom's a few nights because it's closer to the courthouse?"

"Is there anything I need to know, Danny? If not as your secretary, then as your friend?" Anna asked.

"Nope. I'm fine. See you tomorrow." Danny smiled. Danny liked Anna. They went out a few times, but casual dating had stopped months before he had hired her. Both agreeing that Danny was a much better boss than a boyfriend. But they knew everything worked out perfectly, and Anna knew just enough to manage him, allowing him to feel safe at work.

*

"I'm so sorry to bother you this late in the evening, but you are listed as an emergency contact." The security guard looked very uncomfortable. Rumors were Fr. Karl was the oldest, grumpiest priest in the parish. He sure looked like both. Fr. Karl stared at the guard to continue. "Umm, there are some creepy noises from the bell tower, and they asked me to contact you."

"Do I look like a handyman?" Fr. Karl asked.

"No Father... no. god Bless you, sir." The security guard, Al answered nervously, amusing Fr. Karl. "But see your name..." Al really wanted to make sure his butt was covered, now convinced that even with the age and man of God thing, Fr. Karl could snap him in half.

"What kind of noises are people hearing?" Fr. Karl asked, done toying with the young boy. This was probably Al's first job. Although fun, Fr. Karl didn't want to scar him for life.

"All day long, people have been hearing crying from the bell tower, half of the tourists are hoping it's a ghost. Half the parishioners think it's a sign of the second coming. A few say it's just a rusty chain. I personally am hoping it's a ghost. What do you think?" Al asked his new best friend. Fr. Karl sighed.

"Probably not the second coming, and a ghost sounds better than a rusty chain, but I think it's the latter. I need you to guard the door behind me. Don't let anyone follow. I'll be up there a few hours." Fr. Karl said.

"Is it that complicated to fix?" Al Asked.

"Nope. There are just 126 steps. Too damn many for these old knees. And if I take that long, I'm still relevant and needed." Fr. Karl said; Al looked at him with kinder eyes.

"Can I help?" Al asked sincerely; Fr. Karl appreciated that, patted him on the shoulder, then began his painful climb, moaning at every completed step.

Breathless and tired, Fr. Karl locked the second door in the bell tower behind him. After taking more than a few minutes to catch his breath, he smiled. He always forgets how beautiful it is up here—a 360-degree scenic view of the city and waters.

"You know, you could just have called me." Fr. Karl said into the darkness.

"I'm sorry." A voice whispered from the wooden rafters.

"Hello, my sweet Charlie." Fr. Karl said as Charlie flew to him.

"Would you like to pray?" Fr. Karl asked, immediately heartbroken after seeing the tears running down her face. He stretched out his arm, Charlie landed in his palm, and for a good while, they prayed together. "Do you remember all of my prayers that I had to learn in the Seminary?" Fr. Karl asked after a long period of silence. "I bet you do, probably better than me as the years march on."

Karl had met Charlie when he was ten years old. Even as a young boy, he felt a calling to enter the priesthood. His folks told him to pray on it, and if he truly had a calling, he would receive a sign only he could see. Although Karl tried his hardest to be the perfect child, he did have a mischievous streak. And cried and cried when he accidentally locked himself in the bell tower while playing a discreet game of hide and seek with the other alter boys. He thought if a priest or a nun caught him, he would be asked to leave the church he loved so much.

Charlie did her best to let the little boy out of the bell tower without being seen, but Karl saw her. And 80 years and a thousand arguments later, Fr. Karl still believed in two undeniable truths. God, And no matter what Charlie called herself, she was God's angel leading him on the path to becoming a priest.

Charlie has lived hundreds of years but watching Fr. Karl grow old has been one of the hardest heartbreaks in her life. Charlie still saw the young man who would make her listen to every prayer he had to learn and watched every ceremony he practiced for. And no one, not Danny, not even Madeline, knew that once a week, he would pray with her. Once a week for 80 years, neither missing their standing date. They prayed on the phone if either was sick or out of town; this was Charlie's one constant.

"Forgive me, father, for I have sinned," Charlie said. "I really don't remember when my last confession was." Charlie flew around the bells, weaving through the rafters, starting to cry.

"Sit with me." Fr. Karl said. But she would not.

"I made promises I cannot keep." Charlie sobbed.

"Why can't you keep them?" Fr. Karl asked.

"Because..." Charlie sobbed harder, knowing that he was too fragile for the darkness coming even with all that Karl knew. "I think I asked too much of Danny this time. He kicked me out of his apartment. We have had knock out drag out fights before but never like this. When our very basic cores are on opposite ends of the spectrum."

"Is there a middle ground?" Fr. Karl asked.

"Not without him letting go of the delicate life he has so carefully and painfully stitched together. He needs certainty and routines and laws and science. Without these touchstones, Danny is so afraid that he'll become..."

"Ida." Fr. Karl's younger sister was close to her for a very long time. It just got too hard when Ida stopped answering the door.

"And Madeline…" Charlie stopped crying just long enough to catch her breath. "Oh my god, how can I take her hand and guide her into hell. Who does that? But I will do whatever it takes to get Kisseis back. Whatever it takes. I can't see you anymore. Please pray and bless me one more time."

"Charlie, you're being…" Before Fr. Karl could finish, he felt a gentle kiss on his right cheek. Then Charlie just flew away. Fr. Karl followed her tiny glow into the night's sky for as long as he could. Then looked towards the heavens.

Chapter 5

Henry could not concentrate on anything all day long, since his breakfast with Madeline. There was just a familiarity to that girl. More than a customer, or someone he may have crossed paths with, he immediately felt a strange connection to her when Danny introduced Madeline at brunch last week. And the short encounters with her during the week had been like strange Deja Vu moments. But breakfast with Madeline unleashed a flood of fuzzy memories that Henry could no longer ignore.

Mondays were usually Henry's slowest day, so he had no hesitation leaving Jane in the kitchen with his reliable servers. Jane promised to feed Danny or Charlie anything they requested if they ever showed up.

Henry started his vehicle with no particular destination in mind but ended up at a deserted corner of Lake Pontchartrain. He parked the truck as close to the water as he possibly could and sat on the tailgate for a long time. Drawing circles in the water, even though his feet were not touching the lake.

Henry could no longer resist the sweet temptation. He looked around, making sure there was no one watching him, then dove into the lake. The deeper Henry sank, the stronger and more alive he felt. The deeper he sank, the more his human form washed away with the waves, slowly revealing his true form.

Henry reached the bottom of the lake as a storm giant. Almost 26 feet from head to toe, his huge body leaned against a large structure at the bottom of the lake, probably a sunken boat. His blue skin glowed and attracted smaller fishes. This always made him happy, and for an hour, he just sat there and talked to the underwater creatures. Even though Henry could live in different forms in the waters, clouds, and cities as a human, his preference has always been the waters. But he has always lived where his family was, and in this lifetime, it was the city.

As relaxed as Henry was, enjoying being surrounded by the warm waters, Henry kept remembering Madeline or her shadows. He recalled her uncontrollable laughter that only a close friend would know. How could he know it?

In his hours of gushing about Madeline, Danny may have mentioned Madeline was adopted from a local church. Maybe Henry knew her grandmother? It sounded like a decent explanation, but his brain rejected it immediately.

Closing his eyes as the waves gently rocked him, he saw a dream of Madeline drinking with him. Then a tall, lanky guy came in between the two, touched his shoulder, apologized, touched his shoulder again, and then left in a hurry. Charlie seemed to be in the room too. Then Madeline was just gone.

Henry shot up from the calm waters like a missile, too angry to swim; luckily, no one was near his truck as he turned into his human form and slammed the truck's door. He was now certain someone or something had erased her from his memory.

Henry sped towards the city as the crystal clear night turned stormy. The full moon was now hidden behind dark clouds. As Henry's anger grew, so did the winds and the size of the raindrops. By the time Henry reached the Quarter, people were running from the streets, trying to find shelter from the sudden violent pop-up storm that none of the meteorologists had predicted.

Madeline had just closed the blinds at the gallery. She should have left two hours ago when Steven told her to, but he was meeting friends who just got to town, and Madeline wanted to get more work done. She was beginning to feel better and was anxious to try her "move object" spell in a practical setting.

Madeline was startled as the loudest clap of lightning she has ever heard echoed over the gallery. Just then, Henry appeared inside the doorway. At first, Madeline felt relieved. Then he took a step towards her, and Madeline saw a rage in his eyes that was not there when they had shared a lovely breakfast earlier that day.

"Is something wrong?" Madeline asked, instinctually backing up from him as he slowly and silently walked towards her. "Is it Danny or Charlie?"

"What. Are. You?" Henry screamed. The gallery shook. The winds outside howled, sounding like a hundred banshees, burning in a fire.

"I'm Madeline." Madeline shocked herself by how steady her voice was. She was, of course, scared beyond reason, but of his anger, not of him. Somehow, in this moment of madness, she knew, without a doubt, there was a difference. And Madeline trusted this.

"What. Are. You?" Henry screamed the same question again. "What did you do to me? Answer me, little girl." Henry took another step towards her. Madeline put her hands in the air, in a defensive stance, praying it would not come to that.

"Stop. Henry. STOP!" Charlie screamed from outside. Both Madeline and Henry looked around. Just then, there was a large slam against the door, hard enough to swing open... They both raced to the loud sound and found a very pissed off pixie. "It was my spell. I put a forget spell on you because you idiots made me. now calm the hell down." She wobbly flew towards them with wild hair and crushed wings. "I am not done yelling at you, Henry Guidry. I'm going to beat you, you stubborn old storm giant. but I think I have to pass out now...." And Charlie dropped onto Madeline's lap.

The rain pounding on the roof lessened. Henry was confused about many things, but one thing was for sure, his storm had injured Charlie, who must have been flying and got sucked up in the wind. And Henry just melted.

Henry found material to makeshift a bed on Madeline's desk. Henry gently examined his beloved pixie in silence. Charlie had a broken wing, two broken fingers, and a large bump on her beautiful forehead. Madeline instantly understood the true meaning of a gentle giant. Henry kissed her little hand as Charlie now sweetly snored.

"Could you... maybe not tell my great-grandson I attacked you?" Henry whispered. "Our relationship is fragile at best. And I'm pretty sure he would frown upon this... As he should." Madeline nodded, trying not to grin, touching his hand that was holding Charlie's...

"Henry..." Madeline said. "Who or what are the five pillars?"

Page | 65

"I have to go. I just do." Henry said very abruptly, as if he remembered something urgent, still looking at his precious Charlie. "I'm going to send Clara Dubios to take Charlie home with her. She has a little hospital for... special angels like Charlie. I'll plead your case, but she doesn't usually let humans go with the injured. After you see to Charlie, go home. I'll be in touch in a few days. And from the bottom of my heart, I sincerely apologize." The door swung closed before Madeline could say or do anything else.

"Where is she?" Clara Dubios asked about 20 minutes later; the second storm of the night came barging in the gallery.

"Hi, I'm Madeline. Thank you so much for taking..."

"Oh my gosh, Charlie." Clara ran to her, ignoring Madeline's greetings. "What did you do to her? She is the loveliest soul you will ever meet. Did you hit her with an electric fly swatter? Did you roll on her thinking she was a common insect?"

"Excuse me? Of course not!" Madeline was stunned at the unfounded accusations.

"Henry said there was a horrible accident. I assumed he was covering up for the humans again." This Clara chick was the walking stereotype of an evil ruler, snapping nun. Shooing Madeline away three times during the ten-minute examination of Charlie, making contact once. The last hand slap was definitely going to leave a bruise.

"Madeline?" Charlie twitched, opening one eye and moaning a little. "Clara," Charlie now focused more. "Wow, Hi Clara. My friends must have overreacted when they called. I'm so sorry they bothered you." Charlie stared at Madeline, now 10 times more pissed than flying through an angry storm.

"You must come home with me. I can nurse you back to health." Clara sort of bowed, even closing her eyes. Madeline made a mental note to ask for the story of this, betting it was good.

"I will make the human girl take me home and care for me for seven days and seven nights," Charlie told Clara. Only Clara took this proclamation seriously. Madeline, who had a cute, sarcastic comment, was honestly afraid of both of them at this moment so much more than she was when Henry was coming at her.

"Much against my better judgment. But as you wish, Charlie." Clara said, looking annoyingly at Madeline. For the next 25 minutes, Clara barked every instruction imaginable, from bathing and bandaging a Pixie to home remedies. Madeline had never heard half the ingredients.

Clara insisted on at least getting Charlie home and taking care of her for the first night. Madeline had no fight left, so she waved as Clara pulled Charlie away in a little red wagon covered in assorted throw pillows. Charlie stared at Madeline in horror as the distance grew between them. Madeline pulled a facial muscle trying not to smile, but Charlie looked so cute from a distance. Yet, Madeline felt Charlie might snap at any moment.

For the first time in hours, the gallery was quiet. Madeline locked the front door, turned off the lights to the main area, went into the backroom, and started sobbing uncontrollably.

This had been the craziest few weeks ever. Madeline missed her folks, and she knew she had made a mistake inviting Steven for the summer. It was heartbreaking every time he accidentally bumped against her or when they laughed at an inside joke.

At this moment, when Madeline knew she should be researching the five pillars, her mind kept wandering, who was visiting Steven? He said it was Eric, Brian, and Jimmy, and a few "others"... But did Eric's sister come? They were casually dating for a while. Steven did want Madeline to come to dinner with them, so he wasn't shady or secretive. And Madeline knew this, and she said it was all good. And it was. Mostly.

But the strangest part in all of this, magic, made sense to her. It was the one thing she did not question. It felt like an old favorite sweater that got lost in the back of the closet; after rediscovering it, the warm sweater still fits perfectly, comforting you. And you wonder how you went so long without it. Madeline was pleasantly surprised when she realized there were pixies and storm giants in the world. Rationally this should have sent Madeline into a tailspin yet; it just made sense.

"Hey, I know it's late, but ya up to sharing a rum and coke? Will you meet me at my apartment?" Madeline knew the only way she wanted to end the night.

"I'll be there before you, glasses in hand." Jane texted back.

*

"You go. Tell me about your day." Madeline said a few minutes later, clicking her glass to Jane's.

"Ooo, that means you have something huge…" Jane grinned, all knowingly.

"Or, I just care about your day…" Madeline tried to hide her smirk behind her glass, but Jane was right as usual.

"Fine," Jane said. "I don't hate rooming with Steven as much as I thought I would. I absolutely love Henry, and even though the stove is 300 years old and he doesn't seem to have any gadgets from this century or last… Which is just plain weird; I absolutely love his kitchen. The hostess is a little bitchy, but the bartender makes up for it. I'm done, you go."

"Shall we discuss bartender dude in greater detail?" Madeline asked. Little curious, little procrastinating.

"Another night, when there will be more to discuss." They both laughed.

"So…" Madeline began. "I…" She honestly did not know where to start.

"Oh. My. God, you and Steven are back together."

"No. don't be stupid." Madeline said. "But since you brought it up, has he said anything?"

"No," Jane said. "I think he would rather pull off his toenails one by one rather than discuss you with me."

"I never asked, in all those months, did you miss him?" Madeline asked. Once upon a time, Jane and Steven were very close, before Jane had to lead team Madeline.

"I did," Jane admitted. "But that was a huge bridge to burn. He did the one thing I told him not to when he told me he wanted to ask you out…

but for what it's worth, I think he is a good guy who made a mistake that he'll regret for the rest of his life. Men suck."

"They do indeed." Madeline sighed.

"If not Steven. Please tell me you're doing late-night booty calls with Danny." Jane said.

"Noooooooooooo," Madeline said, although not too offended.

"Then can I?" Jane asked

"I…" Madeline took a swig. "I… would like, to call, dibs…. On Danny." Madeline covered her face in embarrassment. They both busted into laughter.

"I KNEW it." Jane boasted. This was the second guy Madeline ever called dibs on. Jane was the one who called dibs, just to be polite, like there was a world where men would pick Madeline over Jane. And they giggled for a long time. Jane assumed this was Madeline's big news. Because even though Madeline was a huge flirt, it took a lot to get her to really like a guy.

"But that's not my news…" Madeline said after the long laughter finally trailed off. "I am discovering that I have some weird abilities…"

"Like… singing? I do love you, but it's definitely not singing…" Jane said.

"Like," Madeline paused. "magic stuff."

"I definitely need to drag you out more if you been hold up in here learning card tricks," Jane said.

"Look." Madeline pointed to the candles on the table. They instantly lit, one by one.

"Ha! You got those l.e.d. remote control candles," Jane said.

"No, I did it, using a spell I learned," Madeline said.

"Stop it. We have been just overindulging lately. You're tired, horny, emotional, and tipsy. We are going on a 30 day cleanse starting tomorrow." Jane said, raising her voice.

"And I can move objects, look," Madeline said, knowing she had to keep going to convince Jane. She moved a pillow from the couch to the chair. "And I can open doors." Madeline opened and closed the front door. "I haven't figured out how to do the dishes with one finger swipe yet, but it's on my list." Madeline nervously laughed, hoping Jane would follow suit, Jane did not.

"I can't process this. I know I'm into yoga and home remedies and maybe even love potions, but." Jane now look horrified as Madeline's heart broke. "I need to go for a walk." And she left her best friend crying as she closed the door behind her. Jane didn't know where she was going but walking always helped clear her head. And this magic crap was just so out of the blue. Jane usually knew Madeline's thoughts before they were spoken.

Jane ended up by the river near Jackson Square. Sitting on a hill, Jane stretched out, looking at the moon, pulling grass.

"Hey, weirdos jog here at night. It's probably not safe." He ran up the hill, leaving the jogging trail.

"Who on earth runs at 3 am?" Jane asked, recognizing the voice. She was very glad it was a familiar one. It was just then Jane remembered that pepper spray might have been wise on this late-night, unplanned walk.

"Oh, I have had insomnia since I was 16," Danny said, sitting by Jane. "I run at night. Drives my family crazy. But it's my thing. You can't sleep either?" Danny asked.

"I just got in a weird argument with Madeline," Jane confessed.

"About Steven?" Danny was immediately embarrassed. It was none of his business.

"Naw," Jane said. "I'm suggesting she has a summer fling..." Jane laughed; even in the darkness, she felt Danny blushing. We just... I think she has been reading too many voodoo novels."

"A fine town to explore things that go bump in the night," Danny said.

"So tell me, Mr. #1 sexiest lawyer in the city, what is your opinion on voodoo and magic?"

"Henry?" Danny blushed again.

"Of course, Mr. Sexy! He's very proud."

"At least he is proud of something," Danny said. "I'm sorry. Henry is great. I do love my great grandfather. I do. He was both a mother and a father when I needed."

"I'm sorry, I didn't know you had lost your folks," Jane said.

"I haven't, not physically." Danny sighed. "But we are getting off-topic. I actually was raised on voodoo... the religion. I loved it as a child. Every Sunday felt like a community celebrating nature and all the good in the world. I didn't know there was anything dark or sinister about voodoo until I was ten. And I saw a late-night movie. I had no idea what a voodoo doll was or why they came with needles."

"So, I won't confess I may have bought a couple..." Jane said. "Do you not practice anymore?"

"To Henry's disappointment and greatest, I mean second, greatest sorrow, no," Danny said. "He wanted me to take over uniting the community. My mom was actually following in his footsteps. She got sick, and through a series of unfortunate events, I am now one of New Orleans sexiest lawyers." He grinned.

"That HAS to make up for the voodoo thing." Jane smiled. "So you're not a believer in voodoo and magic?"

"Actually, I am." Danny confessed, "I have seen magic used in so many acts of goodness. My mom used to put on these huge elaborate puppet shows for us. And of course, I thought this was normal until I saw a puppet show at school and complained to my mom that the teachers used string. Mom just said she knew a little magic. And I thought it made her special."

"So, What was the disconnect?" Jane asked.

"Ha, that's a discussion for another time," Danny said. Offering a hand to pull Jane up from the grass. "I'm going to force you to let me walk you home. Only drunks, pick pocketers, and lunatics are out this late."

Danny did not say another word for the rest of their outing. He just nodded a good night as he slipped into his apartment, leaving Jane in the courtyard at an imaginary crossroads.

*

Jane opened the door and stood there for what felt like an eternity, thinking. Madeline tried not to cry; she honestly did not know if Jane would ever step into her apartment again. But just like that. There she was.

"So... I ran into Danny." Jane began. Madeline had no intention of interrupting. "I pegged him as a type-A personality, Which shouldn't be offensive because you always say that's what I am. We like structure and facts and hate recipes that use pinches or dashes or says cook till done. Who writes that on instructions? But for some reason, the lawyer boy believes his mother is magical, like Bewitched twitch nose move toys magical."

"Oh...." Madeline said, almost saying something she probably shouldn't. Still, for a moment she was lost in thought, If Henry was a storm giant, and his mother was magical, what was Danny? Madeline blinked, needing to focus on Jane.

"So, if Danny believes in magic, I'm willing to listen to you," Jane said. "But then again, he's jogging at 3 am, so I'm questioning his sanity... But for argument's sake, what else can you do, Miss Thing?" now looking Madeline in the eye and locking the door behind her.

Tears rolled down Madeline's grinning, appreciative face. Madeline pointed at the record player. Soon, it played a favorite song of theirs, and Madeline started dancing around the room.

At first, Jane was confused. Then Jane caught an unobstructed view of Madeline, and her jaw dropped. Madeline's wheelchair was rolling without her pushing the wheels. Her arms waving in rhythm to the music, and it was the most beautiful sight Jane has ever seen. And just like that, Jane believed in magic, or at least in Madeline. And they drank and laughed and danced together in the tiny apartment until early dawn.

There was so much more to tell Jane. But Madeline needed one more night just dancing with her best friend.

They ignored the alarm that went off at 8am. And the one they reset to 9am. But by 10, Jane and Madeline knew they had to get going. Crawling herself off Madeline's couch, Jane kissed her cheek and dragged herself to her upstairs apartment without saying a word.

After yawning and stretching, Madeline transferred to her wheelchair. Surprised that she felt rather spunky after an all-nighter but also a little guilty, she dreaded the first thing on her to-do list. Madeline just had to do it, praying it would not be that bad...

"Good Morning," Madeline said, trying to sound extra cheerful as she opened the door to Charlie's apartment.

"Morning?" Clara snapped as she was fidgeting with a second blanket on Charlie's bed. "It's almost dinner time." Charlie looked absolutely miserable, but not from her injuries. She gave Madeline a cold, dead stare.

"I would love to sit with Charlie today," Madeline said, trying to sound pleasantly assertive without being offensive.

"Notes. Food. Medicine. On the table. Do not harm a hair on her head, or 30 witches will find you and skin you alive," Clara said in a voice that sent chills down Madeline's spine. Madeline knew she meant this, literally. "I pray you to feel better, and it was such an honor serving you." Clara's voiced sweetens as she bid Charlie farewell and left after giving Madeline one last lingering dirty look.

"Where the hell have you been?" Charlie asked, sounding a little less pissed but still annoyed.

"I'm going to be honest; Clara scares the hell out of me." Madeline grinned until Charlie gave in to a tiny smirk. "Besides, I figured your boy toy would be waiting for you."

"Danny?" Charlie said. "I think he's out of town or something." Charlie didn't want to get into that.

"Nope," Madeline said. "Jane saw him jogging at 3 am. I wonder what that's about."

"No Idea." Charlie fibbed. She knew he jogged and did paperwork when he was upset. Good. He deserves a few sleepless nights.

"Oh, look," Madeline said. "Danny just texted. He is drowning in paperwork and won't be around for a few days. Should I tell him you're hurt?"

"NO!" Charlie said, angrier than she wanted to sound, taking Madeline a bit by surprise. "I mean, he would just hover, and I really do need to focus on helping Kisseis, and I have two gigs this weekend. So please don't mention it to Danny."

"Ok," Madeline said, a little confused but decided that maybe Charlie was in more pain than she was letting on. "What can I do for you today?"

"Please go find Henry and see if he figured anything out," Charlie said. "And even though he should cook all my favorites for the next three weeks out of sheer guilt, tell him, we are good. Technically it is y'all two's fault, but I forgive you both."

"How big of you," Madeline said; Charlie laughed until her ribs reminded her otherwise. "Since secrets are bad, don't you think you should tell me the secret I'm hiding from myself?"

"I've been crossing a few lines that I never thought I would, lately. Please do not ask me that again. I would do anything to find Kisseis, and as much as I love you. I love her more. So, don't offer me a way out right now."

"I'll go find Henry. Then I have a work thing and a social thing, but when I come back, I will tell you where Henry ran off to, and you can tell me about dear Kisseis." Madeline smiled.

*

"Why, hello stranger, I haven't seen you in minutes." Jane cheerfully greeted Madeline at the door of Henry's restaurant. "Henry surprised us and announced he was closing for a few days. He said something had to be drained and re-piped. Steven and the group invited me to lunch; I might try to catch up with them. Please come."

"I had a few questions about some pieces I found at the gallery, and Danny said Henry was an expert in 1900s art," Madeline said. This was sort of true. "You go. I did promise to join them tonight, so now you have to come too. Please. First group outing with his friends in a long time." Madeline begged. Jane nodded and rushed off.

Madeline made her way to the kitchen where Henry was chopping onions. "Hi," Madeline said awkwardly.

"Clara said Charlie is on the mend," Henry said. Not looking up. "Some people jog when they are upset; I cook." Madeline laughed, making the family connection. "I am extremely sorry about last night. I will personally be cooking your meals for the rest of your life, and probably your children's." Henry said as Madeline smiled. Henry now focused on chopping celery.

"I'm sorry for whatever part I played," Madeline said. "Charlie seems to think it was huge. By the way, Charlie says you are forgiven if you feed her for three weeks." It then occurred to Madeline that there were 21 small pans out. Henry winked at Madeline as he continued prepping the vegetables. Most of them Madeline recognized, a few she did not. She watched him in silence for a long time. He was amazing; every cut so exact and smooth. Every vegetable thrown in separate bowls, landing in pretty patterns.

"I am," Henry chose his words very carefully." "I am a storm giant. I am a pretty decent magic-user. And I have not thought about it for a century, but I am a pillar."

"What is a pillar?" Madeline asked.

"A pillar is a person who has mastered a specific skill, craftsmanship, or type of magic and serves as a teacher to those seeking a better understanding."

"I guess I should ask, what is your area of expertise?" Madeline asked.

"it's like a vampire having to be invited to a house; you have to ask with an opened and uncorrupted heart before I tell you. Ordinarily, I'm not supposed to even reveal that I am a Pillar. But for Charlie."

"I'm not going to like this, am I?" Madeline asked. Henry kept working in the kitchen, hiding a smirk.

"I'm a pillar, and I hold the knowledge of time magic."

"Henry, I ran into Jane, she said there was something broken. I have seven minutes. Do you want me to look at it, and can I grab a PO boy to go, please?" Danny yelled as he came in from the dining room. The silence was broken as he swung the kitchen door open. And the three just stared at each other in awkward silence for a long, long time.

Chapter 6

"Please don't do this, Henry," Danny said after looking around the kitchen, realizing there was nothing broken. "There are only two reasons you would ever close the restaurant, and I don't see any repairs being worked on."

"Madeline, Please go to the back office; I'll be there in a few minutes. I need to have a word with my grandson." Henry said.

"No, I actually think Madeline should hear me out," Danny said. Madeline didn't know whether to stay or to go, but she seemed drawn to them both and felt she belonged exactly where she was. "Did you get a book, Madeline? I assume that was your weird argument with Jane last night." She nodded.

"She has a strong aptitude for it," Henry said.

"My little sister did too. My dad said that hundreds of times. Abigail's aptitude for magic." Danny said. "Did he not tell you about his dear sweet Abigail?"

"Please don't, Daniel," Henry said, trying not to get emotional. "This has nothing to do with Abigail."

"Everything has to do with Abigail!" Danny raised his voice, "magic could not save Abigail. Or mom. And now Charlie is sucking you into her personal crusade. And that's fine. Because you know the risks, but Madeline has nothing to do with this."

"Madeline has everything to do with this." Charlie appeared out of thin air, looking a little ragged, but her voice was strong. "Kisseis is my daughter, and I would kiss the devil's hand to get her back. How can you not help me, Danny?"

"How can you ask me to, Charlie?" Danny whispered and asked her... "If I die, who would Ida have left?" then told everyone, "I have to go to my mom's now because she swears she saw Abigail in the woods and would not stop crying until I agreed to go find her."

"I'll go with you," Charlie said to everyone's surprised. She calms down faster when we are both there." Danny nodded, tired and frustrated, accepting a temporary truce. Danny looked at Madeline, almost saying something but choosing not to. And they left.

*

"Why didn't you ever tell me you had a daughter?" Danny asked softly halfway through the drive home.

"Because I have loved you since the moment you were born," Charlie said. "I always planned on telling you, just when you got older. Then Abigail died, and your mom got sick. And you turned your back on everything magical, but me and I just could not risk losing another child."

"I'm sorry..." Danny said. About to say something else when...

"Danny..." Charlie started screaming as they drove up the long driveway. "DANNY." He stopped the car and ran towards the house. The entire home was engulfed in flames.

Danny sat in the car, in shock. Charlie took charge, turning into human form. She called 911, she talked to the police. She told them how many people they should search for—one for certain, two unlikely but on the off chance.

"Ida's not in there. I physically felt my heart stop for a minute when Abigail died. And I just knew. But Ida, she's not in the house." With no feelings like he was presenting a cut and dry case in front of a judge, Danny said, staring at the fire being slowly suffocated with water.

"Should I call Eugene?" Charlie asked.

"Yup. If he doesn't answer, which he won't, ask him to call me. Say nobody is hurt, but there has been a terrible accident." Charlie used Danny's phone in case Eugene saw Danny's number and wanted to pick up. He did not.

They waited in front of the house for hours until the last fireman said the fire was officially out. His preliminary assessment of the incident was very strange. He said he has been on the job for twenty plus years and had never seen such flames or heat in a house fire. Stranger, although there was tremendous smoke damage on the second floor, the flames seem to have just burnt on the first.

"Mom, please call me." Danny almost crying, leaving the 10th message to his mom, with no response. "Charlie came with me to see you. We will wait for you a while. I love you, mom."

"I know you've been putting it off, but you need to call Henry," Charlie said, now returning to pixie form.

"I will," Danny said in resignation. "I just need a minute; I'm afraid his controlled anger and rage will consume him. When Abigail died, he knew my dad was useless, so he was strong for mom and me. And when mom got sick, he had a purpose of keeping a routine because mom liked to help him at the restaurant 3 days a week. It has only been in the last few years that she just refuses to leave the house."

"I know," Charlie said.

"When I saw the fire..." Danny screamed in pain. "A tiny part of me thought she finally found the courage to be with Abigail, and I thought I could be happy for her. But now she is even more lost. This will break even the mightiest storm giant. I will go for a walk around the lake. I doubt it, but there is a chance that Ida is totally oblivious to the fire trucks and sirens and is having tea with her dead daughter in the outer woods."

Charlie let Danny go. While he was gone, she flew above the burnt and broken home, looking for a clue or a glimmer of hope. Charlie knew what needed to be said, but she didn't know if she was strong enough to say it. Because it might give Henry false hope and make Danny feel used.

Danny reappeared in front of the destroyed house 30 minutes later, looking like a lost boy. He sat on the second step leading up to the wrap around porch and front door. He quietly laughed, feeling like he was on a movie set, where there was a façade of a house, but behind it was nothing. Except this front hid smoldering ashes and a darkness that the flames reignited.

"Henry..." Charlie finally knew she had to call. Danny nodded in resignation. "Can you come to Ida's?" Charlie said. Danny heard how devastated he was through the phone from 5 feet away. "We think Ida is ok... just please come."

"Can you feel her?" Charlie asked, interrupting the silence, the headlights now the only thing breaking the night's darkness.

"I cannot," Danny said. "Growing up, mom told us that she had an invisible tether linking the three of us... And if we were ever lost. It would always lead us back to her. Abigail was better at using it. I hated playing hide and seek with that girl because no matter where I hid, she showed up within 3 seconds after the count ragging about how quick she found me. After Abigail died, I grew so accurate with mom's tether that I could tell what part of the house mom was in, even when I was in the city. It was the only reason I felt I could leave for college. So I don't know why I can no longer feel mom or why I'm 100% certain she's not dead."

"Henry..." they both said at the same time as a light mist began. It felt like a god was crying. Soon after, his truck pulled beside Danny's. In silence, he walked around the house; the rain grew steadier.

"Ida wasn't in the fire," Henry confirmed after his quick survey. The rain stopped.

Just then, another car was coming slowly up the driveway. Henry assumed it was Eugene; Danny thought it might be the police. They were both wrong.

Charlie smiled. Henry and Danny were taken back.

"Did you tell her to come?" Danny asked Henry.

"No," Henry said. "We parted ways a few hours ago. She said she had plans she could not cancel, but we were going to meet later."

"How the hell did she find the house?" Danny asked, feeling on the defensive. "What if I invited her into our lives? Maybe she's evil, and this is a trap."

"You're not that good." Charlie interrupted. "Think about it. Who showed you her resume from the stack? Have you ever met anyone from the foundation that hired you to run it? Why do I always seem to intercept paperwork from them? Why did they happen to hire you for the exact number you were thinking?" Charlie tried to hide how proud of herself she was. Danny grunted in disbelief, too tired to be angry. "The lengths I would go to find you a nice magical girl." Charlie hushed as the visitor came closer, knowing she might have pushed it a little too far as Danny began muttering. Then they both stopped bickering just in time to greet her.

"Hi," Madeline said, rolling up to the group. "I swear I'm not stalking you, but I felt I was needed, and my car just drove here."

"We can fight about this later, Danny. But this is bigger than Ida, or even Kisseis." Charlie whispered to Danny. "I sent for you," Charlie told Madeline.

Danny, Henry, and Madeline surrounded the pixie in the complete darkness now, with only Charlie's glow lighting the dense forest.

"We should look for mom's Grimoire," Danny said after several minutes of silence. "Maybe it can tell us where she is."

"What's a Grimoire?" Madeline asked.

"It's a book of spells and invocations," Henry said. "All practicing magic users have one, and some have family books that include our history of ancestors. I have our family Grimoire in my office at the restaurant. But Ida's should be here." Henry snapped his fingers, and a cluster of star-like objects lit the dark house with white Christmas lights. And the four silently scattered among the debris.

At first, Madeline worried that her wheels would get caught on the burnt fixtures, but everywhere she'd go, she found a clear, perfectly carved out path for just as long as she needed it. The path disappearing behind her back into chaos after she rolled through. She tried very hard not to giggle.

It was eerie to see what rooms were completely destroyed for a house that just had such a destructive fire and which remained untouched. Madeline and Charlie stayed on the first floor as Danny and Henry explored the second.

Madeline slowly rolled through the first floor; each room looked more destroyed than the last. The kitchen seemed the least damaged. Rolling through the kitchen led to a hallway with a closed-door at the end.

Madeline felt a little awkward pushing the door open. What she found was astonishing. The room was untouched by the fire. No smoke, no burnt marks on the wall. The carpet was perfectly dry, whereas the rest of the house's floors was a muddy puddle of ash.

She felt like she was trespassing, but Madeline was drawn in. She feared her wheels would leave a muddy trail. They did not.

It was obviously a little girl's room. There were posters of Hannah Montana, Taylor Swift, and a bunch of stuffed animals. Madeline softly touched the picture on the nightstand of a very young-looking Danny pretending to strangle his younger sister's neck, both smiling from ear to ear.

"How did you get in here?" Danny startled Madeline.

"The door was just open. " Madeline wasn't frightened, but Danny did seem mad. "I'm sorry. I'll go see if Charlie needs help."

"No..." Danny said. "I'm sorry. My mother sealed this room when my sister passed away. I guess 10 years ago now. Over the years, I've tried to sneak in to get a few things of Abigail's, just as keepsakes. And on better days when mom was cute, the door would lightly shock me. And on sadder days, the door just would not budge. My father has wanted the room for his magic artifact collection. Mom never bothers arguing. She just said whoever figures out a way to get in here must have gotten Abigail's blessing. Then and only then would she even consider changing the shrine."

"I'm sure the fire damaged the doors or something," Madeline said, trying to sound confident, but was a tad freaked out.

"Danny," Henry yelled. "Please come to the kitchen."

"Coming," Danny said. "Anyways, thank you for this. I have always wanted to get this picture. Mom has given me hundreds of posed pictures of us. Still, she absolutely hated this one, and even as bratty kids, we knew it would be our favorite picture."

"Can I keep it safe in my backpack?" Madeline asked as Danny tried to decide how to fit it in his wallet or pocket without bending it.

"Thank you." Danny barely whispered, slipping it into her bag on her chair. Madeline nodded as if now guarding the biggest diamond on earth.

"Now, Daniel." Henry was growing impatient.

"Do you know a Louis Delcroix?" Henry asked Danny before Madeline entered the kitchen.

"The name sounds vaguely familiar, but I'm not sure," Danny said. "Why?"

"His card was on the island," Henry said. "No contact info, just his name."

"Wait," Madeline interrupted, reaching for her wallet in her backpack. "Louis Delcroix." She found his business card.

"The reporter I ran into at the gallery a few weeks ago.," Danny remembered now.

"This is odd," Madeline said, looking at the card closer. "Now it just has his name on it." She compared it to the card Henry was holding. "When he gave it to me, it had all of his contact info. I remember because I wrote it in my book so that I could invite him to the opening, even though he was creepy."

"What do you mean he was creepy?" Charlie asked, now appearing from upstairs.

"The day he came in, he sort of appeared from thin air," Madeline said. "I was 90% sure that the alarm was on and the door was locked before he came in, but all of a sudden, I felt his breath on the back of my neck, and he just introduced himself."

"Why didn't you tell me?" Danny asked.

"Cause I didn't want to tell my boss on my 2nd day this strange story. Hey, I think this guy magically appeared out of thin air. And thanks again for hiring me." Madeline said. Danny looked annoyed.

"Apparently, I didn't hire you exactly. You should take this up with the real puppet master; I'd love you to meet our boss." Danny growled at Charlie. Charlie stared at him, suggesting there might be a more appropriate time to have this out. Henry was distracted, staring at the two business cards, now both with the ink fading.

"Hi, Mr. Delcroix," Madeline called a number from her day planner before getting the other's input. "This is Madeline from Phyllis L Art Gallery; I would like to take you up on your offer to do a feature on our new gallery and me. I look forward to hearing from you."

"Absolutely not!" both Danny and Henry yelled the second they realized what Madeline just did.

"Wow, if possible, you got ballsier," Charlie smiled. Madeline took this as a compliment. The men did not share their enthusiasm.

"Does anyone have a better idea?" Madeline asked, rolling away to continue searching the house.

The four searched the house about five times each before the sun greeted them. Besides Abigail's perfectly untouched room and the business card, no one found any other clues. More disappointing, Ida's Grimoire was nowhere in the house. Henry was pretty sure she kept it in her jewelry box, untouched for years. It was not.

Suddenly Danny perked up, realizing that maybe the book was in Abigail's room. Of course, he thought to himself. He had completely forgotten that Abigail kept her most treasured possessions under her bed. With new determination, Danny marched through the destroyed house, stopping in front of Abigail's room.

He carefully turned the knob, as if entering a sacred space. And it would not turn at all. He screamed from his gut, knowing the room had resealed itself.

"Why don't y'all head back?" Henry asked, or rather told Charlie and Madeline. "I'll stay with Danny for a while. Maybe you can see if anyone has heard anything yet, Charlie. And Madeline, in the restaurant's backroom, there are books and magical items you can learn from. I just can't leave Danny."

Madeline rolled towards her car without looking back. Charlie flew to Danny, leaning against Abigail's door, sobbing uncontrollably, kissing his cheek. And flew to Madeline's waiting car.

*

"Hi," Henry said, finding Madeline in his office hours later, surrounded by books.

"Oh, hi," Madeline said. Feeling very disoriented, not knowing how many hours she had been there. "Where is Danny?" she asked, rubbing her eyes.

"He was going to talk to Eugene, his dad," Henry said. "I probably should have gone with him, but we are oil and vinegar on our best days, and those were many moons ago. But maybe to save face, Eugene will be helpful. Thanks for your help last night."

"I don't think I did anything," Madeline said.

"Danny told me about the picture," Henry said. "I remember taking it. Eugene had asked me to take a family picture for some article about him. He was so mad that the kids were in a goofy mood. He wanted a serious picture of his very prestigious magical children. I finally got one after hours of bribes and threats. Danny and Abigail begged him to use the silly picture. Of course, he didn't. So Abigail stole that picture and kept it on her nightstand. It really meant the world to him to get it back."

"Did you have any insights on what may have happened to his mother?" Madeline asked. "Charlie seems to think it may be related to Kisseis."

"What does your gut say?" Henry asked.

"I think so," Madeline said. "I am just worried this is the tip of the iceberg."

"Agreed." Henry nodded. "So much for magic easing back into society."

"From what I've read, magic was pretty prevalent until the Salem witch hunt in 1693?" Madeline asked.

"My father said it was a horrific time," Henry said. "After the trials, most families tied their magical powers. My parents were of different thinking. They believed our magic was part of our persons. It was like trying to quiet our laughter or asking us to deny how smart we are so that we better fit in. We were encouraged to use magic in our homes, never in public unless saving a life. Slowly our kind found each other, and we built a small community. I'm so glad you found us."

"All my life, I've felt like an outsider because of my disability," Madeline said. "I have always been popular by default, but it wasn't until Jane and Steven that I felt I belong somewhere. That they loved me not only despite my handicap but because of it as well. New Orleans is the first city I just feel energized in. I don't think I've slept in four days, but my mind has never felt sharper."

"New Orleans has many ley lines," Henry said. Madeline looked confused. "They are underground. Stone Hinge is built over a cluster of them. Supposedly they are like magic boosters for spells. Probably why you feel exhilarated. But young lady, let me warn you, it's like a sugar high, and your crash might be very soon and very sudden." Henry winked.

"So, You're a storm giant?" Madeline asked.

"Yes." Henry nodded. "I'm in my natural state in the oceans and/or the clouds. Bad things happen when I get angry, as you saw first hand. So I try hard not to because I truly love this city, and I have grown to love my human side."

"May I ask, Danny...?"

"Oh..." Henry seemed torn. "He is very private about his abilities."

"I'm sorry, I shouldn't have..."

"No," Henry said. "Something shut down inside of him when Abigail died. He blamed magic. Her death was the worse thing that has happened in my 300 and something years old life. But I never blamed magic. Danny resented that magic took her. He resented his mom and me for not being able to use magic to get Abigail back. I wish he had an open, unguarded heart again. I have to find Ida. For me, because she is my world. But especially for him. This loss would shatter him."

"So…. I found a book about storm giants." Madeline continued pressing. "Is everything true?"

"Most of it…" Henry said. "Let's see, I can't remember the last time I had or wanted to explain what a storm giant was. It's hard to describe, like if I asked you what it was like to be human." Henry stopped and thought about it, "I am 308 years old. When I'm in the water in my natural state, I am 26 feet and 7 inches; the 7 inches was a big deal when you had an older brother." Henry smiled a sad smile.

Henry continued to share. He was able to live in the ocean and loved walking at the bottom of the waters. Henry could change his form and live in the clouds, but he preferred not to because he hated the isolation. At least in the waters, fishes would tickle and whisper to him. Henry has been living as a human for so long now that it is second nature. Although he has to watch himself because when he gets emotional, he grows instinctively.

"Danny and Abigail used to love stormy nights because I could make the lightning spell out their names across the sky. They both swore that would be their first big spell they would learn. Ida forbid me to let them play with lightning until they each turn 16." Henry began to become lost in thought, and he blinked away a stray tear. "I can fly… kinda." He tried to change the sadness in his voice. "I kinda step on the clouds at a running pace. I can control the weather to some extent, but I don't like to. I think that's pushing into God's territory."

"Are storm giants better at magic?" Madeline asked.

"No." Henry softly laughed. "My best friend was a warlock growing up. I was obsessed. I read every book. I drove his parents absolutely crazy with questions. After about a hundred years, I finally got the knack for it." Henry said.

So..." Madeline asked when she realized how old he was. "Danny, is your great-grandson?"

"Yup," Henry said. "Ida is my granddaughter. I raised her. Ida's mom, Edith, died a few years after Ida was born... My wife was heartbroken, as was I. But Ida became my biggest blessing and complete joy. I regret I am closer to Ida than I was with our daughter. Millie said it was because somehow, our daughter was my clone. And I don't think Millie meant that as a compliment." Henry grinned.

"Millie was your wife?" Madeline asked.

"Yes, my sweet Millie," Henry said. "We were married for 150 years. I was so sorry she passed before she met Abigail and Daniel."

"Was she... a storm giant?" Madeline asked.

"She called herself a mutt." Henry laughed. "I hated that term, but she thought it was cute. She was part human but had many more magic abilities, all instinctive, whereas I had to study. We wanted a dozen kids but were only blessed with Edith."

"I'm sorry," Madeline said.

"Look, this is my only picture with both of my girls," Henry said. Madeline swore, he grew a little with pride and love. His wife, Millie, looked gorgeous. Edith looks so familiar to Madeline, she guessed she was in her early twenties. Madeline wanted to know more about Edith but decided it might be best to ask Charlie. For a storm Giant, Henry suddenly looked small and fragile.

*

After Madeline had dropped Charlie off back at the apartments, Charlie grew restless almost immediately. There was no way to keep her promise to get some sleep. Charlie wandered into the courtyard, grateful it was one of the few times in the day when it was empty.

The pixie sat on top of the fountain, that was completely dry now; breaking Charlie's heart. She considered following the drains into rumored New Orleans' underworld in hopes of finding Kisseis. Yet fought the temptation, deciding to wait, at least until she was fully healed.

"Holy crap, this is going to hurt," Charlie mumbled to herself as she took to flight, annoyed she didn't think of it before they left Ida's. She crossed herself and flew right back to the burnt house. Ordinarily, this was a lovely fast trip, but with broken wings, every flap made her wince in pain...

Charlie landed on the burnt roof that was still smoldering a bit. During her flight, Charlie fooled herself into thinking that maybe this all had just been a nightmare. Upon landing, reality reminded her it was far worse. Charlie sat on the back deck for a long while, waiting for the pain to be manageable. Charlie wondered how a place with such happy memories of Danny's childhood could turn into a place of darkness and devastation.

Not that Charlie would ever admit it, but she must have dozed off for a few minutes, maybe even a few hours. Now it was completely dark. The only reason Charlie was not outraged at the time wasted was the unexpected forced sleep did make her feel better.

Charlie had remembered about the fireflies Abigail had always told her about. Abigail and Danny got into many arguments about this because Abigail insisted they always talk to her at night. Danny, who was born a lawyer, argued that fireflies do not talk. Abigail would laugh, saying the fireflies would only talk to girls, and they told her that boys were big and loud and yucky. In later years Ida mentioned Abigail's fireflies kept her company at night. Danny and Charlie thought this was another fantasy.

"Will-o-Wisps," Charlie whispered, finally feeling strong enough to enter the woods behind the lake, amazed that she never made the connection. Charlie flew to the furthest part of the lake and went 47 human steps east, as she remembered a tiny adorable Abigail explained the correct directions to her. And there it was, behind a big boulder, a village of Will-o-Wisps.

People assume if you are a magical creature, you know all of the different magical creatures. This was not true at all. At least not for Charlie. She actually thought Will-o-Wisps were a myth until this moment. But there they were. Charlie's first inclination was to march right up and question them about Ida. Luckily she was slow due to her injuries, and she was forced to think and plan every action.

Will-o-Wisps were tiny but powerful magical creatures. 99 out of 100 times, they were mistaken for fireflies. This suited them perfectly. They were unfriendly, at best. If they found you annoying, they would land on you, leaving a burnt mark that supposedly stung like 100 wasps. If they hated you, they just flew right through you, like a tiny fireball, piercing the body clear through.

On rare occasions, they befriended other creatures, mostly for entertainment purposes. On rarer occasions, they'd fall in love with a human, reasons depending on their moods. From they were cute like Abigail, to a murderer who was pure evil, and the will-o-wisps wanted to learn from him. Once they made the random connection with their preferred human, they would watch over them. Charlie could not help but wonder if they watched over Ida too. Sort of like guardian angels, just with very flexible values.

Charlie thought she was very quiet when approaching the village, but the second she set foot on their stone walking path, five Will-o-Wisps surrounded her. And they seemed more aggressive and bitter towards strangers than the myths relayed.

"You have 3 seconds to leave our forest, or we will kill you." One of the Will-o-Wisps surrounding her said. She didn't know which one, not that it mattered. All five seemed to be ready to attack. Charlie could have taken them at full strength, but Charlie felt light-headed just coming from Ida's house.

"I come in peace." Charlie really didn't mean to sound snarky, "I'm looking for Ida." She should have led with that."

"A lot of people come looking for Ida, doesn't mean crap. We will not ask you to leave a third time," the Will-o-Wisp flew directly at Charlie. So close to Charlie's nose, she could feel an excruciating heat, possibly worse than a barefoot walking across a blacktop roof in summer.

"Abigail was my Goddaughter," Charlie screamed, not realizing how unhinged she had become. "And I just... I just need to find Ida."

Two of the Will-o-Wisps kept their positions over Charlie's head as the other three flew away from earshot, looking like they were arguing. A few minutes later, they returned.

"When did Abigail die?" the Will-o-Wisp in charge asked.

"10 years, 2 months ago," Charlie said without hesitation.

"How did our sweet girl die?" the Will-o-Wisp continued pressing, still sounding unimpressed.

"She was trying to summon a beautiful mermaid for her folks. Instead, an evil demon appeared and drowned her." Charlie said, fighting back the tears of anger, rage, sadness, and exhaustion. She prayed there was not a third question; all her diplomacy had just been used.

"Come sit." The Will-o-Wisp said without any warmth in his voice as the other four flew back to their lairs. Charlie silently nodded.

She looked around the village as she followed the Will-o-Wisp. There was a thick sadness in the air. The village seemed to be made up of 20 lairs, bigger than Charlie would have expected from insect-sized creatures. Each house looked like an anthill, surrounding a main communal area where Charlie was now approaching.

The Will-o-Wisp floated above a rock and motioned Charlie to sit on a nearby boulder.

"There are only five of us left." The Will-o-Wisp said. "The others help Ida getaway before losing to the darkness. My only comfort is that they did not die in vain."

"I'm sorry…" Charlie tried to apologize, this seemed to only anger the Will-o-Wisp more.

"Look." The Will-o-Wisp said. "Abigail was my pet. I inherited Ida and grew fairly fond of her, but this is where the blood ties end. We got Abigail's mother to safety at the unbelievably devastating cost of my village. You must leave our sacred area now. Now you are considered an enemy. And if you ever return, you will be treated as such. Leave."

"Wait…" Charlie demanded as the Will-o-Wisp flew towards her, forcing Charlie to back away. "Where is Ida? Who took her? Please tell me." The Will-o-Wisp flew as close to Charlie as possible without burning her, whispered a name then disappeared into the darkness.

Chapter 7

"I'm not sure he is available." Henry and Madeline heard the hostess talking to a man outside Henry's office. "He asked not to be disturbed today for any reason."

"It's fine, Emma," Henry spoke loudly, giving Madeline an annoying sigh. "Come in, Eugene."

"Where's Danny?" Eugene asked, not exchanging any pleasantries whatsoever.

"I thought he was with you," Henry said.

"He did come by the campus earlier, but I was in a meeting," Eugene said.

"Didn't you get his 50 voice mails?" Henry asked. Madeline could see Henry clenching his fists, trying not to grow.

"I got a new phone last week. I thought Ida would have given him my new number by now." Eugene said. "Anyways, I can't find Danny's contact info. He said it was an emergency and he would be here tonight. So where is he?" Eugene asked, seemingly very annoyed that he had to come a whole two miles because he didn't have his own son's phone number.

"When was the last time you spoke to my granddaughter?" Henry's voice got louder and louder.

"A few..." Eugene said, embarrassed talking about family matters in front of a girl in a wheelchair. "Weeks ago..."

"I'm going to grab food." Madeline excused herself as the two men silently growled at each other.

"Look, Danny wanted to tell you himself, but there was an incident at the house, a fire, and Ida is missing," Henry said.

"How bad was the fire?" Eugene asked. Henry's whole body grew three feet, ready to pounce on this human worm.

"I just told you your wife disappeared…" Henry walked toward him, reaching for his little neck. Henry had a second of joy when he realized he could probably snap Eugene's neck in half with just a sneeze. His fantasy was interrupted by a loud thump on his desk.

"Flying with broken wings hurts, Will-o-Wisps real. Live in the north meadow, very angry creatures. They saved Ida. Did not say how. Mentioned something called glÉd. Hello Eugene. I'm going to pass out now." Charlie said, in one breath. Then fell unconscious right where she was.

Henry reached for a pillow on a nearby chair, returning to his smaller size as he picked up Charlie and put her in the middle of the pillow. The gentle storm giant carefully took the pillow to the couch at the opposite end of the office, kissed Charlie's cheek, then turned off the floor lamp that lit the living room area.

"Finished the book. Ida really did teach me all of the basics when I was eight. She will be so excited. Who knew…" Danny sarcastically said while barging into the office, tossing his spell book on Henry's desk. Danny expected that only Henry would be there, disappointed that Eugene was too.

"I knew," Eugene said. Henry put his arm on Danny's shoulder before Danny could say anything he may or may not regret later. "I think I have a book on the glÉd; I'll go get it." Eugene quietly left as no one pleaded for him to stay.

Danny and Henry had more questions than answers but mutually decided to sit by Charlie for a while. As soon as Eugene left the kitchen area, Madeline returned with a tray of goodies.

Danny thanked Madeline for the food. Henry told her what Charlie had said. And the three searched through all of Henry's books for any kind of mention of glÉd while taking turns nursing Charlie for the rest of the night. Not speaking at all, except sharing when they found a lead, that usually didn't go anywhere.

"Why can't we find a single reference to glÉd?" Danny exhaustedly said after looking through tons of books and hours searching the net. "Do we know if it's even real? Maybe the Will-o-Wisps were trying to throw us off."

"I don't think they would," Charlie said, feeling better but still lying down on the couch. "They seemed extremely loyal to Abigail and therefore felt somewhat responsible for Ida. I honestly believe that one Will-o-Wisp risked his life, and possibly his village by telling me that name."

"Could it be in a different language?" Madeline asked, feeling like they were reaching for straws. "If so, there would be 100 different ways to spell the word and twice as many ways to pronounce it."

"Henry, could you do a spell translation?" Danny asked.

"Yup, but I would need the correct spelling," Henry said. "And we have only been considering standard alphabetical languages; this is worse than a needle in a hundred haystacks."

"Do you want me to go check on dad?" Danny asked.

"No, I'm sure if he found something, he would certainly claim it," Henry said, sounding a little bitter but not apologizing. "We have reached a dead end. I think Madeline and Danny should go to work today. Maybe an idea will come to you. Charlie will stay here and recoup. I can take care of her while researching more."

"Please don't ask me to do that while mom is out there, grandad." Danny pleaded.

"Daniel, We both sense she is safe," Henry said, with much sadness. "She hasn't been safe in a very long time. We will find her. You have my word. But this feels like we are being targeted on a personal level. That's why Madeline cannot return here after she leaves today and why I have to let Jane go."

"She's part of it," Charlie whispered.

"What the hell does that mean? Stop playing games, Charlie." Danny's controlled anger was reaching a boiling point.

"I…" Madeline asserted herself. "I need to go let the painters into the gallery and have lunch with Jane because we have lunch, Tuesdays and Thursdays. It's one of our many rituals. After lunch, I will order the window treatments. I will then go home and take a nap. After I freshen up, I will return, and hopefully, you will be able to tell me our next step."

"Then I'm going with you," Danny said.

"What?" Madeline asked.

"If Charlie says you are part of it, you are in danger too," Danny said.

"I think I can take care of myself," Madeline said.

"My great-grandson will not leave this office without winning an argument, so I'm sacrificing you, Madeline," Henry said, half-jokingly. "I actually think it is a good idea, and that will be my one request if you insist on going down this rabbit hole with us." Madeline nodded and left. Danny followed.

*

"it's absolutely ridiculous that you stayed here while I showered," Madeline said while coming out of the bathroom, still drying her hair. "But I was thinking, maybe it's Celtic." Madeline kept talking until she realized Danny had answered the door and told a guy to come in.

"Hey, Jason…" Madeline said in a weirdly higher-pitched voice. "Jason is Steven's evil twin. Danny is my co-worker at the gallery." This was awkward, but Madeline didn't know why.

"I am headed back to Houston and wanted to talk to you before I left," Jason said. "We are making Labor Day plans and wanted to invite you to the lake. You can even bring Jane."

"Can I please bring Jane?" Madeline laughed, Jason knew he pushed it, and he apologized silently. Danny tried to keep his eyes on his laptop as he sensed this was a deeper conversation. "September is a few weeks away. I don't know how busy I'll be here. I know Steven will not miss it, and I'm sure he can always find a friend to take."

Madeline didn't mean to sound bitchy but could not emotionally deal with this today. Steven got Jason in the breakup as Madeline got Jane. Jason was never Madeline's favorite person. But while Steven and Madeline were dating, she and Jason reached a pleasant existence, even with a few late-night meaningful discussions. Madeline was even starting to consider him a close friend. That is until she asked him point-blank if she had anything to worry about with Steven, and he said no. It was their last actual conversation except for a polite greeting at dinner last night.

"Jane and I probably will come up for a day. It's still my favorite spot." Madeline started to feel bad that Jason was in the middle.

"Will you see if Jane…" Jason winked, knowing he was pushing it.

"I will recommend you as a boy toy." Madeline smiled as Jason said his goodbyes.

"Sorry," Madeline said after Jason left. "We probably started a rumor because you were in my apartment when I had the wet hair."

"My mother was the crazy witch who lived in the swamps." Danny blurted out, "And that was before she was actually crazy. This is nothing… Do you… care?"

"Honestly? Probably a little too much still…" Madeline admitted.

"Hey…" Jane knocked and entered. "I wanted to know…"

"Wet hair from being up all night doing magical research. Stop judging me. And Jason still wants to date you." Madeline screamed as a reflex…

"I just wanted to know where y'all wanted to eat lunch, you freak," Jane said. Madeline let out an annoying sigh. Danny and Jane laughed. Madeline couldn't help but notice Danny had a great smile.

The rest of the early afternoon was rather uneventful. Madeline was surprised by how forthcoming Danny was with Jane at lunch. Not all of it, but sharing that his mother was a well-known witch at one time and if she had any questions, he would be happy to answer them. Jane seemed to be comfortable with that, and for now, Danny thought that was all Jane needed to know. Madeline agreed.

"Ok, Danny, I have to ask. Is Henry magical too?" Jane asked excitedly after receiving a text from Henry saying the restaurant's pipes were fixed. Could she come for dinner service?

"Rule one of the magic users. Don't talk about other magic users." Danny grinned.

"I bet you have been sitting on that line forever," Jane said. Danny embellishes a gracious bow. Jane kissed his cheek, then Madeline's then excused herself from their lunch.

"If Henry reopened the restaurant, does that mean he figured something out?" Madeline asked after Jane was out of earshot.

"Probably not..." Danny lost his warm smile. "When we are upset, we throw ourselves into work, for better or worse, Henry cooks. I write closing arguments." He shrugged.

"I guess trying to convince you not to follow me back to the gallery would be a complete waste of time," Madeline asked as they both reached for the check.

"Yup," Danny said, taking the check, returning the cash that Jane had left by Madeline's arm.

"Thank you," Madeline said softly. Danny nodded, purposely touching her hand. And there they sat still, just for a little while.

"Oh shoot," Danny said after receiving a text. "I completely forgot I have court this afternoon. I don't suppose I can convince you to come with me?"

"I don't know," Madeline said. "Ordering window treatments or watching one of New Orleans sexiest lawyers at work..." Danny's face turned beet red. Madeline giggled. "No, I really do have to get to the gallery. Steven will be there most of the afternoon. We will keep the doors locked, and I'll go straight to Henry's after."

"Locked in a store with your ex-boyfriend as demons descend, textbook new suitor's dream." Danny sighed, glad to know he could make Madeline blush too.

"See you tonight, counselor." Madeline gave him a peck on the cheek and rolled towards the gallery. She felt him watching her till she turned a corner; hopefully, he didn't see her uncontrollable grin too.

"Madds, the guys and I did a little clean up this morning. See you tomorrow." Madeline found the note on her desk after arriving at the gallery. She and Steven agreed that there would be a to-do list every week for Steven, and as long as he got it done, he could make up his own hours.

Madeline rolled around the gallery. Usually, she would have been over the moon; the guys did everything on Steven's to-do list and more. But she was kind of looking forwards to having the company.

"Shake it off, Madds," Madeline told herself as her first instinct was to go to Henry's, where everyone was, where she would not have to be alone. She growled at herself. Hopefully, this was one of the hundreds of times she would be alone in the gallery. Madeline reached a compromise with herself, order the window treatments, and then she could go back to the restaurant. She could pick light fixtures tomorrow. Madeline looked around the gallery, tripled checked the locks, and set the alarm before heading to her desk in the back.

Ordering the window treatments took so much longer than it should have. One website had the right colors but not the right sizes, one had a ridiculously long delivery time. And so on...

Against Madeline's better judgment, she decided to run to the bakery five doors down to get a coffee and a Danish. Locking up was a hassle, but she really needed an afternoon caffeine pick up and would be gone 20 minutes at most.

"Crap." She mumbled, seeing the door was cracked opened when she returned. "Aw, it's you..." she smiled as Steven stepped outside and held the door open for her.

"I ran into Danny rushing to court." Steven said, "He said there have been some robberies on this street lately and asked if I could walk you home today. And there's a Mr. Louis Delcroix. He was waiting in your office when I got here." Madeline's heart sunk.

"Why don't you just go back to the guys? You did ask for the day off. I'll just be here 30 minutes at most." Madeline said.

"Because…" Steven said. "Because… Danny specifically asked me to walk you home. It's really no big deal."

"It's probably because he's a lawyer, and he doesn't want to be responsible if I was in a robbery."

"Lie," Steven said without budging; that's the problem when you date your best friend; they know when you lie.

"I'm trying to earn his respect," Madeline was reaching, but it sounded like an excellent argument in her head. "I don't want him to treat me differently because I'm in a wheelchair. You know it's a thing for me." Which it was.

"I really didn't get that impression from him, Madds," Steven said.

"I'll leave at 5, I promise." Madeline pleaded. "It's your last day with the guys before they go home. I will text you when I leave and when I get to the apartments. Please go."

"If you come out with us tonight," Steven made a pouty face. Madeline was pleased to see it was a little less effective than time gone by.

"Ok." Madeline flat out lied but would deal with that later.

"Text me at 5," Steven said, walking back towards the apartments. He gave one final wave, turned the corner, and disappeared. Madeline wondered if it would always hurt a little when they parted ways. But she didn't have time to go there, Louis Delcroix was waiting for her inside.

"Hello, Louis," Madeline said, trying to sound friendly.

"Steven, let me in," Louis said. "He is a pleasant fellow, is he your boyfriend?"

"Naw, he is just doing a few odd jobs for the gallery this summer," Madeline said.

"He sure goes on and on about you like he was madly in love. If he's not your boyfriend, I'd worry about him being a stalker." Louis said, laughing a little.

"He was probably just trying to earn brownie points," Madeline said. "I assume you came by to talk more about an in-depth feature on the gallery." Madeline tried to change the subject; she did not like the way he kept talking about Steven at all.

"Although I am thrilled that you are going to take me up on that offer, that's not why I'm here," Louis said. "I'm writing a news article on the fire at the home of Ida Guidry Boudreaux. I wonder if you could comment."

"I really don't know why you would think of me, or a house burning would even warrant a story," Madeline said.

"Ida was quite famous around here before she became a recluse about 10 years ago," Louis said.

"Unfortunately, I've never met her," Madeline said.

"You work with her son, Danny, don't you?"

"For a little over month now. I really don't see why you even thought of me..." Madeline said.

"You were seen having lunch with him today," Louis said.

"Excuse me?" Madeline said.

"Your car was seen at his mother's house as it was smoldering until the early morning a few days ago..." Louis said.

"My employer lost his childhood home, I dropped off a friend of his, and I decided to stay and try to help." Madeline was trying her best to keep her cool.

"And a few days later, you're on a date holding hands?" Louis kept throwing questions at her. "That seems a bit tacky since no one has seen Ida since. Is she alive? Is she dead?" Madeline was flustered and angry and didn't know what to say.

"Have they found a body?" Louis asked. Madeline slammed her hands down in anger, and the strangest thing happened. Louis Delcroix froze. Just for a second. Madeline was too upset to notice. "How is her grandfather, Henry Guidry, involved? You seem to be at his restaurant a lot."

"You need to leave now, Mr. Delcroix," Madeline said. "Or I'm going to call the police for harassment."

"Oh, that won't be necessary," Louis said in a threatening tone. "You seem like a girl who can take care of herself. I'll be seeing you soon." He got up, tipped his hat, and left. The alarm did not chirp as the door closed behind him.

The moment Louis Delcroix left the gallery's storefront, Madeline locked the doors and turned the alarm on, not that it seemed to make a difference. She turned off the lights in the main area and went back to her office. The whole Louis Delcroix thing was unsettling. It wasn't even as if he was scary. Just extremely icky.

There was something about him that seemed even more creepy than their first meeting. Something different physically. Like powder or concealer on his face and neck. Madeline now remembering it clearer; she noticed the makeup immediately but then became flustered when he started talking about Steven and Danny.

Louis Delcroix's face was definitely different. As if the makeup was covering an injury. And his voice seemed less clear and more subdued than their last meeting. Madeline especially recalled this because as creepy as Louis was, he had a great radio voice. This time, Louis Delcroix seemed to have to work at speaking clearly, almost as if he was in tremendous pain. Madeline wondered if a Will-o-Wisp got to him.

"Hey, Henry..." Madeline called him after taking a few minutes to calm down and finally confirm the order for window treatments. "How's Charlie?"

"She's finally feeling better," Henry said. "I even got her to go home, and she promised to stay in for the rest of the night. I give it a 50/50 chance."

"Did you make any progress on the research?" Madeline asked.

"Nope. You?" Henry asked.

"I thought glÉd might have been Celtic but haven't found anything yet," Madeline said, sounding disappointed. "And Louis Delcroix just came by." Madeline had to hold the phone away from her ear for 5 minutes as Henry scolded her for not calling him the second he walked in. "It was fine," Madeline reassured him.

"Anyways," Madeline tried to explain. "He seems to know everywhere I go, but I didn't feel physically threatened at all. Really."

"I wonder what injuries he's hiding?" Henry asked after Madeline shared her suspicions.

"I'm closing up in a few, then I'll come straight to the restaurant," Madeline said.

"Absolutely not." Henry objected. "Go home, relax. And come by for breakfast; hopefully, I'll have something."

"I do have some friends in town who wanted me to join them, but..." Madeline hesitated.

"Please go," Henry said. "And I'll have my adopted son keep an eye on you; I don't like how much Louis Delcroix knew about your whereabouts. Don't bother arguing; my great-grandson inherited his stubbornness from me." And Henry said goodnight.

Madeline stayed at the gallery for a few minutes more. As she locked up, she sensed someone behind her.

"5 O'clock on the dot, beautiful." He said.

"You always did have impeccable timing," Madeline said. And Steven walked her past the apartments to a local bar where their friends had already gotten a table. Madeline was too tired to argue and decided just to try and enjoy the evening. Always very aware that Henry's cute bartender happened to be at every stopped the group visited.

*

"Are you waiting for me?" Madeline asked, locking her apartment door, finding Danny sitting by the fountain reading the morning paper.

"Well, aren't you full of yourself?" Danny smiled. "But as it happens, you are right, this time." Madeline shyly grinned. "Hey, I'm sorry I ended up not meeting you guys last night."

"I didn't expect you to; I just didn't want not to invite you." Madeline said honestly. "Although I wanted you to see that I constantly travel with five guys in my male harem."

"I get it now; you wanted to audition me." Danny laughed.

"Maybe," Madeline said. "No, seriously, how was your night?"

"I ran seven miles, and I pretty much ruled out that glÉd was Latin or any of the Chinese languages," Danny said. Sounding frustrated.

"Morning, Y'all," Steven said, coming out of his and Jane's apartment.

"I think we are going to grab a quick breakfast at Henry's; please join us," Danny said.

"Naw, the guys wanted to do a last lunch before they head home. See ya!" Steven ran off without making eye contact with Madeline. Madeline seemed a little hurt.

"I told him last night I was ready to think about dating new people, and he told me he was hoping he could earn my trust this summer, and maybe we could try again. Maybe even skip dating and go directly to engaged. That was a super fun conversation!"

"You still love him, don't you?" Danny asked.

"Yup," Madeline confessed. "But each and every time he barges out during a fight, I will worry he is going to cheat. And I don't want to live like that. And it is unfair to him too. Deep down inside, he gets it. It'll be awkward for a few days. But he knows I'm right."

"I'm sorry," Danny said. "When you're ready, you will have to tell me more about these new people you might consider dating."

"Maybe after we find Ida and Kisseis, and I request a new supervisor," Madeline said.

"Let's go find Charlie." Danny smiled. Madeline laughed. "Charlie and Henry need to fix this really soon." They began walking to Henry's.

*

"Hey Charlie," Madeline was so glad to see her, upright in drag form at a corner table. They kissed as Madeline parked to her right, Danny sat to her left. Charlie warmly patted his hand, he nodded.

"Where's Henry?" Danny asked.

"In the back, he's trying to keep it together, but I'm honestly worried about him," Charlie said. "Have you heard from your dad?"

"Nope," Danny said coldly. Madeline wanted to comfort both of them but didn't know how. "Have we considered Islamic languages?" Danny asked. Both girls had, both led nowhere. "Maybe I should go talk to the Will-o-Wisps. Being Abigail's brother…"

"I don't think it works that way," Charlie said. "I am 110% sure that they have cut all ties from us, and you'd be walking to your death. But… But… why didn't I think of this. Tell Henry I'll be back." Charlie popped into pixie form and flew out of the restaurant before Danny or Madeline could stop her.

"Henry's not going to like this at all," Madeline said.

"I don't suppose you could tell him? He seems to really like you," Danny grinned.

*

"Hello Al, We should really stop meeting like this." Fr. Karl greeted the security guard, "At least I had my Wheaties for breakfast and was already at the church for morning mass. Thank God for small favors."

"That's funny," Al said, thinking Fr. Karl was making a religious joke. He was not. "Would you like me to go up the bell tower for you?" Al tried to keep on Fr. Karl's good side. "The parishioners say they have never heard the bells crying from the rusty chain so loud before. Some are worried it's a sign of the second coming, again."

"I probably just didn't oil the chains enough last time." Fr. Karl said, sounding less convincing. "Will you lock the bottom tower door behind me, its always a delicate balance when I'm working on the bells." Al nodded as Fr. Karl patted him on the back.

His poor knees cursed him 126 times as he slowly climbed the steep steps that led to the bells. "You know, you really need to start texting me." Fr. Karl said, out of breath after he closed the second door behind him. He rested a minute, looking out to the bay, feeling uneasy that black clouds were drifting towards them from the south.

"Again, I'm sorry." A voice whispered from the wooden rafters.

"Hello, my sweet..." Fr. Karl said as Charlie flew to him. "What happened? Tell me now, Charlie!" Fr. Karl demanded, his soft-spoken voice turned loud as he noticed every cut and bruise on his angel. "Did Danny do this to you?"

"What? No. of course not." Charlie said. "Have you heard about Ida's house?"

"Yes, I've been praying for her." Fr. Karl said. "I actually was planning to go to dinner tonight at Henry's, hoping I'd run into you or Danny."

"So I need to tell you something," Charlie said. She then went into great detail about the night of the fire from Ida being missing. And Abigail's room unlocking to the strange business card from Louis Delcroix and finding the Will-o-Wisps village.

"Wow, when Ida went on and on about Abigail's fireflies talking to her at night..." Fr. Karl said.

"Of course, Danny and Henry are just beating themselves up, feeling like if they had more faith in Ida..." Charlie said.

"She just has been too far gone for so long. There's no way they could have picked out this one needle in a haystack of a fantasy world Ida has built for over a decade." Fr. Karl said. "How can I help?"

"Do you still remember your Old English?" Charlie asked. Fr. Karl couldn't help but chuckle. "I would think you'd remember it better than me!" Fr. Karl teased.

In Seminary, Fr. Karl fell in love with a prayer written in Old English. This led him to a lifetime of researching and learning the dead language; he even earned a Ph.D. as a linguist. He laughed because he must have read hundreds of poems and short stories to Charlie in Old English. She never found the appreciation but admired Fr. Karl's passion.

"Do you know the meaning of the word glÉd?" Charlie asked.

"No." Fr. Karl said, tapping his forehead... "Wait..." he began muttering as if he was rattling off a list of prefixes and suffixes. "I think... it could possibly be a slang word... a strong feminine noun meaning..." His head was down as he paced. It was on the tip of his tongue; maybe glÉd was from a myth or legend.

"KARL," Charlie screamed the loudest scream. Fr. Karl looked at Charlie then looked towards the horizon. A huge fireball the size of a tire was coming directly at Charlie.

"Bless you, my angel, as you have always blessed me." Fr. Karl said as he stepped in front of the glowing ball of fire to block Charlie's direct hit. What happened next was unclear. Fr. Karl took most of the blast. The tower caught on fire and was in flames within seconds. Charlie was blown 300 yards, landing unconscious on a distant rooftop.

Within five minutes, the whole area was filled with reporters and firemen, and tourists. The church was saved, but the bell tower was completely destroyed. Not a single step survived structurally.

"We are heartbroken to see such a landmark of New Orleans be destroyed by lightning, but we are so thankful that no one was harmed." The mayor announced live at the scene, twenty minutes after the first flames were spotted. On tv, you could see his team surrounding him. Louis Delcroix in the background. "The city will buy all tourists a plate of beignets for the next hour." The onlookers moved on.

Chapter 8

"This is so unprofessional." Madeline, who had her nose in her laptop trying to order light fixtures, complained to Danny, who was behind the bar.

"Please. It's only for a few days." Danny said, refilling her ice tea. Somehow Henry had convinced Madeline to work from the restaurant, telling Jane and everyone else that the paint fumes were horrible at the gallery. Madeline had full access to the kitchen and bar during her stay.

"What the heck was that?" Madeline was caught off guard. For 5 seconds, the ground shook, probably not as strong as an earthquake but definitely noticeable. A few glasses hanging over the bar even fell, shattering.

"I think they are demolishing a building a few blocks over. Let me get a broom." Danny said, thinking nothing of it as he went into the back hallway.

"Hey Mack, can you turn on the news? I just got a weird text from my mom asking if I was safe from the fire." About 15 minutes later, Madeline asked the part-time barkeep, part-time bodyguard. Mack was the one following her group last night. He nodded, clicking the remote.

Danny returned with a broom as Henry peaked his head from the kitchen. Both were drawn to the tv, and the second they saw the mayor's press conference with the church in the background, they looked at each other and left the restaurant like bats out of hell. Madeline wanted to follow, but Mack frowned at her, and the two continued watching the news.

Danny and Henry ran five blocks towards the fire. They weaved through the crowd until the police blocked them from coming any further.

"We are just jumping to conclusions," Henry said, not believing his own words.

"Charlie's phone goes straight to voicemail." Danny hung up without leaving a message. "Hey, I think that security guard was one of Abigail's friends; I run into him every few months at mom's gas station." Danny and Henry pushed to pass the police, most of which knew one of them personally.

"Al?" Danny bent down as Al, visibly shaken, was sitting under a tree. "Do you remember me? I'm Abigail's brother. Can I help you?"

"He asked me not to go up." Al could barely get the words out, almost crying, but seemed very determined to tell his story. "Fr. Karl was up there a really long time, so I decided to check on him. But when I reached the top, I began to hear voices. It sounded like Fr. Karl and a lady. And they were praying, so I decided to leave them in peace. And 10 minutes later... I don't know how anyone else got up there. I've been on duty all day, and Fr. Karl is the only one I cleared to go up. Do you think it was a recording or a video of a female?"

"Yes," Danny said. Al was grasping at straws; Danny let him, blinking away tears. Henry just left the area, finding a nearby building to lean against, trying not to break down. "I bet he was on a phone call."

"I've been trying to tell the police that Fr. Karl and maybe a female were up there. Why did they announce that no one was hurt? Why?" Al wanted answers. Danny had none. None that he could share. None that would bring Al peace. Just then, Al spotted his mother in the crowd and ran to her. Danny felt a heartbreak of ugly jealousy, wishing he saw Ida in the crowd and could run to her.

"Do you sense Charlie?" Henry asked. As Danny leaned against the building next to his grandfather.

"No," Danny whispered.

"Try. Harder." Henry said louder than he meant to. "I have always told Charlie that religion is bad."

"Religion or magic?" Danny asked.

"Do you really want to do this now?" Henry got in his face and immediately regretted it as loud thunder suddenly clapped, and a light midst started.

"No, grandfather." Danny knew emotions were too raw for this conversation. "We just need to find Charlie and mom. I need to find them. To apologize. Please help me, Henry." Danny surprisingly hugged him. Henry began weeping uncontrollably. Other than special occasions and holidays, Danny stopped hugging him for comfort after Abigail's funeral.

"Ok, we will find Charlie and Ida. I swear." Henry said, kissing Danny's forehead. But the rain did not stop. They embraced for a good long time. Henry didn't want to ruin this time that meant the world to him, but if Charlie was hurt, and there was no way she was not, every minute counted. "You are not going to like what I'm going to ask of you now…" They talked for about ten more minutes and parted ways. Danny knew arguing was futile and nodded with tears rolling down his eyes.

By the time Danny reached the restaurant, the door was locked. Luckily most of the lunch crowd had already finished their meals. Mack told everyone, including the staff, that Henry was closing incase the smoke from the church fire got bad.

"Is everyone gone?" Danny asked Mack a few minutes later. The dining area was empty except for Madeline, who stayed, sensing something was going on. One glanced at Danny confirmed this.

"Yup." Mack answered. "What does he want me to do first?"

"Make sure I don't do anything stupid." Danny sighed.

"Crap, Boudreaux. I'm not a miracle worker." Mack grinned. Madeline just learned 20 minutes ago that Danny and Mack have been best friends since they were five.

"I hate to interrupt this bromance, but Mack promised you would tell me what is going on," Madeline said. So Danny did.

Danny told both of them that although he hoped he was wrong, both Henry and he think Charlie was hurt in the fire. It did occur to both of them that there was a chance she didn't survive, but neither was strong enough to say it.

Henry decided that he would go look for her on foot, and Danny would coordinate the restaurant's search party. Henry told his grandson that there was absolutely no way he could concentrate on finding Charlie if

Danny was out on the streets too. Going against every fiber in Danny's body, he agreed, because deep inside, Danny knew as much as he has lost, Henry has lost ten times more.

"Henry has a lot of friends living on the streets. They will help. Charlie has fed most of them twice a week for decades." Danny said. "My secretary and I are going to call everyone who owes us a favor."

"What can I do?" Madeline asked.

"I don't know..." Danny sighed, looking out the window.

"I'm calling my aunt; maybe her crystal ball can help," Mack said.

"You're kidding, right?" Madeline asked.

"Nope, that's how we were busted on prom night for stealing her 65 Mustang," Mack said. Danny smirked.

"Ok, Henry wants me to get a map and tell people who come in what blocks they should search so that we can cover the most ground," Danny said. Looking at his phone.

"I'll grab a map. I think Henry has one on his bookshelf." Mack said.

Just then, Madeline had an idea. "Oh shoot, Jane and Steven locked themselves out and need the extra key I have," Madeline said. Pretending she got a text, "I will be back in 30 minutes."

"Nope," Danny said. Not looking up from his phone, as texts from searchers were starting to fill his screen. "Why can't they come here?"

"They are being difficult." Madeline lied. "I will be right back, I swear."

"I guess if I forbade you, there would never be the first date," Danny said.

"Is it worth the risk?" Madeline said. Touching his arm and zooming off in her chair before he called her on her very questionable scenario, thank goodness Danny was distracted.

Madeline rolled to the apartments as fast as she could, praying that she did not run into Jane or Steven. Fibbing to a distracted Danny was one thing; Jane and Steven would definitely be harder to blow off. Madeline just needed 10 minutes alone. Thankfully no one was in the courtyard as

Madeline rolled to Charlie's door. She looked around to make sure she was still alone, placed her right hand on the doorknob, whispered the unlock spell, and went into Charlie's empty apartment.

"Where did you hide that picture of us?" Madeline muttered. She felt awful going through Charlie's stuff but knew begging for forgiveness would be better than regretting not doing enough. She found the picture in a hope chest by the dresser and slowly trace their image, whispering, "Please lead me to you."

Suddenly Madeline's wheelchair moved quickly forwards and out the door without any human assistance; only stopping for a second, allowing her to shut Charlie's door. Madeline was torn because, on the one hand, Madeline had always hated being pushed around, especially without her permission. But on the other hand, this was really cool. So Madeline just rolled with the latter. With her left hand holding the picture, and Madeline's right hand, on her wheel, just as a precaution, the wheelchair led her through a maze of streets and alleys.

"Hey there." Treeva popped out from a bush. "Where ya going?" the teenage imp was now running backward in front of her. "You're Danny's chick, huh? He wouldn't like you in this area. It's full of homeless people, hookers, and demons..." Treeva said. Madeline couldn't help but giggle.

"I'm trying to find Charlie," Madeline said.

"Can I go? can I? I am so bored. I need an adventure. Will you entertain me, human? Are you human? Anyway, I'm not prejudiced. I hate all non-demons. That's not true, I'm gonna be honest. I've gotta thing for Danny. He is so cute! And ok, I hate Charlie less, even though she is kinda straight-laced for me, but she feeds us well." Treeva said.

"You do know Charlie is a drag queen... and that's straight-laced?" Madeline asked.

"Yup. Yup. Can I go?" Treeva asked.

"Ok." Madeline wondered if all demons were this hyper and pushy or just the teenage females.

"Can I push your chair? We can go ridiculously fast…" the imp pleaded, even trying to bat her eyes, which certainly wasn't as cute as Treeva thought it was.

"Stay behind me and no more talking. I need to focus on." Madeline said. Fingers on her lips as Treeva geared up for another round of questions. Begrudgingly Treeva fell back and followed Madeline in silence. She bounced along because just walking in dead silence was unbelievably boring.

The chair stopped three minutes later at a high rise construction site.

"Do you know Clara, the healing witch person?" Madeline didn't know the correct pronoun. Treeva looked disgusted, "Can you get her, Henry, and Danny?"

"I'm a demon, and she scares me. This is now going on my time card for Danny." Treeva seemed put out but headed back towards the Quarter at a quick pace.

Madeline rolled around the entire building that was enclosed by a chain-link fence. She could sense Charlie somewhere nearby. Going against her better judgment, she magically unlocked the gate.

"Where is Charlie? Where is she?" 15 minutes later, Clara ran up to Madeline, out of breath and angry.

"I think she's on the roof," Madeline said.

"What are you waiting for?" Clara asked and started running towards the structure. Madeline followed, ignoring the approaching sirens, hoping that they would pass right on by. They did not.

"Please exit the construction site with your hands up." A male's voice echoed from a large bullhorn. Madeline followed directions. Clara did not. Madeline was about to turn herself in to the police just as Danny and Henry appeared. Madeline could not hear what they were saying, but after a few minutes of talking, Danny shook both of their hands, and they left.

"We have 20 minutes to finish our scavenger hunt, then we will be trespassing," Danny said, walking past Madeline, hurrying to catch up with Clara. He seemed extremely mad.

"You did good, kid. Life has just made him a cautious worrier," Henry said, now walking fast with Madeline, towards a huge opened caged elevator. The ride up was unbelievably long and silent. Madeline tried to apologize with a cute shy grin, Danny refused to look at her.

Madeline gave up and rolled forwards so when the slow elevator stopped, she would be the first out... The second that the doors opened, Madeline's chair took off. The top floor was a maze of roofing supplies, bricks, tools, and crates of tiles; even if Charlie was here, it would have been a difficult search without Madeline. Luckily the wheelchair went directly to her.

After spotting Charlie in a corner stuck between two pallets of bricks, Clara ran towards Charlie. Henry, Danny, and Madeline watched as she softly moved her to a more open area. Everyone was paralyzed in fear and silence until Charlie slowly turned her head and tried to focus on Madeline.

"I knew you'd find me; you always do. And that's not even your coolest trick. Where's Karl?" She winked at Madeline then passed out. Madeline's heart sunk.

"I'm going to sedate her until we can get her back to Henry's," Clara said, in a less stern but very worried voice.

"I have to go get some more supplies," Clara said after trying to make Charlie as comfortable as possible on Henry's makeshift couch/hospital bed. "Someone should sit with her at all times. Charlie will drift in and out of consciousness. Agree with everything she says. Upsetting her will only make the healing process harder. I'm worried about internal bleeding, so the first 48 hours are critical." Clara touched Madeline's shoulder and left.

"I'll take the first shift," Danny said. Neither Henry nor Madeline dared to argue.

*

"Danny writes closing arguments when he's upset. I cook." Henry said after Madeline found him in the kitchen a few minutes after she returned from the ladies' room.

"Should I go talk to him?" Madeline asked.

"It's better to let him come to you," Henry said. "He is so much like his mother, I think that is what scares Danny most. That something will happen that is so horrendous that he will just snap. I have never seen him look at anyone like he looks at you. And although very different, that's as emotional for him as not knowing where Ida is." Henry said, feeling bad that he made Madeline blush. He scooped a bowl of gumbo for her, and after bringing Danny one, they ate in silence.

"Charlie is asking for you." Danny appeared in the hallway, and Madeline dropped her spoon and rush to her bedside.

"Hey Charlie," Madeline said quietly. Charlie smiled weakly.

"Did you go back and fix it?" Charlie whispered as if asking a secret question.

"Let's not talk about that now." Madeline assumed Charlie was delirious.

"You have to go save Fr. Karl." Charlie insisted.

"Ok, I will try." Madeline hated lying but remembered Clara's stern warning.

"Damn it, Madeline, after a hundred years of friendship, I know when you are being condescending," Charlie yelled, clear as day. "Go back and warn me." Charlie started crying. "get out, don't come back till you can bring Fr. Karl to me." Charlie was inconsolable now. Danny rushed in and laid by her as Charlie sobbed herself unconscious.

"I'm sure she didn't mean it," Danny said as Madeline backed away from the two. Danny assumed Madeline was upset that Charlie was clearly hallucinating. The truth was Madeline was suddenly terrified because, in her heart, she was positive that Charlie had a moment of clarity. And Madeline had no idea what it meant.

Madeline suddenly felt claustrophobic as she left Charlie's side. She quickly rolled to the end of a long narrow hallway that had an exit. Madeline ended up in the tiny garden behind the restaurant. She needed fresh air, no longer able to breathe. Henry watched her from the hallway, both wanting to comfort her and give her space. When Madeline stopped pacing, Henry appeared and sat on a bench facing a huge rose garden.

"My wife would kill me if she knew how much I paid for the gardener..." Henry said. "Millie loved her fresh roses more than she did me, which, looking back, was fair. For 50 years after she died, I tried to keep up her garden. Some years were better than others, but the flowers never seemed as colorful or smelled as sweet. After the hundredth thorn Ida pulled out of my finger, she insisted we hire a gardener. They do look better. But the roses never seem to have the same sweet fragrance as when Millie tended to them."

"Charlie wanted me to go back and save Fr. Karl," Madeline said after a long and thoughtful silence.

"Oh Madeline, Clara warned that there would be so much pain, that Charlie would hallucinate," Henry said.

"This was..." Madeline struggled for the words. "She somehow had a moment of clarity. I saw it in her eyes. Can I show you something?" Madeline asked Henry, he nodded. She pulled out the picture from her pocket. The one that led her to find Charlie on the rooftop. Henry stared at it, almost as if he was in a trance. After a good long while, he carefully flipped it over as Madeline looked over his shoulder, "Love, HG..." Madeline looked confused. Then it clicked. They both gasped.

"I think..." Madeline hesitated. "I think. You need to tell me about time magic."

"Even with everything I know and everything I've seen, I've never met a Time Lock." Henry began. "Nobody I've known has known one. The closest was a 5th removed friend who had died a decade before. As a young storm giant, I just became fascinated with the subject. To me, it's kind of like believing in God. It's a lot of blind faith."

"Just amuse me, to pass the time. Please." Madeline said. Henry was thrilled too. The only other person he was able to talk to about time magic was his wife, and her eyes immediately rolled when he got to the science part.

Madeline had a secret. She never told her parents, or Steven or even Jane. Ever since she could remember, she thought she had very small seizures. She always assumed it was related to her injury. Telling her folks would just open the pandora's box of doctors again.

The "Seizures" were extremely rare. But did seem to happen when Madeline was startled or extremely angry. Madeline tried to track them, but they were so infrequent that she would forget where she wrote about the last one. Describing these episodes lasting a second would be way too long. A jiffy felt more accurate.

On the rare occasions when they did occur, Madeline felt everything come to a standstill, just for an instant, like the world was on pause and only herself was unfrozen. She would blink or hear her heartbeat loud, then without time to process what was happening, the world would resume, like it hadn't skipped a beat.

After Henry finished his long-winded talk of time travel and rare mystical creatures called time locks, Madeline blurted out her secret. Henry felt extremely bad, being a storm giant and knowing dwarves, and witches, and elves, but this was hard to believe, even for him.

"Old English. It's Old English. Charlie told me." Danny appeared in the doorway. "I have a friend at Tulane that may help. I'm going to run over and try to catch her before morning class." He hugged Henry and kiss Madeline on her cheek, then kind of blushed. "Please call me if Charlie wakes up again." Danny left through the gate in the garden. Henry was still lost in thought as he and Madeline return to his office where Charlie was now sleeping.

"Please tell me what you are thinking." Madeline pleaded as she sat by Charlie, watching Henry fiddle with something at his desk.

"Ok, let's try something." Henry finally let curiosity get the better of him. Danny would be so upset, but Henry was willing to risk it. Henry was

99.5% sure absolutely nothing would happen. Charlie would get a good laugh that her hallucination sent them on such a bizarre goose chase. And end the thousands of questions swimming in Henry's brain.

"Before you start, you need to sign this book," Henry said as Madeline rolled to his desk. "Morality contract." The book looked to be 100 pages. Madeline flipped through it. "The highlights are, don't screw with any historical events, and you cannot make more than one hundred dollars on a stock tip or gambling in a day. But since this was written a long, long time ago, I sort of question the financial ethics." Henry smirked. Madeline didn't realize it, but she physically shook when signing it.

Henry got up and stared at his bookshelf that wrapped around the entire room. He brought back a leather-bound skinny book called 'Time magic for toddlers.' "What can I say? Time Locks are quirky. Plus, the book titles are magically updated every 50 years. Even magic has to keep up with the times." Henry chuckled. Madeline was already too lost in the book to appreciate his humor.

"Ok…" Madeline said about an hour later. She was absolutely lost in the book while sitting at Henry's desk. She didn't even realize that Clara had come and gone and manage to get Charlie to take a few spoons of broth. Henry also had time to think, "Let's try a teeny tiny jump." Madeline said.

"So, upon reflection…" Henry said. Madeline frowned. "I've waited all my life to meet a time lock… I just thought they'd be older and wiser. And they would know their stuff. I'm not comfortable sending you to the unknown… If something happens to you, I don't think I could live with myself. And I have somehow lived through some unimaginable things."

"I could learn under your supervision," Madeline said. "Or in a few days or weeks with my friends after a few cocktails. When curiosity gets the best of me and I announce my new party trick… and like you said, I'm probably not."

"You always get your way, don't you?" Henry asked.

"Except for my mom, pretty much," Madeline said. Henry laughed.

They made a plan, going over it 14 times. Madeline started counting on Henry's 5th run through. Henry wrote out a simple spell from the book. Madeline's goal was to jump exactly two minutes into the future to Henry's kitchen, where he would be waiting. Henry kissed Madeline on the cheek and backed away. Madeline slowly began chanting the spell.

*

"See Henry, nothing… happened," Madeline said, not realizing she was, in fact, now in the kitchen. "I'll be damn…"

"I'll be damn." Henry greeted her by the large brick stove.

"I'll be damn, what?" Jane cheerfully asked, entering the kitchen, ready to prep for lunch.

"You were right, Jane." Henry thought quickly on his feet. "Your friend is indeed charismatic and gifted, but she really cannot crack an egg, can she?" Henry and Jane seemed tickled. Madeline was annoyed that, one, it was indeed true, and two, surely Jane and Henry had better things to gossip about than her lack of cooking skills. Madeline stuck her tongue out at both of them.

"Did Madeline tell you the bad news?" Henry asked Jane. "They found mold in the walls at the gallery, so I offered Madeline to use my back office until it's safe there. I'm going to go clear off my desk." Henry left, not allowing Madeline time to answer.

"Hey, I can fix your lunch every day." Jane was excited. Madeline was torn because she really wanted to be near Henry and Charlie while she healed, and of course, having Jane just a room away was the dream. But she needed a day to be alone and process. "Not to add to your plate, but Steven kinda waited up for you last night. He didn't think you came home… he's a little heartbroken… You know I'm the president of Team Madeline, of course, and I can't wait to hear the story, but I must confess he seems different and sad. Even when his boys were here, he seemed less annoying, less rowdy.."

"Charlie drug me out, and we ended up staying at her friend's B&B. nothing inappropriate, I'm sorry to say…" Madeline sadly confessed. She could not explain to Jane what just happened when Madeline didn't understand it all herself.

"I have to run to the butcher; wanna come?" Jane asked, seemingly satisfied with Madeline's story.

"Naw, I have to set up my makeshift office," Madeline said; Jane winked and left. After Madeline was sure Jane was gone, she made her way to Henry's office and was glad to see Henry feeding Charlie a few more bites of broth before she quickly drifted back to sleep.

Henry was sitting by Charlie as Madeline returned to the back office. Charlie was sleeping again. Madeline felt guilty but was thankful not to have to face Charlie just quite yet. Charlie's first question would surely be about saving Fr. Karl, and Madeline now had a thousand more questions with not even one answer.

"Are you ready to talk about it?" Henry asked. He left Charlie's side, covering her with a blanket, and sat in an armchair near his desk where Madeline was now sitting,

"Not by a very long shot," Madeline said. "Although I might have a list of 100 questions by tonight."

"And I shall try to answer each and everyone," Henry said.

"I've seen my share of time travelers movies; I can't just go back and save Fr. Karl, can I?" Madeline asked.

"If it worked that way, I'd already have signed all my worldly possessions to you. Abigail would be sitting with us, I'd be retired, and Ida would have taken over the kitchen by now. Sadly it doesn't work that way..."

"I should have retired twenty years ago. Ida was going to take over after both of the kids graduated from high school. Then we lost Abigail, and Ida kept saying that she still wanted the restaurant when she got better. I would run this restaurant another 200 years if I knew Ida would be able to take it over then and find some happiness here..." Henry said.

"I got it..." Danny burst into the room. "glÉd is an Old English word for a Strong Feminine creature burning coal living with ember fire flames...

You're not going to believe this next part. Even when Old English was commonly used, glÉd was an obscure word, mostly used in mythological stories..."

"Like?" Madeline asked.

"No. that's impossible..." Henry scratched his head... Henry started pacing, scaring both Danny and Madeline, just a little. After about 10 minutes of intense silence and thinking, Henry ran to the left bookshelf as Charlie rolled over, groaning in pain. He ran his finger over 50 book spines before pulling one out.

Henry opened the dusty book on the desk near the lamp where Danny and Madeline could look over him. He carefully turned each brittle page, dreading each cracking sound; the book was filled with extinct creatures that once terrorized different parts of the world. Henry stopped halfway through and pointed to the right page. Danny and Madeline looked on in shock and disbelief.

Chapter 9

"That's a..." Madeline said.

"Dragon," Danny said. "Isn't that impossible, Henry? I thought all the dragons became extinct centuries ago..." Henry sat in silence, at a loss for words.

Madeline started reading the story beneath the illustration of the dragon. "Until the year 1000 AD, dragons, humans, and magical users lived in a somewhat peaceful existence on the European continent, as dragons mainly lived in the north. When the dragons started getting more adventurous and grew increasingly callous about human life, this started a Dragon War that would last 300 years. Many thousands of lives were lost, but when the humans and magic users finally figured out how to combine their weapons with spells, they somehow manage to slay the tribe of 50 dragons."

"Is that true?" Madeline asked.

"I wish it had ended there," Henry said. "Everything would be different now. Maybe my father would have been blessed enough to have met Ida."

"I don't understand, Granddad." Danny looked confused.

"You need to tell him the rest, Henry. He has the right to know; it matters, now more than ever." Charlie piped up from her corner bed, drifting back into slumber before finishing her thoughts.

"My grandfather, Vodrich, actually was one of the military leaders in the dragon wars," Henry confessed.

"Why didn't I know this?" Danny asked.

"It is just something I was taught not to talk about." Henry fibbed a little; the truth was Danny stopped listening. If Henry said that, Danny would have probably left the restaurant right then, Henry couldn't risk it. Not now.

Henry continued his story, trying to avoid family minefields. "During the war, every time a dragon was slain, its fang was taken, for the leaders to keep count. After three years and so many lives lost, the leaders decided that 49 fangs were good enough and proclaimed that the war was over, the continent was saved, and all the dragons had been killed."

"My grandfather, Vodrich, disagreed, believing it was too dangerous to leave even one dragon alive. So, of course, he was asked to leave the council. To my grandmother's dismay, Vodrich spent the next 200 years looking for this one last dragon, the leader, if you will."

"Vodrich just never came home after one of his scouting trips... His younger brother, Gezdor, who was very sweet but not very smart, followed Vodrich everywhere, believing his brother would always protect him."

"Gezdor came home alone after they had been gone for two months, telling everyone that my grandfather died a hero. That he killed the last dragon, but Vodrich sadly died from wounds. This brought my grandmother somewhat peace. Vodrich had made Gezdor promise if anything happened to him, Gezdor must get home safely. And to tell Vodrich's wife whatever she needed to hear to bring her peace and end his personal war, the one Vodrich himself was too weak to."

"My father had a brilliant mind, and every time Gezdor told the story, it was just a little different. My mother assumed sweet Gezdor was just having trouble putting the horrible events together."

"But the more my father dug, the story just didn't add up. Gezdor finally confessed that the dragon killed his brother right in front of him, slowly and painfully, blaming Vodrich for the wars. The dragon cursed Vodrich's family for 10 generations. It said they would never have one storm giant die of old age; not one would know a peaceful life... Then the dragon let the injured brother go, thinking he would tell the horrendous and bloody tale then die soon after; no one knew the bloody truth but Henry's father. My father told Gezdor a hundred times how proud his brother would have been of him."

"But Gezdor died soon after that. Most think it was from his injuries; some think it must have been from a curse. My father wholeheartedly believed Gezdor willed himself to death. Because he thought he had betrayed his brother by telling my father the truth, which is a horrendous way to die. This brought tears to my father's eyes every time he thought of sweet and so innocent Gezdor."

"My father, Brogant's, first instinct was to seek revenge for his father, uncle, and the other thousands of lives lost." Henry continued telling his story. "But he really took to heart what Gezdor told him on his death bed and believed his father would want his family safe and at peace."

"Brogant manage to convinced his mother to move to the New World, and for 100 years, they found happiness. My dad fell in love with my mother, and they were married within a month. My brother John and I always laughed because they were like teenagers in love, until the very day he passed on. I, of course, secretly prayed for that kind of marriage. Looking back, it was the only prayer that was answered." Henry said.

Danny looked down, trying to hide his expression. He didn't remember an uncle John. An unexpected sadness rolled through him...

"In 1698, humans started disappearing in central America. People had all kinds of explanations, but the magic community knew it was a hundred times worse than anything humans could imagine. Of course, my dad was asked to organize the search party and eventually, the killing of the mysterious creature, which, of course, was the dragon."

"My father did not want to go, but he, of course, felt it was his duty to finally end what his father died for. My brother and I, who were raised in a protective, pretty damn sugary existence, thought it was about time we sowed our oats. We both begged to go with him. My father probably downplayed the job, so my mother didn't give it a second thought when my brother asked to go. Plus, as much as it pains me to say, John was really stronger and just had that military mindset that was lost on me,"

"But I really did want to go. My dad was my hero. So I asked. He didn't even pretend to think about it. Just no. That was the only time I was truly angry at my father. He told me he was taking John because I was soft and gentle like Gezdor. And he gave me $100, which was a ridiculous amount of money to open a restaurant, for me, and my mother, and our future. It took me a century to really appreciate what he was trying to do."

"Although my father had a brilliant strategic mind, he could never have predicted what happened," Henry said, now pacing a little. It was such an important story for him. Maybe more important for Danny, especially now, but it was horrendous to have to tell out loud. He had heard it only once. Brogant was just strong enough to tell it once, And that was enough to give Henry nightmares for the rest of his life...

"Everything about this battle was ten times harder than what my dad had thought. My dad promised that he and John would be gone three years max. They were gone almost 11. My folks were relatively young before dad left, and he promised mom they could try for a girl when he got back, no matter how many boys they got by accident. This always made mother laugh. I, sadly, would remain the youngest."

"Finding a dragon somewhere on a continent is, in fact, as daunting as it sounds," Henry said. "She was angry. And hungry. Most of the dragons in Europe stayed in their main tribes, and you could track the towns they slowly took over. This creature, Fuego, as the people named it, attacked frequently and would leave a trail of a thousand miles of the dead, uneaten bodies. She was not hunting for survival; she was killing for sport or revenge or both. And from all accounts and information patched together, Fuego was stronger and used more magic than the dragons in Europe, combined."

"The other problem was Europe already had an active military. And the magical community was strong and was mostly accepted by humans, so an alliance was easy. Central America did not have a unified military, and by now, magic users pretty much kept to themselves."

"But my father and John were relentless, Dad said John blossomed into a fine, smart leader right in front of his eyes. They spent 5 years putting together an army they could call on when the time came. It was difficult at first, but the more spiteful Fuego became, the more men who volunteered. The magical community was just as hard to gather. Still, if they had any ties to Vodrich or Gezdor or the dragon wars, even by 2nd or 3rd generations, they eventually volunteered." Henry said.

"Our only blessing was before my dad left. He made displacement boxes, one for him and one for my mother." Henry pointed at a glass case on his fireplace mantle; in it was two wooden boxes, the size of a hand.

"What are displacement boxes?" Madeline asked.

"Mom told me that story. I always thought it was a fairy tale." Danny smiled sadly.

"No matter their distance, they could magically and instantly send each other small stuff, mostly letters. Food was more difficult, but I made special bread that traveled pretty well. Sometimes I'd get adventurist, once, I thought quiche would be a good idea. Dad replied with a note saying, "Just bread from now on, please, son.' Mother laughed because, for the next month, her letters smelled like rotten eggs with spinach."

"It was a strange time, but my mother really believed that Brogant was doing God's work, and as long as she heard from him a few times a week, it was tolerable. I felt a little guilty because my life was going so well. The restaurant was extremely busy. I began courting Millie. My heart was ready to marry her after the first date. But I wanted John to be my best man and my folks to dance at my wedding. My sweet Millie got it; we lived in sin for six years. She never pushed. Just teased that they better come straight from Central America to the chapel."

"During the ninth year, the letters slowed down. Dad and John had done as much preparation and gathering of volunteers as they could. It was time to end it. They needed to get back home. Dad had been encouraging John to go back to New Orleans for the past five years so he could start a real life. By then, dad had built up a council of advisors, so he was not alone and felt John could step down from his duties. John refused." Henry said.

"It took them better than a year to set everything up. The plan was to lure Fuego into a canyon, get her stuck in magical quicksand, and just kill her with spells and weapons. It sounded like a simple job, but it had so many moving parts, the timing had to be down to the second. No one knew how long or even if the quicksand would trap her. The canyon had to be the perfect size for maximum damage. and hundreds of other things I can't even begin to imagine."

"Dad had studied all of the military actions in Europe. They killed 15 dragons this way. So his council approved the plan. Dad wasn't totally convinced because even though it felt like a solid attack, they really had no idea of the strength of the dragon."

"But the military was a few weeks from just going rogue. The death toll had tripled each year that Fuego was on the loose and the people had reached their breaking point.'"

"Henry," Charlie said, now groaning from the pain of sitting up. "Let me tell Danny this part. You shouldn't have to." Charlie said in a sweet, thoughtful voice.

"Neither should you, my love," Henry said. He walked over to Charlie and stroked her cheek until she unwillingly went back to sleep again.

"The battle began perfectly as planned." it took Henry ten minutes to start again. Madeline and Danny just sat in still silence, respecting Henry's quiet thoughts. "Fuego was lured to the canyon. For a short time, she was stuck. "

"The military began the attack first; they had made a thousand arrows filled with poison. The same poison that killed 5 dragons in Europe. Fuego didn't notice; none of the arrows even broke the skin. Then they tried guns and cannons. The dragon shook them off like it was one annoying little nat."

"Then the magical users got involved. First, the dwarves threw poisoned blades, the water nymphs showered her with acid. The shaman chanted, The priests and nuns prayed. The Pixies flew closer, dropping magical bombs on her... At first, dad and the council thought they might be making progress because Fuego just stood there."

"Then the storm giant threw lightning bolts at her—one after another after another. And everyone else joined, using their spells or remaining weapons; the people say they felt the ground shook for thousands of miles for hours. We felt it too."

"Then the weapons all fell to the ground, magically taken out of each of the military hands. The dragon started laughing. "The lightning bolts actually tickled. That was nice." Fuego took a deep breath, then blew fire at the military section. The priests and nuns raced to them with healing powers, but it was just a sea of ash."

"The dragon stood up on her hind legs, shaking herself clean from the sand. She requested to talk to Brogant. My father gave John a letter that he wrote to my mom and hugged him."

"I am Brogant." My dad screamed at the towering dragon over his head.

"I told your father his family would know no peace for 10 generations." The dragon said.

"My father got on his knees and whispered a prayer for his family and waited to die. What happened next was far worse than death. The dragon turned and shot John with a breath. He died instantly. Til this day, I believe I heard my dad scream the moment that John died."

"The dragon took pleasure at my dad's pain. For 30 minutes, she watched my dad scream. Then just as my dad manage to stand up, still, in shock and completely disorientated, the dragon burned both of his legs. "Don't worry, one by one, everyone you love will join your eldest son in hell. My revenge has just begun." It was the last thing my dad heard before he blacked out."

Henry poured himself a drink. Danny remembered Ida saying Henry drank a lot for a long time until Millie told him to stop or she would leave him. Danny had never seen him drink more than just nursing a single glass. Ever.

"The bad part about being married for 200 years..." Henry stared at the glass of cognac he was holding, Twirled it. Smelled it. Then slowly poured it back into the decanter. "Even though she up and leaves you by dying, she is still always in your head."

"Charlie was the one who got my dad back to my mom after his injuries," Henry said in a broken voice; he sniffs the empty glass one more time before putting it down. "There's a bunch of conventions this week, the restaurant is overbooked, I need to get to work, Clara is going to help with Charlie during lunch and dinner service."

"Henry…" Danny called to him as he left the room, "Granddad! damnIt"

"Let him go, Daniel," Charlie weakly said. "Let him calm down. He still has vivid nightmares about John."

"How could I not know any of this?" Danny asked.

"As broken-hearted that he was that you rejected magic…" Charlie said, "He was thankful that he never had to tell you your history."

"I just want my mom," Danny said, sniffing away tears.

"I'll help you find her, this I promise." Charlie said, trying to sit up… "just maybe not today." Charlie winched from pain.

"I'll help find Kisseis, of course, I will. I just didn't know, Charlie. I just didn't understand." Danny apologized.

"I know," Charlie said. "Can you go get me a glass of milk, sweetheart?"

"Yes," Danny said, leaving Charlie and Madeline alone.

"I'm sorry." Charlie whispered." I know you can't save Fr. Karl. So don't spend the next 48 hours researching how…"

"I… totally… Was planning to." Madeline laughed just a little. Charlie tried, but it hurt too much. "I have so many questions…"

"And I have so many answers," Charlie said. "I just don't think I should be answering them while on a morphine drip. But I do need a favor."

"Name it," Madeline said.

"Danny just lied his butt off," Charlie said. "That boy isn't coming back with my milk. I guarantee you, he has left the building, through the back way to avoid Henry. He has a hothead; it's in his DNA. Can you just go with him?"

"I can do that." Madeline patted Charlie's hand and left. Charlie waited until she heard the back exit beep and the door shut. When Charlie thought she was finally alone; Charlie stuffed her mouth with part of a blanket covering her and began to sob. uncontrollably, not caring that every tear hurt. "Please don't let it be starting again." She looked up.

"Hey," Madeline said. Danny hadn't gotten far. He was leaning against a building four doors down from the restaurant.

"Who sent you?" Danny asked.

"Charlie…" Madeline hesitated. "But for the record, I would have come of my own free will, eventually." Madeline extended her hand; he smiles shyly, slowly taking it.

"So, how are my family introductions going?" Danny smirked. Then got very serious, "Oh… I should have listened to Henry more… I've been awful to him for years. But he kept showing up when my mom couldn't believe when my dad had no interest. Henry showed up. I'm going to find mom. For me, for my future kids, but mostly for him."

"What can I do?" Madeline asked, softly entangling her fingers with his.

"I feel like I should say let's get food or let's go listen to a band," Danny said. "So you don't think I'm a total freak. But there is somewhere I want to go…"

"is there food, at least after?" Madeline asked. Danny nodded, "Then I'm in."

They walked hand in hand a few blocks south. Madeline's wheelchair rolled along, not being pushed at all. Rolling in perfect time with Danny's steps.

"Oh, nope. Nope, nopity nope." Madeline said. As they stared at a run-down house on the edge of the Quarter, near the cemetery.

"Let me get this right," Danny paused, trying to hide how amused he was, "You learned magic in 24 hours; you've won the heart of an ancient storm giant. You were just told a wild story about dragons, and you saved a pixie, All in less than a month, and this freaks you out?"

"I'm complicated," Madeline said.

"You're not serious?" Danny asked.

"What if…" Madeline said. "The fortune-teller tells us something horrible?"

"Like?" Danny asked.

"Like, I'm gonna have eight kids," Madeline said.

"That actually would be cool, means I don't have to bring my A-game when courting you." Danny laughed as Madeline playfully hit his stomach.

"Or that you won't meet your soulmate for five years." Madeline teased but realize that would make her sad.

"Then I'd know she was a fraud, and we should just have gotten pizza." Danny whispered in her ear, "You need to tell me when I can kiss you because I think one kiss will seal this for me." Madeline looked down, it wasn't fair not to tell him about possibly being a time lock, and as much as she knew she and Steven were over, she wasn't sure her heart had gotten the memo.

"I just need a little time," Madeline said.

"Usually, I'm not a patient guy," Danny said. "But something tells me you are worth the wait." Playing with her fingers…

"Ok, explain the fortune teller thing," Madeline demanded, trying to change the mood because she wanted to kiss him with every fiber in her body.

"Ida just always went to this one, Madam Rosalie, for years," Danny said. "I think they were even friends. I know it's a long shot, but I thought maybe she could sense Ida or tell me where to look. Holy crap, this sounded logical in my head. I just need to be actively looking for my mom. So she can sense how hard I'm trying; maybe it will give her hope."

"Then, let's go in," Madeline said. Trying not to look into those puppy eyes of gratitude.

Madeline and Danny tried not to laugh as they walked into the little house, but it looked exactly like a scene from every movie with a psychic. From the shag carpet to the beaded curtains to the big crystal ball on the felt cloth covering a dining table.

"Hello?" Danny called out.

"Hello, I'm Madame Rosalie..." she said, backing into the room as if trying to announce herself. She spun around with a beaming smile, took one look at Madeline and Danny, and her whole personality changed, "I'm sorry, I didn't realize how late it was. I'm closed."

"But the sign says psychic readings 24 hours a day," Danny said, pointing to the blinking neon sign in the window,

"We also have the right to refuse any customers."

"Look, My friend is having a really bad week," Madeline said. "We are trying to find his mom, Ida Boudreaux."

"I cannot help. She is coming. GlÉd is coming, get out. She's going to kill you, Madeline... and then she's going to take everything from you, Daniel. Now get out.." Madam Rosalie reached under the table for a shotgun. They left without looking back.

They walked two blocks in complete silence, still holding hands. Danny could sense how scared Madeline was.

"I think you owe me an apology," Danny said, trying to lighten the mood. Madeline looked at him, puzzled. "Bet having eight kids with me sounds mighty attractive now..." Madeline forced a grin as he kissed her hand. "Mack just texted me an SOS. He and Jane are on break at our favorite hole in the wall pizza joint." They headed that way immediately, with no discussion.

"So, I am sorry, that was just a bad idea. I'm so desperate I thought a psychic could find my mom." Danny said after taking a few steps.

"I saw this dateline special." Madeline really wanted to find a logical explanation. "Psychics would have cameras in the room so they could google and Facebook their clients' information before they consult with the spirits. That's why there's a 30-minute wait."

"And I am big shit around here, so she probably knew my name and remembered the bad stuff that Ida told her. Even her name sounded hokey, what a joke." Danny said, hoping to convince her.

"I'm sure it was your big shit..." Madeline said. They laughed a little then finished the walk in silence.

For Danny's 13th birthday, Ida gave him a psychic reading. Which was so much better than the 3 video games he begged for. But as always, Henry snuck them to him. Danny had absolutely no interest in going to this madam Rosalie, but Ida looked so excited, so he just sucked it up and went.

It was the longest 45 minutes of Danny's young life. Most of what she said was general crap she could have learned from Ida. He enjoyed sports. He was highly intelligent. He loved being a big brother, and his mother was his favorite person...

Then the reading got uncomfortable; Madam Rosalie said Danny would suffer a great loss at 15. He would meet the great love of his life at 27, and he would fall in love with her instantly. She would be more hesitant about starting their relationship even though she was already head over heels. Danny needed to be patient because their first kiss would begin a great but tragic love story. This made the 13-year-old Danny throw up a little in his mouth.

Danny blinked, looking away from Madeline as they walked towards the pizza joint. Danny hadn't thought of that reading in years, or what Madam Rosalie did next. Because Danny was staring at the clock above her head, he knew he had 23 minutes left of his reading. Still, after Madam Rosalie laid down the next tarot card, she got a very concerning look, made up some happy ending then asked him to leave.

Danny didn't mean to, but he accidentally pulled his hand away from Madeline's. Madeline tried to shake the sting of rejection; anyway, Jane was waving them to their table. And Mack was beside her. And Steven was besides Mack.

"This has to make up for the psychic thing. Best. First. date, ever!" Danny whispered in Madeline's ear as he sat down by her. He grinned and stopped thinking of Madam Rosalie, just for a moment.

"So..." Mack hesitated. Danny nodded to go ahead after they ordered pizzas and beers. "I worry that Henry is losing it. Gentle or Band-Aid?"

"Band-Aid," Danny said after sipping his beer. "We are all friends here, go." He felt safe with the company.

"Ok, Ummm, all in one shot." Mack leaned towards him. "Henry fired Brian, burnt a roux, he keeps pouring glasses of cognac and pouring them out then angrily mutters to himself. He accidentally knocked over the picture of Millie on the bar, and he came completely unglued, shattering a glass he was holding."

"Then he made a customer cry because she insisted a steak was overdone. But Emma comped the meal, so they left thrilled. It's supposedly trendy if a chef yells at you." Mack shrugged, "I've seen him blow his top before, mostly at us, but this was something I haven't seen. Henry seems like he's very close to just exploding. Or worse... he seems defeated."

"That was a big Band-Aid; thanks for just ripping it right off. This game was better when we were ten." Danny said. "Have we ever asked for the gentle truth?"

"No, no one wants to be the first to give in... But wait, there's more!" now Mack added jazz hands. Jane and Madeline thought it was cute, Danny not so much. "Charlie is on the warpath; she refuses to take any more pain meds until someone can find Fr. Karl's obituary."

"That ought to be easy," Madeline said.

"One would think..." Mack said. He had one more thing that wasn't so awful, but Mack could tell Danny had reached his limit. "Oh shoot, I have to get back. Can I see you tonight, Jane? I get off about 2?" Mack asked. Jane nodded.

"I'll go with you. See ya." Steven offered and left without speaking to Madeline.

"Why are you playing footsie with Mack under the table, and why is Steven following Mack?" Madeline demanded, trying to be cute to try to distract Danny, who had gotten very quiet.

"Oh, you were holding hands under the table, so come on down from your high horse, Madds..." Jane playfully accused. "Listen... in Henry's defense, the steak was perfectly cooked. But look, there is this other minor thing... When Henry fired Brian, the other bartender... Steven was kinda right there..."

"No. no. No... no. No." Madeline said very loudly.

"And with the gallery on hold..." Jane said. "He does need the cash for grad school. He made your favorite perky peach drink as a sample of his work. Mack swooned a little. I couldn't stop it."

"Mack is a trader. And will be dealt with." Danny said, trying to hide a tiny smirk. He got his wallet out and waited for the bill.

"You are never going to call me again, are you? Thanks for a first date. I can just email you gallery business." Madeline said. Hoping Danny would smile and kiss her on the cheek, but she knew there was a chance he would run screaming. He kissed her on her nose.

"I have to go check on Henry and Charlie. Mack and I have been after Henry to fire Brian for months. He was drinking more than he was pouring, so I guess there's your silver lining. I shouldn't like Steven, I know, but I do, and I trust him for some reason. If he needs a job until the gallery gets going again, it's fine." Danny said.

"Henry has blown up at customers before. But the wanting to drink bothers me; I know it shouldn't, but it does a lot. Ida says he's a mean drunk. Millie was the only one that was never afraid of him, and she set him straight a few times in his life. And I know its sounds odd that Mack would bring up the roux, but Henry's emotions are tied to his cooking. He hasn't burned anything in 12 years, especially not a roux." Danny confessed to the girls. "I was going to ask you if I can come to find you later tonight?" Danny asked Madeline. She smiled shyly.

"That was a booty call if I ever heard one," Jane said.

"Nope, Mack showing up at your door at 2:17 is a booty call. You can set the alarm." Danny laughed. Jane blushed just a little.

"You look so upset, honey," Jane said after Danny was out of hearing range. "I thought you'd be ok with Steven..."

"It's not that. Ok, it's a little that..." Madeline said. "But some weird stuff is happening, and all I want to do is kiss Danny, but I've got these secrets, and my ex-boyfriend is now everywhere. I think Danny is keeping something from me. I know I'm all judge-y because I'm pretty sure my secret is bigger than his. But the fortune-teller just doomed our future, so I should not care..."

"Wow, that's a lot, even for me," Jane said, trying not to look at her watch.

"You have to go." Madeline sighed.

"I have to go," Jane said. "Come hang at the bar..."

"So Steven can make me drinks? It is a perfect ending to my date with Danny. " Madeline laughed.

"Will you be ok, Madds?" Jane asked. "Go home, go to sleep. I'll come to check on you after the kitchen closes." Jane got up, and they both left the restaurant. "Oh, by the way, I'm not ignoring the fortune teller story, just waiting for time to enjoy it; who the hell goes to one on the first date?" Jane now screaming as they parted ways on the street.

Madeline closed the door to her apartment. It felt like she hadn't been home in a week. She didn't bother turning on the lights. She just crawled onto the couch and decided to make a phone call.

"Hi, daddy..." Madeline said, trying to sound cheerful. "No, I'm not crying... no, don't wake mom... that's not true, I also call you daddy when I need money... I promise I'm not upset. I'm just a little homesick... no, you cannot fly in to buy me lunch every time I'm a little sad... Can You? I'm kidding, dad... Jane is good. I'm glad she's with me too... I just wanted to tell you I miss you... Yes, I'll call mom more... I wanted to say I love you, daddy." Madeline prayed that she hung up before she started sobbing.

Chapter 10

Madeline woke two hours later, eyes still puffy. She was covered in a blanket. Jane must have been by as promised. Madeline looked at her phone, hoping there was a text from Danny, there was not. She wished she could have laid there, but she knew she had to check on Charlie.

Madeline rolled by the restaurant's front window. For 10:30 pm on a Tuesday, the place was packed. Mack and Steven were behind the bar, surrounded by a crowd. Steven had paid his way through school, bartending. He did the whole twirling glasses, tossing bottles thing. Madeline used to hate watching him because his skills and that cocky smile got him about five numbers a night.

Jane appeared from the kitchen and ordered something from Mack. Steven pointed, and everyone laughed. Jane bowed. Steven spotted Madeline from the corner of his eye. He shrugged; his eyes invited her in to join them. She half-heartedly waved, then was gone by the time Steven looked up again.

Madeline rolled towards the back entrance, cursing all the way because it seemed like a better option than crying. She had no idea why that scene made her feel so horrible and disconnected. She was in a new city with her two best friends. Ok, one who broke her heart but still, in theory... And she was falling in love with one of New Orleans sexiest lawyers... and she had never felt so confused and alone... she wanted to hide in Henry's garden for a while. That was not in the cards.

"Madeline, Madeline, get your butt in here," Charlie screamed. Madeline didn't know how Charlie knew the second Madeline had set foot in Henry's garden, but boy did she.

"Hi," Madeline said faintly as she rolled into Henry's office. At least Charlie would comfort her.

"Where the hell have you been?" Charlie was mad. Not cute mad but angry mad.

"With Danny, like you told me," Madeline said, the wrong thing...

"He stormed past here two hours ago." Charlie was screaming. "Did Mack tell you I can't find Fr. Karl's obituary? I cannot find it."

"I'm sure it's in the paper; I'll look now," Madeline said. Trying not to cry.

"I looked, Henry looked, Mack looked. Clara looked. Danny pretended to look. But I'm sure you can find it." Charlie snapped. Madeline sniffed and reminded herself to breathe.

"When was the last time you took your medicine?" Madeline asked. Ducking in case Charlie had something to throw.

"If God wants me to take my medicine, he can show me Fr. Karl's obituary..." even Charlie knew that was crazy. "I just need to send flowers and go to his funeral, I just do. Madeline." Her tone softened just a little. "Did you know to Henry's dismay, Fr. Karl officiated Millie's service. That was his first one. Henry always said if Millie just didn't believe in God, she would be the perfect creature. " Charlie was trying so hard not to scream from the pain.

"If you take your meds..." Madeline said. "I'll go to the church first thing in the morning..." Charlie angrily took the pills from Madeline.

"You look as bad as I feel," Charlie said after a few minutes, not really feeling better, but at least the room had stopped spinning. "I'm probably going to blackout in two minutes, but do you want to talk about it?"

"Yes," Madeline said. "No. can I just lay beside you for a bit?" Charlie motioned her to come closer.

The whole week must have drained Madeline because she felt like she was in a coma for the rest of the night. But no matter how deep her sleep was, she could feel his warmth. And Madeline felt safe.

She guessed Danny had come in about 10 minutes after both she and Charlie had crashed. Danny sat on the couch beside Madeline all night. Not saying a word. Just stroking her hair while doing work on his laptop. Only getting up to make Charlie drink every hour.

At around 6 am, Madeline moved closer to him, stared at him for a long time. Danny was still working deep in thought. She playfully startled him when she tenderly stroked his cheek. Then Madeline kissed him, passionately and with her heart. The whole room lit up when he smiled. He didn't have time to reciprocate or to say anything at all...

"Congratulations... I'll sing at the wedding. now go find out about Fr. Karl." Charlie said, dead serious... "And not together..."

"I'm going to walk Madeline out, and then I'll fix you breakfast," Danny said very loudly, drowning out Charlie's demands, backing out of the room motioning her to hush. Charlie literally growled.

"hi..." Madeline whispered as they slipped out into the rose garden.

"Hi..." Danny grinned, kissing her soft lips.

"Five minutes, Daniel, or I swear to god I'm going to the church myself," Charlie screamed.

"In a perfect world, we would have the whole day..." Danny said sadly. "But my secretary says if I don't come in this morning, she would report me as missing. Mack told me last night that right after he left us at the pizza place, Henry called him, saying he had prepped everything for the week, left instructions for the nightly specials, and would be back in a few days. He even left his phone on his desk. Henry always has his phone on him in case mom calls. Even in the kitchen, which is a no-no. Mack tried to ask where he was going, but he immediately hung up. So I have to help Jane cook dinner service this week..."

"You cook?" Madeline asked, a little surprised...

"I've got tricks you haven't seen." Danny smiled. Madeline melted. "I'm not creative like Henry or Jane, but I know our menu and have mastered most of Henry's dishes."

"Are you ok? Really..." Madeline asked quietly.

"Nope. Not by a very long shot." Danny said, sadly. "But I have to keep it going. I have five opened cases. And this restaurant is our blood. I cannot not be ok now. I just don't have time. And all I want to do is be with you and talk to you. And maybe go on a date without our entourage... hopefully, Henry will come back in a better mood with a plan to find mom and other stuff..."

"You mean the dragon not killing me? And not taking everything from you?" Madeline uncomfortably laughed...

"What a mood killer," Danny said, not able to laugh this time. "Henry will be back. He's the only one in my life who wouldn't just bail, besides Mack and Charlie.."

"And now you have me, too." Madeline hugged him.

"I'm getting dressed..." Charlie screamed. "Oh, never mind... I don't think my leg should be bleeding that much."

"I'm going to the church before she explodes." Madeline pouted a little. They kissed again. "I'll let you know what I find out."

"I'll feed her breakfast, wait for Clara, then head out. Can I check my schedule and try to meet you for lunch, even if it's late?"

"You better," Madeline rolled slowly away. "Hey, despite what you may hear, I don't go around kissing guys..." Danny put his hands on his heart and backed into the doorway.

As Madeline rolled past the apartments, she felt someone lurking. "Oh, you've gotta be kidding me." Madeline sighed as Steven walked beside her with a gym bag. "Why are you up so early?"

"Jane. Mack. Very loud." Steven said. Madeline burst into laughter.

"At least it's not the camping trip," Madeline smirked. "I just kissed Danny." She accidentally blurted out.

Steven was silent for a long while. "I was hoping I'd have a little more time, but here is my case. You look at him the way you used to look at me. The way you don't look at me anymore." Steven said. "And it kills me, but I know I caused it. And I always thought maybe if you had a fling with an asshole... we'd have a clean slate..." Steven whispered.

"But I think... I think he's the real deal. And I can tell he is already in love with you. How could he not? You still don't get that, do you? But... But the most devastating part is I know you, and I know the moment I told you I cheated, the connection we had, long before we started dating, shattered." Steven said.

"The worse thing is," Madeline confessed. "You were my person. Probably more than Jane. You promised you would always be my person. And you broke me. And I lost a boy, which sucks but more, I lost my person. Then I was alone, And that's why I hated you so much for so long. I miss talking to you."

"I'll do better. I know I can never be your person again, but I'm not gonna lie, you probably will always be mine." Steven said. "I love working at the gallery, and last night was just crazy fun. That's the best gig I ever worked. I know Danny is a part-owner at the restaurant; his graciousness isn't lost on me, so I'm not going to do anything to screw this up. I promise, and maybe one day you will feel like you can talk to me."

"Did you get any digits last night, buddy?" Madeline asked. Steven cringed. Madeline smiled to herself; that didn't hurt. "See, too soon." They both laugh. As they began walking in opposite directions. "Can you not tell Jane I kissed Danny? I want to." Madeline yelled as Steven crossed the street.

"I totally already texted her." He grinned, bowed, and disappeared into a building. Madeline slowly rolled towards the church. This was as close to closure as Steven and Madeline would get. And for the first time in 268 days, talking to him didn't hurt at all.

Madeline giggled when her phone dinged with a text saying, "Probably too soon and a desperate nerdy move but... hi."

Madeline could not stop grinning for the next two blocks; she was falling in love and could finally admit it. She hoped she would see him at lunch... "hi." Texting back, almost sending a heart emoji but thought that was a bit too much.

Then Madeline turned the corner. Seeing the burnt tower brought all the horrible feelings that kissing Danny made her forget, just for a little while, back to the surface. She had no idea how Charlie survived that. Madeline just sat in front of the church for a long time. The tourists kept walking by, snapping photos.

"Excuse me," Madeline said. Getting tired of people taking weird selfies in front of her. "A priest just died up there, show some respect." She yelled at a young guy that almost fell into her lap from his weird poses.

"No, lady, I'm not a creep. It was just a cool lightning strike; no one got hurt. Do your homework, geez." The guy walked off. A feeling of dread washed over her.

Madeline rolled towards the entrance; she didn't want to get in line for a tour; she just wanted to talk to someone in the office. Rolling through the church forced Madeline to remember that one of her aunts used to pray over her so she could walk and be whole. Madeline blinked, not wanting to go down that rabbit hole.

"Hi," Madeline spoke, making herself come back to the present day. "I was wondering if you could tell me when funeral services for Fr. Karl is. Where we can send flowers or a charitable donation that he might prefer." Madeline smiled at Sarah, the receptionist.

"I'm sorry, there isn't a Fr. Karl in our parish. Could you be at the wrong church?" the little old lady asked.

"Fr. Karl, the priest that died in the bell tower during the lightning strike. Oh wait, I think he was retired. Maybe he is on another list." Madeline said.

"Young lady, I've worked in this office for 30 years. No one died in the fire, and I know every priest in the City of New Orleans, I have never heard of a Fr. Karl. There's a Fr. Kelly and a Fr. Kendal, but not a Fr. Karl."

"look, I finally kissed a guy I really like. I cannot see him again until I find out when Fr. Karl's service is. I just really need this information now so I can kill the dragon and have eight kids with this man," Madeline blurted out, realizing she may be losing it... "I'm sorry. It's a silly scavenger video game thing. I am very competitive. But Fr. Karl was supposed to be a real clue." Madeline thought fast. "Is there a priest I can talk to?"

"No, honey." The lady said. "They are all on a morning retreat. There is a prayer room with pictures of all the fathers who have conducted mass here with their names etched in stone in the back of the church. You might look there. I don't really approve of video games, but you're so cute and spunky; I hope you win. And you should ask for extra time... because... you know," Madeline just nodded a thank you. Nothing else seemed appropriate in a church.

Madeline slowly made her way to the prayer room. Echoes of tours could be heard through the long hallways. Madeline walked into the cozy, beautiful room, expecting to be disappointed, but to add to her confusion, Fr. Karl's name was the 5th picture Madeline happened to look at. He was exactly as Charlie described. The years of service matched. She felt bad like she was committing a sin, but she snapped a photo of his portrait and name, softly tracing the engravement curve, and left the church.

"Hi," Danny answered on the 1st ring.

"Hiii," Madeline said. Trying to sound normal, which made it so much worse. "I'm not supposed to call a boy I just kissed for two days... awkward."

"Madeline, what's wrong?" Danny asked. Madeline explained that no one seemed to remember who Fr. Karl was. His funeral wasn't listed in upcoming services, but his name was engraved in the prayer room.

"I have a really bad feeling," Madeline said.

"I have another hour here, but I managed to clear my afternoon; I can come straight there; do you want Mack to keep you company until I can sneak out of here? I could call him."

"No." Madeline sounded unsure, but... "I'll see what I can find out."

"Hey, see if you can talk to a security guard named Al," Danny said. "He knew my mom and Abigail. Fr. Karl befriended him recently. He was pretty shaken up when I saw him after the fire."

"Ok..." Madeline hung up before she said something stupid or needy or both.

Danny sensed this and tried to get through his to-do list faster. As soon as he had gotten into his office, he explained everything to his assistant, Anna, about Henry and Charlie, Madeline and Ida, well, kind of. They agreed to try to do everything from the restaurant except meetings and court until Henry got back.

"Call Treeva; she can be your runner for two weeks and offer a bonus if she stays on track," Danny told Anna.

"Everything you need to sign is done. Eric will meet with the new clients at three. I'll print out everything you did last night and drop it off later. Which, by the way, looks to be three days of work, so I think you are caught up! All I ask is that if we work from Henry's, you send me home with a doggie bag every night, or it's just cruel.." Anna smiled. "And Danny, you've never looked so miserable but so giddy." Danny patted Anna, who was sitting in his chair and left.

*

Madeline must have lost herself in thought because, by the time she exited the big courtyard in front of the church, she spotted Danny hurrying up the sidewalk. He grinned at her then was sadden by the looming blackened tower.

"There's Al, in the front of the church," Danny said. Taking Madeline's hand quickly but softly.

"Hey Al," Danny said.

"Hey." Al lit up. "You're Ida's son."

"Yes, I am," Danny said, trying not to stare at Madeline, now understanding her bad feeling...

"Do you know she still insists I come by every week for a batch of cookies?" Al was just as happy as he could be. "It's weird, no matter what time I show up, they are oven-fresh and warm."

"Mom always was good about that." Danny sniffed, Madeline squeezed his hand. "I mean, she is, is good." Danny winked at Madeline, hiding a tear. "I'm sorry you were here on the day of the fire," Danny said, trying to push through it.

"Oh, I wasn't. it was my day off." Al said. "I wish I was, I don't think I could have done anything because the fire department was here within two minutes, but boy did I love the sound of that bell "

"Al, do you know a Fr. Karl?" Danny asked, wanting a yes but had little hope.

"Nope. And I try to remember the names of all the priests. Most of them are very friendly and appreciate my personal greetings but not all." Al said. "Please send my love to Ida; she's one of my favorite people."

"Mine too," Danny said. Madeline could hear his heartbreak, as hers broke for him. "I'm working at our restaurant this week; if you come in with a few friends for dinner, tell Emma you are my guest, and she will take care of you." Al grinned and walked away.

"You are a nice guy, Daniel Boudreaux," Madeline whispered, stroking his hand. "What do you want to do now?"

"What I want to do now and what I have to do now are two very different things." Danny sighed as they started walking towards Henry's. Madeline babbled when nervous or anxious. Danny. Did. Not.

They walked about a block in silence. Then Danny stopped, leaned down, and kissed Madeline for a few minutes. "Charlie probably isn't going to let that happen again anytime soon. I needed to do that, in case there was any doubt that I didn't want to continue what you started." Danny said. Madeline giggled a little. Then they continued to walk towards the restaurant.

"Madds, Madds, Danny, Danny," someone yelled, Madeline turned, Treeva running towards them. Danny smiled, thinking she was just excited about the job Anna had probably just told her about. "I know what attacked Charlie and Father..." Treeva yelled as she crossed the street, about two buildings down from them...

"Close your eyes, Madeline, please... damnit, now." Danny suddenly screamed as a feeling stormed over him. But it was too late. He couldn't stop it. About 10 feet away from them, something attacked Treeva . Something invisible. Something massive with claws. Two strikes, and she fell. Gashed opened from head to toe, people were screaming. Danny rushed to Treeva's bloody body.

"Madeline." He yelled. She froze. "Madeline, my love, I need you. Please... I need you to call 911, go get Clara, and stay with Charlie. Do not come back out. You have to stay with Charlie... send Clara to help me. Madeline!" Her whole body shook, but she managed to nod and dialed 911 while rolling to the back entrance of the restaurant.

"Lock the door behind me," Clara screamed, already leaving the garden as Madeline came in yelling for her. Madeline sat in the hallway for 47 minutes, alone. Charlie was quiet. Hopefully, she was sleeping. Madeline was in shock.

Danny told Madeline later that Clara did her most powerful healing spells as he tried to stop the bleeding, but there was just too much blood, too many wounds. Treeva probably died instantly.

The police sent Frank, head of special investigations. Frank was a close friend of the family; he and Danny even had a monthly racket ball game. Danny suggested it might be a random shooting. Frank agreed, promising the body wouldn't have an autopsy. Danny asked that Treeva quietly be buried by Abigail's memorial statue and to send him all the bills. They talked about 15 minutes more as the cleaners erased the scene.

When Danny finally came to the garden, soaked in blood, Madeline was waiting for him. He was so strong and took care of everyone for the last hour. But when he saw Madeline, he fell to his knees, sobbing.

Madeline could barely think, but she knew what she had to do. She helped Danny back to her apartment, started a bath, undressed him, and softly washed away the blood as he cried. After he was all clean, Madeline kissed Danny's forehead and closed the door behind her. Danny wanted to get out of the tub, but he physically felt too weak. So he slid down, under the water, and laid still.

After an hour, he quickly sat up. Danny had no intention of staying in the water that long. But he did. He suddenly hurried, blinking the water out of his eyes, dried himself off, and put on the fresh clothes Madeline had put by the sink.

"Hi," he said weakly as he came out of the bathroom. But Madeline was not there.

Her spell book that was on the coffee table was gone, replaced with a note. "I'm moving back to Houston. The dragon cannot take me away from you if I'm not yours. P.S. probably nerdy desperate move but, I wanted you to know I think you could have talked me into having eight children and I don't really like kids."

*

"I'm sorry, Danny. I just didn't know what to do." Clara whispered to him outside of Henry's office, still had Treeva's blood on her clothes, "If Charlie doesn't calm down and take all of her meds, she's going to die. Plain and simple."

"She has ripped stitches, dislocated bones I've set. She pulled out four I.V.'s in the last hour." Clara continued. "All of her tiny veins are beyond repair. She's begging me to heal her magically, but I just think it's too late. IF she can heal naturally for 24 hours, she might be strong enough for the spell, but it would still be risky. And she keeps talking to Fr. Karl and Abigail. Then asks for Madeline, Kisseis, Henry, or you. You were the last person I wanted to call, but I could not just watch her die without trying…"

"I know." Danny covered his face in defeat and sighed. "I will try to settle her down. But I need you to do something for me, and you're not going to like it." Danny explained. Clara volunteered Mack, but Danny had already asked him to run the restaurant for the day. Danny knew he couldn't. Clara finally agreed at left madder than normal. Danny went into Henry's office where Charlie was and closed the door behind him.

For the last 30 minutes, Madeline had been trying to start her car. The brand new car her folks bought her for graduation. So their daughter would always have the freedom to go home to them from where ever she was, without worrying about engine problems. With tears streaming down her face, she hit the steering wheel repeatedly. Knowing the next hit would start the car and get her the hell out of this damn city.

"So." Clara climbed into the locked passenger seat. "Danny sent me. He asked me to be kind and understanding and hold you while you cry. But that's not really my thing... So suck it up, buttercup, and let's go back in."

"Nope," Madeline said, still crying, still banging on the steering wheel. Her palms were now raw and bleeding.

"So, you think you're being stalk by a dragon, but she respects state borders, so if you go back to Texas, she'll just give up?" Clara asked.

"Nope. I'm 99% certain that I'm going to die in Texas." Madeline said. "But he won't have to watch. Jane won't have to watch. Even Steven... Jane would heal. Steven would be angry for a very long time, but he would do the stuff he knows I would want him to do, like go out... find a nice girl, slightly uglier than me, but... he would move on. And one day, I'd just be this chick he knew in college."

"But if I die in front of Danny, I think it would kill him. I mean, literally, kill him." Madeline continued. "So many people love him and need him; his heart can only take so much. I saw that when he was running towards Treeva ... I'm just a girl he kissed once. That's really not worth dying for..."

"if... if the kiss is from the love of your life, it is..." Clara sighed. "I have known Danny all his life, mostly through Ida and Henry. He's a popular guy. Ida has hundreds of pictures of him in tuxes; he goes to parties and events for work. But Ida was always worried because, by 11:30 pm on most nights, he is either on the phone with Ida or helping Mack and Henry close up. Ida doesn't believe he has ever loved anyone, and that breaks her heart."

"Do you love him?" Clara asked.

"More than I ever thought possible..." Madeline said.

"Would you risk your life for a day with him? Or an hour?"

"Yes..." Madeline said without hesitation...

"Then why don't you love him enough to let him have that choice too? Danny needs you, and so does Charlie." Clara sighed. She touched the steering wheel, the engine started up immediately. "I still don't like humans, but you seem better than most. If you tell anyone we had a heart to heart, all your hair will fall out." Clara laughed but made Madeline suddenly very nervous.

Madeline sat in her car for another hour, crying for Treeva . She needed a bit more time... but she did text "Hi" to Danny. He sent back a heart emoji instantly and without hesitation.

*

"Stop Charlie, for the love of God, please lay down," Danny yelled.

"Charlie..." Clara screamed in frustration as Madeline rolled into Henry's office. Madeline was so sad about Treeva , but there was something tangible she could do.

"Clara, we will not need you until tomorrow. Please text me her exact medicine and feeding schedule." Madeline asked. Clara was too tired to argue; she nodded and left.

"Danny, why don't you go for a run, hang out with Mack for a bit, then come back, or go home to sleep. I'm gonna nurse Charlie back to health, or kill her trying. We are going to have 24 hours of silence and stillness so Charlie can get better." Madeline said.

"Please come back, Danny, and soon. I'm sorry I bit you!" Charlie pleaded, slightly scared of Madeline at this moment.

"Madeline and I just had our first fight, so I really should do exactly what she says..." Danny rubbed Charlie's head. And left, touching Madeline's arm as he passed.

"I'll be back with dinner," Danny said as he mouth thank you to Madeline. And he stared at her a few minutes from the doorway, in complete adoration.

"Fr. Karl..." Charlie asked.

"Nope. 24 hours of silence and stillness... then we can talk about whatever you want." Madeline said.

"Ida..." Charlie asked.

"Nope," Madeline said.

"You're not playing, are you?" Charlie asked; Madeline shook her head. Charlie was irritated but thankful. "If you're not going to entertain me, I'm going to sleep, geez…. I love you, Madeline." Charlie barely got the words out before she crashed.

Charlie was a good patient for the rest of the day and into the night. Mack brought them a snack at about eight. Madeline kept herself busy by reading some of Henry's books. As interesting as they were, Madeline couldn't help but wonder where Danny was. He didn't have to come back, but Madeline was hoping he would.

"Go to the garden; Danny asked me to sit with Charlie for a bit." Mack came in just before midnight.

"Before we deal with the wrath of Charlie, tomorrow, which is going to be bad," Danny said, leading Madeline to her private table. "I thought I'd probably owed you dinner…" Madeline had never seen such a gorgeous sight; the candle lite dinner wasn't so bad either… the two stayed out there all night. And for a minute, everything was easy.

As the sun began peaking through the trees, Madeline smiled stupidly, feeling someone was next to her. She rolled over in the long patio chair, looked at the figure towering over her, and screamed instead…

"Charlie called me. I'll be in there for an hour. Comb your hair." Clara was as delightful marching into Henry's. Madeline wondered where Danny had gone. She stretched for a moment then transferred back into her wheelchair.

Madeline quietly rolled through the hallway. She heard Charlie talking to Clara. Madeline smiled because Charlie's voice sounded strong. Then continued to the kitchen where Danny was lost in thought, chopping vegetables. Madeline stared at him for as long as she could, then let out an uncontrollable happy squeal. He stopped, grinned, and greeted her warmly.

"Can I asked you one thing?" Madeline asked shyly. "Was last night… how you got… that?" Madeline pointed at Henry's framed copy of the sexiest lawyer's cover.

"Yup. New girl every week. Two if it's a slow work week and I'm bored." Danny said, trying to keep a straight face until he saw Madeline really thinking about it.

"Madeline!" Danny knelt to her level. "Mack, who has far more connections in the city, nominated me as a gag. He got Ida on his side. They guilted me into it. If I showed up at their party in a tux, the organization would donate 5k to my favorite charity. I took my mom; that was one of her happiest nights in three years. That is the only reason Mack isn't dead. Ok?" she nodded, and he kissed her until she believed him, without any doubts.

"Did you get any sleep?" Madeline asked.

"Not really... but I did have a few hours of sheer bliss," Danny smirked. Madeline got very shy... "I actually don't sleep more than 2 hours a night since Abigail died. Three hours if I'm exhausted. It's probably not a great sleep cycle, but I get a lot done." Madeline didn't know why but this made her sad.

"I got three kinds of fish for the seafood bisque..." Jane said, bursting into the kitchen. Mack and Steven followed, less enthusiastic, "Good morning sunshine," Jane greeted Madeline with an approving interesting look. Madeline grinned; she couldn't help it.

"Thanks for coming in early, you guys," Danny said. "I can't believe we had that last minute booking, 30 for a business lunch. but before that, omelets for everyone."

"Hey, Charlie!" Jane said 20 minutes later as everyone was finishing up breakfast. Madeline had told Jane she was out of town. "How was your trip?" Charlie showed up in drag queen form in the kitchen. Danny and Madeline were very surprised that she was already up. Danny insisted she take his chair and Immediately started another omelet before Charlie could refuse.

"It was a rough trip," Charlie said. "But I'm glad to be home." Madeline felt her sadness and squeezed her leg. Jane started clearing the dishes as Danny went back to prepping vegetables.

"Thank you for breakfast, Danny; I think I may try to make it to 11 o'clock mass." Charlie got up. Madeline noticed she was still very unsteady on her feet.

"Henry is out of town; I was hoping you could help me today." Danny stared at her; she avoided eye contact.

"I do have a bunch of things to do today... I'll call Treeva for you; she always wants a quick day job." Charlie said. Danny hadn't had the heart or strength to tell her what had happened to her friend yet.

"You know," Madeline said. "I should go check on the progress of the mold remover at the gallery. Will you walk with me, Charlie, on the way to the church?"

"Sure," Charlie said without an ounce of enthusiasm.

"I do have a check to get to the painters. Can you come in Henry's office, Madeline? It will just take a sec." Danny said to Madeline, she followed. Jane and Steven thought they just wanted a moment. Charlie knew they were conspiring to handle her.

"I will tell Charlie about Treeva later today." Danny pleaded.

"Oh, I don't know if I can do that. If she asks..." Madeline said.

"Just a few hours..." Danny pleaded. "Between Kisseis and mom and Fr. Karl and now Treeva ... it's too much for her, right now..."

"It's too much for you too," Madeline said, touching his chest tenderly. "Let me tell her about Treeva tonight."

"it's my thing... besides, I'll be fine. I have eight future kids to live for." Danny smirked.

"I'm burning that note." Madeline grinned. They kissed and went back to the kitchen.

"Charlie said she would see y'all later," Jane said. Danny sighed. Madeline excused herself and hurried to catch up with her.

Danny and Mack looked at each other. Mack winked at Jane then excused himself.

"Hey…" Madeline's chair quickly caught up to Charlie, who was already halfway to the church. "Charlie, Charlie… stop."

"Do you know when Fr. Karl's funeral is?" Charlie asked, stopping very abruptly.

"No," Madeline said.

"Did you find Ida?" Charlie asked.

"No," Madeline said.

"Are you going to tell me why Danny made his sad puppy frown when I mentioned Treeva ?" Charlie asked.

"No," Madeline said.

"Are you going to tell me why Mack is following us?" Charlie waved him to come closer.

"I actually didn't know about that one," Madeline said; Charlie began walking again.

"Stop, Charlie," Madeline yelled. "We'd need to tell you something about the church…."

"You have 30 seconds," Charlie said, very annoyed. Mack and Madeline tried to softly explain. That did not go over well. Charlie charged into the church, Mack and Madeline followed nervously.

"Hello Sarah," Charlie greeted the receptionist.

"Hello, Charlie. Have you been on tour? We haven't seen you in a month of Sundays." Sarah said. "Hello again," looking at Madeline, "Did you ever win that scavenger hunt?" Madeline nodded.

"I brought you coffee last week, Sarah," Charlie said.

"Really?" Sarah was a little confused but tried to hide it. "Time just passes too darn quickly these days, doesn't it?"

"I just really need to know when Fr. Karl's funeral is. And if you need ushers…" Charlie said.

"I told this young lady that we don't have a Fr. Karl. Oh my goodness, am I on candid camera?" Sarah asked. "Is Fr. Karl a celebrity dressed as a priest? As long as he doesn't curse, that would be funny." Mack grabbed Charlie's hand before she made a fist…

""I can show you his room," Charlie said, now walking past the reception area towards the outdoor pavilion, pass the meditation pond to the house.

"Stop Charlie, you should not be back here," Sarah said.

"Hi, Charlie,"

"Hey Charlie, can you call bingo next week?"

"Thanks for fixing the sink, Charlie."

Three priests yelled at her as she walked by them. She kept walking, trying not to melt into a puddle.

Charlie walked into the house where many of the priests lived and went straight to the dormitories. Sarah, now trying to keep up, was huffing very loudly. Charlie named the father's who lived in each of the 10 rooms. If a priest was home, they greeted Charlie by name. a few even asking where she had been.

"This was his room," Charlie whispered, pointing at the last door.

"No, Charlie…" Sarah said. "This has been a junk room for 25 years."

"This. Was. His. Room." Charlie said louder with every word. Madeline tried to reach for her, but Mack mouthed, "She needs to do this."

"See, the padlock is so old, it's rusted," Sarah said, and stepped away from the door, honestly scared of Charlie now.

Charlie closed her eyes, said a prayer, placed her hand on the doorknob. The lock clicked, the door slowly opened, and there was Fr. Karl's room.

On the bulletin board, to the left, was a picture of a pixie that Fr. Karl drew when he was ten. Charlie was inconsolable.

"Sarah," Mack said. "Can you go get Charlie some Juice, please?"

"Yes, yes I will…" Sarah said, "Fr. Karl, he brought me doughnuts every Thursday… how did I forget that?" Sarah scratched her head.

Mack helped Charlie outside to a bench near the meditation pond.

"Should we call Danny?" Mack asked.

"Not yet…" Madeline said.

Charlie sat on the bench, rocking back and forth as Mack stroked her back. After about 20 minutes, Charlie patted both of them a quiet thank you. Her silence and sudden calmness were almost worse than her cries. After Charlie wiped away the last teardrop, she stood up, continued towards the church, slowly and with a specific purpose. Mack and Madeline followed.

There was a small tour group in the prayer room when Charlie went in. After an unexpected breeze from seemingly nowhere, the tour suddenly finished and wandered away even though the tourists had just gotten there.

Besides Charlie, Madeline knelt in front of Fr. Karl's picture as Charlie said, "Let us remember you…" Her fingers followed his name etched in stone. White light shadowed her trace until his whole name glowed.

"Hey, there's Charlie and Mack behind the news reporter on tv," Jane said. Turning up the volume in the kitchen about two hours after Madeline and Charlie left that morning.

"During the clean up of the recent bell tower fire, workers were heartbroken to discover the body of Fr. Karl Summers. He was one of New Orleans's most loved priest who served the community for over 75 years. Details of the Funeral Service will be announced later today."

*

"I have a confession," Jane said. As Madeline returned to the kitchen where Jane and Danny were relaxing after a busy lunch service. "When you said you were going to help while Henry was gone, I thought you would be in the way… but you are better than most chefs…"

"I've got the skills, baby…" Danny grinned. He smiled even more, when Madeline rolled up beside him and put her head on his shoulders. Madeline had something to tell Danny, but her two favorite people's banter was just too adorable.

"I'm trying to figure out why your very cute friend here is a lawyer and not a chef…" Jane said

"Because." Danny said, now playing with Madeline's hand. "Because Henry and my mom wanted me to be a chef. And I wanted to be a rebellious teenager that really pissed off Henry without disappointing my mom. Which sounds ridiculous now. Luckily I'm ok at the lawyer thing. The big cases pay for my lost causes. But don't you dare tell Henry I'm decent at it. Or that I really enjoyed it." Danny made Jane pinky shake.

" I just do scheduling, pay bills, and am the busboy when he's here," Danny said. His voice trailing off… "Hey, how's Charlie?" Danny asked Madeline.

"I happened to be with her when she found out about her old friend, Fr. Karl's death," Madeline said, very carefully. "She said she just wanted to be alone. I walked her home and told her you would bring her an early dinner and sit with her a while." Madeline said. Danny looked grateful but still worried.

"Umm, I ran by the gallery just now, and there's seems to be a problem with the mold… Do you have an hour to come to look?" Madeline asked. Danny smiled because he was hoping it was a cute code to get some alone time. Madeline didn't smile back.

"It should be a slow night…" Danny said.

"I got it," Jane said.

"Please call me if it gets busy; Mack will also call me whining if you are too busy to flirt with him."

"Ha!" Jane said, kicking them out.

"At worse, I'll close and clean," Danny promised. Jane honestly loved the kitchen so much she was thrilled to be on her own.

"Please tell me that was code because you really wanted to be alone with me.." Danny teased, walking towards the gallery... As Madeline frowned.

"Kiss me," Madeline demanded before they turned the corner. "Remember, you really like me. And that I did go straight to you, after I kinda poked around... but mainly straight to you..." Madeline explained. His goofy grin disappeared, and he ran towards the gallery.

Madeline caught up with him as he stood in front of the gallery; the doors had been completely torn off. The metal frames look like it had been run through a paper shredder.

"Go back to Henry's, tell Mack to come," Danny demanded.

"Would you like me to roll backward and bow too?" Madeline asked.

"Madeline, just go to Henry's now," Danny said.

"Cuz I'm a girl or cuz I'm in a wheelchair?" Madeline asked.

"Cuz, I'm falling in love with you," Danny yelled with a little less sharpness.

"Oh my god," Madeline said. "Mack said you'd say anything to win an argument..."

"I would!" Danny said. "But it happens to be true... Madeline, please go back to the restaurant..."

"We can either both go in, or both go to Henry's..."

"Are you always this stubborn?" Danny still was screaming but... less.

"This is me being cute, cooperative, and compromising." Madeline was still mad, but Danny just couldn't stay angry.

"Can I go in first?" Danny asked.

"I'm stubborn, not stupid, of course, I'm making you go in first," Madeline said, in a softer voice.

The inside was ten times worse than anything Madeline could have imagined. The walls had huge claw marks, the floors looked like it had potholes. The reception desk was torn into four, the pieces tossed around like tissue paper. Chairs broken, glass from the light fixture shattered.

Danny kissed her head. There was nothing to say. She sniffed as he motioned her out the door. Madeline used a simple spell to border up the doorway. As they walked hand in hand in silence, back to Henry's, Danny was at a complete loss. All he knew was that there was a legend that the restaurant was the only safe place in New Orleans where evil could not attack. He prayed this was true.

After walking half a block, Madeline's phone rang. "Hello?"

"Madeline, this is Mack. Can you try not to react?"

"I'll do my best, but I cannot promise," Madeline said. Now stopping by a street sign and turning away from Danny, which Danny did not like.

"Is Danny with you?"

"Yes," Madeline said.

"I..." his voice broke. Madeline took a deep breath and started fidgeting with her wheelchair. Danny noticed and squatted down. "I need you to get him to the downtown memorial, basement, special ICU. It's Henry and other stuff but mostly Henry. Danny can lose his shit with me later, but right now, he just needs to hurry so he can say goodbye to his great grandfather." Mack hung up.

"We need to do something, my love." Madeline cuffed Danny's face and kissed the swelling tears appearing in his eyes; he knew the instant she looked at him.

They took a cab downtown, thinking it would be faster, but Danny decided to get out and run after hitting traffic from a parade. Madeline's wheelchair kept up. They raced through five streets, three corridors, four hallways, and two elevators and finally spotted Mack at the end of a hall.

"Listen, Danny." Mack forcefully stopped him before he barged into Henry's room. "The doctor will be right back. He's in really bad shape,..."

Mack could barely get the words out. Danny told Madeline that Mack could say absolutely anything to anyone; he did not have a diplomatic bone in his body. Danny shoved Mack away from the door, Mack shoved back. "He lost his left arm… and eye… they wanted to put him in an induced coma, but he refuses until he sees you… And Danny, Ida is in there."

Mack moved away from the door. Danny went in. Mack and Madeline watched as Ida stood up from a chair and Danny ran into her arms. Then he went to Henry's hospital bed, kissing his forehead.

"Did you know that when I was six, my dad beat me up, he actually broke my arm for eating the last cookie?" Mack told Madeline as they waited in the hallway. "I told Danny the next day at school because he just would not stop asking me what had happened. I even tried to punch him in the groin to shut him up and make him go away. But he kept hounding me. Exhausted, I blurted it out." Mack said.

"The next day, Henry picked me up from school. And I never saw my dad again. Henry always wanted to officially adopt me, but there was so much red tape. I told him the moment that he picked me up from school, he became my dad, and Danny became my brother. No paper needed." That's the most Mack had said to Madeline in two months. They hugged.

*

"Hi, Henry." Danny bent over him, trying not to show how devastated he was. Henry was the biggest man Danny had ever seen in his life, but now laying in a hospital bed, he looked so tiny, so broken.

"Did Jane do good this week?" Henry asked.

"Yes, granddad," Danny said. For the first time, he didn't argue. "Her roux is the perfect color."

"I'm leaving Mack a nice nest egg and half the restaurant. Please don't decide important decisions by arm wrestling; you know it's not fair. Madeline gets all my books. Let her work out of my office. It's protected. But you and Ida get everything else," Henry said. "And here…" Henry put something in his hand. Danny gulped.

"Granddad," Danny rubbed his eyes.

"I brought your mom back, my lovely granddaughter. She looks so much like my Millie. Maybe I should go see my Millie soon."

"No, granddad, I need you." Danny's voice was so shaky.

"And Daniel, nurture her…" Henry said. "Don't make her choose because Madeline will always choose you. But she can do both. She's going to be great at both, and she will always come back to you. Madeline will be challenging but worth every fight. Just. Like. Millie."

"I don't know what that means, granddad," Danny said, now sobbing.

"Go feed your mother; she said she has been eating, but I don't believe her. And send Madeline in." Henry ordered.

Danny kissed his hand, ushered Ida out, and nodded Madeline to go in, squeezing her hand as they passed.

"Very nice," Henry said as Madeline made herself float up so Henry could see her. "I brought you the book. It's on the chair; only a time lock can read it."

He then started screaming in pain. The nurses rushed to his side, kicked Madeline out, and closed the door. Madeline quickly slipped the large book into her little backpack; it fits snuggly like the backpack was made to hold it.

Henry always said he wanted the biggest, loudest, wildest wake in New Orleans's history. If it wasn't, it sure came close.

Chapter 11

"Everything looks good for re-opening," Madeline said as Danny looked for something in the refrigerator. "Jane is picking up all the food in the morning. I'm going with her. Mack and Steven are busy going to five liquor stores. Every drop in the bar was drunk at the wake."

"So..." Danny sat in front of Madeline, closing her laptop. "Mack said he would stay with Ida tonight. I thought maybe we would go see Charlie's first show back since everything... grab a bite, then... find something to do..." Danny tried to kiss her, but she moved back.

"Anna wants you to call her asap. I think they need you to confirm you'll be back Monday." Madeline said, looking down.

"Madeline, you haven't hugged or touched me since the wake," Danny whispered in her ear. She moved back again, away from him.

"I wanted to wait a few weeks until you got back to your real life, but I don't think we ought to see each other anymore," Madeline said.

"Okay," Danny shrugged. Madeline had prepared herself for Danny's anger or maybe begging, even a little crying... but not indifference.

"Good, that was easy." Madeline pretended to be relieved.

"But... Look, We should kiss goodbye, one for the road..." Danny was playing her. She needed to stay strong. "I know, just a simple, friendly hug. One last hug. I won't even grab anything." Danny smiled. Madeline avoided eye contact at all costs.

"Okay. No hug. I get that. I mean, look at me," Danny grinned, knowing he was wearing her down, "Okay, here is my request. Just shake my hand, look me in the eye, say goodbye, and I will spend the rest of my life loving you from afar." He put out his hand; she was determined to see this through. But when their hands touched, their pinkies intertwined, Madeline melted.

"Please let me go," Madeline begged. "This way, you will hate me, but just a little. You won't be able to stand the sight of me when you know the truth..." But looking into his beautiful eyes, she blurted her secret out.

"I... I... killed... henry." Madeline said, hiding her face; she truly believed it was her fault. "He was helping me figure out who I was. And that's what got him killed."

"Did he tell you that?" Danny asked.

"No, but..."

"Were his last words to you in anger?"

"No, but Danny," Madeline cried... "He was in so much pain, maybe he was confused, maybe he thought I was someone else."

"Come here..." Danny said. Madeline shook her head no. "Please. Come here." She couldn't help but be drawn to him. "This is not the time. You will know when I'm asking for your hand. There will be flowers and a band and maybe fireworks, but Henry gave me these," Danny showed her something in his wallet. "And he left you all his books... with his dying breath, he had nothing but love and complete adoration for you. And I will be happy to remind you that every day for the rest of our life."

"All cards on the table?" Madeline asked.

"Yup."

"Okay..." Madeline thought for a second. "I'm gonna disappear for 10 seconds; when I reappear, I will be sitting on the island."

Danny watched as Madeline blew him a kiss and vanished into thin air. He should have been more afraid, but he just counted to 10.

"Ta-dah..." Madeline proudly announced before she realized she had landed in the sink...

"Wow, maybe Henry was indeed slightly confused," Danny said. "He said you would be really good at something; I hope this wasn't it..." Madeline gasped, pretending to be offended as Danny pulled her out of the sink. "We'll work on it..." he carried her back to her wheelchair after kissing her a few minutes on the island."

"I'm sorry, Mr. Boudreaux," Ida came into the kitchen as Danny was setting Madeline back in her chair. "You did say she could come here whenever she wanted?"

"I certainly did," Danny said. "Hi mama, I'm so glad you came by." Danny hugged Ida, and she tried to hug him back.

"Hello, young lady," Ida said. "Are you Abigail's friend?"

"I am, but I'm also Danny's friend," Madeline said gently.

"Oh," Ida said.

"Mama, Remember I told you all about Madeline and how much Henry just absolutely loved her to pieces and that I thought you would too."

"And that she would make me a grandma." Ida giggled with delight.

"I said," Danny cringing, a little embarrassed. He winked at Madeline. "If we were blessed enough one day in the distant future." Madeline should have felt uncomfortable, but it was sweet.

"Where's Granddad?" Ida asked. "Is he still in the hospital?"

"Yes, mama, but he is not in pain; he told me he has never felt better," Danny said with a heavy sigh.

"Danny, when can I go home?" Ida asked.

"Remember, I'm taking a few weeks off, and I thought we could spend some time together," Danny said. "We are going to the zoo tomorrow!"

"I would absolutely love to come if I am invited," Madeline asked.

"I'm sorry, dear, usually I would, but tomorrow is family day." Ida said. "Me, my husband, Henry, Abigail, and Danny. But maybe next time."

"I would absolutely love that," Madeline said.

"I think Danny has to help get the restaurant ready for y'alls big re-opening," The nurse saw it was just too much for Danny. "Let's go get ice cream." Ida grinned. Madeline rubbed Danny's shoulder as they left.

"She is just worse than I have ever seen her," Danny said. "Ida usually has at least a few conversations about my present life. Asks what case I'm stressed about, asks if Mack and I have gone out lately. Asks if Charlie could come to dinner. Before she drifts back, but... "

"It's probably just the loss of Henry. I'm sure she is trying to get back to you." Madeline said. Neither believed it, but Danny appreciated the thought.

"I'm going to help Charlie get dressed for her performance. She still feels off, poor thing." Madeline softly kissed him. "AND... I will be making up for my lack of affections after dinner," Danny moaned as she rolled away.

*

For the 1st time since Henry's death, Danny was completely alone at the restaurant. He looked around the empty kitchen, slid down from the island he was leaning against, and came unglued for 20 minutes.

Madeline did not kill Henry, but something certainly did. And as much as Danny tried not to think about it, he knew the evil wasn't done with Charlie or Madeline or even him. He stood up and punched the refrigerator, immediately regretting it, leaving four knuckle dents.

"Hey," Danny said, pacing back and forth, calling someone. "Please don't talk me out of it... You know I've been sitting on the letter for a week..."

"She's just not getting better... I know Henry wouldn't want me to, but mom's going to need 24-hour care... I want to be around more, if she recognizes me once a day, it's worth it. Eugene will not return my calls. Mack ran into him yesterday; he told Mack he knows Henry was like a father to him and he was sorry for his loss... Not a damn word asking about his wife or me..."

"Charlie told me she is afraid to go out." Danny continued. "Charlie has never been scared of anything. I just need to watch over all of them because I'm not marrying Madeline before I know my future family will live happily ever after..."

"Can you believe I love a girl more than my job? Nope, she will try to talk me out of it. I have to do it before I lose my nerve." Danny paused and let out a loud sigh. "Okay, Please deliver my leave of absence letter today. I also recommended you be placed with Levits with a 10% raise. Thanks,

Anna," Danny tossed his phone across the floor. Mack caught it and helped Danny up.

"You're paying for that dent," Mack said. "Did you do it?"

"Yup," Danny said.

"Do you regret it?" Mack asked.

"Oh, so damn much," Danny said. Running his fingers through his hair.

"Wanna start training Monday?" Mack asked.

"Yup," Danny said.

"Are you going to tell Madeline why? The real truth?" Mack asked.

"Probably not..." Danny said.

"Damn, you are, indeed, as dumb as you look," Mack said and left.

*

"We just had a three-course meal. How can you be getting yourself a big bowl of ice cream?" Madeline teased as Danny was rummaging through her kitchen.

"One day, you will understand when I say I'm just a 500-pound nerd stuck in this body." Danny laughed. "Besides, I plan to work it off very soon. No, do not answer the door!" Danny hissed as someone knocked.

"What if It's your mom?" Madeline asked.

"Tell her we are practicing for grandbabies?" Danny grinned.

"Danny! What if it's Charlie? She was feeling blue, so I told her to come by after her 2nd show." Madeline said.

"She can come back in 15 minutes." Danny hissed again. Madeline blew him a kiss as she cracked the door opened, immediately regretting her decision.

"hi." He said, "Can I come in?"

"This is a really bad time," Madeline was trying to hide the visitor from Danny.

"I really need to talk to you." Steven pushed his way in.

"Oh, hey Danny," Steven said.

"Just… one… boring…. normal… date… night…" Danny sighed. He looked slightly irritated but not mad. "Actually, I should go check on mom… I'm taking my bowl of ice cream with me."

"Are you coming back?" Madeline asked.

"Ah, yeah… I'm understanding, not an idiot." Danny kissed Madeline's cheek. And closed the door behind him.

"This better be an epic moment in your life because, for once, we were having a normal date night. Danny and I have these huge events and stolen passionate moments… but never like falling asleep to the tv, we were going to watch tv after ya know…"

"You're right, too soon," Steven said. "But as my person, I need you to tell me what this means….." he pulled out a leather journal he just received. It looked exactly like Madeline's.

 "Oh my god, you know what they are, you have one." Steven stared at her as she tried to pull off a fake confused look. He started pointing at her and screaming.

"How far are you?" Madeline asked. Steven and Madeline may or may not have had a reputation for being extremely competitive.

"Just a few spells in," Steven said.

"That's adorable…" Madeline said. Steven rolled his eyes.

"I've been doing research; they say magic is coming back; if it's true, I might change my Master's focus," Steven said. "Some are supposed to be more powerful than others. Do you know anyone else who got a book?"

"Nope," Madeline said.

"But…" against her better judgment. "Maybe next week we can clean up the gallery while practicing… Since Henry's death, Danny's a little overprotective, but he's going back to work full-time Monday. So we should start too. I really do need to get the gallery back on track."

"I can't believe vandals did that much damage," Steven said. That's the story she had told everyone.

"More ice cream," Danny said, reappearing with an empty bowl. Madeline was glad he came back.

"I am sorry for barging in, Danny, family stuff," Steven said. "I'm sure I'll see you all weekend at the restaurant, but I'll be there 10 am Monday, Madds…" and he left. Madeline cringed as she sensed Danny was about to say something.

"We can fight, or we can mess around…" Madeline shrugged. Danny gave in, not prepared to open his own can of worms.

*

The next three days were crazy. Danny and Jane cooked, and Mack and Steven took care of the bar. Madeline helped organize the staff and answered the phones. The shortest wait was an hour and a half, both Friday and Saturday, from lunch until 11.

Charlie kept saying she was coming over, but she never showed. The last time she was at the restaurant was for 10 minutes during Henry's wake; she sang one song and left. Madeline asked her to stay longer, but she confessed she couldn't and ran off. And hadn't been by since.

Madeline tried not to worry, but Danny just looked miserable during the re-opening. He was always gracious to the staff, exchanged cute banter with Jane, mocked Mack, and always touched Madeline tenderly as they passed each other. But his mind and heart were somewhere else. He missed Henry.

During a short break, Madeline found Danny sitting at Henry's desk.

"He wanted you to learn your craft in his office." Danny told Madeline as she hugged him, "He said you would be protected in here,"

"I'm almost ready." Madeline sighed. "It still physically hurts to be in here."

"Oh shoot, text from the nurse," Danny said. "Mom won't calm down until I go say goodnight."

"Let me go," Madeline said. Danny nodded gratefully. Hiding his head in his hands.

Madeline ran over to the apartments. Ida was standing by the fountain.

"I'm sorry, I know you and Mr. Boudreaux have your hands full this whole weekend, but she has been extra agitated tonight, so much so that I'm scared she might hurt herself." The nurse said.

"It's fine," Madeline told the nurse and went to Ida.

"Hi, Ida," Madeline said. "Danny is very busy tonight, but he was hoping you would let me hang out with you a while."

"Is he in court? He is such a good lawyer." Ida said.

"He is," Madeline said.

"Don't let him give up being a lawyer; he loves arguing more than cooking even if he won't admit it," Ida said. Madeline laughed, knowing it was probably true.

"You're the only girl he has ever let in..." Ida said. Madeline sniffed. "And Madeline," Ida took her hand and looked straight into her eyes. " I've been trying and trying to remember to tell you this, but... She is trapped. That bitch has figured out how to use an avatar, a willing avatar. Henry said I had to remember to tell you. I'm sorry I forgot."

"No, thank you for telling me. But I don't know what that exactly means, please tell me, Ida," Madeline pleaded.

"No, too scary..." Ida frowned, then was lost again. "Well, hello dear," Ida smiled, "I'm sorry, but it's kinda late for a playdate for Abigail. I think we might go to bed, good night. Say goodnight Abigail." Ida leaned down and made the invisible girl wave. The nurse touched Madeline's arm and led

Ida back into Danny's apartment. She had no idea how Danny had been doing this for 12 years.

Madeline was suddenly filled with an overwhelming feeling of dread. For some reason, she knew Ida had one moment of clarity and that it would probably be her last.

Madeline slowly made her way back to the restaurant, glad to see that it was finally dying down. The tables were all still filled, but no one was waiting.

"Can I have a virgin pina colada, extra pineapple-y?" Madeline propped herself behind the bar. She was thirsty, upset, and wanted to avoid Danny just for a minute.

"The fact that you still don't drink a lot has been one of my biggest failings in life," Steven said. Mack laughed too. "And she drinks virgin pina Coladas when she's upset, which is just damn weird..." they both laughed. Madeline made faces at them.

"Hey, Mack..." Madeline said. "Can I ask you a very odd question?" Mack nodded. "Danny once told me that Ida's greatest pet peeve was cursing, and she washed y'all mouths out regularly?"

"Yeah... and Danny got caught more than me. It was awesome." Mack smiled.

"And she has never said a bad word? Even after she got sick?" Madeline asked.

"Nope," Mack said. "Why do you ask..." Just then, Danny snuck up behind her and took a drink from her glass. Madeline winked at Mack, and he dropped it.

"The nurse texted mom is in bed. Thank you, Madds." Danny looked a tiny bit less sad. Madeline did not. "Jane wanted to cook everyone dinner at midnight. They really earned it today."

"I think I'm just going to go home; I'm a little tired," Madeline said.

"I'm an idiot; you've been doing everything for me for the last three weeks, you must be exhausted," Danny said. "Let me tell Jane we are leaving."

"Absolutely not," Madeline said. "This was an amazing success. Henry would want you to celebrate with your staff. Just wake me when you come in." Madeline quickly left, trying to hide how upset she was but Danny knew something was up. He would just stay to make a few toasts. He couldn't help but wonder what Ida did... Madeline was usually unflappable, so it was probably huge.

After leaving the restaurant, Madeline found Charlie sitting in the dark at the table by the fountain as she rolled through the courtyard. Without asking, Madeline took the extra cigar, cut and lit it. Inhaled deeply and blew out slowly, and smiled.

"When the hell did you start smoking cigars?" Charlie asked, very amused.

"I once lost a bet with a boy..." Madeline laughed.

"I'm sorry I haven't been around." Charlie sighed. "I needed a little time. My favorite person was Fr. Karl. My second favorite person was Henry. And even though I wasn't that close to Treeva, it hurts that she was caught in the crossfire. It's just a lot." Madeline started fidgeting and looked down, "Spit it out."

"You're mourning... I can't put anything else on you." Madeline said.

"I am going to be sad for another week," Charlie explained. "Then I'm going to be angry for a very long time, like blowing stuff up angry. Mourning Charlie is easier to talk to than angry Charlie unless you want to blow something up than I will be your girl." Charlie grinned a little.

"This is probably the strangest thing I am ever going to ask you," Madeline said.

"Oh honey, we've been friends for centuries; I think it's not."

"Has Ida ever cursed?" Madeline asked.

"Fr. Karl cursed more than Ida…" Charlie giggled.

"Ida usually rambles about Danny and Abigail, Right? Not much about anything else?" Madeline asked.

"Yup," Charlie said. "90% Danny and Abigail. Then me, Mack, and Henry, the fireflies. Never about her husband, unless it's a reference to a family outing or anything else… why?"

"I just had a very strange conversation with her about avatars. Danny had a rough day; I didn't want to tell him until I figure out what it meant. It's probably just weird babbling. …"

"Wow, that's not usual Ida verbiage," Charlie said. "I'm curious; what exactly did she say?"

"She looked into my eyes; I feel like it's the only time in the past two weeks that she acknowledged me. As a person, she recognized, not as someone Danny keeps introducing her to." Madeline said. "She said Henry had a message. She kept forgetting to tell me, but she was trying very hard because Henry said it was very important. And then said: She is trapped. That bitch has figured out how to use an avatar, a willing avatar…"

"Definitely not her usual chatter," Charlie said. "She actually said the word "Bitch"?"

"Yup," Madeline said.

"Oh, that's not good, it might be nothing but… wow."

"I tried to ask her to explain, but she reverted back to being with Abigail, and I didn't want to push," Madeline said. "What if it was a warning from Henry? Or, more likely, what if it was the last movie she saw on cable just before I visited her, and I'm making this into something to avoid my own crap?"

"Madeline, one thing I can tell you about yourself, your instincts are always dead on. It's actually pretty damn annoying. Let me do a little digging… I'd usually run to Henry or Fr. Karl on something like this… they both made up my north star," Charlie sniffed and took the last drag from her cigar.

"I'm sorry, I should not have told you my crazy crap." Madeline felt bad.

"Your crazy crap has saved our butts numerous times, so I'd listen to it all damn day. But stop replaying it in your head," Charlie ordered as Madeline looked down, annoyed that she was called out.

"Let me think on it a few days," Charlie said. "Danny, look Madeline, it's your boy toy, Danny." Charlie suddenly changed the subject.

"You are as beautiful and as subtle as ever, Charlie," Danny said, kissing her forehead while glaring at Madeline.

"You are supposed to be having dinner with your staff…" Madeline said.

"And you are supposed to be in bed," Danny said. "I doubled their tips; they worship me." He grinned. "I just really wanted to watch you fall asleep tonight."

"Okay, I'm leaving before I puke; that's a line if I ever heard one." Charlie laughed, but still with so much sadness. "Can we have lunch in a few days, Madeline? I'm almost done being alone, and I'll think about your question." Charlie got up, whispered something to the fountain, maybe a prayer to Kisseis, and disappeared through her closed doorway.

"What question?" Danny asked Madeline...

"Can you please just hold me?" Madeline said, leading him to her apartment.

"Yes, my love, yes," Danny said.

*-

"Oh. My. God. This is the best omelet you have ever made!" Madeline said.

"Seriously, Jane," Steven said, making her try a bite.

"I guess it doesn't suck." Jane shrugged.

"How are you even on your feet?" Madeline asked. "Danny and Mack purposely decided to close the restaurant today to give everyone, especially you, a day off before the restaurant goes back to its normal hours. So you decide to make us breakfast, you freak. Not that I'm complaining. This omelet is divine."

"I don't know," Jane said. "There's something magical about this kitchen. I want to cook all the time! I'm really grateful for this opportunity, but Henry was just so talented, I'd have been his sous chef for as long as he would have had me. His death was so unexpected and tragic. That must have been a horrific car accident."

"Yup. Should have never happened." Madeline sighed.

"How is Danny, really?" Jane asked.

"I think he is even sleeping less, if that's possible. Henry was everything to him." Madeline said. "Last night, he was determined to stay in bed all night because he thought it was sweet and romantic and would cement our relationship. At two, I caught him playing with my hair. At three, he was watching YouTube videos of dogs that sing. At four, he watched an info commercial on knives muttering how a knife should never both cut a tomato and a can. To save our relationship, I kicked him out at five and made him promise never to spend the whole night with me ever again."

"See, if you did that with me, we might have never broken up...." Steven grinned. Both Jane and Madeline threw their napkins at him. Jane mouthed: way too soon, dummy.

"Jane!" Danny walked in, "Do you not understand what I meant by a day off, Sunday?" Danny grinned, sitting by Madeline.

"The kitchen was spotless when I got here, so I assume that is what you did after you had the argument with the infomercial..." Jane said. Danny bowed his head in shame, smirking a little.

"How was breakfast with Ida?" Madeline asked Danny, stroking his cheek.

"Umm, she is usually more lucid in the mornings..." Danny said. "She didn't even ask me about my day or anything. But she did ask about you, Madeline, and asked if you were safe."

"I told you! Mothers love me." Madeline grinned nervously.

"Charlie!" Jane greeted her as she walked in. "Do you want an omelet?"

"No thanks, I actually wanted to talk to Madeline for a quick second. And I think I left something in Henry's office. Can you help me look for it, Madeline?"

"I can help. I like helping." Danny said.

"It's a girl thing, but thank you," Charlie said. Danny felt his suspicions were confirmed as he heard Henry's door slam shut....

"Don't freak out," Charlie said after she knew the door was completely shut.

"Than don't sneak me away from my boyfriend, take me into the room of a newly deceased mentor figure and say 'don't freak out...'," Madeline hissed.

"Are you curious or not?" Charlie said.

"Yes... No... Maybe..." Madeline said. "What if we decide Ida was having a really off night. All the bad stuff was horrific supernatural accidents. I can go back to running a new gallery and date a really cute lawyer boy."

"Then you... would not be Madeline Jourdain..." Charlie said.

"Okay... Go..." Madeline growled.

"So, it really bothered me that Ida said, bitch," Charlie said. "I honestly did not think she knew the word. And I just cannot believe she would know, let alone use, avatar in a sentence. I checked tv listings, the movie hasn't been on this month."

"I know," Madeline confessed. "I looked this morning..."

"My girl..." Charlie said. "So I researched the definition of avatar. Hindus believe an avatar is a manifestation of a deity or released soul in bodily form on earth that can be controlled by its god, even if it's trapped."

"I'm confused, Charlie," Madeline said.

"If... if Ida just said the word bitch, I would be curious," Charlie said. "If she mentioned the word avatar in passing, that would really stump me... but the thing is, Henry didn't know the ending to the Central American

Dragon War. And the ending… the ending has always kept me up at night. And hearing Ida's words just sent my head into dark places."

"After the dragon killed John…" Charlie began. "It took Brogant and me two years to get home. Henry and his mom were so happy to have him back that we decided to tell them that John's death was not in vain. That the others rallied after they saw John die and killed Fuego. What else could we do? Henry just wanted to know he could go on and try to find happiness without dishonoring John's memory."

"Brogant wanted to make it okay for Henry to be happy, so he did. Henry and Millie finally got married. Brogant really tried to be thankful to be home, but he could not get over John's death. Mary said he would wake up screaming almost every night. His leg got a minor infection a few years later. I could have probably healed him. But Brogant begged his wife and me to let him go be with John. Mary said it was the kindest thing we could do, so we did."

"The legend said…" Charlie continued. "Fuego just disappeared from the canyon. And because enough people wished it was true, it became true, and everyone assumed the dragon was killed,"

"Of course, that's not what happened. Every single person and magical being involved in that fight was slaughtered. Except for the water nymphs who were waiting about two miles away, with a second attack. They had a backup plan." Charlie said.

"My Kisseis was there, trying to help. They knew Brogant would have never agreed. Brogant wanted Fuego dead, as did the water nymphs, don't get me wrong. They wanted Fuego dead too. But in case the army and all the magic users were not powerful enough to kill the dragon. Maybe the water nymphs could at least trap and imprison her."

"Do you believe that?" Madeline asked.

"Absolutely not…. I assumed something went wrong and truly believed my daughter died. I should have looked. Why didn't I look harder? " Charlie cried. "But then Kisseis showed up. And I just was so focused on her, I could not see the bigger picture."

"You're saying…" Madeline said, "You think, Kisseis has been keeping the dragon in prison for centuries, and now not only is she breaking free. Now, this dragon can transfer her powers to her disciples to carry out her revenge on Henry's family, including Danny?" Charlie nodded.

"Fr. Karl was hit by a fireball." Charlie cried. "I see it every time I close my eyes. Treeva and Henry had gashes…"

"The gallery had claw prints on the floors……."Madeline said.

"What happened at the gallery, Madeline?" Charlie questioned her friend.

"You just…" Madeline stammered. "And I needed to prioritize heartbreaking disasters, and comparatively, the gallery seemed like a minor nuisance."

"Not if the dragon was looking for you," Charlie said. "Damnit, Madeline."

"This is a lot," Madeline said. "Danny is returning to work tomorrow. I'm going back to the gallery. Then we can figure things out."

"Nope," Charlie said. "Nowhere but here or the apartments till we know what this is. For you and Danny both."

"Why?" Madeline asked.

"Because they are protected. It's why Brogant bought these two blocks." Charlie said.

"What am I supposed to tell him?" Madeline asked. "' I just found him. I just found my heart, Charlie."

"Give me a day to think," Charlie said.

"Can you help me with something tonight?" Madeline asked.

"You mean the magical book hanging on your wheelchair for the last month? Yup." Madeline wanted to smile, but she couldn't."

"Hey Jane," Charlie said. leaving Henry's office. "Can I still get an omelet?"

"But of course," Jane screamed from the kitchen, never sounding happier.

Madeline sat at henry's desk still for a while. "You were supposed to teach me. You promise to make me strong..." Madeline mumbled in a soft cry. Covering her face.

"Now I will, now I will teach you, and I will make you fierce, for us, and for our future." Madeline looked up; it was Danny.

"Close the door, my love." Madeline sighed.

*

"I know it's a lot; I will leave you to your thoughts," Madeline said.

"Please don't, I feel better any time you're near me, even when I'm upset," Danny said, wiping a tear from her cheek.

"How mad are you at me?" Madeline asked.

"You should have told me last night, Madeline," Danny said. "I looked at you, and I knew something was off; I should have pushed. I hate that you didn't run to me when you were scared, or nervous, or even felt a little off. Even Mack said you looked a little freaked."

"I just wanted everything to be okay; I just wanted a relaxing Sunday with you before you started back to work tomorrow. Then Charlie and I would try to figure out if it's even true..." Madeline said. Danny started squirming.

"Daniel?" Madeline asked.

"Madeline, see, I know your name too." Danny smiled. "Let's christen your desk." She was not amused.

"You are going back to work tomorrow? Right," Madeline asked.

"I took a leave of absence," Danny said, rubbing his forehead.

"Why? You love being a lawyer," Madeline said. "So, tomorrow after breakfast, you were going to?"

"Practice magically blowing stuff up with Mack as part of our training... " Danny grinned; it was a little cool.

"Were you going to tell me?" Madeline asked.

"Right after you told me there was a dragon with a 1000 year grudge after us OR after you admitted you started a kiddies learn magic club with Steven?" Danny asked, trying to keep a straight face. "I saw him slip the journal into his back pocket the other night,"

"I would like to christen my desk now, sir," Madeline said, trying to be cute, wanting to avoid a fight but... "Danny, your mom told me you like arguing more than cooking."

"Something tells me I will constantly be arguing for a very long time." Danny teased.

"You hate magic," Madeline said.

"It's a tool. I didn't get that until now." Danny explained. "And for a very long time, I had no use for it. But now, it's a tool that I need to achieve a specific goal."

"What if," Madeline asked. "What if I love it and I'm really good at it?"

"As long as you come home to me every night, I will be your biggest supporter, cross my heart that you now own..." Danny whispered. Madeline nodded. "But I do have one kinda big condition..." Madeline got very nervous because he looks serious.

"I would like to sell the gallery... Wait. Let me present my case before you argue yours. Come with me." Madeline growled but followed Danny. They wandered through the hall, outside, around the rose garden to a nice size building in the back that she had never noticed before. Danny opened the locked door with a glance.

"Henry was a packrat," Danny said. "He would get a kick out of it if you and Steven turn it into a gallery of magical artifacts.

"Yes!" Madeline kissed him. Her first inclination was to argue, but she decided to let him have an easy win. Danny really did want to compromise and try to let her continue her dream job while keeping her safe. She knew he wanted her on protective grounds, even if it was for a little longer.

"There is one more thing I need to show you," Danny said. "Do. Not. Scream." Danny led Madeline back to the kitchen. "Order an omelet." He whispered as he joined everyone at the table. Mack had just come in, nursing a black coffee.

"Jane, can Danny and I share another omelet?" Madeline asked.

"Sure, babe," Jane said.

"Wait for it," Danny told Madeline. She was a little confused, but then it happened.

"Well, holy hell," Madeline said, trying not to squeal. "Who sees it?"

"When I point it out, we all will. I thought you might enjoy it the most." Danny said. "Being around Henry must have jump-started her knack…"

"No way!" Madeline gasped as everyone stared at her. Danny laughed.

"Hey, Jane?" Danny asked.

"Yes, chef?" Jane said.

"Are you going to add hot sauce next?" Danny asked.

"Yes I am… why do you ask?" Jane was a little confused. Everyone else was trying not to laugh, now realizing what Danny was doing. Except for Steven, who had his head in the sport's section. Mack tapped his shoulder.

"Remember when I told you I'd explain to you everything I knew about magic? Just the ugly truth? We should start with what a knack is and why you should ask us for a raise right about now." Danny said.

"A knack magically enhances a skill that you already have mastered and helps you to physically do something as fast as you can think about it. Like in the back of your mind, if you know you will need hot sauce, it appears right in front of you, so you don't have to stop what you are doing to go get it off the shelf. You, my friend, just got a knack!" Danny said. Jane looked up in amazement, fear, intrigue and shock.

"No," Jane screamed, scaring the hot sauce to float down to the counter. "You're messing with me?!?!"

"Think about it. You should be dead on your feet. Did you burn anything all weekend?" Danny asked. "Did anyone send anything back?"

"Holy shit." Jane said. "I think I need to sit down for a minute."

"How do you know so much about magic, Danny?" Steven asked.

"He minored in the history of voodoo and magic in the New Orleans culture in college because he thought it would get the girls," Mack teased.

"You'll have to let me know how that works out for you," Madeline giggled. Charlie busted out in unexpected laughter, then apologized.

"I really just know the basics," Danny admitted to Steven. "But if you have any questions, I'd be happy to try to answer them. Henry was always curious about that stuff, so I find myself drawn to it now." Madeline squeezed Danny's leg.

"I don't know a hell of a lot, Jane," Danny said. "But knacks are probably the purest and most basic gifts of magic, and Mack and I would love you to be our executive chef. We decided this before your knack kicked in. I just wanted to make sure you knew that!"

"Mack told me you were taking a leave of absence; I thought maybe... you would want to be the executive chef. I was hoping you would keep me around in any capacity, bottle washer included, I have just fallen in love with this restaurant." Jane sniffed.

"Naw, we would be so honored if you'd be a chef. Although I will substitute on your days off, I need to take care of my mom and other family crap for a while. But I would ask that you keep Henry's signature dishes as a personal favor." Danny said. Jane was speechless, squeezing his shoulder. Danny looked at Charlie; she winked at him...

While Danny was talking, Mack had snuck off to get a bottle of champagne to toast their new chef. Jane and Madeline cried. The guys suggested that they go on a carriage ride or a jazz club that afternoon to celebrate, but Jane just wanted to cook and figure out this knack thing. She made everyone promise to, at the very least, pick up dinner later. They also toasted to the news Madeline shared about the new gallery next door to the restaurant.

After Jane fed everyone as much as possible, Mack and Steven decided to go shoot some hoops. They wanted Danny to go, but he decided to go check on Ida. Charlie went with him. Madeline found herself drawn to Henry's office. For as many decades as Madeline would work out of that room, it would always be Henry's office.

Madeline quietly explored her new space.. She knew Henry would want her to feel like she belonged in it. Like she was a continuation of his goodness and legacy. Madeline loved his family pictures scattered throughout the large office with a sitting area. Many were of Ida, Danny, and Abigail, or any combination of the three; Charlie was in a few. There were a couple of Millie and one of Henry's parents and brother. Madeline let herself hope that one day there would be added pictures of her newly found tribe.

Madeline continued rolling around, following the wrap-around floor to ceiling bookshelves. There were at the very least a thousand books. She spotted a hidden door camouflage by books; she cracked it opened.

"Henry, you dog." Madeline laughed. It was a state of the art walk-in humidor. With a flat-screen saying the exact temperature was 70 degrees Fahrenheit and other info. Extremely high tech and ritzy for an old storm giant.

Madeline knew more about cigars than she should. The hazards of dating a rich college frat boy. She, embarrassingly, knew most of the high-end brands, but she didn't recognize most of these, which only made her more curious.

In the corner was a logbook, in it listed every cigar that ever passed through the room, where Henry got it, and who smoked it. The list of names was jaw-dropping, a true testament of who Henry was. Because Henry didn't have a single picture of any of the chefs, politicians, or celebrities listed in that book in the office, just his family.

"That room is going to get me in more trouble than this magic stuff," Madeline muttered as she closed the door.

Madeline was suddenly overcome with sadness. For a week, Danny had been telling her that she needed to clear off at least part of Henry's desk.

She had been helping do all of the restaurant's paperwork at the coffee table. And was getting a crick in her neck. Still, that seemed less painful than clearing his desk.

After doing everything Madeline could to put it off, she magically moved Henry's leather chair from his desk with a heavy sighed. Her eyes welled up in tears. And Madeline had to remind herself to keep breathing.

She very gently pushed his chair to the corner, near the cigar room. She draped one of his aprons over the chair's back and set his chef's hat in the seat. Then Madeline very solemnly rolled into Henry's desk, which looked too high for her, but fit perfectly.

"Kill the dragon, marry the girl." Danny had been watching her for a while now, completely awestruck.

"How's Ida?" Madeline asked as Danny sat down in front of Henry's desk.

"I got in trouble because I would not let my baby sister win at tic-tac-toe. My dead sister, by the way." Danny ranted. Madeline let him. "I promised myself if mom came back, if she just came back alive, I would stop being a whiny bastard about her fantasy world, oops."

"It's just not that easy, my love," Madeline said.

"It should be." Danny sighed. "One heartbreaking subject to the next... have you ever looked at the book?"

"You mean..." Madeline said. "The book that Henry probably died getting me, that I'm supposed to be able to read. Nope. I was going to put it off for another year... or four."

"Madeline, it's time."

"Can't we enjoy one Sunday afternoon?" Madeline pleaded. "Fee each other beignets. Making other couples bitter at how disgustingly in love we are, then go home for a long nap, falling asleep listening to jazz."

"I want," Danny said. "A million Sundays like that. I want that more than anything I have wanted in my life... But..."

"But what?" Madeline asked.

"Ida…" Danny hesitated… "Ida told me… I have to kill the bitch before it takes you away from me." Madeline sighed, covering her face as the backpack floated up from the back of her wheelchair and landed on the desk. It gently pushed out the book. The empty bag returned to Madeline's chair.

Chapter 12

Madeline traced the book's outline as Danny silently encouraged her, "Have faith, you restored mine." Danny whispered. Madeline smiled as he touched her hand. She opened the cover and was immediately drawn into the words, they spoke to her.

Danny, however, had a different reaction. He was immediately overcome with nausea, vomiting, and dizziness. The letters on the page made him feel seasick. He blinked, turning his eyes away, trying to refocus on Madeline. Still, it was as if Madeline became one with the book. The harder he tried to focus on her, the worse his head hurt. His screams of pain snapped Madeline out of the story she was being sucked into. She immediately shut the book and rolled to him.

"Danny!" Madeline yelled. He crawled to the sofa, rubbed his eyes, and grinned stupidly when Madeline's face was clear and gorgeous again.

"Hi. You sure are pretty." Danny said, sounding a little goofy. "Guess there was a reason Henry said only you could read it…" Madeline looked like she was about to cry. "Madeline, I found one of Henry's books on time locks. I knew there was a chance if it was written by a true time lock, and I looked at the writing, it would make me ill. The books are written in a completely different measure of time."

"Then why did you stay?" Madeline asked sadly.

"There was no other option. I certainly was not going to leave you." Danny said, now kissing her cheek, calming her down. "Tell me what you read. I'm completely ok, I swear."

"It's a diary," Madeline said. "From a slave girl. From 144 bc… She said her master is making her write it for me… she specifically named me… I think it's in Latin, and I'm using a spell to translate it. Are you sure I didn't break you?" Madeline asked. She looked excited and intrigued and lost and so sad all at the same time.

"I changed my mind, which I rarely do, so enjoy this moment, Miss Time Lock," Danny said. "I think we should go get beignets, make other

Page | 185

couples hate us because of how madly in love we are. Then we might take a nap, falling asleep to jazz music… or not. Then Jane and Mack and you and I can have dinner. Then after a few more naps, I'll go for a run, and you can read a little more. Ok?" Madeline nodded, still shaking inside but so grateful for him.

Danny tried very hard to give her a wonderful Sunday afternoon. They did go to Café du monde, but Danny seemed on edge being in a large crowd, so Madeline tried to hurry up a little. She felt so sad when Danny accidentally let out a sigh of relief when they reached the apartments again, which marked the beginning of Brogant's block.

Jane made a five-course dinner that evening. Every bite was a taste of perfection. Danny and Mack had to finally physically remove, ever so gently, Jane from the kitchen by eight. Madeline was pretty sure Jane would not have left otherwise, probably ever.

"I am…" Danny said after kissing on Madeline a while. "I'm going to tell Ida good night, go for a nice run, come back and clean up the kitchen, then we can go to the apartments, ok? And Madeline, this is now your home. Henry's office will be your sanctuary." He winked and left.

"Welcome back, Madeline," the book began as she curled up on Henry's sofa. "First, I'm sorry for making Danny sick. Just don't let him read the book, and he'll be fine." Madeline got chills but pressed on.

"I guess I should start with the basics. My name is Lucia. I'm a 14-year-old girl. I live in Rome in 144 bc, I'm not a very good writer, but master says it's important for us both. I've tried to put a translator spell on this so it will be easier to read. I hope that this book finds you in good health, and I hope you have a kind Master."

"Wow." Madeline gulped.

"I was sold into slavery when I was three because my father thought I was possessed. My first three masters thought the same. Luckily because I could blink away, I have never been beaten that bad or felt a man pushed against me."

"What the hell?" Madeline said.

"Please keep reading, Madeline," Lucia said. Madeline almost poured herself a drink but decided not to. " My current master is kind and says if I write this diary and we can pass our knowledge to you, he would release me at 21. It will be too old to find a husband, but it's something."

Madeline closed the book in disbelief. She rolled into the kitchen and puttered around for a while. She stopped, looking at a picture hanging on the wall of Henry and Danny.

"Hi, daddy," Madeline called as she poured herself a freshly made cup of coffee, even though no one had been in the kitchen in hours. "You always say I should be in bed when you are grading papers watching the very late-night show. I come by it honestly... redoing the gallery's budget... I am disappointed, but we just found a better location... Hopefully, this week... the downside is, they asked If I could work seven days a week till we got back on track. So I cannot come home this weekend....

"But I'm really happy, dad... and I just wanted to tell you." She continued. "I am thankful that I have a good life. No, I'm not drunk. Dad, when I come home in a few weeks, I want to bring a boy; I think this is the one... He is really good to me. You are going to love him. Yes, I will tell mom. Soon. I'll talk to you in a few days... You go to sleep, too! Love you. Night."

She replayed the conversation in her head. Madeline desperately wanted to tell her dad about the magic thing. She has always told him everything, just in short, parent-friendly versions. Madeline just could not think of a dad-worry-free version of this... Madeline washed out her coffee cup and returned to the sofa where the book was waiting for her.

"Hi again, Madeline," Lucia said. "Your father sounds so loving... But now its time to get started. Master has given us three spells to start with, you have to do them, perfectly, 50 times each. If you mess up, even on the 49th one, you must start over. Master is very strict about these things. Thankfully he just yells, no beatings. The first spell is pausing time for 25 milliseconds..."

Madeline practice for hours on the three spells and must have fallen asleep because she was wrapped in a soft blanket when she woke. The pillow holding her head was her favorite from the apartment; Danny must have gotten it. There was a second blanket on the other couch, too, but no bodies underneath it. Madeline tried not to frown, but... she missed kissing him goodnight and had much better dreams when she fell asleep in his arms.

*

"Nope," Madeline said, finding Jane in an empty kitchen with her head between her legs. "You can't get fired your first day. Danny would be so grumpy. I'm finally getting some regular loving, so, suck it up, Summers, take one for the team." Jane just burst into uncontrolled laughter.

"And to top it off, Mack said he likes me," Jane said.

"That bastard..." Madeline said.

"You're just mean before your first cup of coffee," Jane smirked. "When we started fooling around, I was just doing this for the summer, and he was just the bartender... I like him, maybe a lot, but if I had to pick, I'd choose this, a million times over."

"Cuz, you look so damn happy." Madeline teased. "If you are that worried, ask Danny to give you a contract."

"Mack said that too," Jane said. "I just think it would go against the spirit of this kitchen."

"Then keep it casual with Mack until you are sure..." Madeline said. "He's not Brian..."

"This is a much more enjoyable conversation when it's about you and your weird hang-ups." Jane grinned.

"Oh, We don't have time to open that box. I recently stuffed so much more in it," Madeline said.

"You do seem off, Madds, for a few days now," Jane said. "I know I hurt you when I freaked out about the magic journal... But I'm here. I'll listen."

"There's just a lot to figure out. And I'm sad Danny took a leave of absence. He looks so defeated after he sees Ida. And I would like to get the new gallery up and running asap. I'm annoyed that trying to learn magic and opening the gallery, two of the most exciting things that have ever happened to me. Two huge wonderful things that I should be focused on 24/7, I should be motivated but instead I just want to be with him, hanging out." Madeline said.

"Well, speak of the devil," Jane said.

"Good morning, chef." Danny and Mack said in sync, arriving with a gorgeous bouquet of roses for her. Danny stole one and presented it to Madeline.

"Thank you both," Jane said. "I'm so thrilled to be here."

"So thrilled, she just hyperventilated." Madeline teased.

"Please leave my kitchen," Jane said.

"Yes, chef." Madeline kissed her cheek. "I'm going to run home, shower, and come back. If Steven comes by, can you tell him the back door to the new gallery is opened? Hey Jane, odd question, do you know where I can get a clock like that one?" it was a digital clock with milliseconds. Mack said there was an extra one in the pantry, and he would find it and leave it in Henry's office. Madeline left, winking at Danny.

"We REALLY are trying to be responsible adults, but I'm like a silent partner, so I don't think I need to be here at this meeting..." Danny said. "Jane, you got this. Henry said you have twice his talent than when he started after he watched you finish your 1st meal service." Danny hugged Jane but was fidgeting like a boy to be excused.

"Wait, you promised I could be the silent partner. We can flip for it, Tails you win... Go. Just go..." Mack said, pretending to be annoyed but actually very please; his best friend hadn't had a natural smile in years. Danny ran to catch up with Madeline before Mack finished.

*

"Wow..." Steven said.

"This seemed less daunting when Danny showed it to me yesterday..." Madeline sighed.

"I counted; there are more than 200 trunks," Steven said. "More stuff in the raptures. Everything is labeled. Henry was an organized hoarder. But all the trunks are locked. Have you seen any keys?"

"Nope," Madeline said. "Have you tried to, ya know..."

"I just felt weird about it," Steven said.

"I know..." Madeline said.

"You knew him better; you should try to open one," Steven said.

"You tried, huh?" Madeline teased. "Ok," Madeline lightly touched the lock on one of the trunks, expecting it to open. After all, she was, well, almost, an all-powerful, time lock; how could the closed trunks just not pop open with a gentle touch? They did not. Steven snickered.

"Maybe, these are family trunks..." Madeline didn't know how she knew that. "Hang on." She sent a text to Danny.

"So, Madds....." Steven said. "You know I've been struggling to find a direction for my Masters in history. I think I want to transfer to Tulane and focus on voodoo and why magic disappeared and is now returning slowly..."

"Do you really believe in all that?" Madeline looked down...

"I do," Steven said. "And you do too. I can feel it. Look, If I get accepted to Tulane, I can move to the other side of town, and you never have to see me again. But I would like to continue working at the gallery and bartending. I have no idea how it works, but Jane and I love being roommates. And I just feel like I'm supposed to help here."

"If you are serious," Madeline said. "You go do something with Danny. Like a guy thing. I want him to know you have no feelings for me."

"I will tell him I will never try to win you back because I know I've lost that right. and I will mean it with every fiber of my being. But I'm not going to lie to him and say I have no feelings for the best and most favorite person I know. But for you, I will start sleeping around again..." Steven said.

"You're an idiot!" Madeline said, more amused than annoyed. "Look, if he is really ok with you working here, then I would like that because I do miss pre-dating us. I just never want him to spend a millisecond wondering about my intentions. The thing is, I love him. I love him without fear. If he asked me, I'd go to the courthouse and marry him today."

"That can be arranged," Danny said, hearing the whole conversation, which Steven made sure of; Danny sneaked up behind her grabbing her shoulders. "Welcome to the family, Steven! Mack says you're the best bartender he has ever seen."

"That was a horrible way to male bond." Madeline pouted. Danny tried to kiss her, but she playfully pushed him away. "Just try to open the trunk…"

"Is she always this bossy?" Danny asked.

"Pretty much," Steven said.

"I'm not going to like this friendship, am I?" Madeline asked. They grinned. To add insult to injury, Danny opened the first trunk with just a glance.

They sorted the trunks into different categories with a bit of magical help, including weapons, books and records, jewelry, figurines, china, bottles, and photographs. Henry also had one trunk marked for Jane, Charlie, Danny, Mack, and Madeline.

"Why don't I…" Steven said. "Put y'alls trunk in Henry's office?" Danny nodded gratefully. "I have to go change into a bartender now, but tomorrow, we can start logging everything,"

"Thanks!" Madeline said.

"Hi," Danny said quietly after Steven left the building, hugging Madeline tightly. "I should go check on Jane and my mom." Danny looked emotionally drained, "I come in here about once a month because there are extra dishes in the back. Our trunk was not here then; it's a little spooky. I keep expecting to see him around every corner. Henry had another 100 years of life, easily." Madeline kissed him softly…

"Why don't you go relax in the office. I'll go check on Ida and Jane, and I'll bring dinner back, and we can open Henry's trunk, or I can show you my time lock tricks, or we can do absolutely nothing." Madeline said. Danny agreed without argument; this scared her a little.

*

"Look, My love actually sleeps," Madeline whispered to Danny, napping on the couch. She had just returned from checking on Ida, who was having a bad night. And Jane, who was having a good night. Jane even made up a tray of goodies when Madeline was at Ida's for her to take back to Danny... Madeline quietly sat the tray on the coffee table, kissed his forehead, and turned off the lamp.

Madeline rolled up behind Henry's desk. She smiled; Mack had left the digital clock as requested. Even though all she wanted to do was curl up with Danny, she knew any free moments she had, she ought to use studying. The next spell Madeline had to learn was to send a small object .7 seconds into the future and make it reappear in the same spot. This was much harder than it sounded.

"You're overthinking," Danny said about two hours later, as he watched her from the couch.

"Did I wake you?" Madeline frowned.

"A two-hour nap for me is like a five-hour nap to anyone else," Danny said. "Thank you. I didn't have a nightmare. I usually do. It must be the angel watching over me..." he said, now coming up behind her. Madeline softly giggled, "But I really do think you're trying too hard; Spells should roll off the end of your tongue without thought or question. When a spell has wiggle room, it will do exactly that."

Madeline tried 100 times more, each time better, each time with more confidence.

"Only 500 more spells to go..." Madeline sighed in exhaustion. "The next is a displacement spell. I will pop in and pop out..."

"As amazing and entertaining as that sounds..." Danny said. "Do you remember the first time we talked all night when you were still in

Houston? You told me that because you were paralyzed, you felt better and more on point when you got eight hours of sleep?"

"No. Must have been some other girl." Madeline shrugged. "Oh my god, how many chicks in chairs do you talk to? I've heard about these fetishes..."

"'Madds....'" Danny said. "I'm serious, I think that no matter how crazy it gets. We should try to have dinner together around nine every night. We should have non-restaurant/ gallery/magical conversations with our friends. And I'll tuck you in at midnight every night and wake you up at nine every morning..."

"Wait, that's nine hours." Madeline laughed.

"Sometimes, it is about me." Danny winked.

"We can start this when the gallery is open and after I finish the book."

"No." Danny slammed down his fist. It sounded louder than it meant to. He was worried that it scared Madeline. It did not. "I just need to keep a routine as much as I know you need more sleep to be at your best."

"Because... because... my reaction times are directly connected to my health..." Madeline said, a little pissy. "So, if we get into a 72 hour battle with a dragon, you're going to send me to take naps?"

"If I have to, you're damn right I will," Danny said. "Look, as your boyfriend/future husband, I should not tell you this because I'm sure you will use it against me at some point. But, between the book you were sent and the Time Lock thing, you will probably be one of the most powerful magic users of this century. I just want to make sure we have every advantage..."

"Can't I cast a sleepless spell on myself?" Madeline asked. "That sounds like a thing..."

"No," Danny said. "Definitely not a thing, but nice try."

"Ok..." Madeline knew what he was trying to say without scaring her. "Let the record show, I made a compromise. I'll try very hard to get...

seven hours of sleep. Don't get used to it, Boudreaux. By the way, didn't everyone get the same spell book?" She faked a smile.

"Eight hours, Madeline. And everyone got different books that match their inherent qualities," Danny said.

"Aren't you going to show me your book?" Madeline asked.

"Nope," Danny said. "I'm going to check if everyone wants a late-night drink to toast Jane and to opened Henry's trunk." He walked away.

*

"Thank you very much," Jane said. as everyone gathered around the chef's table in the kitchen. "Let's raise our glasses, to Henry."

"To Henry." Danny, Madeline, Charlie, Mack, and Steven clicked their glasses together, then raised them to the heavens.

"He would be so proud to know you are our chef, Jane," Danny said quietly. "But he would be so touched that you have become such a good friend to me personally. Cheers to a very long and successful career. To Jane."

"To Jane..." everyone clicked their glasses with hers. Danny disappeared for a minute as the group mingled and returned with the trunk. Madeline quietly transferred into his lap and snuggled her cheek against his... "He left gifts for all of us. Charlie, can you please hand them out. I don't think I can..."

"I will, Daniel. I will..." Charlie said, kissing Danny's other cheek.

"To Steven," Henry wrote, "These books will help you with your Master's Degree. Everything in them are true." Steven gulped, looking for Madeline for an explanation. She winked.

"To Jane," Henry wrote, "I lied, I did write down all my recipes. Your knack will translate what 'cook till done' means, your natural instincts will improve on all of these dishes. Make them yours." Jane sobbed unapologetically for the rest of the night.

"To Mack." Henry wrote, "Here is my compass so you can always find your way home. Remember, business partners, second, brothers, first.

You are, in all the ways that matter, a Guidry." Mack and Steven tried to nod manly at each other, sniffing a little.

"To Charlie," Henry wrote, "Here is Millie's rosary, of course, I didn't throw it away... I must confess I sincerely hope there is an afterlife. Having Millie gloat about being right for an eternity sounds kind of wonderful."

"I'm sorry y'all, but I... g'night." Charlie kissed Danny's head and left. Madeline tried to get up from Danny's lap, but he held her tighter.

"To Madeline." Henry wrote, Mack took over for Charlie. "This is the key to my office, your office now. It will open anything in there that needs to be unlocked. There will be a lot in the office for Danny too. I trust you to find them and give them to him as the need arises. I want to give you more, but you seem to have stolen the one thing I love most in this world; please be good to him, and make him be good to you. Occasionally he will need to be reminded." Madeline sobbed.

"To Danny," Henry left him three things. Henry's personal spell book, a family "Guidry" book, and a framed picture of Danny, Abigail, Henry, and Ida that Danny had never seen before. "Accept your gifts, for they are indifferent, Your heart makes them good. Your heart makes them honorable."

"I'm sorry, I thought I could do this, but I need air..." Danny gently set Madeline in her wheelchair... "I can't breathe."

"Danny," Madeline said thoughtfully as he was trying to leave. "I'm going to have another drink with my friends, help Jane close up, and I plan to be home at midnight. Please be there so I can drift asleep in your arms with peaceful thoughts."

"Yes, my love..." Danny nodded with tears streaming down his face and left.

*

"Morning, Chef," Danny said arriving in the kitchen. "Do you realize we are booked for the next three weeks? Won't you consider taking a full two days off, instead of just a few lunches when Mack literally has to drag you out kicking and screaming?"

"I was in the middle of deboning a chicken last time... it was a very personal moment," Jane laughed. "Actually, I was going to ask if I could have next Thursday off. A friend of Madeline's and mine will be in town for the day, and she planned a whole girl's day for us."

"Hmm... I mean, sure." Danny wondered. "Have you seen Madds?"

"She went into the office about an hour ago," Jane said.

"Thanks..." Danny said. "Are you sure you don't want to do something crazy like take that Friday off, too?" Jane made a disgusted face.

Danny wandered into the office, Madeline was not there. He sighed, trying not to be angry. He went to sit in his chair in front of her desk. And waited...

About three minutes later she appeared with a bagel and a coffee, she screamed when she saw Danny looking directly at her, not amused the least bit.

"I'm sorry," Madeline decided just to try to look really pitiful.

"I'm gonna regret this," Danny sighed, rubbing his forehead, "Where did you get that bagel, miss Time Lock?"

"I've been very good for the..." Madeline stammered. "I've been very good all morning; I deserved a bagel... from... New York City.... The argument sounded so much better in my head... you are gorgeous when you look really pissed."

"Madeline..." Danny said. "I know I'm overprotective, and you have to believe I'm trying to keep my emotions in check. I realize that you have to practice. And I know I use this excuse too much, but I worry I'm going to lose you... Can you just tell me when you are practicing?"

"Here's my offer, Boudreaux," Madeline said. "I will be more careful, and I will tell you about my plans to practice on any given day... but I have been a little hurt that you don't trust me enough to tell me what you are, like in magic terms. I know you're mourning Henry and taking care of Ida, and that's a lot, so I'm trying not to push. I just wish you trusted me as much as I trusted you. I'm in this, with all of my heart. And that's a huge thing for me…"

"It's me… I don't trust myself." Danny said. "I'd walk on fire if you tell me it was ice. The thing is… if I had started training with Henry from a little boy, like he wanted me to, maybe I'd be prepared. Maybe I wouldn't be living in constant fear… I just had to relearn everything in the last month that once would have been purely instinct. I just needed to know I could bring something to the table…"

"That's not fair to me at all. If you weighed 500 pounds and couldn't do a single magic spell, I still would believe you owned the moon. I'm sorry you don't trust me enough to help you train. Maybe I should train alone too, in case I'm not good enough either." Madeline said sadly. "I'm going home for a while." and left.

"Hey," Jane appeared in the office's doorway a few minutes later. Danny had his head on the desk, moaning. "Because I'm your friend too. A mad Madeline is easier to deal with than a hurt Madeline. It's not fair to you, but she has trust issues, which she got the hard way. You must be something else because I never thought she would let herself love anyone, like for a really long time, if ever…."

"Don't lie to her and don't hide stuff, especially if you think it's for her own good." Jane continued. "Listen to my advice, young one, and she's pretty much an easy lay. You may quote me on that." Jane said. "Wait an hour; she'll be ready to hear you." Jane disappeared back into the kitchen.

"Hey," Danny called Mack. "Can you train at 2? No, we'll meet you there."

*

"Did you just show up at my door with a scale, Daniel Boudreaux?" Madeline literally shrieked when Danny came into the apartment a few hours later. "Wow… I put on two pounds. I don't have time to find an accessible gym…"

"Come here. Please come here." Danny said. Madeline was still very upset, but extremely curious about where this could possibly go. Danny looked embarrassed as he stepped on the scale, so Madeline casually glanced at the screen.

"No... you're doing some kind of lawyer voodoo argument to confuse me." She said, reading the scale for a second time.

"I was 250 pounds by the time I was 10. Mom decided to keep me from recess because I kept breaking the swings." Danny said. "I did inherit a few storm giant traits. Mostly the bad ones... We are a proud, heavy, stubborn people, and sometimes we push away the ones we love most when we feel we are spiraling."

"How is that possible?" Madeline asked. Still staring at the scale in disbelief.

"Our muscle mass is denser..." Danny said. "I'm about 50 pounds over my normal weight—25 from my family drama, 25 from Jane. I don't fly commercially. I don't go to amusement parks, and that's why Mack and I always drive big trucks; it's just easier. Mack, who knows every single thing about me, doesn't know how much I weigh... Madds, you're the first girl I've been with. I never trusted anyone before ..."

"Come on," Madeline said. "That can't be true. Look at you. Women stare at you all the time. Honestly, it's a little intimidating,"

"Have I ever looked back? Even once?" Danny asked.

"No," Madeline whispered. "I would not be with you if I didn't trust you 110%."

"I always teased Henry because he said after his first date with Millie, he was done. I couldn't imagine anyone falling in love that quickly. Or anyone wanting to... Til the moment I saw you."

"Ok," Madeline whispered, now playing with his hands.

Let's see," Danny continued. "Ida thought if I studied, I would be a powerful mage. Henry thought I would be a full storm giant. I'm something in between."

"Can you live in the clouds and water?" Madeline asked.

"Nope, but I do swim like a fish, and I can hold my breath underwater for 30 minutes," Danny said. "Henry thought it was 'cute.'"

"Can you control lightning?" Madeline said.

"Nope," Danny said.

"See, now we have a problem..." Madeline teased. "I was digging the lightning thing..." Madeline pulled him closer and kissed him.

"I'm freakishly strong." Danny continued, now putting Madeline in his lap with no effort. "I can see almost as well in the dark as in the day. And... let's see, I'm agile, like Olympic gymnast level, agile... And I learn physical spells instantly."

"I should have told you all of this the night we had dinner in Millie's garden." Danny apologized. "I was just nervous because I've denied my abilities for so long. I'm honestly still scared."

"I think..." Madeline said. "You are trying to be as honest as you can. But I think I'm still being lawyered."

"Ouch. What? About my love?" Danny teased,

"Nope. But I have a feeling that you are modest about your newly developed abilities..."

"I do have to keep up with you..." Danny smirked, "Do you... want to start training with us?"

"Yes, Please." Madeline grinned and clapped her hands. "But... this is totally coming out of my sleep time."

"Madeline!" Danny sighed while hugging her.

"That's cool," Madeline said a few minutes later. "I guess my mom did buy me pots and pans." Danny laughed as Madeline came out of the bathroom, finding him making a quick lunch.

"So..." Danny waited after they finished eating, and Madeline was doing dishes. "There is this one other really tiny thing..."

"You are so lucky you cook." Madeline was too exhausted and had too much to do to get mad.

"Mack and I were asked to leave the gym... the day we started training. We argued that it was like fencing; they disagreed." Danny said as fast as he could. Madeline gave him a dirty look. "We have been training on Henry's property..."

"The one that's 30 miles away from here?" Madeline asked. "The one you've been waiting to take me to for a romantic weekend? The one you refuse to go to because we have absolutely no protection from the fire breathing avatar while we drive back and forth for at least an hour when there is no traffic? That property?"

"Yes," Danny smirked. "That sounded so much worse when you said it, using facts and distance and stuff. But I think we should call a truce, and I won't ask you about the day you are planning with Jane."

"I'll accept the plead deal, counselor," Madeline said.

"So, I was thinking, the next part of your time lock thing..." Danny said. "Good practice, maybe we could stay out there a few nights a week. Doing non-training stuff..."

"No," Madeline said. "I'm not ready." She nervously wiped the counter.

"But you are," Danny said. "I would not ask you if I had any doubts. You said it's the same spell. You think about where you want to go, you add the perimeters, and blink. I'll just be a passenger."

"Oh... I don't know, love." Madeline said.

"I do think we might need to master this if..." Danny touched her cheek.

"If I do this without killing you..." Madeline said. "No more driving out there. Neither of you. Either I'll always go, or I'll transport you both." Danny crossed his heart.

Madeline gave Danny a kiss, took his hand, thought of Henry's property, focusing on the porch that Danny had told her about, and blinked. The next thing she heard was Danny's giggling. Unbashful giggling.

Chapter 13

"That. Was. Wild…." Danny said. They landed perfectly on Henry's porch.

"Oh, Danny, it's beautiful." Madeline sighed, looking at the beach 100 yards from them.

"It sure is," Danny sighed, staring at her. "Maybe we can build a house out here. Our kids will love being raised by the water."

"Danny…" Madeline said. She had a few things that were extremely hard to talk about. This was one. "Since you've been honest with me… I have been avoiding this; at first, it was a funny joke between us, having eight kids. I never considered having kids before I met you. Not when I went to four baby showers last year, not even when Steven and I thought maybe we would go the distance." Madeline fiddled with her wheelchair.

"But the thing is, I don't know if I can have kids… and until three months ago, I didn't care. Now I care so much. I want to have like two kids with you and see how that goes… I want it in our future more than I thought possible. But if it's a deal-breaker, I get it. Family has to be so important to you."

"I'm a 500-pound mutant. Why would you assume if we had any problems, it was you? If later on, we want to see doctors we can, or if we just wanna try every day for like at least 25 years, I'm just that committed, No deal breakers, Madds, ever." Danny grinned, just as a truck drove up. "Besides, I'm pretty sure we still have to raise Mack." Madeline sadly smiled. She never ever wanted to find her birth parents until this moment.

"Glad to see you finally manned up, hello lovely Madeline," Mack said as Danny got into the bed of the truck. Madeline followed; her wheelchair floated up, parking beside him. "My work out area or yours, first?" Mack screamed from the cab. Danny shrugged.

They drove about five minutes south. Mack stopped and hopped out. "This is Macky's happy place." Both of the men laughed, following

Madeline off the truck. Danny tried to hide his embarrassment as the truck's suspension seemed relieved. Madeline thought it was cute.

"Henry and I shared a love of firearms," Mack said. "When I was 16, I started feeling my oats. I went to juvie—stupid kids stuff. After I got out, Henry decided I needed a project. Every Saturday for a year, we worked on this range. Henry taught me how to shoot and be a man. After the year, when the range was finished, we both still showed up every week, like clockwork. We missed once during a hurricane. The last time we were out here was 12 days before he passed away."

"He taught me to respect weapons," Mack said. "But I think he was preparing me to protect our family if the need ever arose, I could probably hold my own."

"For once in his life, my friend is modest. This is the one thing he doesn't suck at." Danny teased.

"Gear up, Daniel..." Mack smirked. "Full course, three shots each. Loser closes up Friday night."

"Henry would love how we decide things." Danny laughed.

They high-fived each other and then got serious. There were two giant bays with tires stacked 15 feet high. They were set up identically with 10 steel targets scattered downrange. Danny and Mack stood up in their starting positions, both counting down from three, firing their first shots on go. Madeline was surprised how in sync they were and enjoyed mentally counting the dings as the bullet hit the steel.

"Damnit." Danny laughed. He pretended to pout, letting Madeline comfort him. Danny had finished a second earlier than Mack, but he missed two targets, whereas Mack shot the course clean, with no misses. "I've got to stop betting nights; I'm not used to having a girlfriend..." Danny said. Mack laughed, but Madeline could tell they both missed Henry.

"If you load onto the truck, we will continue the tour," Mack said. They drove in silence for about 8 minutes. Madeline watched Danny's demeanor change from a sweet boyfriend to something else. Nothing

Madeline was afraid of; he just became more serious and more focused than she was used to.

"It took us a while to figure the best set up." Danny took her hand as Madeline floated down from the bed of the truck. "We cleared this acre, and when I'm training, we throw up a soundproof dome,"

"There are 30 magical steel targets. We can tell them to set up in a pattern or randomly. As I hopefully hit them, they disappear. After I finish a course, I get a printed report on how fast, powerful, and accurate I did. You can make me blow up stuff, but the nerd in me still needs that spreadsheet." Danny said.

"You are an embarrassment to badass soldiers everywhere," Mack said.

"Some targets are marked good guys, so I have to try not to hit those." Danny continued, ignoring his friend. " Sometimes I shoot from here. Sometimes Mack makes me run and shoot, carrying weights."

"Wanna do a few run-throughs?" Mack asked.

"Yup," Danny said.

"Remember, you need to read the targets better. Not everything needs your more powerful blast. Little mean dogs, small warning blast, charging rhinos, bigger blast." Mack yelled as Danny approached the targets. "Three. Two. One. Start scenario."

It was nothing like Madeline had seen before. The fiery blasts ranged from a kiddie pop gun to fireworks to a really big, loud, shake the ground, boom. Danny ran through the obstacle course, firing different blasts from his right hand.

"Again." Mack's usual mellow tone turned into a military Sargent. "You hesitated on the third target." Danny looked down, kicked a rock that flew farther than it should, shook out his hands, and nodded to start again. Danny and Mack continued this for two hours.

Madeline got Danny to wink at her twice. She always teased him that he smiled at her too much. Madeline had been so busy at the gallery, restaurant, or learning spells that minutes or even hours would go by without her thinking of the dragon. The dragon that had taken so much away from Danny in such a short time. It was obvious to Madeline at this moment that Danny probably never stops thinking about what he had lost already and what was still at stake.

"Good day." Mack fist pumped Danny. "I'll figure out how to add Madeline to our training. I told Steven I would pick up four cases of beer before Happy hour. I'll close tonight. I like knowing you owe me," Mack punched him, touched Madeline's arm, and walk toward his truck.

"No more driving out here, Macky," Madeline said. "I'll be your personal teleporting service." He grinned and left.

"Can we share a beer on Henry's porch and watch the moon rise?" Danny hugged Madeline as they slowly walked back to the cabin, but he still felt distant.

"How is it possible that you and Mack are so meticulous at the restaurant, but the cabin looks like a frat house after a party?" Madeline teased, coming out of the cabin with one beer. She found Danny on the big lounger, asleep. She smiled, remembering he said that training was the only thing that drained him.

Madeline floated from her wheelchair and stretched out beside him. Danny instinctually reached for her and laid his head on her stomach. She sighed, wishing they could stay in this bubble, noticing the waves were getting rougher.

Madeline looked at her backpack, reached out, and her book glided into her hands. She held the book away from Danny, making sure he would not be able to see the writing in case he suddenly awoke. The writing that had made him so sick the first time she had opened it.

"Hi again, Madeline!" Lucia said. "I'm so glad you made up with cute Daniel. Master says he is not to be angered with because he is very strong and might beat you." Madeline looked down and giggled as drool dripped from his chin."

Master is very pleased with your progress with displacement. I, myself, am having a little trouble. I can't seem to focus. He says I have too many voices in my head distracting me." Lucia said. "He's going to give me a few more weeks, then he may have to shake them out of me. I hope not. Master says you should continue to work on displacement for the next two weeks and go further than you thought possible. The more you displace, the better. He wants you to practice until it becomes 2nd nature to you."

"I don't know what this means," Lucia continues. "But master says if you displace from your sacred property, it's almost impossible to be followed. Safe travels."

Madeline sent the book back into her bag. Danny rolled over and sighed. "I'll be back, love," Madeline said softly. "I'm going to pick up dinner and check on Ida. Do not leave this seat." Before he could argue, she blinked away.

"We are going to have to have ground rules on this blinking thing," Danny muttered to himself and dozed off again...

"Hey." Madeline appeared to Jane coming from Henry's office.. "Mack just said you guys officially had the night off, and I should chase you away if you came in." Jane said.

"How beautiful is your glasshouse, chef?" Madeline teased. "Can we get two plates of pasta to go? Please? I just checked on Ida, and I needed 10 minutes at the gallery to schedule a delivery, then I am out of here. Hey, is Danny scheduled to open or close tomorrow?"

"Let's see. close." Jane said, looking at the schedule on the refrigerator.

"I think..." Madeline said. "I'm going to try to kidnap him for 24 hours. Can you tell Steven he may play hooky tomorrow?"

"Enjoy!" Jane said. kissing her cheek, handing her a bag of food. "Have a fabulous day off. You really do deserve it. And remember, the world would not end if he missed one closing. "

"I'm pretty sure his head would explode." Madeline giggled and left the kitchen. Because no one was in the hallway, she blinked back to the beach where Danny had a set table waiting.

"Where are you?" Madeline asked softly as they finished a quiet dinner, hugging his neck.

"Wasting my time, thinking about stuff I shouldn't," Danny said. "I need to train more. I need to figure out where the avatar is because at least if we can sever the ties, maybe we can help Kisseis retrap the dragon until I figure out how to kill it. And I am going to kill it. For my family, past, present, and future."

"Do you think," Madeline asked? "That I can just send it into another time?"

"No," Danny said. "I think that would mess with the timeline too much. I think we need to get rid of the avatar first. If we did that, I would feel like I'm actually moving forwards. Right now, I feel like I'm slowly sinking in quicksand, and I'm constantly so angry. My biggest fear is that I'm gonna use the 'Henry died, mom's crazy and dragon's coming" one too many times with you."

"Do you know what will buy you a month of free passes?" Madeline asked. Danny shook his head. "I got us, a full 24 hours off. No restaurant. No gallery. Your mom is having a good evening. I even booked a room."

"You know we shouldn't get a room in the French quarters, later on when it safe..." He argued.

"Listen, it's sorta further than around the corner," Madeline said. "I read a little more from my book; it says that I need to blink as much as I can until it becomes second nature. And I should travel further... but he also said, if I left from protected grounds, it would be almost impossible to trace..."

"I can be a focused, obsessed jerk for a month?" Danny teased, not really wanting to go but knowing Madeline deserved this and so much more. "I do have to work tomorrow night." He added that. Madeline giggled, took his hand, and blinked.

*

"Please say something." Madeline pleaded. "It's a little extravagant, and I did pull from my savings to pay for this room. And I'm suddenly ridiculously nervous. Like, I hope you are still into me, now, when it's just us, away from the craziness. Because if you aren't, I might die of embarrassment. You hear about adrenaline junkies."

"Please shut up and kiss me, right now," Danny said. He magically made the wheelchair float upwards to him.

"I remembered you always wanted to see the Eiffel Tower and other structures around the world. During one of our all-night phone calls, you said you never thought you could fly for personal reasons. I just wanted to bring you here..." Madeline had somehow blinked them perfectly to their hotel room's balcony, facing the famous monument.

"One, this is the second-best view I have seen in my life," Danny said, "Two, I propose this counts as a three-month anniversary trip, so it will be my gift to you."

"It's really expensive... and I know you are on a leave of absence...." Madeline argued.

"How can I say this without sounding like a dick?" Danny asked. "I'm kinda set for life. Any kind of life we choose."

"Damn, You just get cuter and cuter." Madeline teased. "What would you like to do with me for the next 24 hours, Mr. Boudreaux?"

"I would like to change our reservations to three nights," Danny said. "And... Can we just... walk the city, holding hands, without worrying about anything. And eat at two restaurants that Henry had on his bucket list?"

"Next week, I will help you displace around the world, I will create all kinds of crazy challenges for us, and you can help me train. And I will probably be an even bigger ass. So I apologize in advance." Danny said. "Because the more time I spend with you, the more you become my world. But right now, in the city of lights, I want to enjoy being so madly in love with you."

*

"You disappeared for three days; you should be in a better mood." Steven teased.

"Can I tell you about the best weekend I ever had because I haven't seen Jane yet? It was the most …" Madeline gloated.

"Stop. Can we do general terms, like – good date. Bad date…" Steven pleaded…"Moving on… How can you be so bad at this? Didn't you have a whole class on color?" Steven asked.

"Then you do it." Madeline mocked. "I just need the caffeine to kick in, then I will decide the color of the walls. Leave me alone. Go open a trunk."

"And for the record, I was in an excellent mood until now." She mumbled, now glancing at the door. Steven got a weird vibe and decided to sit at a table near her, opening one of the last trunks that needed to be inventoried.

"Hello Madeline," Louis Delcroix said, coming into the gallery.

"Hello Louis, we really are not open yet. We are shooting for end of October, early November, at the latest." Madeline said.

"I'm sorry you had to relocate; what happened?" Louis Delcroix asked.

"They found mold in the walls. It was cheaper to move."

"I heard it had been vandalized beyond recognition.. like someone or something was after the owners." Louis Delcroix said. "Anyways, I'm writing an article on Henry Guidry's life, May I interview you?"

"I only knew him in passing, but he seemed like a very kind man," Madeline said.

"You seemed to be a regular in his restaurant since you moved here. I just assumed you knew him better." Louis Delcroix said.

"My best friend was his sous chef for a while, before she had to take over due to his tragic death. I probably eat there more than I should." Madeline said.

"How did he die again?" Louis Delcroix asked.

"It was a fatal car crash," Madeline said, trying to keep her cool. "But I'm sure you knew that."

"Medical reports say he died from unexplained gashes all over his body. People say you were at Henry's death bed,"

"Are you accusing me of killing a sweet old man?" Madeline asked.

"No. Of course not. You tiny little thing. I just can't figure out why you were with the family at such a personal time. That seems kind of more than a casual customer thing." Louis Delcroix said. "Between us, are you involved with his grandson?"

"This is embarrassing, but I do have a tiny crush on him, but Danny's probably dating three or four lawyers or models; I hear he is quite the catch. I mean, have you seen him?"

"He is seen coming and going from your apartment like he lives there." Louis Delcroix said.

"You seem to know a lot about me, Louis," Madeline said. "That makes me a little nervous. Maybe I should get to know you better too."

"But I'm getting off track." Louis Delcroix said. "Did you know that there's a legend that Henry Guidry was the patriarch of a powerful magical family, and now his great-grandson is taking over?"

"Sounds like a wonderful New Orleans urban legend," Madeline said. "I'll have to ask Danny about it when I see him again. But I'm sure if my boss was some powerful, scary guy, he would probably frown upon your digging."

"Ma..." Danny walked in, grinning at her.

"Thanks for coming to sign the invoices, Danny." Madeline interrupted him. "I told you they could wait till I saw you next week. This is Louis Delcroix, he's doing a story on your grandfather."

"We really don't want any more press Mr. Delcroix," Danny said. "He was a very private man. As am I."

"Oh, I don't know, his restaurant's cigar room was legendary, as is your career as a lawyer and as a bachelor. Why did you leave your job? You were on track to be the youngest partner at one of the best firms in the south.

"Off the record," Danny said. "Henry left me more money than I, my children, and their children could ever use. He invested well. And now I can focus on his restaurant and my personal causes."

"How is your mother? I was so happy to hear she was not in the fire." Louis Delcroix said.

"She had forgotten to tell us she was going out of town," Danny said. "But I have been meaning to catch up with you. Would you happen to know why she had your card at her house?"

"I just thought a once new Orleans socialite turned recluse would make a fascinating story, but she just didn't seem to have all her marbles when I visited. She told me this crazy story that Henry was a storm giant, and her son was a powerful mage." Louis Delcroix smirked. "I wonder what stories she would tell if she was kidnapped and tortured?" Danny took a step forward, Madeline grabbed the back of his shirt.

"Your employee sure is handsy." Louis Delcroix said.

"I just had the floors redone; I wouldn't want blood on them. " Madeline said.

"I think you should go now," Steven, who was sitting in the back, piped up.

"Sure." Louis Delcroix said. "Stay safe Madeline, I'll be seeing you soon."

The moment Louis Delcroix stepped out of the gallery, Danny raised his left hand, the doors locked, and the curtain closed.

"What did he want?" Danny asked.

"He was fishing, but so was I," Madeline said. "I was hoping he was the piece to our problem, but he's just a creepy reporter looking for a story."

*

"You're an idiot…" Mack joked as Steven walked by Henry's office and knocked.

"Hey, come in. I think Madeline ran home for a while. We are doing paperwork. And by we, I mean me, while Mack mocks me."

"No, I'm just saying I am questioning your judgment if you chose to leave the hotel room. How do you not know about room service…" Mack caught himself. "I'm sorry, that was weird."

"It's fine… sorta…" Steven laughed. "I wanted to tell you something, in full disclosure." Danny invited him to sit. "I got my letter telling me who my academic advisor is…"

"Professor Eugene Daniel Boudreaux?" Danny guessed; Mack smirked.

"Madds says he is kind of a jerk, so I wondered if you think I should try to switch, I don't want any conflicts, and my loyalty is here," Steven said.

"Naw, from an academic standpoint, he is the best," Danny said, trying not to sound bitter. "If it comes up, can you say you work mostly for Mack, and we have little or no interaction? He has lost the right to know anything about my mom or me."

"Sure thing," Steven said.

"I'd probably avoid mentioning me too." Mack laughed. "I was Danny's bad friend growing up. On second thought, you might not mention that you work here, at all." All three laughed.

"Hi mama, I was just coming to see you. Please come sit with us." Danny said as Ida appeared in the doorway. "Go grab lunch if you want," Danny nodded to the nurse.

"Are you and Mack smoking in Henry's office again?" Danny and Mack both hugged her, laughing.

"No, mam, not since you used a switch on me." Mack teased. "Have you met our friend, Steven? He's helping me run the bar." Ida nodded, Steven smiled.

"Danny, I've been worried about you. I haven't seen you in a long time. I was afraid the avatar got you." Ida said.

"No, mama... that was a bad dream, you should only have good sweet dreams." Danny didn't look at her. "Remember Madeline, and I were out of town for a few days. We called you a lot. You laughed because we were eating snails." Danny said.

"And you sent me that picture of you in front of the big tower. You looked so happy. It's the only picture I have of you where you look truly happy since Abigail died." Ida said. Danny sniffed.

"Would you like a grilled cheese, mom? You know it's the only thing I can cook." Mack said.

"I would like that," Ida said. "Can you ask Henry to call me?"

"I will, mama," Danny said. Ida kissed his cheek and followed Mack out.

"I don't know what bothers me more, her days being lost in a fog, or her seconds of perfect clarity," Danny said, taking a sip of coffee leaning back.

"Can I ask you something?" Steven asked after giving Danny a few minutes to think. "How... accurate is Louis Delcroix and the facts in the book that Henry left me?"

"Pretty accurate, unfortunately," Danny admitted.

"Listen...No matter how I say this, I'm gonna sound like a jerk...." Steven said. "But Madeline will always be my business. And she is really bad about asking for help. Will you let me know if she needs anything?"

"Yes, I will. Can you let me know if you see Louis Delcroix around here? Even if he is harmless, he knows a few things that he had to do some digging to find out, so I don't think he will just go away. If he is ever ballsy enough to come to the bar, maybe be extra friendly..."

"Indeed."

"You're a research geek, huh?" Danny had an idea.

"I'm bringing Charlie lunch," Madeline said, popping her head in the office a few minutes later. "And, I do not approve of this friendship. If you are trying to figure out how to handle me with Louis Delcroix, neither of you will have a moment of peace for a month." She announced and rolled away. Both men were cautiously amused.

*

"Thank you for bringing pastries from my favorite bakery!" Charlie said. "I miss Paris so much." That's the first time Charlie had smiled in a month.

"Are you back full time at the club?" Madeline asked.

"No..." Charlie said. "They said either I need to commit to five shows a week, or I'd be put on rotation, which is like being put out to pasture. I got an offer today for a gig as a backup singer on a big concert tour. I'm trying to decide what to do. When I'm singing, I'm sad; when I'm not singing, I'm angry. I used to wonder how Ida could have just snapped. Now I kinda get it..."

"Charlie..." Madeline said.

"I'm just venting... I'll be fine," Charlie said.

"No, Charlie, turn around." Charlie turned around and fell to her knees, and started sobbing. The fountain had started again, and Kisseis appeared, kneeling in front of Charlie.

"Mom, time feels odd in the catacombs; I didn't know I was gone that long. I really needed to tell you that." Kisseis said. "I could only get away for two minutes, but I wanted to tell you I love and miss you; and I needed to give Madeline her book."

"Kisseis," Madeline said. "Wait, I have questions. Is the dragon controlling an avatar? Is she trying to break free? Is she coming after Danny?"

"Yes, all the avatars. Yes, to everything. It is worse than you can imagine." Kisseis said.

"I'm a time lock. Can I blink to where you are holding the dragon?"

"No. not yet. I have to go. The book will have more answers. If I don't come back, will you take care of my mom? Promise Madeline," Kisseis said. "I didn't mean to leave her, but I had no choice."

Page | 213

"Mom... Mama. Mom, Please look at me." Kisseis begged.

"Don't go Kisseis, I don't care about anyone else anymore. I just need to be with you," Charlie screamed.

"I love you, and I'm trying to get back to you, mom. Please read the book, Madeline. They are calling me. I have to go." And Kisseis flowed back into the fountain.

Madeline tried to help Charlie up, but she refused. "You could have frozen time. You could have blinked to go with her. You did nothing. Now I have truly lost everything and everyone that matters to me. Please leave me. Go just go." Charlie screamed at Madeline. Madeline took her book and rolled back to the restaurant, not wanting to upset Charlie anymore.

Chapter 14

When Madeline returned to the office. Mack had rejoined Danny and Steven in the sitting area; they all looked guilty as hell like they got caught by a teacher.

"I just don't want to know," Madeline said, touching Danny's leg as she rolled towards Henry's desk. The boys laughed, shrugged, and continued smoking their cigars. Danny kept talking to them but watched Madeline sadly, sensing something was off. Her mood had completely changed from 24 hours ago when they were still on their romantic vacation. Madeline knew she should kick everyone out, but she wanted Danny to be happy for a little while longer.

"Madds, I...." Charlie ran into the office, then noticed the boys were there too. "I'm very sorry. That visitor just upset me." Charlie didn't want to get into it.

"I know. We are good." Madeline said. "Thanks for getting me that book; I have a feeling that it's going to keep me up a few nights, but I definitely will be discussing it with you soon."

"Charlie, have a cigar with us," Mack said.

"Next time, Macky, next time." Charlie faked a grin and left.

"Want us to leave, Madeline?" Mack asked.

"Naw, finish your smokes; I kinda like the noise," Madeline said. Danny tried to make eye contact with her. She pretended to be swamped in paperwork. Madeline could sneak the book onto the desk and felt a little relieved as Danny was being sucked into a football discussion.

She stared at the book that Kisseis brought her for a really long time. Unlike the spell or the time lock journals, there was a sense of familiarity, which honestly crept Madeline out. She kept tracing the outline of the book's cover with her finger. Madeline debated on opening the book in front of the guys but feared incase something reached out and grabbed her. Still, curiosity finally got the better of Madeline.

Madeline took a deep breath, opened the cover, and muttered, "What the hell?" and was suddenly overwhelmed with confusion, disbelief, and a little pure joy.

"Hey, we should go prep the bar for tonight," Mack told Steven while giving Danny a stern look. Steven tried to make eye contact with Madeline, knowing she was upset, but she did not lookup.

The door closed without anyone's touch after Steven left. Danny sat in front of Henry's desk, Madeline handed him the book. He opened the cover and was speechless.

"It's definitely my handwriting," Madeline said. "My mom hates the way I make my A's." Danny waited for a better explanation.

"Kisseis dropped in while we were having lunch." Madeline hurried with her story as the tiny vein across Danny's forehead reappeared. "She said I needed my address book. And other stuff about the dragon and avatars. Charlie had a meltdown... it was kinda heartbreaking. Charlie wanted me to follow Kisseis. Maybe I should have..."

"And... you thought letting me smoke a cigar and shoot the bull about sports was important?" Danny raised his voice.

"Yes, Daniel Boudreaux, I did. My first instinct was to blink away and hide and figure it out by myself." Madeline said. "But I feel safe here. I knew you were here. So I came here. And you and Mack looked so normal and relaxed.."

"Can I at least have a minute to gloat about the name and info, if loss return to..." Danny grinned stupidly.

"Danny... there is more than one avatar, and Kisseis said the dragon is breaking free. I don't think Kisseis plans to make it out alive. She sounded like she was trying to give Charlie some kind of closure." Madeline blurted out.

"I knew there was a possibility there could be more than one," Danny said. "Have you looked at the rest of the book?"

"It seems to be my address book. I have never seen it in my life, but I know it's mine." Madeline said. "I have so many questions. Why did Kisseis have it, and how is it suppose to help us? Stop Smiling!"

"kill the dragon, marry the girl. I'm glad you are not going to hyphenate." Danny said. "I'm going to talk to Charlie. Maybe she will remember something. Then I'm in the kitchen. I told Jane I would help her tonight. We are overbooked. You are not leaving this desk till you figure out the book, are you?

"Nope," Madeline said. "Kisseis looked so scared. And I'm pretty sure Charlie has reached her breaking point..."

"I'll leave you to this today," Danny said. "But dinner at 10, home by 12, and tomorrow we train all day." He kissed her forehead as she stared at her book.

"Hey, can you buy me about 400 index cards?" Madeline asked.

"Wow, that's what I get for telling you I'm rich... you're crazy. As you wish, Madeline Jourdain Guidry Boudreaux ." Danny stared at her for the longest time, then left.

*

"Hey, love," Madeline said as Danny reappeared in Henry's office. "Are you on a break?"

"Madds, it's 11, it was so busy, I worked an extra hour.' Danny said. "Wow, your desk is very serial killer like." Madeline had spent the last six hours writing every name and address from her book onto index cards; there were close to 400.

"One, I do owe my mom an apology, my handwriting is indeed horrific," Madeline said. Danny was amused. "Two, there is not a single last name in this book. Not even for my mom and dad, just first names and the initials of their last. Some are only initials. Why would I do that?"

"That actually seems like a smart time lock thing," Danny said. "How were you sorting them?"

"The tiny stacks are the names and addresses I recognize." Madeline sighed, "The other 20 stacks are not."

"Everyone's waiting for us for dinner..." Danny said.

"But look," Madeline argued. "I was extremely social for the last four days. I think I can miss one dinner, please?" Madeline asked.

"This is really important to you?" Danny asked.

"I think it's a big step in the right direction," Madeline said. "Besides, you know we can't do what we talked about in Paris until we get this done."

"Ok. That argument is not fair. At all....." Danny kissed her. "You have less than an hour..." Danny said, straightening out a new gold chain around Madeline's neck hiding a ring. "I'll go have dinner with everyone, clean up, then we will go home."

"I guess it's a bad time to ask for 30 more minutes on top of that to review my bids to paint the gallery?" Madeline said, half kidding, but if he gave in, she totally would. Danny just shook his head in frustration and went back into the kitchen.

As her attention turned back to her desk, she noticed one card had fallen from one of the stacks and placed itself right in front of her. She tried to get back in research mode, but she had gone cross-eyed by this time and decided to join the others after hearing their warm laughter.

-

"In our 22 years of friendship, I have never heard Mack giggle. I find it extremely disturbing." Danny said after Madeline blinked them both to Henry's property the next day, near the gun range.

"Be nice!" Madeline teased Danny.

"By the way, Congratulations!" Mack kissed Madeline's cheek.

"We just didn't want the dragon to take years away from us like she did Henry and Millie," Madeline said. "It's a little sad because we really do want to share our joy, but Danny thinks I'll be a bigger target if we announce it. I personally think he doesn't want to give up his sexiest bachelor title..." Madeline said.

"I was going to nominate him again this year. Lawyer turned successful restaurant owner." Mack smirked.

"Oh yes, Please." Madeline laughed.

"I do not approve of this friendship." Danny grinned. "I won't talk to Steven, if you don't talk to Mack..."

"Are you going to tell anyone else?" Mack asked.

"Not yet..." Madeline said, trying to hide her sadness.

"Soon," Danny promised. "We just have to get rid of the avatars. I hate that they could be anywhere, anyone. But we'll figure this out," Danny hugged Madeline, staring at Mack very concerned.

"So..." Madeline said, trying not to spiral. "Do I really need to learn to shoot?"

"In a perfect world, you won't," Mack said. "In a perfect world, Danny won't have to shoot either. I'll shoot, he'll blow stuff up, and you'll freeze stuff so that I can shoot more, and he can blow more stuff up. But... we just would feel better if you had different ways to fight. Plus, it would annoy the hell out of Daniel if you were better at weapons than him, and bring me so much joy."

"If I can shoot better than you, in a month, I can go to seven hours of sleep?" Madeline grinned.

"Absolutely not. I have a feeling you can do anything you set your mind to." Danny said.

"Ok. Let's get started." Mack said. And for three afternoons a week, Mack taught Madeline to shoot both a handgun as well as an AR-15. Mack and Danny love watching every time she did a full course. Madeline would lean low in her wheelchair, gracefully rolling to each target. The faster the shot, the faster the wheelchair would roll forwards, anticipating her next shot...

Madeline never particularly liked guns, but she learned to respect the strength and accuracy of shooting. She really enjoyed hanging out with

Mack. Mack enjoyed knowing she was almost as good as Danny. And Danny slept better at night, knowing without a doubt, Madeline was holding back, just a little.

*

"You have to stop giggling," Danny demanded.

"It's just so damn cool," Mack said as Danny, Mack, and Madeline entered the office from the rose garden.

"Hey, Madds," Steven said from the couch. "We really need to get Wi-Fi at the gallery. Where have y'all been?"

"Because I'm living in the French Quarters, they are trying to teach me self defense," Madeline said.

"Wish I thought of that when you were living off-campus," Steven smirked. Madeline rolled her eyes. "Can I go next time?"

"Yes," Danny said.

"Yes," Mack said.

"Uh, no," Madeline said. "What are you doing here anyway?"

"I am trying to set up my online stuff with Tulane," Steven said. "And I'm finally reading Henry's book. It's amazing. History of magic, by H. H."

"Steven, did you mess with my cards?" Madeline asked, rolling to her desk.

"No, but I am dying for an explanation," Steven said.

"It's a puzzle Henry left me," Madeline said in frustration. "Hey, who is HH?"

"Harry Houdini," Steven and Danny said at the same time.

"History geeks, quick, where did he live?" Madeline asked.

"New York…" they sang together again.

"Why?" Steven asked.

"Just cuz," Madeline said, staring at a card on her desk that said Harry H, and his address in New York. This made Madeline giggle a little but really didn't help much.

"it's a slow Sunday. Can I see if Jane wants to take off?" Mack asked Danny.

"Good luck with that!" Madeline laughed.

"Says the girl at her desk." Mack teased.

"Go. Enjoy the day!" Danny said.

"Congrats again, you guys," Mack said and left.

"I think I'm going too." Steven wanted to ask what Mack was congratulating them about and figured Madeline would tell him. But maybe he wasn't ready to hear it.

"hi," Danny whispered, going around to hug her waist behind the desk. She enjoyed a moment of tenderness then pointed at the Harry H. card. He grinned.

"But that doesn't really help us," Madeline said.

"Then let's start over; I'll do a spreadsheet," Danny said. Madeline laughed at his cuteness.

They spent the rest of the day and evening working on the addresses and running back and forth to the restaurant. Danny did recognize about 45 more of the addresses as colleagues or friends. Still, besides that, Madeline felt like she had gotten nowhere.

"Hey, I wanna break my own rule," Danny said as he wiped down the island. "Let's go find the perfect sunrise, Miss Time Lock. A little training exercise for you. Little make out session for me. Kind of like a win/win, to be honest..."

As much as Danny loved watching the sunrise on three different continents that night. He enjoyed watching Madeline gain confidence with each jump more than he ever thought possible.

*

"Morning..." Madeline said, entering the kitchen, expecting only Mack, Jane, and Danny.

"Madeline Jourdain," Danny said, "This is my boss, Mr. Leon White. Madeline is running The Guidry Gallery."

"Hello," Madeline said.

"Oh, the gallery, your pet project." White said to Danny, then turned to Madeline, " Well, Aren't you a cute thing?" Mack turned his back in fear of the train wreck. "I'm trying to get your boss here to come back to the firm as a full partner. He keeps saying he is so tempted, but he has family matters he needs to take care of. Every week I try to sweeten the pot. I am even down to 55 hours a workweek, and he can have his pick of two secretaries, one for brains and one for beauty..."

"Leon," Danny watched as Madeline's heart broke a little. Still, he and Madeline did agree to not share their relationship with anyone besides Mack for now. Danny just didn't realize how hard it would be. "I really do need to help Mack until we figure out all the in's and out's of the restaurant. Plus, I do have some pressing family matters that mean everything to me. And do require my full attention." Danny apologized with his eyes, Madeline softened a little.

"Nice meeting you, Mr. White," Madeline said. "Have a good day, Danny." Mack tried to hide a laugh with a cough as they all heard Henry's door slam.

"Leon," Danny said. "I really meant it when I asked for a year's leave. I have found something I love so much more than the law, and Henry told me that I should hang on to it if I find it. I actually thought this would be harder, but I think you should go ahead and look for my permanent replacement."

"Ok, Boudreaux..." White said. "But I'll be back. You'll miss us." They shook hands, and White left.

"Hey, can you guys do a midnight dinner in the rose garden, invite Charlie and Steven too? It's really important," Danny asked Jane and Mack.

"I am very sorry." Danny went into Henry's office and shut the door behind him.

"Shh!" Madeline hissed.

"Don't shh me when I'm trying to apologize; I'm like wrong once a decade..." Danny said.

"Come here." Madeline was at her desk. "How did we not see this card?" Danny stared: H.G. French quarters. with a date and a symbol.

"But look..." Madeline showed him the date on the back of her Time Lock book. "Kisseis said I need to meet with 5 pillars to become strong enough to fight the dragon. Maybe the other four are in here too?"

"Wow... That's wild." Danny said.

"Yes," Madeline said, staring at the cards. "It's a start... but there are still so many questions." She covered her face in frustration.

"Hey, I am really sorry," Danny said.

"It was part of the plan that I agreed to," Madeline said. "I didn't know it would be this hard. And I miss my folks. They are so upset I have not invited them to see the new space, but I don't think it's safe for them here. It's killing me that they haven't met you in person."

"And I said it didn't matter, but I want to wear Millie's rings, and I want to be introduced as your wife... my best friends don't even know we are married. You are the best thing that has ever happened to me, and we can't even walk across the street. I'm just sad."

"Come here," Danny said, picking her up from her wheelchair. "I couldn't go another second without being your husband. And in Paris, it was just us, and everything was simple... and it was too easy to stop by Vegas on the way home. I should be, but I'm not sorry. But if you have any regrets at all, we can get it annulled, and I'll wait another 100 years for you."

"Nope, best wedding ever. You are stuck with me." Madeline grinned.

"And now that you can blink, we can go to Houston more, Ok?" Danny asked.

"Maybe meet your in-laws in person before you say that. Mom's a lot." Madeline giggled. "But seriously, you should have told me you missed being a lawyer."

"I know," Danny sighed. "I really do. I was thinking maybe after we find the avatars, I'll start a small firm."

"As long as I hire your secretaries. Seriously." Madeline grinned.

"Will you meet me in the rose garden tonight at midnight?" Danny asked.

"Yes, husband," Madeline said.

"You are going to stare at your address book until then, huh?" Danny asked.

"Yes, husband. Help or get out." Madeline teased, "But we can blink to a destination of your choice for lunch..." Danny moaned happily and left.

Madeline was very surprised to find a three-piece band in the garden when she arrived at midnight. They were already playing as Madeline rolled to the elegant table setting where everyone was already sitting with drinks.

"I wanted to thank everyone for coming; you truly are my family." Danny stood up and sniffed. "You have seen me through my darkest hours, now I would like you to share in my light and happiness. Please lift your glasses to my bride, Madeline."

"To Madeline." Everyone said. She had no words.

The evening was perfect, and no one seemed that surprised. Everyone showered them with love. Everyone danced, Charlie sang. The food was scrumptious, and the skies twinkled with more stars than normal. It would be a bit longer before Danny could introduce her as his wife to strangers. But everyone that mattered knew. And for Madeline, this was a compromise she could live with.

What no one realized was that this was Charlie's last performance for a long time. She later said it was the perfect way to let go of her old life, searching for something new.

*

"Morning, my love," Madeline said. She hugged and kissed Danny finding him sitting at her desk in Henry's office.

"I was hoping you would sleep in today. You haven't slept a full night in a week.." Danny said.

"I did not have the proper incentive to stay in bed this morning." she giggled and kissed him again. "Besides, I had to let the painter and the cable guy in."

"I wish you would hire an assistant. Steven is only going to be there a few hours a day now that school has started.." Danny said. "At least hire another part-time runner."

"It's not in my budget," Madeline said.

"Wish you had married a rich nerdy guy who would give you the moon. Oh, wait." Danny grinned.

"I know. but it's not me." Madeline said. "I want the gallery to be something I create myself, actually using my degree that I worked very hard to get. And hopefully, it will be something Henry would be proud of. It also gives me an incentive that I'll just be a gallery owner one day, and you'll be a lawyer... Ya wanna train later? I'm free by 3."

"Damn, you're gorgeous and smart. Yes, wife, 3 o'clock." Danny said. "So barefoot and pregnant for ten years, probably isn't going to happen?" he yelled as she left, going back to the gallery. Danny loved hearing her sarcastic laugh.

*

"Daniel..." Mack said, coming into the office a little while later.

"Macky..."

"We missed you at racket ball this morning," Mack said. "But I did crush Frank."

"Ah yes, racket ball, three blocks over. I remember jogging there. Do you remember when we jog places? And we ate at holes in the walls, and we were not worried about a fire breathing dragon trying to kill me. Fun times."

"You mean, before Madeline…" Mack said. "When you were an angry 27-year-old virgin tight ass lawyer? Yup, damn fun times. It still kinda creeps me out when you smile."

"She's just… my everything," Danny said. "Honestly, do you think I'm overreacting?"

"Honestly," Mack said. "If I didn't see Henry's injuries, I'd think you were off your rocker. But those gashes give me nightmares at least twice a week. And I only saw the ones on his arms. The thought of Madds or you…" Mack sighed. "You're not overreacting. I wish you were,"

"What?" Danny immediately knew Mack was hiding something.

"Frank told me…" Mack said. "He's been seeing more blood sacrifices lately. Most are dumb teenagers with pig's blood. But there was one last week that was the real hardcore deal. And he thinks it was to an ancient creature. I do think we should step up security around here. I'd rather be safe than sorry." Danny hung his head down, rubbing his forehead.

"I'll do security." Charlie flew in and grinned.

"No," Danny said. "Absolutely not."

"Why?" Charlie asked.

"Because I almost watched you die twice," Danny said. "Please don't ask me again, Charlie."

"I cannot explain it, but I'm stronger when Madeline is nearby," Charlie said. "Remember in the Prayer room, when Fr. Karl's name lit up, and everyone started remembering him again. I thought I had broken the spell myself, but the more I replay it in my head, the name didn't light up until Madeline and I joined hands. What if we are more powerful together?"

"But still…" Danny said. "I have already asked too much of Mack; I can't begin to think what I have asked of Madeline."

"I can do this, or I can go out and look for Kisseis. I need this, Daniel." Charlie was being honest.

"I don't like it, but it's a solid plan. We are better with Charlie's eyes out there." Mack said. Charlie nodded. Danny reluctantly agreed..

*

"I can't believe y'all made that bet." Madeline howled in the restaurant's kitchen as Jane made a stir fry lunch for Madeline and Steven.

"You never answered. $20 is at stake." Jane said.

"We got married because we are madly in love," Madeline said.

"That's it?" Steven asked.

"Yup. I'm sorry I'm not with child, you freak." Madeline said.

"Damnit." Steven handed Jane a twenty.

"Thanks, Steven, best wedding blessing ever." Madeline laughed. "How was your first day?"

"Interesting... it's going to be intense." Steven said. "Your father-in-law is mighty proud of being related to Henry."

"Holy crap, I have a father-in-law," Madeline said.

"And..." Steven said. "From time to time, he will bring in prominent guest lecturers from the magical community, including his son."

"You need to tell Danny," Madeline said.

"Can't you? Like during a kiss or..." Steven smirked.

"Take one for the team," Madeline said. "He hasn't made his frowny face at me in two whole days."

"Fine," Steven said. "But that's your wedding gift."

"Hi Chef," Danny said, entering the kitchen, sitting by Madeline, putting his head on her shoulder, picking a bite from her plate.

"How was your first day?" Danny asked Steven. Steven smirked.
Page | 227

"Anyways…" Madeline said. "I do have something I want to tell you guys."

"What is it, Madds?" Jane asked, feeling like it was serious.

"Wow, telling y'all I had to get married would have been easier," Madeline said. "You guys know magic is slowly coming back, and I got a book?"

"Yup," Jane said.

"I got a book too." Danny tried to help.

"It seems that…" Madeline stumbled.

"They need to know all of it so that this can really be your safe space," Danny said.

"I can do extra stuff," Madeline said softly. Danny burst into laughter. She playfully hit him.

"like…" Jane asked. Steven looked very interested.

"I can teleport." Madeline shrugged.

"Wait…" Steven said. "if Henry's book is accurate, only time locks can teleport, and they are extremely rare."

"Look," Jane said. "Danny has convinced me that magic is real. And Steven has been helping me learn about knacks, but this is a whole freakier level."

"Oh my god. Think about it; you keep saying you hear Madeline in the hallways, but she's gone when you try to find her." Steven said.

"But there's more, isn't there?" Jane's first instinct was to go for a walk, but when her eyes met Madeline, she just knew. Madeline started crying.

"It seems…" Danny hesitated. "Henry was killed by an evil spirit who is very determined to end his family line."

"So you married him?" Steven unexpectedly screamed.

"Yes! I wanted to know I was married to him, even for a few months, and then I'm going to save him or die trying." Madeline pounded her fists on the table, and the lights flickered.

"Madeline!" Steven said.

"You have my word, Steven, Mack, and I plan to sacrifice ourselves if it comes to that," Danny admitted.

"I can kinda see that." Jane sniffed.

"This block is safe. No evil should be able to attack me here." Danny said. "But that's why Madeline and I haven't explored the city. Why I can't introduce her as my wife. We don't know who or what is involved. We have to be extra careful in the quarter. For now, they are only after Charlie and me. Charlie, for reasons I can explain later. Madeline will be a target when they figure out how powerful she is, and or they figure out we are married."

"Madeline and I love you guys so much that we agreed y'all needed to know everything," Danny said. "If you wanna resign, Jane, we can talk about you opening a restaurant anywhere you want, and I'll be a very silent partner and investor. Henry would insist. And Mack can find you a gig at a better bar in a second, Steven."

"But there would not be here, and here is where you and Madeline are, so no," Jane said. "I am still a little freaked out, but I do trust you, Danny … we can do some cool stuff, huh?" Jane asked Madeline.

"You have no idea." Madeline grinned through tears.

"I'm sorry," Steven said. "I shouldn't have questioned why Madeline married you. You've been nothing but kind to me. I would like to stay too."

"I would be disappointed if you said anything less," Danny said. "Why don't you take Jane somewhere? I'll do dinner service."

"Do you trust me?" Madeline asked Jane.

"Yes." Madeline giggled and took her hand, and blinked.

"Wow," Steven said. "Where do you think they went?"

"I don't think I want to know," Danny said.

"You truly love her, don't you," Steven asked.

"She's going to live a long and exciting life. And she's gonna do great things. I'm going to see to that." Danny sighed sadly.

"Did you know I once asked her to marry me?" Steven said.

"I did not,"

"She probably didn't because she didn't count it as a real proposal, which I get. Anyways, I asked. And Madeline said she would love me for the rest of her life but could not marry someone she didn't trust. And knew I was probably asking because I did something bad and felt guilty." Steven said. "Which, of course, I had. And then she said... she would marry once, and would trust him unconditionally. I think she's expecting a lifetime from you. Don't disappoint her." Steven left the room.

Danny reached into his wallet, put Henry's ring on his left pinky, sighed, and wandered into the office. He stared at the books on the shelf and decided to pull all the books on time locks. Danny stacked them on a chair when he noticed something. All of the books on time locks had a funny looking handwritten symbol inside the cover. He ran to Henry's desk, opening Madeline's address book.

"Yes..." Danny said, smiling. "Thanks, granddad." He found four other addresses with that symbol.

*

"Come back to bed, wife," Danny said, rolling over, staring at her at the small dining table surrounded by books and notebooks.

"I can't sleep," Madeline said.

"Even better. Like I said, come back to bed, wife." Danny laid there a minute, grumbled, and got up, pretending to be heartbroken that she was not rushing towards him... He went to the kitchen, dished out a bowl of ice cream, then went to sit by Madeline. Feeding her a bite.

"I'm not sure about this time lock thing," Madeline admitted. "Displacing around the world, is one, very cool thing. But traveling through time feels like such a great responsibility. There are so many rules, from having to fit in with clothing and dialect to not changing timelines. Even my wheelchair has to change every time period. What if we just stayed in this apartment for like 100 years?"

"Ok," Danny said. "I got my girl, I got my 3am ice cream. The 13-year-old me says I have met my life's goals."

"Ok," Madeline said.

"But..." Danny said. "That would mean... we couldn't travel without worrying or see your parents, ever. Or build our dream house, or fill our dream house with kids. We couldn't even do something as simple as grabbing a beer with our friends across the street. What has thrown you off? You have been so focused lately?"

"I was watching you sleep, and I knew, even though I would prefer not to, I'd die for you," Madeline said. "And I would be very mad at you for a very long time if you died saving me, but I'd get it. It's just killing me that you and Mack made this crazy pact,"

"He is the most loyal person on the face of the earth." Danny said. "But he is the most loyal to..."

"Henry," Madeline said.

"He wants to end this for us, of course, but for Henry also.. Mack says I have no choice in the matter but Madds, if you have to decide," Danny said, looking down, playing with her legs. "He already saved my life once. I owe him. He promised one day, life would be worth all my losses. I could not see it as an angry, depressed 17-year-old. but damn if he wasn't right."

"Guess I'm gonna have to step up my game and save the both of you arrogant but very cute fools," Madeline said. And they kissed for a long time.

"Let's go over the rules, again..."

*

"This is weird," Danny said.

"Beautiful, but very awkward..." Jane said.

"Henry always said he was planning to try," Danny said. "It was even in his final business plan to me."

"We don't have to do this once a week, do we? I feel like I'm being punished?" Jane asked.

"I do get the principle," Danny said. "But this is just unsettling. Maybe monthly?"

"I could do that." Jane agreed.

"Madeline!" Jane and Danny screamed. Madeline appeared in the cabin's doorway with two bottles of wine and three pizzas. She floated down the steps where Jane, Mack, Steven, and Danny were sitting around a small fire on the beach.

"Are y'all loving your day off?" Madeline asked.

"Nope," Danny said.

"Not even a little," Jane said.

"look, I got your favorite pizza from New York and your favorite wine from Napa Valley. Stop being brats." Madeline teased.

"What have you been doing today? I haven't seen you relaxing on the beach with us..." Jane smirked.

"I've relaxed, watching my light fixtures being installed, learning spells, and training with Mack." Madeline shyly admitted. "Not everyone can be partners at the hottest restaurant in New Orleans."

"Are you going to try to explain to her again that by marrying a Guidry, she's a partner too?" Jane teased.

"It's just not worth it." Danny laughed.

"Eat. Drink. And be merry. I'll be right back," Madeline kissed Danny twice. He thought that was odd but didn't question his luck.

"So, we agree?" Jane asked Danny and Mack as Madeline disappeared into Henry's cabin.

"Yup," Danny said. The restaurant stays open 7 days a week. Only the weak need time off." Danny and Jane clicked their glasses together as Mack laughed.

"Madds?" Steven said, finding her pacing in the cabin. "What are you doing?"

"Nuttin," Madeline said, avoiding eye contact.

"lie!" Steven shrugged.

"Oh, how I love hanging out with my ex-boyfriend.." Madeline annoyingly sighed. "My book says I need to start practicing, ya know."

"Are you trying to distract your husband, in case you don't come back? But hey at least he has pizza?"

"And his favorite wine," Madeline said. "Ok, I heard what that sounded like; shut up."

"Danny," Steven said. "Would you come in here?" He yelled out the door, then shrugged, "Hey, You wanted us to be friends..."

"But not when it's inconvenient for me," Madeline smirked.

"See ya on the flip side, Madds," Steven said, kissing her cheek and leaving the cabin.

"Trader," Madeline screamed as the screen door shut.

"Hi," Danny said. "Whatcha doing?"

"The book thinks I'm ready to try time travel," Madeline said. "I'm scared I won't be able to come back to us; I really like us," Madeline confessed.

"You will always be able to find us, this I truly believe," Danny said. "What is your first task?"

"Going forwards in time anywhere from 1 to 15 minutes," Madeline said.

"You did go forwards 2 minutes with Henry," Danny said.

"Then he died," Madeline whispered.

"Madds... That's not what happened. You have to know that." Danny sighed. Lifting her chin, making her look at him. "You got this. Try 3 minutes. I'll be waiting..."

"Yes, husband," she gave a weak smile. Madeline focused on the new spell she had just memorized, added her location and time frame, and blinked. Danny never told her those were the longest three minutes of his life.

"Hi..." Madeline grinned exactly three minutes later. Hopefully, she would get used to the feeling. It felt like being shoved through a keyhole, a very tiny keyhole.

They practice this for the next week, gradually feeling comfortable with 15 minutes blinks forwards in time. The book says although it's possible to travel back in time centuries, you should only travel 15 minutes maximum into the future. Madeline never broke this rule. And Danny always waited for her to return exactly where she left him.

*

"It's a little funny," Madeline said from behind her desk.

"Did you at least apologize?" Jane asked.

"I said I was sorry that he didn't have a sense of humor," Madeline smirked

"He's very upset that you are sleeping less and less," Jane said.

"I need two weeks nonstop at the gallery; I can practice my normal spells there," Madeline said. "Steven agreed he would help all weekend, And I have to keep training with Mack in the afternoons. So the only time I can practice time jumping forward... is at night... when Danny is asleep. Which was fine. Until he caught me."

"You do look tired, Madds," Jane said. "Ok, It's a little funny, but you really cannot skip sleeping."

"I can certainly try." Madeline shrugged.

"It's dead, Jane," Danny said, coming in. "Not even magic can save that refrigerator. Henry should have replaced it ten years ago. The sales guy is coming at 11. Merry Christmas."

"There is another thing…" Jane said. Danny sat down on the sofa. Madeline floated to sit in his lap. He pretended to resist but hugged her waist, but Madeline sense he was still pissed. She kissed his cheek, he grinned a little. "Last night, we had a few complaints about a flying cockroach."

"What?!?" Danny asked. "No, No, Please say you are kidding."

"Charlie says she gets bored watching the door, so she just decided to fly around the dining room. But even that got boring," Jane said. "So she…"

"She what?" Danny asked.

"Charlie…." Jane hesitated. "Started using the table's legs as the obstacle course, flying, weaving faster and faster through them. Most of the customers were delighted. Except for one older lady who repeatedly tried to swat her. Which did not go over well. Mack comped her, and I think I have to cater her grand daughter's sweet 16."

"If I laugh, are you going to divorce me?" Madeline asked.

"I can't. I forgot to make you sign a prenup." Danny teased, kissing her softly. "I'll talk to Charlie," Danny told Jane.

"Hello?" a man appeared at the door and came in before being invited. Danny quickly but gently set Madeline back in her chair and winked.

"Jane," Danny said, sounding like a boss now. "Please meet with the sales guy, get exactly what you need, and ask if there is any way we can get it today. The extra cost for same-day delivery is fine."

"Yes, Chef," Jane said and left.

"Hi, dad." Danny sighed at the guest. Madeline tried to leave, but Danny asked her to stay with his frown. "This is my… Madeline, She's running Henry's gallery." Danny snapped a pencil he was holding.

"Oh…" Eugene did not seem thrilled with her. "That's a mighty big job for a person in a wheelchair. I hope my son is good to you."

"He is." What else could Madeline say?

"Can I speak to you alone?" Eugene said.

"Actually, Henry left Madeline his office, so we are her guests…" Danny said.

"Why, that dirty old devil, guess he wasn't as hung up on Millie as he claimed," Eugene smirked.

"Dad!" he pounded his fist on the coffee table. Madeline swore he grew a little.

"Danny!" Madeline forced him to make eye contact until he calmed down. "I do have some work at my desk; nice seeing you again, Eugene." Madeline left the sitting area.

"Dad, it has been a very bad morning; why are you here?" Danny rubbed his face,

"I just wanted to check on you and your mother," Eugene said.

"I don't even know how to answer that," Danny sighed, frustrated.

"Hey." Madeline had to answer the phone. "What? Not that I can recall, but I haven't really looked. No. no. I'm in a meeting, and you should not drop by now. Can you text me that info? I certainly will. I can do lunch at one. Thanks!"

"I think we are interrupting Madeline; let's go talk in the dining area," Danny said.

"Ok," Eugene looked annoyed as hell but agreed. Danny pushed him out and closed the door behind him. Madeline sat at her desk for three minutes longer to make sure Eugene was not coming back. Sent Danny an "I love you" text and began a frantic search.

"The 200 Most Unknown Yet Most Influential Men in the History of magic," Madeline muttered to herself, "You've got to be kidding me."

Madeline's first instinct was to look for the book that Steven told her to find shelf by shelf, but then she wondered.

"I need the book, " Madeline said in her office, "'The 200 Most Unknown yet Most Influential Men in the History of magic." Madeline grinned as a very thick book from the top shelf floated to her.

"Henry did have it!" Madeline texted Steven.

"Wow," Danny came back in. "I don't know how to apologize for my father."

"Believe it or not, I've heard worse," Madeline said.

"That makes me so sad." Danny hugged her.

"Besides accusing your wife of being a gold digger and having a fling with your great grandfather, what else did Eugene want?" Madeline asked.

"If possible, the conversation got worse," Danny said. "He says if I agree to be a guest lecturer in his History of magic in New Orleans class, he would give me full custodianship of my mother. He wasn't brave enough to finish the threat, but I could have really hurt him."

"What are you going to do, love?" Madeline asked.

"I don't know Madds," Danny said. "You know I want custodianship of my mother. I must confess that I'd consider it ordinarily, just to get him out of Ida's life. Currently, if he got a wild hair, he could take her to who knows where. And I would have no say. But it's not safe for me in a huge unprotected lecture hall. You know Eugene would turn it into a circus to get more PR for his department."

"Why don't I blink you to the cabin, and you can go for a 10-mile run to clear your head?" Madeline offered. "You have had a bad morning, and I apologize for being stubborn."

"Wow," Danny laughed. "You kinda apologized but not really."

"I'm charming like that," Madeline said.

"I actually would love to go for a run," Danny said. "I hate being this angry. He is such an awful human being."

"He can't be that awful, he made my favorite person, ever," Madeline whispered. They hugged.

"But Madds," Danny said before they blinked. "When I get back, we are talking about your sleep schedule, and why you would rather spend a few hours with that book on your desk than coming on a jog with me, I can make it fun." She giggled and blinked.

Madeline returned to her desk a few minutes later, touching the spine of the newly discovered book, "Find any mentions of Henry Guidry." She ordered. The book turned to page 386 and found a full-page article about Henry. Madeline sniffed. Touching a young picture of Henry, never noticing how much Danny looked like him. Besides the captions, under his picture was the tiny symbols that Danny had noticed in her address book.

"Book," Madeline touched the page, "Find me all the entries with this sideways P symbol," Madeline asked. It found all five, Madeline knew, without a doubt, these were her pillars and they were the path to finding Kisseis .

*

"She's sleeping," Danny said.

"Are you sure?" Mack laughed. Clicking their glasses of cognac and smoking cigars in Millie's rose garden.

"So, I revised my will," Danny said.

"I really don't want to do this, Daniel." Mack sighed.

"In the case of my and my," Danny whispered. "… After our untimely death, I set up a trust for Ida. I'm giving my shares of the restaurant to Jane, and you get everything else."

"I'd rather beat your butt at racket ball for the next 50 years; it's the little things in life that bring me true joy." Mack teased.

"I'm pretty sure if I'm dead, he'd lose all interest. But If Eugene becomes a problem…" Danny said.

"He won't take Ida away from me," Mack said. "I'll see to that. Do you think our girl is ready?"

"Mentally, she is…" Danny said. "Madeline has done everything in her Time Lock book perfectly a hundred times over. But she's nervous. And she's a little angry and sad that this is our first year of marriage… And I get that. We went to her parents last weekend; you could just tell she was trying to make the most of being together."

"You got everything?" Mack asked.

"Yup," Danny said. "Steven did a really good job researching the time frame and what we would need to fit in. Will you make sure he get's Henry's books?"

"When are you leaving?" Mack asked.

"Tomorrow, from the apartment," Danny said. "I wanted to leave from Henry's office after Madeline said goodbye to Jane, but she said that would be too hard on her, and she needed a clear, focused mind."

"You should be back tomorrow afternoon, right?" Mack asked.

"Yup," Danny said.

"I've got Jane and I tickets to a late burlesque show; it's non-refundable. Don't miss your dinner service, or you'll owe me $150." Mack said, punching his shoulder then disappearing into the building. Danny sat in the garden for another hour by himself, wishing he could end the dragon without Madeline but knowing he could not.

Chapter 15

"Hi, mom," Madeline said as Danny ran to check on Ida. "That's not true... I don't always call Dad... We did too. I'm glad you and daddy love him. No, he's not at all like his playboy profile online... Please stop googling him, mom... That's not what I meant; I want you guys to come when we can have a relaxing weekend; the gallery's opening day will be crazy and stressful. We'll see you for Thanksgiving, I promise... we will really try. Ok, I love you, mom." Madeline hung up and cried.

"We can start our adventure tomorrow," Danny said, overhearing her call, hugging her tenderly. "Today, we can stay in bed and hide under the sheets and listen to music and argue about what kind of house we want, today or for as many days as you need..."

"Nope," Madeline said, pulling herself together. "Let's make sure we have hundreds of days like that."

"Hey, come here." Danny pulled out Millie's ring from his wallet, placing it on her finger. He then moved Henry's ring from his pinky to his ring finger, "We can be married there." He winked. She nodded, took his hands, and blinked.

*

"Oh my god, Danny! We did it. It's spectacular, love." Madeline could not believe she had blinked them to a top of a mountain in Tibet, hopefully in the 1920s. Her joy was short-lived as she turned around, finding Danny looking green and throwing up.

"It felt like..." Danny said between throw-ups. "You pinched my nose and pulled me really fast through a water hose. A very long, tangled, knotted water hose. Bad time lock wife, bad." He laid flat on his back until the world stopped spinning. Madeline felt bad for him but hoped it would click very soon that it was 10 below, and she was absolutely freezing.

"Can you get up, love?" Madeline asked about 15 minutes later. Danny hopped up, almost feeling normal. Rubbing her arms to warm her. "That must be the monastery." She pointed 200 yards to the East. As they walked towards the structure, Danny held her hand, her wheelchair now looking like a wicker love seat with a high back.

It took them a long time to figure out how to get thru the gates as an iron fence surrounded the monastery. Madeline spotted the tiny doorway with a finding spell. She would have stared at the door all day if she wasn't freezing. Danny finally grew impatient and knocked for her.

"Hello?" Danny said. as a monk peeked his head out. "We are here to see Kushemi." The monk almost shut the door until he saw Madeline in her wheelchair. He opened the large door, signaling them to follow him.

"Sir," the monk bowed. He backed out of the small room, and Kushemi appeared from the shadows. His picture in Madeline's book did not reflect his grandeur. He stood 9 feet tall with piercing bluish-grey eyes and boney hands. His crazy wild white hair and the unkempt dress did not match his eloquent English accent.

"Ah," he smiled. "The most powerful time lock and her warrior. Welcome." He sat down on the floor, they joined him at his request. The monk who had brought them in now returned with tea.

Kushemi spent the rest of the day showing them around the monastery and introducing them to the 20 monks. There was a one-room cabin behind the property he described as perfect for newlyweds. Despite having no electricity, no running water, and no bed, Madeline and Danny would always remember this cabin with the fondest of memories.

"Please join me at 6 am. And we can start our training Madeline, and if you would like, you can train with the monks, Danny." Kushemi said in a quiet, welcoming tone, bowed, then left the newlyweds to their new home.

For 7 days a week for the next six months, the two had a very strict schedule. Danny would train in martial arts with the monks. Madeline would often have to make Danny soak his whole body in the hot springs behind their cabin after his long day. And found herself wrapping his bleeding hands a few times a week.

Danny seemed to enjoy cooking simple but tasty meals over an open fire and found himself feeding more and more of the monks every passing night, which he enjoyed. The monks remained mostly silent but grew to have great respect and fondness for him.

Kushemi and Madeline clicked from their first meeting. And although it went against everything she believed in, she tried very hard not to argue or question his methods. Kushemi was the pillar of the mind. Although she was very skeptical because most of the exercises were very frustrating. Madeline truly believed that Henry had a hand in picking out the four other pillars she needed to learn from.

Kushemi said he had five exercises that would really strengthen her mind. Madeline found each exercise stranger and harder than the last. But every time she considered quitting, she would see Danny in the distance and just mutter through her tears. Madeline was thankful Danny insisted on visiting each pillar with her. They had had many fights about Madeline visiting the pillars alone. Danny finally put his foot down, and Madeline knew it was one battle that she would not win.

The first of Kushemi's exercises was meditation. This was harder than it should have been. Madeline had never realized that she was either thinking of to-do lists for the gallery, restaurant, spells or having impure thoughts about Danny. Like 24/7. But Kushemi made sense, explaining that meditation can exchange anxieties, fears, and hatred for clarity, concentration, and calm. A time lock needed this, as well as a powerful magic-user.

Madeline promised herself she would do this every morning. A well meaning promise that she did not keep. However, she did meditate before a lot of battles, both magically as well as personally. Madeline tried to teach Danny a few times. It just never took.

Kushemi's next exercise was taking water out of different shaped glass containers with a shallow spoon. The spoon-like scoop would barely fit into the opening. The object was to scoop all the water out without spilling a single drop. This taught Madeline patience, focus, and slowing down her heart rate.

Kushemi hid his amusement when Madeline tried to cheat occasionally by using magic. He would always catch her in the act and make her refill the jugs. Madeline hated admitting that this did improve her eye-hand coordination. But it was still annoying. Sometimes Kushemi would let Madeline compete with Danny. She even beat him a few times.

Throwing needles was probably Madeline's most mentally challenging exercise. It was like darts except 10,000 times harder. She had to take regular sewing needles and throw them through the glass. With the exact speed and power, the tip of the needle hit and pierced through the glass. With too much or too little throw, the needle would impact the glass at the wrong angle. This exercise really strengthened her attention to detail and taught her that all of her spells and attacks had to be exact and precise.

Kushemi was pleased the first time that Madeline did it but pushed until she could do it 9 out of 10 times. It took a few months, but she finally did it. When she thought she successfully completed his challenge, he would make her do it faster while singing or telling him a story about her life.

"Kushemi," Madeline said.

"Yes, Madeline?"

"I've been trying very hard not to argue with your techniques in honor of my mentor..." Madeline said. "Danny will tell you I like arguing."

"He already told me that..." Kushemi's eyes sparkled with humor.

"I don't think I need to do a physical obstacle course," Madeline said.

"I disagree," Kushemi said.

"My wheelchair won't even fit through the maze,"

"Please put on your knee and elbow pads," Kushemi said, now raising his voice. Madeline hesitated. Without warning, Kushemi scooped her from her wheelchair and placed her in the middle of the maze. "If you don't think the first thing your enemies will try to destroy is your wheelchair, you're wasting my time."

"It will always have a protection spell," Madeline argued.

"98% of the time, that will probably work," Kushemi said. "Is that good enough for your adoring husband or your future children?" Madeline hated that he was right. It took her three hours to complete the first course. Her time got better each run, even though the course changed itself and got harder.

The obstacle course forced Madeline to make quick decisions while being in physical pain. Although she would never admit it, it was the exercise Madeline was most proud of. And the only one Danny loved to watch so much that he would stop training and watch from a distance.

The last exercise boggled Madeline's mind because Kushemi did it every day. He had a large punch bowl filled with a hundred identical tiny red beads. Mixed in the bowl was a single bead that was two shades of different red. Kushemi could walk by the bowl, And pull out the single different color bead every time. Quickly, with no hesitation. He said when Madeline could do this, she was done.

During the third week of training, Kushemi and Danny discovered they shared a love of chess. And on many evenings after Danny had finished feeding the monks, Kushemi would invite Madeline and Danny to his office. For hours, Danny and Kushemi would play chess and talk as Madeline studied her spell book.

"I always thought yetis were a myth," Danny said.

"And I thought storm giants were," Kushemi said, both amused.

"When I was nine..." Kushemi began telling Danny and Madeline his story after the 4th month. "My parents were shot and killed in the forest near here. I sometimes think I still hear their voices in the howling winds. They raised me to fear humans. But I had been shot in my leg, and my mother's dying words were 'Do anything to live, son.' So when this elderly monk found me and offered to wrap my leg, I went with him."

"The five monks living here were nothing like my tribe had described," Kushemi said. "They were kind, fed, and helped heal me. They allowed me to stay in the cabin you're in now. Wanting me to know I was a guest and not a prisoner. After I healed, Woenang, the eldest monk, spent months with me, looking for my village." Kushemi paused for a long time.

"When we finally found it, the village was burnt to the ground," Kushemi said. "All the bodies were piled in a mass grave. I recognized my brother's on top. I cried for a year, Woenang held me for a year. He took me as his son. He taught me to read, write, and pray, always saying I taught him so much more than he taught me. I always thought I would leave after Woenang passed on. I guess I was waiting for my true purpose," Kushemi quietly stared at Madeline.

As the days passed, Danny and Kushemi's friendship for each other grew. Madeline cried when Kushemi announced she was done after he beat Danny at one final chess game. Madeline asked if they could return for a fall retreat every year, and Danny shook his hand as they parted ways.

"Madeline," Kushemi said as they hugged for the last time. "Please remember to meditate before you use your powers in anger." Madeline kissed his cheek as Danny bowed then the couple blinked home.

*

"Are you really not going to feed me?" Madeline asked Jane in the kitchen.

"You were gone six freaking months," Jane screamed, a little kidding, a little pissed.

"Technically, we were gone seven minutes. Do you want me to tell you every time I leave the building?" Madeline asked.

"Pretty much." Jane kissed Madeline's cheek, setting a bowl of etouffee in front of her. "Seriously, What was it like?"

"It was really incredible," Madeline said. "Kushemi is one of the kindest souls I have ever met. He even taught me to meditate."

"So, he's a miracle worker?" Jane teased.

"I was a bit skeptical," Madeline admitted. "But I already feel more focused with my spells. I was a little nervous about being alone with

Danny for that long, but it was really good. There was this one thing, I was late a few weeks. And we hoped it was nothing. Kushemi had me doing some physical workouts, so I thought that may have screwed up my cycle. And I guess it had. And when it turned out to be nothing, we were both a little sad."

"Isn't that the worse thing..." Jane said. "Speaking of which, John wants to come to visit. I did tell him about Mack. And Mack about John. Will you and Steven hang with him after my boss suddenly calls me into work?"

"We will," Madeline said. "But in full disclosure, I'm on team Mack, now." She grinned."

"Hi chef," Danny walked in.

"No, that man buns gotta go," Jane teased, touching his hair. "But I do dig the beard."

"You said you liked the long hair." Danny accused Madeline.

"In 1920s Tibet, it was hot..." Madeline said. "Now... I reserve judgment." They all laughed.

"Hello?" a young man entered the kitchen after Danny waved him in. "Are you Madeline Jourdain?"

"I certainly am," Madeline said.

"Please sign here." The young man handed Madeline an envelope, thanked Danny for a tip, and left.

Inside the large envelope was a cover page and a letter. The cover page just said Williams and Davidson's law firm had been hired to keep this letter in a lockbox for 100 years. With instructions to deliver it to Madeline on this day. And upon delivery, the terms of their contract were finished.

"Danny," Madeline said. "Look at the handwriting."

"How. Why?" Danny asked. "Read it, love."

"Dearest Madeline," Madeline's whole body now physically shook. Jane wanted to comfort her, but Danny stopped Jane, sensing Madeline had to read it.

"Dearest Madeline," Madeline forced herself to continue. "A few minutes after you left, we were attacked by an avatar. I tell you this as a warning, not a cry for help. As your teacher, I ask that you meditate for three hours before planning future actions. I forbid you to travel back in time; you must accept the battles you must lose to win the war. Stay true to your heart, your teacher first, friend second, Kushemi."

"I can save them." Madeline's voice became very focused and cold. "You can come. Or stay. I hope this isn't a deal-breaker. I'd risk our marriage for very few things. But this is one. I have to try to save them. I have to try to save Kushemi."

"We should stop by the land and gear up," Danny said, not looking at Madeline directly. Knowing if he looked at her, he would just come completely unglued. Before Jane could say anything, they were gone.

*

Against his better judgment, Danny let Madeline blink back three times, each making him sicker, making Madeline angrier and less focused. Each time the monastery was still smoldering. Madeline was willing to risk a paradox, but Danny was not. He just hoped she would forgive him.

On their last blink, Danny tried to comfort her, but Madeline was inconsolable. Frustrated, Danny started digging individual graves with simple headstones, knowing all of the monk's names. In silence, Madeline began to help him.

The hardest body to bury was Kushemi's. His was the only body with the distinct claw marks. Danny could tell Kushemi fought the entire length of the battle with everything he had in him.

Danny was very confused because there was another body besides Kushemi's that he didn't recognize. He tried to show Madeline, but she was not speaking to him. So in Danny's grief, he dug an extra grave, trying to put it out of his mind. Madeline was in no mood to comfort him, and by then, Danny had lost the ability to think clear thoughts.

They stood in silence until the cold overtook their senses. Whenever they had blink together before, Madeline would intertwine their hands. This time she barely touched his shoulder.

"I think," Madeline said after they were safely back in Henry's office and Danny's head stopped spinning. "I'm going to the cabin to meditate. Can you tell Jane we are back?"

"Madeline," Danny said. "One more blink, and we would have messed up the timeline."

"You don't know that," Madeline said, trying not to cry.

"Please be home..." Danny said, but she had already blinked away. "... by midnight, my love..." his anger and sadness made the lights flicker.

Kushemi had told Madeline that when she got home, she needed to pick out a meditation spot. She promised she would, having no idea her heart would break doing this. Madeline remembers telling Kushemi she had the perfect spot. In the little pavilion at the end of the pier, where Danny and Abigail carved their names as children. Where Danny said, Henry would suddenly appear, back from the seas.

Madeline rolled to the end of the pier and took a deep cleansing breath; she was still full of rage. Still, it now felt targeted, no longer misdirected at everyone, mainly at her poor husband.

Danny had vowed to keep Madeline following the time lock rules, no matter the personal cost. Which was exactly what he did today. Madeline burst into tears, now realizing what it cost him and that her stubbornness made it harder.

Kushemi also tried to teach her how necessary it was to review battles through clear, unemotional, critical eyes. Madeline's heart grew heavy, but she knew what she had to do. She closed her eyes and walked through the smoldering monastery. Feeling every death... then watching Kushemi kill the avatar with his dying breath. That was the body that

Danny was trying to show her. Madeline wondered if the dragon was going after all the pillars?

She meditated three hours as Kushemi asked. Her sadness and anger were still very raw but she knew before she did anything else, she had a promise to keep.

Somehow Madeline had got home before Danny. She guessed he had thrown Jane out of the kitchen for the night and cooked dinner service to try to manage his anger, for a little while, which he had. By the time Danny got home, Madeline had lit candles and put on his favorite jazz record. And that night, they mourned Kushemi together.

*

"Wake up, Madds, sweetie," Danny said, trying to gently shake her. This was the 7th night in a row Madeline had had a night terror.

"I'm sorry." Madeline woke up just enough to feel Danny's arms around her. she backed into him, trying to touch as much of his warm body as she could... Danny kissed her shoulder. "I don't want to be a time lock. It has cost us too much already. Please don't be a deal-breaker."

"Madeline, no deal breakers. You know that." Danny whispered. "I need you to try this one thing with me, ok?" Madeline nodded. "Can you get dressed and blink us to your meditation spot?" she shook her head no and hid back under the covers.

"Wow, I can't believe you're going to be known as one of the most powerful witches of the 21st century....." Danny laughed. "Please, Madds."

"You'd think you would be nicer to me," Madeline growled, flipped the covers down, uncovering her head. She slowly got up, Dressed, and made a thermos of coffee. All the while still growling. Then she hugged Danny and blinked.

"I forgot how gorgeous sunrises are here," Danny said in the pavilion.

"That it is," Madeline said. "Why can't we just live out here? We could homeschool the kids; we could tell them we are the last people on earth. If we don't really push education, they'd never know." Danny smirked.

"I just want to give you the world," Danny said.

"You are my world," Madeline whispered. "Please don't make me risk it by being a time lock."

"Try this one thing for me, sleep on it a week, and if you feel that strongly, we can look at safer options, but I don't think there are any," Danny said. Madeline nodded.

Danny got down and sat crossed legged against a crossbar on the pier and ask Madeline to lean against his chest. He kissed the top of her head.

"I'm going to show you something Kushemi taught me. For you.." Danny whispered. "But you have to swear on Henry's love for you; you will never do this without my guidance,"

"You're scaring me, honey." Madeline sniffed. "I swear." Sensing how serious he sounded.

"I want you to go to the deepest meditation you can, go back to the monastery at the moment of Kushemi's death. Then take my hand," Danny said in a forceful tone. And he waited. It took Madeline more than an hour to control her breathing enough to reach this state; Danny waited patiently, stroking her hair. She finally took his hand.

"How do you think you could have saved him?" Danny asked.

"If we have stayed 15 minutes longer," Madeline said in a strong voice.

"Play out the scenario," Danny said, regretful for the pain this would cause her.

"No..." Madeline screamed in terror. She continued making scenarios—all ending with three of their deaths. Danny finally had to call her back to him, knowing she would have done scenarios all day long. Trying to find the one that would have saved Kushemi and the other monks.

Danny held her as she sobbed. Danny shook in fear because she did exactly what Kushemi told Danny she would do. Exactly why Kushemi told Danny not to do this unless Madeline had completely lost faith.

"What if I just blinked back to Houston and had not come to the French Quarters at all. Maybe if I never met you." Madeline sobbed, "I could do that if I knew you and Henry were safe." She closed her eyes and meditated on that scenario... But found herself watching the news with Jane... all of new Orleans was now burning... she screamed again, seeing Danny's burning body on top of Henry's.

"I don't understand; why are you doing this to me?" Madeline covered her face, now very angry.

"To show you not everything is your fault. I had to prove to you that the dragon was going to go through with his vendetta whether we are together or not. And by giving up... you are sealing our fate, but by fighting, we are creating a new one."

"Why didn't Kushemi show me how to do that? Why did he give you that power?" Madeline asked.

"He loved your heart," Danny said. "But with this, you can second guess everything. How many new scenarios did you just think of? To try to save Henry or Kushemi?" Madeline looked away. "Your gut and your passion are your strengths as a powerful witch, Kushemi told me this." Danny hesitated.

"But they could be your downfall as a time lock. He warned me that most time locks take their own lives because they cannot live with the guilt of taking the wrong path. Honestly, this scares me more than the dragon. Do you know you still apologize to Henry in your sleep?" now both in tears.

"Ok..." Madeline said, kissing away his tears. "Can you go for a run? I will meditate some more, then I'll decide what I can handle."

After the day of meditation, Danny kept his promise and didn't push Madeline for a week but watched her very closely. Danny and Mack trained every day, maybe even harder than before. Madeline joined them a few times but mostly kept to herself. Mack was shocked at how much Danny's fighting skills had improved.

*

"Hello." John knocked on Henry's door. Danny and Mack were doing paperwork in the couch area as Madeline looked up from her desk.

"Oh my god!" Madeline smile. John went to Madeline and hugged her. "I heard you were coming to town."

"We have a two-night gig at the dump. I was going to ask Steven If he wanted to sit in for a few sets."

"I'm sure he would love to." Madeline said. "how was your tour of dive bars?"

"The playing was good," John said. "Everything else sucked. Then I get home; you and Steven are no longer the "it" couple. Jane is…"

"A lot can change in a year. Look, Jane is really good now. Don't…" Madeline chose her words carefully.

"I know. I just…" John's voice trailed off, remembering they weren't alone. "How are you anyway? You seem sad. Jane said you were madly in love. Are you still?"

"I actually am." Madeline grinned. "I'm just stressed about the gallery. I have to pick an opening weekend soon, and I have a lot of personal stuff going on." Mack gave Danny a judgmental look.

"You guys have to come to the gig tonight, drink a little, dance a little," John said.

"Oh, how I would love to dance with him in a crowded bar," Madeline sighed. "But I think my boyfriend has to work all weekend."

"Even better, Jane, Steven, you, and me. For old times sake." John smile, "Last one standing wins."

"For so many reasons, that isn't going to happen." Madeline teased.

"Hey." Steven popped his head in. Steven and John shook hands and hugged. "Jane said you were getting in today."

"I'm sure we are bothering these restaurant owners; let us show you the gallery." Madeline rushed them out.

"You need to tell her today," Mack told Danny after the others left.

"How am I supposed to take another thing away from her?" Danny sighed.

"Hey," Charlie flew in. "Who's the gorgeous guy with Steven?" Mack threw a pen across the room.

"Oh shut up," Danny said. "My wife cannot introduce me. I can't even take her dancing,"

"On the bright side," Mack said. "When you tell her about Ida and the gallery, she probably won't wanna dance with you. Ever again." He grinned.

"What did you do, Daniel?" Charlie asked.

"I need to tell my already devastated wife..." Danny said. "That I would prefer she not open the gallery. Until the dragon is taken care of... and I'm considering teaching a class for Eugene so I can have full custodial rights of mom."

"When mommy and daddy get a divorce, I wanna live with mommy time lock," Mack said in a kid's voice.

"We will be nice to the rest, but we will always love your 1st wife the most." Charlie teased too. "Seriously, how is she? She's not eating in the kitchen, She's not reading the morning paper in the courtyard."

"I don't know, Charlie," Danny said. "She hasn't had a night terror in a few days, but she tosses and turns all night. I think she will be ok, but I'm scared that every battle will shatter and slowly change her golden heart. " Danny flopped back.

"Excuse me." Jane walked in, followed by John, Madeline, and Steven. "I wanted to introduce John to my boss, Danny, and this is Mack."

"What?" Madeline asked. John gave her a dirty look. "I get confused with her many men. Oh, that IS the Mack you were asking about." everyone laughed but Jane.

"And this is Charlie," Jane smiled.

"The Pixie," John said, "Jane can't stop talking about you." Charlie giggled.

"We are going for a quick lunch. Would you like to go with us, Mack?" Jane asked.

"That would be delightful," Mack said. And got up. Danny tried not to laugh, but Mack had never used the word delightful in his life.

"Come on, Madds," John said.

"I really do have to wait for deliveries today, but I would love to see you again before you head home." Madeline tried to hide her sadness that she could not even go to lunch.

"I'll leave tickets at row call for tonight if you change your mind," John said and left.

"Come sit by me, wife," Danny said as Madeline tried to leave to go back into hiding in the gallery, but Danny made such a cute face she couldn't resist. She floated to him and sat close.

"What's the deal with John?" Charlie asked.

"Let's see," Madeline said. "Actually, they were engaged. I have an ugly unworn maid of honor dress in the back of my closet. John landed a tour two weeks before the wedding. Jane said he could go if he promised not to drink or bop his groupies. He said he could not make that promise. And wanted to date other people for 18 months."

"Jane loved him so much that she thought maybe... he would change his mind," Madeline said. "The problem is, I'm friends with his guitarist, so I know the stuff he got into. It was definitely more than casually dating other people for a while. But... He finishes the tour this month; I guess John just wanted to see if anything was still standing."

"What do you think she will do?" Charlie asked.

"It's good she invited Mack to lunch," Madeline said.

"And I have to say, she's been upfront with Mack about John, so either way, they'll be on good terms," Danny said.

"How have you been, Charlie?" Madeline asked.

"A little worried about you, kiddo," Charlie admitted. Madeline wanted to say she was fine, but she didn't like to lie.

"I'm okay." Charlie continued. "Getting used to this magic being out is a little bizarre; I can't believe I can now fly down the street in pixie form... I get a lot of stares, but actually, less than my drag queen alter ego. The strangest thing is about half the people who see me as a pixie really recognize me and ask if I'm still singing in drag."

"You have such a following," Danny said. "Are you sure you're going to give up your singing career?"

"Yup. At least for now. It just makes me sad." Charlie said. "Are you already tired of me hanging out in the restaurant?"

"No," Danny said. "But please try to hang at the bar. You have to stop flying through the restaurant. I had two calls from the health department this week. Luckily it was Jordy. He asked if you were our new trained flying cockroach."

"Jordy is dead to me." Charlie teased, sort of. "I'm just bored. and I find myself wandering the streets at night looking for something that would give me purpose again."

"You are careful, Charlie?" Madeline sounded more scared than she meant to.

"I am. I promise. Plus, I'm trying to adjust to being my pixie self all the time. Which is actually harder than it sounds." Charlie said. "Drag queen had a purse and a makeup bag... Trying to carry a cell phone is a pain in the ass. They are big frigging things if you are 6 inches tall." Danny and Madeline laughed. Which did not help the situation.

"Then this sticky little human child tried to catch me and put me in a mason jar," Charlie said. "So I made her ponytail fall out."

"Charlie!" Danny howled. Madeline started giggling. Danny blinked away a tear, not realizing how much he missed her laughter.

"Hello, Danny." Eugene walked into the office. Madeline tried to quickly wiggle off of Danny's lap, but he hugged her to stay.

"Hi, dad." Danny sighed.

"My department is throwing a gala for magic returning. I wanted to invite you and Charlie and your... Madeline. And I would love to buy a dress for Ida." Eugene said.

"I'm pretty sure I'm washing my hair that night," Charlie said.

"You don't know when it is, Charlie,"

"Exactly,"

"Dad," Danny said, putting Madeline back in her chair. "I don't think Ida can go to a gala."

"My board members really want to meet a Guidry," Eugene said. "Then you and your lovely girlfriend of the month can be my guests."

"Absolutely not!" Danny said.

"It doesn't have to be Madeline," Eugene shrugged. "I can fix you up with one of my grad students. They are very... friendly."

"I can assure you, he will not be doing that," Madeline said, having reached her limit. "I'm the scary controlling girlfriend they warned you about. I stole this office from Henry, as you said. I wonder what else I could do with my feminine wilds." Both Charlie and Danny choked on laughter.

"Danny," Eugene tried to ignore Madeline. "Attend this gala or guest lecture one class, and I'll divorce Ida, giving up all rights to her."

"Do you hear yourself?" Danny turned emotional unexpectedly, even to himself. "I can't help dad, it is complicated and unfair, and any other father would be so upset that I feel like I have the weight of the world on my shoulders.

"Do you get that I have to mourn Ida every day when she goes to be with Abigail instead of staying with me? And Henry left, then Kushemi. People keep leaving me. Even when they don't leave physically, they all leave me emotionally." Danny scratched his forehead, worried he had said too much. Madeline knew he unintentionally meant her too. This snapped her out of her self-pity.

"Look, Eugene.." Madeline floated up to his eye level, Eugene took a step back, Charlie giggled. "Danny will teach one single class, and he gets custodial rights starting now. The class will be taught in my gallery; it will not be promoted or recorded. Mack and Charlie will see to this. Broken cameras and phones are on you. And I ask that you never set foot in Henry's office again. Because it is my home now."

"I'm taking Charlie shopping for the rest of the day, I have an idea on your phone problem." Madeline said. " and I think we should pick up Italian tonight, Mr. Boudreaux." She winked at her husband. "And Danny, I'm sorry, but I've fallen way behind on Henry's gallery; I hate to ask, but I think I need to put the opening on hold indefinitely." Madeline avoided eye contact. Danny knew that was a flat out lie but was so grateful.

"Unbelievable." Charlie laughed at Danny and followed Madeline out of the office.

"So, she makes this ridiculous offer for you," Eugene began a rant. "Tells you she can't seem to hang two pictures on opening Henry's gallery, goes shopping instead of working, and expects you to take her out tonight?"

"Yup," Danny said and let out a long deep breath. "She is kind of magnificent. Let me get the papers on Ida. They are in the safe in the kitchen." Danny ran, so relieved to be getting this done. He didn't think anything about leaving his dad in Madeline's office.

Chapter 16

"Dang, I did marry out of my league." Madeline giggled as Danny came out of the bathroom in a suit. He kissed her at their dining table and went to the kitchen. "Are you nervous, love?"

"Naw," Danny said, returning to Madeline with a bowl of cereal. "I just want to get it over with and enjoy the rest of the day off with Jane and Mack. Double date night, Baby. Except for blinking to the city of our choice, it's kinda nice and normal."

"Hey," Madeline said, answering her phone.

"Is Danny still there?" Mack asked.

"Yup." Madeline sighed, knowing her happy, peaceful morning had come to an end.

"It's a shit show over here," Mack said. "There's a line of people for five blocks. I'm calling Frank to help with crowd control."

"What can I do?" Madeline asked.

"Keep your husband calm," Mack said.

"Anything else? Anything? I'd rather do anything else… seriously." Madeline said. She could hear Mack smirked before he hung up…

"Wanna go back to bed?" Madeline asked. "I'll do that thing…"

"There's not a good way to answer that…" Danny said. "The nerd in me says that must be a trick question. But as your husband, I have noticed you pick your palm when you're hiding something."

"I do not," Madeline said, now separating her hands, slightly annoyed, slightly amused that he called her out. "Macky described it as a shit show. Line back to the church." Madeline waited for him to explode.

"You know…" Danny surprised her by smiling. "We knew this would probably happen. You got me legal custody of mom. You figured out how to do this class on sacred ground. By this afternoon, we will be in Napa. I can suck it up for a few hours.."

"Hi, mama," Ida knocked on the door, and Madeline let her in.

"Can I come to your class, Danny?" Ida asked. "You're so handsome when you speak in front of a crowd."

"Mama," Danny hesitated, but this was the first thing she had asked for in months. "It is going to be so crowded, I am even trying to convince Madeline to stay away." Which was true.

"Why don't," Madeline suggested, "You come over for a little while after it starts, and we can watch it from the gallery's office. If he has too many screaming fans, I'll make sure we get home safe and sound."

"Can we, Danny?" Ida asked.

"Yes, mama," how could he deny his two loves?

"Why don't you and Ida finish having breakfast. I'm going to check on Mr. Mack," Madeline said. Ida grinned; Danny was trying very hard to stay in his happiness bubble. Still, it was sure easier when it was just him and Madeline cuddled on the couch.

"This is bad." Madeline blinked to Mack, who was in the gallery with Jane. "I bought 15 minutes before he comes barging over." Madeline looked through the blinds. People were overflowing from the sidewalk into the streets.

"15 minutes was very optimistic on your part. Your husband just texted me, he can't leave the apartments because of the crowds; go get him." Jane said. Madeline sighed and blinked. A minute later, they were back.

"Guess you chose wrong, we could be home right now." Madeline tried to lighten the mood. Danny was amused but growing more upset by the minute.

"Frank!" Danny and Mack said as Jane let the cop in.

"You must be this idiot's lovely wife," Frank said. Madeline didn't mean to giggle, but her heart kinda melted; she had never been referred to as Danny's wife before, not in public.

"How bad is it?" Danny asked.

"I'm pretty sure you'll be nominated to lead the main parade for Mardi Gras. Way to go on keeping a low profile for a year," Frank said; Mack laughed, Danny pretended to bang his head against a column.

"We do have a list of the 100 students who are supposed to attend, would that help?" Madeline asked.

"Yup," Frank said. "You just went on and on about how gorgeous she was... I'm glad I assumed wrongly that she was just going to be a pretty face." Danny smiled. "Mack and I will check everyone at the door. And we will politely ask everyone else to go away. I'll have a backup on standby."

"Madds," Danny asked. She was staring at her phone. "What's wrong?"

"Oh, just a stupid ad." Madeline slightly fibbed. She would wait to tell Danny after the class and probably Napa. In the crowd with the other grad students, Steven sent her a picture of Eugene and Louis Delcroix in an intense conversation. This would absolutely push Danny into free fall, and the class was starting in a half an hour.

Frank and Mack finally got all the students seated. It only took 15 minutes longer, which was kind of amazing considering the size of the crowd. Steven made sure to sit in the back in case he was needed. After Danny pleaded with Madeline for a few minutes, they made a compromise, and she went into the office. She could still see and hear everything, but no one could see her. That made Danny feel a little better.

"Hello, I am Daniel Guidry Boudreaux, and welcome to your pop up lecture, Magic Returning." Danny smiled. The class clapped, Mack and Frank stood in the back. "As you know, in the last two years, magic has made a comeback. In this class, we will talk about what it means in our daily lives and..."

"We just want to ask you questions, Mr. Boudreaux." Someone screamed.

"But look, I made a very impressive PowerPoint presentation," Danny said. Everyone laughed. Madeline could imagine what a great presence he must-have in the courtroom. "Ok, but they must be intelligent questions on the topic." Everyone clapped and raised their hands.

At first, the questions were very general. And Danny was at the top of his game; the class hung on his every word. He explained about knacks and magic users and how everyone could learn the basics of magic.

Ida came by for a little while with her nurse, but she was foggy again by then. Danny looked so sad as the nurse walked her out. Madeline smiled lovingly at him as he tried to get back on track.

"What do you think about the New York Times Best Seller, "Magic for the Everyday Housewife?" Steven asked, hoping to help Danny. This opened a very robust discussion about how magic was indeed mainstreamed now. Which slowly turned into an intelligent debate on whether or not magic had the power to change the whole of society.

"But remember, magic itself is not good or bad; it's what the user's intentions are," Danny said. And for about 30 minutes, Danny felt good, and the class was engaging. Then it went downhill.

"I just have to ask, are you involved, Mr. Boudreaux?" a girl asked from the back.

"I would rather not say, all three of my girlfriends think I am." Danny tried to be cute for Madeline, but he realized how bad it sounded unless you knew him very well. Mack thought it was funny as hell.

"I'd like to be your 4th." She giggled, so did half of the girls in the room. Madeline was not one of them.

"Madds, he's not Steven," Jane whispered. She was now sitting in the office with her best friend . "You would have never married him if he was, you know that." Madeline exhaled slowly, nodded, and leaned against Jane.

"He teases that one day he might pop, turning into a clone of Henry. Now would be a good time," Madeline told Jane, they tried not to laugh, but they could not help it..

"Mr. Boudreaux, can you tell us more about your family?" a man asked in the second row. Steven quietly got up and went to talk to Mack. Both Madeline and Danny noticed immediately. "Wasn't your grandfather a storm giant and a powerful magic user. Haven't you taken his place as a mobster pulling the strings to our city? Why did you seal his hospital records?"

"Why am I being asked to leave by your security? Why does a lawyer even have security?" Mack was behind the guy now. Steven had whispered to him that the uninvited guest was not in the graduate program. "Why are you hiding a wife you married a month ago? Is it because she's in a wheelchair? How did Henry die? And who is Kushemi?"

"Hey." Charlie flew up to the stage, nudging Danny off. "I'm a pixie; I'll take 20 questions, so make them good." She grinned. Every hand in that room shot straight up.

Madeline found Danny in Henry's office a few minutes later. "That was indeed a shit show." Danny poured a drink and gave Madeline a sip. "You know I'm not…"

"I trust you completely," Madeline said. "But we do know Eugene planted that guy, so he must want something. I think he is in co-hoots with the slimy reporter…" Madeline showed him the picture of Eugene and Louis Delcroix that Steven took and kissed him before he yelled. "It's going to come out that I'm your wife. Would it be so bad if, for now, the world thought you married out of pity?"

"Madeline, I'm not doing this," Danny said, raising his voice. "You told me every guy you dated made you self-conscious about being in a chair. And I promised I never would. No."

"But… Don't be my adoring husband." Madeline said. "Look at it from a strategic point. Wouldn't I be less of a target if I was a poor helpless thing instead of a powerful witch who could send you to Siberia if you got a girl's digits?" Madeline grinned. Danny sighed, knowing she was right.

*

"Hey Frank," Steven said a few days after the class. "Can I fix you a drink? You caught me before closing." Steven was wiping down the bar.

"Naw, I'm still on the clock," Frank said. "Is Danny here?"

"I think he just left, but Mack is in the back," Steven said.

"Hey…" Frank said. Entering the kitchen where Jane and Mack were playfully flirting.

"This better be good, Franklin." Mack teased, but took one look at Frank and sighed.

"Where's Danny?" Frank asked.

"He went home," Mack said. Frank turned and left the kitchen; Mack knew he should follow.

"Shh, do not answer the door, Madeline, as your 500-pound husband, I forbid it." Danny laughed from the couch a few minutes later as Madeline threw a robe on.

"Love…" Madeline said in a tired voice, knowing this was bad, "It's Frank and Mack." Danny hopped to his feet as they came in.

"So. I'm sorry, Danny, but it's about Eugene, and I wanted you to hear it from me," Frank said. Danny exhaled and nodded. "There was a car bombing at the university. There were 10 witnesses. Nine of them had the exact same story. Eugene and a man were talking in your dad's car. After the man got out, the car exploded seconds later. There were nine witnesses, nine general descriptions of your everyday Joe."

"The 10th witness was a nun; her story was slightly different." Frank continued. "She said Eugene and a man were arguing. The nun heard screaming but could not make out what they were saying. When the guy got out, he leaned in the car, said something, and the car exploded while the unidentified man was still touching the car. He somehow walked away unharmed. I tried to get a description from the nun, but she kept saying he was so ugly, it scared her.

"I'm going to run the DNA with my guys tonight," Frank continued. "But… the car was parked in Eugene's spot, and all of the witnesses described him perfectly. I am sorry, Danny. I'll check on you tomorrow." Madeline thanked him and closed the door.

"I know I have a heart," Danny said after 10 minutes, Madeline sat by him on the couch as Mack sat on the island. In silence.

. "It leaps every time I see Madeline. It hurts every time I walk through the restaurant expecting to see Henry. It broke for Abigail and broke again for Kushemi... And I am upset that a person was murdered. But for the life of me, I do not have one fond memory of Eugene." Danny said. "I'm going for a quick run, just twice around the block. I swear."

*

"My wife should not have thrown such a beautiful memorial service for a man who was downright cruel to her." Danny said as he, Mack, Charlie, Jane, and Steven went back to Henry's office from the gallery where the simple, very short service was held.

"I'm just sad that Eugene spent his life looking for the most powerful witch, and he never knew. I really wanted to tell him." Mack smirked. "Where is Madds, anyway?"

"Hey, I'll be right back," Jane said after receiving a text. She winked at Mack, squeezed Danny's arm, and gave Steven a dirty look.

"Madds!" Jane screamed as she found Madeline on her couch, looking like she was dying.

"I just need ice. I googled it, I think I have appendicitis. It really hurts, but I think if I put ice on it, I'll feel better. Ask Steven to bring me ice, please. Please?"

"Can you sit up?" Jane asked.

"Yup," Madeline said. she tried and failed, moaning loudly. "Nope."

"You need to tell Danny, and he can take you to the emergency room," Jane said.

"He. Cannot." Madeline snapped. "I need the pain to stop for a minute so I can think. We have not talked about unscheduled emergency room visits while a dragon is trying to kill him yet. That wasn't on the what newlyweds should chat about list."

"Steven's bringing ice, ok?" Jane fibbed but tried to calm her down...

"Madeline Jourdain Guidry Boudreaux." Danny appeared two minutes later.

"That doesn't sound like Steven. That sounds like a very angry husband." Madeline said, having her eyes closed...

"Madds, you're burning up," Danny said, feeling her forehead... "Oh honey."

"I just wanted you to have this day to mourn your dad even if you didn't think you needed to. At first, I just thought I was having bad, bad cramps, please don't be mad." Madeline's voice radiated pain as she curled upon him.

"No, I'm not mad." Danny kissed her forehead, his lips burn from the touch.. he stared at Jane and Steven, Charlie, and Mack, who just came in; his eyes showed fear. "Madds, Mack is going to call ahead to the hospital, then we are going to blink, ok, my love?"

"We cannot," Madeline said. "It's not safe for you." She screamed with another wave of pain. This made Danny want to come unglued because he knew she had a ridiculously high pain threshold. "I'm not going unless you swear you are not coming with me. Swear it, Daniel."

"I swear," Danny had no choice.

"I will go with her," Mack said. he went to her and forced Danny to move. "Can you blink to the basement of the hospital where..." he took her hand? She weakly smiled at Danny and blinked.

Mack called about 20 minutes later. Madeline, of course, had blinked them perfectly to the hospital then immediately passed out. They rushed her to surgery.

Danny pounded the coffee table in anger and frustration. It broke in half. "She was trying so hard to convince me that if we had this block, Henry's land, and she could blink to her folks a few times a year, maybe it was enough... maybe we could just be. And after Kushemi died, I wanted to believe it. But reality says otherwise." Danny now pacing.

The average length of this surgery was an hour. Madeline's took four. The doctor facetimed Danny saying it would have killed a normal person 24 hours earlier. This was meant to make Danny feel better. It did not.

Danny explained that there were extenuating circumstances that Madeline needed to be home. Still, Danny could hire round the clock care and absolutely anything they needed. The doctor said she was not quite out of the woods yet and had to stay at least 48 hours more to finish at least one round of the strongest antibiotics they had. And that her infection was so bad, Madeline might require a second.

Danny told himself the moment she woke up, he would be able to breathe again.

"Hey, beautiful wife," Danny tried to smile the first time he facetime Madeline after she woke up. Mack held the phone up.

"Stop frowning Danny, I'm good," Madeline said sleepily. "I'm feeling better, I'm thinking of blinking Mack, and I home after I take a tiny nap."

"You cannot leave until the IV's are done," Danny said. "I'm being good by ignoring every fiber in my body to come to the hospital, so you need to be a good time lock and stay put." Madeline nodded and unintentionally fell asleep.

"Thanks, Macky," Danny said. "Jane is going to bring you food... I wish I could be there... I finally got the girl, Mack."

"And I finally got a sister," Mack said, looking at Madeline. "We'll be home in a few days. She'll call you when she wakes up."

Madeline had a few setbacks that night but was feeling better by the next day.

"Get a room." She sighed when she woke to find Mack and Jane on the couch next to her the next morning, and tried to laugh, but it hurt so much.

"Hello, I'm Dr. Waters; I'm here to change Madeline's bandage. Can you both wait outside?" The new doctor requested.

"Actually," Mack said. "She's my sister, and she gets nervous around new people. So I think I'll stay."

"I'm gonna go," Jane said, kissing Madeline's cheek. "I'll be back tonight." Mack walked Jane a few steps and put one foot out the door to hug her bye.

"MACK, run with Jane now!" Madeline screamed just before a loud explosion silenced her. The sound of broken glass radiated through the hospital, shaking its foundation. Mack grabbed Jane, carried her to the end of the hallway, and ran backed to Madeline's room, now in flames.

*

"Oh, you've gotta be kidding me! Unbelievable." Madeline slapped her hands in the muddy swamp water that was up to her ribs, now trying to sit still because of the tremendous amount of pain in her stomach. Madeline must have blinked as she was being attacked in the hospital. "Probably not good to sit in the mud with an opened wound. Oh damn... Mack." She covered her eyes, knowing she had to solve one problem at a time.

Just then, something very strange happened, a canoe floated right by her. Charlie flying beside it.

"Charlie, Charlie, Char..." Madeline screamed, waved, wondering why the pixie was not screaming back. Then Madeline passed out.

Madeline struggled to open her eyes again but knew she had to. "Charlie, where's Danny?" for a minute, she had forgotten where she was. She tried to sit up from the dirt floor, but her side still hurt. Charlie was in the other corner of the hut talking to the most adorable little girl Madeline had ever seen.

Madeline also noticed that Charlie and the young girl spoke a different language, one she had never heard before. Madeline closed her eyes and did an understanding language spell.

"Hi, I'm Kisseis, and this is my mommy, Chenoa Enemene." The little girl grinned and giggled. Kisseis must have been four. She had wild hair intertwined with leaves, skin radiating broken light as if looking through a magical waterfall. "What's your name?"

"My friends call me Madds," Madeline said.

"Here is a flower just for you. Do you have a daughter I can play with?" Kisseis asked.

"Not yet, but I hope she is as cute as you," Madeline said.

"Kisseis, go pick some berries for our guest but do not go too far; you've gotten in trouble already this month for exploring," Charlie said, kissing her cheek.

"Ok, mommy," Kisseis said and ran out of the hut. Madeline's heart melted.

"She's precious, Charlie," Madeline said.

"Why do you keep calling me Charlie? My name is Chenoa Enemene." Charlie thought about it. "But I do like the Charlie name; maybe I'll use it in my next life. Tell me, what are you, and are you in some kind of trouble?"

"I…" Madeline screamed in pain and disappeared. Madeline didn't remember blinking, but she felt an involuntary one pulling her away before she could finish talking to Charlie. The next thing Madeline knew, she was in the middle of Canal Street as cars were racing towards her. She took a quick breath, thought about Henry's office, and blinked again.

*

"What's the difference between a queen and a king?" Mack and Jane found Danny in the kitchen stirring a pot of soup and carrying on a very odd conversation. "We are temporarily in a tiny apartment, so I need to make sure it fits until we build a house. Umm, Do you have any for larger people?" Danny whispered as Mack and Jane circled. "I would like that delivered today… do you have sheets too? High thread count. Perfect. Someone will be there. Thanks."

"Hey," Jane said.

"Hey," Danny said. "Did Mack check out, ok?"

"I think he has a concussion, but the doctors say he's fine," Jane said.

"I said I am." Mack snapped.

"Danny." Jane hesitated. "Were you just buying a mattress?"

"Yes, I was," Danny said and went back to stirring. "Madeline has been meaning to buy one for months. Not to brag, but I keep breaking her futon." Danny grinned to himself. "She's gonna be hurting when she gets back in a few hours. She'll need bedrest and food. I'm cooking her favorite soup."

"Daniel." Mack whispered, "I don't think she is coming back."

"Yes, she is," Danny said. "She's coming back in about an hour. She has to. She promised we would be married for centuries, and we would have eight children, and they would be grossed out at how in love we are even when we are old and wrinkly. If you don't believe that, I need you to leave, Mack."

"Daniel," Mack said. "You weren't there."

"Thanks for reminding me," Danny said. "I hadn't thought about not being there for my wife in eight seconds." Danny slammed a pot down.

"That's not what I meant," Mack said. "I was going to go back in the room to try to get her out but she slammed the door shut. The last thing I saw was a fireball an inch from her nose."

"Ouch!" Madeline screamed, then cussed. It sounded like she was in her office. They all ran and found her awkwardly sprawled out on her back on Henry's desk. In a muddy hospital gown with a huge bloodstain holding a flower.

"No. no touching. Not even by cute husband... I hurt." Madeline said as they all ran to hug her. "I just need these questions answered before I pass out yet again... but I better wake up in my apartment with my husband holding me. If I wake up in a hospital, someone's going to get it! Are Mack and Jane, ok?"

"Yes, you saved us, Madds," Mack said.

"Janie, you good?" Madeline asked.

"Yes, sweetie. Now I am." Jane sniffed...

"Was my hubby mean to you, Macky? Cuz I'll kick his butt, not right now, but first thing after I feel better." Madeline said, still with her eyes closed. Mack laughed.

"Naw, he was a good boy." Mack stroked her hair, nodded to Danny, and left; Jane followed suit.

"hi…" Madeline whispered. "Can you carry me home? Blinking on drugs is hard." Danny smiled but was too emotional to speak.

*

"Wow," Charlie said, coming into the apartment. "So, lawyers are very bad with spatial awareness?"

"It's cute…" Madeline said. "He tried. Danny said he was so upset when he measured for a new bed, he wrote down the wrong measurements. Then he was too embarrassed to send the mattress back when he realized it took up ¾ of the apartment. He's going to have a guy take it to Henry's and store it until we build a house out there. Do not tease him. He's still fragile. This is the 1st time in 48 hours he has left my side. Thank god Jane had to cater that wedding, or he would not have left."

"How are you feeling?" Charlie asked.

"I'm about 55% better," Madeline said. "Getting swamp water in my incision did not help. That was a fun explanation with the nurse Danny hired… I think I'll be back to full strength by next week. Nurse says two. But Charlie, now that I have you alone, I do have something I need to tell you.."

"Go, kiddo," Charlie said.

"Chenoa Enemene. Chenoa Enemene. Chenoa Enemene.." Madeline groaned, reaching for something on her nightstand, then gave up and called it with magic. She gave the flower to Charlie.

"You know I'm not your personal beetle juice, right?" Charlie giggled a little, then got a sad look and exhaled slowly. "Thank you for this. I can't find these kinds of flowers anymore. Kisseis was obsessed with these and had to pick every single one she saw. They were all over my house and annoyed the crap out of me. Now I'd sell my soul to find one on my floor."

"I'm gonna save your daughter so I can have mine." Madeline said. "in a few weeks, I'm going to tell Danny I'm ready to visit another pillar. He has been trying so hard not to push. But when I was attacked in the hospital, I realized that even as high as I was from pain killers, what I learned from Kushemi and the guys probably saved my life as well as Mack and Jane's. I need to see this through."

"Good. I can't wait to have my two girls with me." Charlie grinned but was very reserved. Madeline forgot that Charlie had faced the dragon before and lost.

"So…" Madeline raised her eyebrows.

"So," Charlie looked confused.

"So, Chenoa Enemene." Madeline raised her eyebrows again.

"Yes Madeline Boudreaux?" Charlie tried to hide her amusement.

"I unlocked you. I broke the spell. You are supposed to tell me everything now."

"I forgot how sweet and innocent you are in your youth; it's sickening." Charlie laughed. "Come on, a powerful time lock witch would never share all her secrets with anyone. Especially her younger self, who just has enough power to screw up everything. You will be wised beyond your years, but Danny and I are going to have to drag you kicking and screaming most of the way."

"What can you tell me?" Madeline asked.

"The hut was the first time we ever met," Charlie said.

"That's it?" Madeline asked.

"You made me promise to tell you stuff on a need-to-know basis." Charlie shrugged.

"I feel like I should be able to break my own rule," Madeline said.

"Nope," Charlie said. "Older you, knows younger you too well."

"Charlie, I need to know, did we hurt Henry? Is that why we took his memories? It keeps me up at night."

"No," Charlie said. "I swear that he actually made us for his own peace of mind. I truly believe he would want you to know this. I miss him so much. He would be so proud of you and so happy that you married Danny."

"Look, it's Chenoa Enemene." Danny reappeared at the door, and crawled onto the bed. He literally had nowhere else to go in the apartment. "Did she tell you anything good?"

"Nope," Madeline said.

"You need to take your meds and go to sleep, little time lock," Danny said. Madeline wanted to argue, but she was still in considerable pain. "I'm gonna walk Charlie out. No blinking." Madeline was already halfway out after Danny covered her.

"That's one sick little girl," Charlie said as Danny closed the door to the apartment.

"Her high tolerance to pain is a double edge sword," Danny said. 'I'm going to have to watch that in training and in battle."

"Why can't Clara zap her?" Charlie asked.

"She can," Danny said. "She just cannot promise Madeline it won't affect anything else. Madeline has never had a regular cycle, so she freaked out and ended that conversation. I think she is a little better today, but I told her that I'm calling Clara if she passes out again. If it is between her and our imaginary children, it will be the simplest, quickest call I'll ever make. The upside is this really scares her because she knows I'm dead serious, so she has been doing everything the nurse has said."

"I know she will be ok," Charlie said.

"You do, don't you?" Danny said.

"I meant..." Charlie laughed. "But you do deserve a break. She will be back to her stubborn self in no time." She kissed his forehead. "Do you want to talk about Eugene?"

"Not even a little bit," Danny said. "I get paralyzing waves of grief for Henry and Kushemi. I dream of Abigail and Treeva . I keep waiting for a delayed reaction for losing my father, but he was an awful human being. How sad for him that I have no tears for my own flesh and blood."

"Speaking of flesh and blood…" Charlie said. "Have you told Madeline about your growth spurt?"

"Nope," Danny said. "Not until I figure out what it is and if I can control it. It only happened… once."

"And it happened when Madeline was attacked two miles away?" Charlie asked.

"Yup," Danny said.

"You knew this was a possibility. Henry told you." Charlie said.

"Honey," Madeline yelled. "Come and entertain me."

"Saved by the time lock." Danny grinned, leaving Charlie scratching her head.

*

"She's hot and smart and very funny... by the way, you still really look like crap," Steven said.

"Oh, how I do miss our pillow talks. Can we discuss your new conquests after I can wear jeans again?" Madeline said as they went into henry's office with a pizza, now noticing a gorgeous blonde in a skirt and jacket. She was sitting on the couch. Madeline suddenly felt underdressed in one of Danny's T-shirts and pajama bottoms.

"Elizabeth?" Steven smiled, very surprised. "I was just thinking about you."

"Steven?" Elizabeth asked. "What in the world are you doing here?"

"I work at the gallery and bartend at the restaurant. This is my best friend, Madeline." Steven said, grinning stupidly. "Elizabeth and I met last night at a college thing when Jane and I were hanging out. What are you doing here?"

"I'm meeting an old college friend, Daniel," Elizabeth said. "I'm going to try to convince him to teach a class. I heard he was really good at the pop-up event. We used to joke that we wanted to run a department at a college. I'm actually in town to accept a job at the university to run the magic graduate program this year. I love California, but this offer is just too good." Although Madeline found this fascinating, she could not help but wonder if she had combed her hair this morning or this week.

"I'm sorry, I assumed you were a student when I ran into you last night, " Steven admitted.

"The dean wanted me to try to blend in to see if it's going to be a good fit before I excepted the job." Elizabeth grinned. Steven grinned. Madeline tried to stay impartial.

"Coffee. Black. I remembered." Danny said, returning to the office. Letting out a long disappointed sigh when he saw Madeline but kissed her head anyways. "I'm so sorry that you can't meet my wife today, Lizzy; she's at home recovering from almost dying with not one but two infections with a busted appendix." Danny introduced Madeline to Elizabeth.

"Hi, "Elizabeth said as Madeline shook her hand. "I've heard wonderful things about you."

"Me too," Madeline said. "Danny was so happy to hear you were moving back. We'll let you guys catch up. I think Steven and I will go finish lunch at my desk. I hope to see you again soon, Elizabeth."

"Love…" Danny said. "I thought you were taking another few days off."

"I just wanted to have lunch with Steven. and to pick up some books, two hours tops. I promise." Madeline grinned, touching his hair, and rolled towards Henry's desk.

"See you soon, Elizabeth," Steven said then followed Madeline.

"So. Many. Questions…" Madeline hissed under her breath. Steven avoided eye contact. "Hey, have you been at my desk?" Madeline asked in a quiet voice.

"Nope," Steven said, getting a piece of pizza for her. "Why?"

"It's probably nothing," Madeline said, noticing two books had been pulled.

"You still wanna do this now? Steven asked.

"Speak in general terms..." Madeline said. "It really bugs me."

"More than being attacked?" Steven sighed.

"Kinda..." Madeline shrugged; Steven beat his head on the desk. Danny noticed and smirked. "How did I go back that far, and why wasn't I able to stay?"

"Did you ask Charlie what year that was??' Steven asked, almost whispering.

"She said, and I quote 'a long, long time ago'," Madeline said.

"I could not find any definite answers in my research, but 'I'm thinking maybe the drugs distorted your focus when you..." Steven suggested. "And you said there were very strict rules, so you probably got kicked back to Canal street when you were somewhere you were not supposed to be. Like time threw you up."

"Very nice imagery... " Madeline teased. "So no more drugs for me."

"Madds! That's not the solution." Steven sighed louder than he meant to.

"I wanted to say it was a pleasure meeting you, Madeline," Elizabeth said, coming towards Henry's desk. "I didn't realize how late it was; I need to head out. Danny said maybe in a few weeks he will cook for us."

"I'd loved that," Madeline said.

"I actually have to go back to campus too. Would you like a ride?" Steven asked.

"Thanks," Elizabeth said. Madeline gave Steven a disapproving eye roll as he left.

"Madeline..." Danny said. They were alone again.

"I've been very, very good, haven't I? Two whole weeks, in bed, actually sleeping. It's a little sad." Madeline grinned, whispered, and hugged him. He tried to hide his delight at her being able to float to him again. "And, if you don't frown at me, I won't frown back that you neglected to tell me that your 1st love is absolutely gorgeous."

"The nurse said you needed three weeks in bed. And Elizabeth is almost as gorgeous as my wife, but not quite, poor thing..." Danny said. "Hey, I meant everything that I told you about her. We were very good friends then we went on a few dates. I did really like her, but I knew I was waiting for someone else. I think I was in love with you even before we met.."

"Good answer, counselor," Madeline whispered, kissing him. "Wanna talk about the storm giant books on my desk?"

"I will, but not yet." He smiled sadly. "I used to tease Henry that I'd rather the sex talk than the storm giant talk... I..."

"Excuse me, are you Daniel Boudreaux?" a delivery guy asked Danny to sign for a package.

"If they are 24 long-stemmed roses from a groupie, you are in so much trouble." Madeline laughed.

"Dear Danny, start training, my love, Madeline," Danny said. In the box were two Japanese swords. The most magnificent handcrafted weapons Danny had ever seen.

"It's my handwriting," Madeline said. "What did future me do? Or was it past me? Please tell me this makes more sense when you're not on pain pills."

"Nope," Danny said. "Wow, these were custom made for me. The grip fits my hands like a glove. Mack is going to die."

"How old are you guys?" Madeline giggled.

"13." Danny could not stop staring at the swords.

"Danny, you know there's a pillar in ancient Japan," Madeline said. "Maybe future me is telling us we have to go study now."

"Then future you would know what a huge fight present us is about to have," Danny said. "I truly believe, if we blinked now, especially that far back, it will kill you; when your 110% back in the game, we can talk about it. Not before."

"But... I need to save the world today, so you can teach and lawyer and stuff." Madeline shrugged, completely confused, and was starting to ache again.

"Let's get you back in bed," Danny said, seeing the pain in her face. "But I am taking my swords with me..."

"And my books..." Madeline pleaded. He reluctantly agreed.

*

"Look at you..." Jane gushed. "In jeans and a blouse... combed hair..." Madeline entered the kitchen feeling completely healthy for the first time in a month. "Want some gossip?"

"Yes, please." Madeline grinned as she grabbed some fruit out of the refrigerator...

"Steven hasn't slept at home in three days," Jane said. "I think he really likes her. He wants our... approval."

"Nope," Madeline said.

"I kinda love her." Jane shrugged.

"See, I love her too." Madeline laughed. "We need another girlfriend here more than he needs to..."

"Agreed," Jane said.

"Speaking of doomed relationships, I think Danny is done with me."

"I don't believe this at all, but you haven't had a meltdown in months, so go, entertain me," Jane said.

"I don't think he has ever slept in our new bed," Madeline said. "Like at all. Every time I wake up, he's reading or watching tv or just sitting there on his side of the bed, looking like he is waiting for something to happen.

And I was cleared last week to you know... and he doesn't even wanna cuddled. It feels like we are off and I... have done this before... and...What if guys get tired of me after a certain point."

"Madds," Jane said. "You are in denial. You have no idea how close you came to dying, and I'm not even talking about the avatar. Although we do need to get drunk and talk about the fire breathing dragon at some point. Do you remember throwing up for two days straight?"

"No," Madeline said.

"Do you remember having a fever so high that you carried on a whole conversation with Kushemi?" Jane asked.

"No," Madeline said.

"Do you know you popped your stitches four times in seven days?"

"No," Madeline whispered.

"Danny does. He is probably afraid to touch you, seriously." Jane said. "I'm actually currently praying you don't bleed out or throw up in my kitchen because I just cleaned the floors. Madds..."

"Ok," Madeline said.

"Hey." Danny walked in.

"Your dumb wife would like to know why you are not ravishing her body. She has been cleared for all of two minutes. She is kinda hideous, but you told me you could get past that. Don't you love her anymore?" Jane mocked. Danny laughed. Madeline threw her head on the table in horror.

"I..." Danny said after kissing Madeline's neck, despite her playing hard to get. "I broke our scale." He announced.

"I have no idea what that has to do with reassuring me, but the scale probably just needs new batteries," Madeline said.

"No." Danny sighed. "I meant in a more literal sense like I stepped on it, and the scale broke into four pieces..." Madeline floated into his lap. "I have broken three chairs, two doorknobs, and I had to restock the bar twice yesterday because I kept breaking bottles. All within a week, So yes,

I, in fact, do not want to touch you or cuddle with you, and I haven't slept in our bed in a month. But it's not because you are hideous Madeline. It's because I am. My body is changing into a storm giant, and I'm pretty sure I could snap you in half if I rolled over you while I was sleeping." Danny stormed out of the kitchen. Madeline waited a few seconds then followed.

"hi." She entered Henry's office and locked the door behind her. Danny was sitting on the couch, Madeline floated to him. "We are going to make out, then we are going to have a little fight, then we are going to make out some more after you admit how wrong you were for hiding something this big from me... then we'll figure this out. Got it, Daniel Boudreaux?"

"Damn, I even missed bossy you." Danny grinned and held her for a while.

Chapter 17

"Madds?" Danny whispered, sitting up from the couch to a dark office, only seeing a silhouette of her at Henry's desk. He wrapped himself in the blanket that was covering him and went to sit by Madeline. "How long have I been out?"

"Four hours," Madeline said, "I actually thought you might make it to five but... nope." Madeline grinned.

"Why am I wrapped in Henry's hideous quilt?" Danny asked, now looking at his attire. "Wasn't it at his cabin? Wife, did you blink? You said you would wait a few more days before blinking,"

"Do you wanna fight, or do you want to know why that blanket will allow you to sleep by me every night?" She asked. Madeline did a little research and figured out that storm giants who marry humans have enchanted items around the house to keep them in human form.

"...Thank you," Danny whispered after realizing what Madeline had done. "It would have killed me if I couldn't fall asleep in your arms every night. I think I can figure everything else out. But the thought of not sharing a bed hurt. What are you looking at now, my love?"

"The five pillars," Madeline said. "I think we've been looking at it wrong. Kisseis said I needed to visit them. And you were coming along for moral support, But I think it's so much more than that. Kushemi said we were stronger together. That's why you grew the instant I was attacked at the hospital. You knew."

"That makes sense," Danny said.

"As awful as it was losing Kushemi," Madeline hesitated. "I feel like we both learned so much. We completed all of his tasks, he answered all of our questions. And we were able to finish his tests. Then Kushemi blessed us."

"I agree," Danny said.

"I don't think ancient Japan is our next pillar. I think we as a couple need to finish something first." Madeline said. "You were right. I am not strong enough as a time lock to blink to the pillar of weapons yet. I am pretty sure visiting Charlie that far back made me so much sicker."

"I have so many unanswered questions, and you need to learn how to live as a storm giant. Maybe before anything else." Madeline continued. "Now, It's so much more than killing the dragon; it's about how we live our lives. I have basic questions like, should I even see a human doctor if the drugs make me that vulnerable? I think only a pillar could answer this."

"What are you saying, Madds?" Danny asked.

"I don't think we are done with the first pillar," Madeline whispered.

"Honestly, I don't know if I can..." Danny sighed. "I won't want to leave him again."

"Will you think about it. I would love nothing more than if you told me I was wrong."

-

*

"Speech, speech." The small crowd in the restaurant demanded.

"Um..." Danny started.

"You've been on sabbatical too long if that's all you've got, counselor." Some guy yelled from the back. The 20ish people laughed.

"Thank you all for coming to my surprise birthday dinner," Danny said. "I was not expecting this at all." He stared at Madeline, who was sitting on the bar. "I've had a really rough year, but I am definitely thankful for my bride, Madeline, and our new head chef, Jane. Henry would have loved the energy and sheer joy they have brought to the restaurant and to me. Now, Eat, drink, and dance, please!"

"He looks happy," Jane said, standing behind Madeline. "Has he decided?"

"No," Madeline said. "I'm thinking maybe I can do this one by myself, it's too much for him. I can go for a month and learn everything and teach him when I get back."

"Madds…" Jane said.

"Wife," Danny surprised and hugged her, kissing Jane's cheek. "Thank you, guys. This really means a lot. Now please, come meet everyone." Danny put Madeline back into her wheelchair and pushed her into the crowd.

The dinner was perfect. Everyone enjoyed themselves, even though Madeline kept sneaking back to the bar. And Danny kept finding her. she really did hate crowds, but it was nice that Danny kept wanting her by his side.

"You really just want to be perched on the bar and gossip about my friends with Jane, don't you?" Danny finally asked.

"I really do, but we are gossiping about you and Mack too if that helps," Madeline said. Danny laughed as she waved him away.

"Hello, ladies," Elizabeth said. "Mack. Steven." The guys were behind the bar too.

"Thanks for coming." Madeline hugged her.

"I honestly have never seen Danny this happy; cheers to his better half," Elizabeth said.

"Would you like to dance, Elizabeth?" Steven asked. She nodded.

"We should tell him he has our blessings," Jane said.

"But he's so much nicer when he's all squirmy and filled with doubt." Madeline laughed. "What if he doesn't cheat on her?" She whispered.

"It means… he learned his lesson," Jane said.

"They do make an annoyingly attractive couple." Madeline grinned.

"I wish you would see yourself as we do," Jane said.

"Although, I indeed would kill for her figure," Madeline admitted. "I'm jealous of her career. You're head chef, Steven is getting a Master's. And I'm stuck. I came to open a gallery and wanted to get my Ph.D. by 30. And let's face it, even if we... eliminate our big obstacle, I know him. Danny will go back to working 70 hours as a lawyer, and I will end up running the restaurant and raising the kids..."

"This doesn't sound bad at all, but I really would love a few years with just him, while he still thinks I'm cute. No dragon. No avatar. Enjoying our lives. But until we finish this pillar bs, I'm stuck. But I can't say, let's go visit your dead grandfather, who you love more than anything. Who does that?"

"Madeline!" Jane said.

"He's behind me, isn't he?" Madeline hung her head. "I'm sorry, my love. Steven made me a drink. It probably had a lot more alcohol than I requested because he thinks I'm funnier when I'm drunk. I say stuff I shouldn't. and he forgot tonight I'm trying to be a very good lawyer's wife."

"Dance with me." Danny smiled.

"No. it's embarrassing in front of your work friends." Madeline said.

"Please," Danny begged and picked her up. He carried her to the middle of the room. Charlie began to sing, and everyone danced. "Let's have a really fun night and enjoy our friends."

"And tomorrow we'll go... I'm sorry I've been stalling. It will be hard, but I forget your whole life is on hold, too. I know that not being able to move forward on the gallery is killing you. And I will never work more than 60 hours a week. But I have a feeling you will need to promise me that too." Danny stroked her hair as they kissed.

*

"Perfect landing, Madds," Danny whispered. "But a little worse going through. Madeline?" Danny was now laying flat on his back on the pier on Henry's land. "Say something, honey."

"New rule, no time traveling for three months after major surgery and/or the day after drinking just a little too much." Madeline moaned, "Stop smirking; I can feel you smirking, Daniel Boudreaux."

"Are you bleeding?" Danny asked, now opening one eye, inching towards her.

"Naw stitches actually held up. I'm already feeling better." Madeline sat up slowly and called her wheelchair to appear. She took a deep breath staring at the ocean as Danny stood up. He walked towards her, smiling. "How are you?"

"I'm ok," Danny whispered. "Can we sit out here for a little while?" Madeline nodded, rubbing his back.

"When we get home, I think we should start looking at floor plans for the house; why would we not want to look at this view every morning?" Madeline said, trying to distract him. He was grateful, took one more deep breath, and they began walking hand in hand towards Henry's cabin.

"Hello," Madeline knocked on the door after watching Danny try to make a fist for what seemed like a lifetime.

"Why, hello." An old lady answered the door; she looked like a much older Ida. Danny gulped. "I'm Millie, you must be Charlie's friend, Madeline. Please, Please, come in." Madeline had to pull Danny into the cabin he had been in a million times. "This is my very handsome husband, Henry."

"Hello," Henry turned from the stove. This time Madeline gulped too. "Charlie said you might be stopping by because you wanted to learn magic. Unfortunately, this is a bad time for me."

"Actually, it's the perfect time for him," Millie said. "He has nothing to do for the next two years than to watch me die."

"Millie Louise Guidry!" Henry scolded.

"That's better," Millie said. "He hasn't raised his voice since the doctors diagnosed me. Anyways, Charlie said you've come a long way. I fixed you up a guest room. I'm sorry dear, does your husband talk?"

"We've just had a very long trip," Madeline said.

"Why don't you go rest until dinner time, and my Henry will be back to his warm self." Millie said. "I think Charlie is visiting tonight."

"Thank you so much," Madeline said.

"I'll let you name all our children and pick out the design of the house if you send me home right now!" Danny whispered a few minutes later. "I thought I could do this, but I don't think I can, Madds. I didn't know Millie was sick. I never asked Henry how the love of his life died. How is that possible? Maybe I'm exactly like my father."

"Love," Madeline said. "You're spiraling. We can stay tonight, and if you feel that strongly, I'll send you home tomorrow, and maybe I can blink to you at night. I just feel like Henry isn't done teaching me."

"Can't you just tell them I'm a mute?" Danny said, half kidding.

"Oh, please, can I?" Madeline giggled. "Charlie would love that too."

*

"That was the best meal I have ever had." Madeline gushed. "And my best friend and my husband are chefs." Henry grinned softly. Millie struggled to get up. "Please let me clear the table. And wash the dishes. It's the only thing I'm allowed to do in the kitchen." Millie nodded in gratitude.

"Are you a chef, Danny?" Millie asked.

"I think of myself as a cook; I can follow instructions," Danny said quietly, still very uncomfortable.

"So Madeline," Henry said. "Why would you like to learn magic?" He leaned back in his chair, looking at her. Millie grinned proudly, knowing her husband needed a project.

"I..." Madeline struggled for words. "It was not until this year that I discovered that I may have... gifts."

"Are your folks' humans?" Henry asked.

"I was adopted," Madeline said. Danny played with her hair. "10 doctors say I am. Although none have been able to tell me why I'm paralyzed."

"The things she can already do are amazing," Danny spoke, still very shyly. "With training, she will be a force of nature."

"Do you also want to learn magic?" Henry asked Danny.

"I do," Danny said.

"Are your folks' humans?" Henry asked.

"My father was..." Danny said. "He recently died."

"I'm sorry," Millie said.

"We were not close," Danny said. "He was not the man that raised me..." he coughed. Madeline silently encouraged him to continue. "My mom comes from a long line of magical users."

"Hello," Charlie opened the door, flew in. and greeted everyone with a kiss. "Henry," he smiled. "Madeline, how have you been?"

"She'll show you her scar later," Danny said when Charlie kissed him.

"Millie, how are you, my love?" Charlie asked.

"I have had a few good days," Millie said. "And you were right. Madeline is delightful. I love that the cabin is full again and that Henry has agreed to teach them." Millie winked at Henry; he growled a little.

"Have you found Edith?" Henry asked.

"No." Charlie sighed.

"Ungrateful, stubborn child," Henry growled in anger.

"I wonder why she's so stubborn?" Millie laughed. "Charlie, will you help me to bed? I think I did too much today. And will you say Rosary with me,"

"I will." Charlie followed her into the bedroom.

"My wife wants me to teach you, so I will. We start tomorrow." Henry said and disappeared into his room. Danny blinked away a stream of tears as Madeline finished clearing the table.

*

"Before we start, I need to get some supplies; why don't you both come with me?" Henry said the next morning after they had breakfast.

"Are you coming, Millie?" Madeline asked.

"No, I'm a little tired, but will you pick up some material and two spools of thread for me? Henry hates buying sewing stuff." Millie said. Madeline nodded and made a list of what she needed.

"Maybe I should stay with Millie." Danny offered out of the blue. It took a minute for Madeline to realize why. She felt bad for not thinking of it too.

"No, son." Millie winked at him. "It's a very smooth ride; you'll have a great day." Danny could not explain it, but he trusted her completely. For a second, Danny swore Millie knew exactly who he was, and he felt safe with her. Danny breathed a huge sigh of relief after he got in the Model T without his weight crushing the tires.

"The next time Millie is feeling up to it, we'll have to take you to our restaurant in the quarters," Henry said as they drove into town.

"May I ask what Millie is suffering from?" Madeline slowly inquired.

"Her muscles are getting weaker, causing her pain. Some days it's excruciating. The nights are even worse." Henry said. "I want to take her to a specialist in New York. But she says herbs and prayers are helping. Millie promises she will go if our daughter Edith goes with us. But Edith left with a boy to go to California last year. She doesn't even know her mama is sick."

"I'm sorry, Henry," Madeline said. Danny stared out the window in silence. They drove for about 30 minutes. Madeline had no idea until this moment how much she had missed Henry, how much she wanted to tell him, and how many questions she hoped he would have answers for. This must have been a tenth of what Danny was feeling. Madeline scooted closer to her husband, putting her head on his shoulders...

"I hate leaving Millie too long. Madeline can you go buy the sewing stuff, Danny can go buy eggs, and I'll go buy vegetables?" Henry asked them when they reached the open-aired market, they both nodded.

Madeline was too lost in thought to pay attention to where she was going. The only material the lady had that met Millie's criteria was the exact pattern to Danny's enchanted quilt. This gave Madeline chills, but she hurried back to meet Henry and Danny.

"Hello, little girl." Two big fellows suddenly appeared in front of her, blocking Madeline's path to the truck.

"Can you move, please?" Madeline asked, hoping for the best, preparing a shock spell if they touched her.

"It's rare to see a Chinese cripple around these parts." One guy said.

"I will ask again because my husband says I'm meaner than I look. I really don't want any trouble," Madeline said, more annoyed than anything.

"I hear the chinks are mighty sweet." The other guy said. Then, Madeline heard Danny running towards her, Henry a half of step behind.

"Let's touch her breast..." One of the guys reached towards her. Madeline lifted her right hand to cast a painful but not deadly shock spell. Before she could, Danny jumped in front of her wheelchair, growing to ten feet. This caused a huge commotion, people began staring.

"Monster, monster, freak, kill him!" The crowd gathered, yelling and pointing at Danny. Henry cast a confusion spell, breaking up the crowd even before Danny returned to normal size.

"Henry, do you trust me?" Madeline quickly asked, Henry nodded. Madeline took him by the hand and Danny by the neck and blinked.

She blinked perfectly to the porch where Millie was knitting on the swing. Upon their unexpected return, Madeline looked pissed, Danny looked embarrassed, and Henry looked absolutely delighted.

"I'm sincerely sorry, Henry." Madeline began. "I should have told you I was a time lock last night. It's ridiculously complicated. I hope you will still consider training me."

"Yup," Henry said. "And now I won't half-ass it just to please my wife, which I was planning to do," Henry smirked. "But I would like to know exactly who your husband is. Storm giants aren't common around these parts." Henry's tone changed to serious.

"Henry Guidry, open your eyes, look at the boy!" Millie said. "He's the spitting image of you 150 years ago." Millie turned to Danny. "I was trying to figure it out since you arrived last night. I knew you were much too old to be Edith's son, but since your wife is a time lock... maybe great-grandson?"

"Great-grandson, mam," Danny whispered.

"Oh Henry," Millie said. "My Edith is alive! That's something." Millie thought for a second, motioned Henry to help her back into the house, hugging Danny on the way, winking at Madeline.

"So," Danny said after Henry closed the door behind him. "How mad are you?"

"I..." Madeline said, her anger had lessened. "They were punks. You know I could have taken care of them with my pinky, especially since training with Kushemi."

"That was before you almost died, twice," Danny said. "Both times of which I was stuck at the restaurant. Whether you like it or not, I will always punch any guy who is inappropriate with you. But because their backs were turned..."

"You thought..." Madeline said. "They were avatars." She floated up to him and touched his cheek. "I'm sorry, I wasn't thinking."

*

"Why do you look so upset, Henry?" Millie asked as Henry sat her in their bed and laid down, staring at the ceiling.

"Because…" Henry said. "I've been watching Madeline. She is ridiculously talented for her age and says she only has been training for less than a year. Did you notice how effortlessly she moves in her wheelchair? That is a sign of a powerful witch. At the market, Danny came completely unglued when two punks approached her. it felt like a strange and unwarranted overreaction."

"The Guidry men are indeed protective and jealous," Millie said. "How many bar fights did you get into as a madly in love youth, my dear Henry?" she smirked; Henry sighed, unable to argue.

"This was different. Danny's eyes showed fear, not anger, not jealousy." Henry said. "They both seem highly intelligent and responsible. They probably have hectic, good lives. I don't sense an ounce of malice in her, but Danny seems very uncomfortable around me. So if they both came here, they must be preparing for something that scares them to their cores."

"Then you, sir, better teach them." Millie winched from a sudden pain.

"What if," Henry hesitated. "If I promise to train them both if and only if you would see the doctor in New York? We know Edith is alive…"

"Then you wouldn't be the man I waited seven years to marry," Millie said.

"God damnit, Millie," Henry raised his voice.

"Edith is going to come home," Millie said. "And she's going to need us, Maybe for the first time in my wild child's life. I'm going to be here. I'm going to welcome her with open arms. And so are you."

*

"I'm sorry if we woke you," Henry said as he came out of the house, finding Madeline on the porch swing in the moonlight a few weeks later.

"Actually, Danny woke me up before he went for a run on the beach," Madeline said. "Millie's having a rough night, huh?"

"I am one of the most powerful wizards in the world, and I can't cure her. It doesn't seem fair." Henry said, swirling the ice in his glass. "Don't tell her I'm drinking. She thinks it makes me mean and cynical."

"Does it?" Madeline asked.

"No, I truly believe…" Henry said. "She has a spell on me… and I'm less mean and less cynical when I'm around her."

"Danny told me the same thing very recently," Madeline smiled. "You've never admitted you were a wizard before."

"Let's play a game," Henry said. "I get to ask you two questions, and you get to ask me two."

"Oh, I don't know." Madeline hesitated.

"Please," Henry said. "I can't help my wife, but maybe I can help you. I have decided that when you and Danny leave, I'm going to have Charlie erase your time here from my memory. So nothing I do will affect our timelines, ok?"

"Ok," Madeline sighed, very conflicted. "Two questions."

"Why is Danny so warm with Millie when he can't even look at me, and why is it that when you look at me, you always look like you're about to cry?" Henry said. "Like, the exact look you are giving me right now."

"That's your two questions, Mr. Wizard?" Madeline giggled.

"That's one question, with two parts," Henry argued.

"Please don't ask me to speak for Danny," Madeline said. "But I do feel sadness and guilt when I look in your eyes. You are my mentor in the future, and I think I did something that brought harm to you. Can you just… remember to not help me when I show up at your door?"

"Does Danny believed you brought harm to me?" Henry asked.

"No, but…" Madeline said.

"The second question," Henry said. "What are you preparing to fight? You and Danny constantly make time for Millie, but if you aren't with her, you're training, practicing, or thinking about a spell. Danny is the same, maybe even more focused, if that's possible. You're young; you're obviously madly in love. What could overshadow that?" they sat in silence for a long time.

"Damnit," Henry suddenly grew a foot in anger. "How could... I have been so focused on Millie. And she was so happy when you appeared at our door. I was not thinking clearly... its not a family reunion. It's the dragon, isn't it?" Madeline looked down.

"It's worse," Madeline whispered.

"One," Henry said. "I don't want to know, but you do have to believe this, If I died saving Danny or you, it was a mighty fine death. And I know I'd do it 100 times over. " Henry opened his arms, Madeline floated to him and began to sob uncontrollably. "Let it out, let me replace sadness with strength. Two, now that I know what we are fighting, I can better train you."

"My turn," Madeline said after pulling herself together. "Can I do anything for Millie?"

"If you can..." Henry said. "Stay until my daughter comes home or... You and Danny bring her so much joy; she deserves so much peace and love, especially now. And I'm so happy you are here. Watching Danny train is a gift."

"That's good," Madeline said. "I'm pretty sure Danny sucked most of your joy away during his teenage/early twenties years."

"You cannot tell me more about him?" Henry asked.

"I could," Madeline said. "But you need to try to break through to him. He's kinda worth it."

"I'm just not good with children. Millie says Edith is my clone; that's why everything was a fight. I counted on the fact that Edith loved her mom more than she hated me." Henry said. "It hurt less when I thought we had all the time in the world."

"Is Edith your only child?" Madeline asked.

"Yup," Henry said. "Millie had a rough pregnancy. And almost died during childbirth. Storm giants make big babies. She would have risked everything to give me a houseful of kids. I was not willing to take that risk. I made myself a potion... never told her... and we never got pregnant again. Wow, that's the first time I admitted it out loud. Maybe I am a mean drunk; even now, I don't feel an ounce of guilt. My decision gave me decades more with her.

"Can you not tell my husband?" Madeline said. "We want eight kids. And it took him two months to get over a minor health scare with me."

"I'm sure he would argue your definition of minor. But since our conversations are limited to the weather right now, it probably won't come up." Henry said. "But I suspect Danny would feel exactly like I do."

Madeline sniffed. "Second question, can I send people away from danger? Like if we are in a battle and someone is in the line of fire, can I have a spell ready to blink them out, even if it's without me?"

"No, Madeline, for hundreds of reasons." Henry sighed, very worried.

"Hi," Danny ran up the stairs and hugged Madeline. "What did I missed?"

"Nothing." Madeline faked a smile. Henry looked down. "Let's go back to bed, my love. Good night, Henry." Madeline kissed his cheek.

"I meant to tell you at dinner, you both have mastered basic magic. Take a day off tomorrow, then we start offensive and defensive spells," Henry said. "And Madeline, we are not through with your last question by any stretch of the imagination..."

As promised, Henry did give Danny and Madeline the next day off. But when they resumed training, it was very structured. Henry seemed more serious; he pushed harder and expected more from the two.

Henry had a daily schedule now, whereas the first month was a little more whimsical. A typical day was getting up at dawn with two hours of exercise; Henry and Danny loved this. Madeline did not. They finally gave in and let her do an hour of warm-ups with them, then an hour of meditation by herself. Millie tried to join her in meditation about twice a week.

Although he constantly growled at them for giggling, Henry secretly loved watching Millie and Madeline laughing uncontrollably on the pier when they were supposed to be serious and centered.

Spell theory and construction was a little dry for Madeline, which of course, meant Danny excelled in it. He learned much quicker than Madeline, but she had a natural gift. After Madeline learned something once, she could recall it in her sleep, without doubt or hesitation.

Following lunch, Madeline always spent an hour with Millie as Danny practiced controlling his storm giant side. This was very frustrating for him. Danny had never struggled with learning anything in his life.

"Can I suggest something?" Henry asked.

"Sure," Danny said.

"Maybe…" Henry said. "You don't want to be a storm giant…"

"Of course I don't; I have told you this a million times since I was 15, granddad." Danny blurted out, immediately feeling regretful. It was the first time Danny had called him granddad. They both exhaled, now sitting side by side on the beach. "When I was 15, I, we, lost someone we both completely loved and adored. And I begged you to save her, and you couldn't."

"I don't think I blamed you." Danny continued. "Maybe I did. I don't know. I did blame magic. And that drove a wedge between us. But for the record, you always showed up. When my mom couldn't, when my father wouldn't, you came to every game, every ceremony. I didn't know there was a reason you were trying so hard to train me. I don't even think you knew on a conscious level. If I started training at 15… If I just knew…"

"Then…" Henry sighed; he had so many questions that would remain unanswered. It was touching how far Madeline and Danny would protect Henry from an obviously tragic series of events. Henry would try not to make it harder. "I will start with the basics, and soon you can live in the clouds and swim with the fishes."

"I just want to kill the dragon and live happily ever after with the girl," Danny whispered. Henry stood up and offered a hand to him. Danny smiled and took it.

The rest of the afternoons, and sometimes late into the evenings, were spent practicing offensive and defensive spells. For Madeline, Henry really stressed the importance of pinpointing where she could inflict the most damage. How she needed to summon energy around her instead of using all of her inner power. This would allow her to fight longer without exhausting herself.

Between training with Kushemi and Mack, Henry was already impressed with Danny's fighting skills. So they focused on defensive spells, force fields, and helping Madeline summon energy that they both would need.

"Come to bed, Henry," Millie whispered, catching Henry staring at the moon through their bedroom window late one night. "I'm feeling pretty good. Come be with me, husband."

"I," Henry turned, startling Millie. Millie could count the number of times her husband had cried on the one hand. "They are good, very good. They balance each other's weaknesses perfectly. But I don't think it's enough. I think they will both die trying to save each other. "

"Then try harder," Millie said as he curled up beside her. Millie could not recall the last time her storm giant looked so small.

By the 5th month, Millie's health had significantly declined. Even though Henry had made her a wheelchair, she was uncomfortable in any position other than lying down. They brought a bed into the living room so Millie could listen to Danny and Madeline study at the table and watch them train from the window.

Henry had run out of book learning, so they practiced battling when they could. But by this time, Madeline and Danny were really more focused on making Millie as comfortable as possible. Henry was truly touched by their love for her.

"Ok," Henry said. "I feel I have one more thing to teach you both," Henry announced one night after dinner. He cleared off the table and grabbed a box of items from his room. He laid five items out: A journal, a knife, a blanket, and two rings.

"My address book!" Madeline said.

"Write your name in it and your address, and if lost, you will always be able to find it," Henry said.

"Can I use my full name and my address?" she showed Henry, using her full name. She would legally change to Madeline Jourdain Guidry Boudreaux and the restaurant's address. Henry showed Millie. They both beamed with pride.

"Ok," Henry said. "We are now going to learn how to enchant items. I picked out a few I thought would be most helpful. But through the years, you'll collect and surround yourself with these trinkets. They can protect you, defend you, or even help you find your way back to each other. Enchanted items work better if they are handmade or have sentimental value."

"I forged this knife, and I would like Madeline to keep it on her wheelchair at all times," Henry said. He taught Madeline a spell, she repeated it, waving her hand above the knife. The knife would always detect magical threats and would attack immediately when Madeline called upon it. Danny liked this idea more than she did, but Madeline understood the value.

The next item was another quilt Millie had made. She called Madeline to come to sit by her. Millie only knew the basics of general magic but had learned a few important spells to care for a storm giant husband. Most she had already shared. The last was how to enchant quilts. Henry really didn't need a special quilt to lay with Millie anymore, except when he was really upset. So they just had one hanging around, like an old favorite sweater. Danny, who hadn't quite mastered keeping his human form yet, would find comfort under these quilts made with Millie and Madeline's love. Danny would always prefer to use them, long after they were needed.

"These rings were my parents..." Henry sighed, thinking of moments with his father. "There's a time lock spell that will link you forever. Danny will always be able to find you and you to him, no matter where you are......."

"That seems kind of a big commitment from a quickie Vegas wedding." Madeline sniffed, grinning at Danny. They always regretted that Henry was not at their wedding. Now he kinda was. They read the spell together and sealed it with a kiss.

One very late night, about six months after they had arrived, Millie had her worse day yet. They finally got her to take the pain medication, which she had been adamant about not taking because she heard it was addictive. Millie finally gave in because there was only one thing worse than her pain, seeing the agony and heartbreak in Henry's face.

"I'm just saying that they have made critical decisions based on a coin toss." Madeline tried to distract Henry and Danny as they sat on the porch after Millie finally went to sleep.

"So, I left my 200-year-old restaurant to them?" Henry laughed.

"For the record, you told me not to make important decisions arm wrestling; we assumed coin tosses were ok." Danny laughed too.

"Hey boys," Madeline said, interrupting their laughter, their backs facing the ocean... "Turn around, Henry."

"Hi, daddy." Edith appeared on the second step of the porch, looking 10 months pregnant. "Charlie found me. Is mama..."

"Go lay with her." Henry could barely speak. "She probably won't wake until the morning, but you look tired too. Go lay with her, daughter. She will be thrilled if you are the first person she sees when she opens her eyes." Edith hugged him and disappeared into the house.

"She made it home." Henry exhaled slowly, looking up at the stars, visibly shaken. "Millie... Millie might keep holding on to meet the baby, but... I think she will let herself find peace soon."

"Henry," Madeline whispered. "Can I blink and bring a doctor to her. Maybe the one in New York... Or I'll blink with her to New York, and I'll come back for you... What am I thinking? I'll blink you both at the same time. You can carry her." Madeline was babbling, and she knew it, yet she could not stop herself. "And after I drop you off, I can come back and stay with Edith."

"Stop, sweetheart." Henry softly touched her cheek. "No. for a hundred reasons." Henry sighed. "Storm giants believe if you die in battle or surrounded by love, it is a perfect death. Thank you for helping give Millie a perfect death."

"Please don't send me away now, Henry," Madeline pleaded.

"You have a dragon to kill and galleries to open, and babies to make. Although I do stand by my opinion about the babies. Huge heads..." Henry grinned then sniffed. "It helps to know you will become a powerful witch in my office, and we will meet again.

"But you know, It's time to go, my beloved time lock." Henry said. Madeline rolled to the pier, not hugging him, not looking back. She was not strong enough to do either.

"Granddad," Danny said after losing himself in the silence for a minute. "We can stay a little while longer."

"I'm pretty sure there's a time lock law against meeting your mother when she's an infant," Henry said. "I'm probably breaking a pillar oath or something. But I wanted you to know, I think Madeline will try to sacrifice herself in a misguided attempt to save you and Mack and to ensure our family linage goes on..."

"I know. That won't happen." Danny assured him. "Because of my stupidity and stubbornness, I won't apologize later, but sorry about the scratch on your 66 convertible."

"Daddy... I need help. I thought I had another week..." Edith screamed from inside the cabin.

"Funny thing about the circle of life." Henry got up, kissed Danny's forehead, and disappeared into the cabin. Danny hesitated for a moment, then ran to the pier where Madeline was waiting to blink them home.

"Office or home, my love?" Madeline asked as she took his hands.

"Home, I need to go home with you and hide from the world for a day," Danny said.

Chapter 18

"Do not answer the door, Madeline." Danny sighed. "You promised me 24 hours on our fluffy mattress, in ac, with all the store-bought ice cream I could eat, before we had to face the real world again."

"Shh!" Madeline teased, throwing on a robe.

"Are you Madeline Boudreaux?" a delivery guy holding a package and a helmet asked.

"Yes, I am." Madeline sighed, thinking of her last letter from Kushemi. "Thanks."

"Hi, Madeline." Ida spotted her before she closed the door.

"Hello Ida, how are you?" Madeline hugged her. Sometimes Ida liked being hugged, sometimes not. Today she did, and Madeline was thankful for that. Ida looked so much like Millie.

"I'm fine." Ida said. "I'm sure missing granddad today."

"Me too." Madeline sadly agreed.

"Is Danny home? I wanted to know if he and Abigail wanted to go to the zoo today?" Ida asked. now bubbly.

"He actually has to work all day, but I bet he will cook you a huge breakfast tomorrow morning," Madeline said. She hated lying to Ida, but she knew Danny needed a minute to shift into his real-life again.

"Ok, will you give him a hug from me?" Ida asked and followed the nurse back into her apartment.

"' You put on pants; why did you do that, husband?" Madeline teased.

"You killed my buzz," Danny said, playfully sticking his tongue out at his wife. "What did you get?"

"A package…" Madeline said. "I thought it might be from Henry, but it's not his handwriting."

"We agreed," Danny said. "After visiting each Pillar, we would take a few days off. Check-in with each other, have dinner with our friends. Take my mom and my dead sister to the zoo. You know normal stuff young couples do."

"I wish I could have warned Henry about Abigail, but as a time lock, I couldn't," Madeline said.

"I know," Danny said. "It was the one thing I wanted to tell him. Hoping maybe subconsciously, he would have stopped her that day. But I knew it wasn't fair to put him in that position. Besides, I think it would have changed too much. I would have gone to college on the east coast. Never gotten to know Henry or..."

"Are you ready to talk about it?" Madeline asked. "We spent six months there. You must be hurting."

"But I've got a pretty girl and ice cream, so I'm pretty damn good," Danny said. Madeline was not buying it. "Ok, you are checking in. I get it... I was expecting to train with Henry alone. I tried to prepare myself to see him. I was not expecting Millie. I think time with her was well spent. She reminded me so much of Ida before the accident. Millie made me promise to try not to be sad for her. She kept telling me that she had a great life. And she was old, so her death wasn't a tragedy. And I keep trying to remind myself of that. I just wished Millie's last days weren't filled with so much pain."

"I miss him, but I do feel better about Henry. I think I'm finally becoming the man he wanted me to be," Danny continued. "Although he is worried about you. He thinks you will try to steal my sperm, give me a son, and sacrifice yourself when killing the dragon. Breaking the Guidry curse so I will somehow live happily ever after, without you..." Danny took one look in Madeline's eyes and knew it was true.

"I really don't have to steal your sperm; you're kinda easy." Madeline teased. He no longer was in a teasing, flirting mood.

"I'm going to pick up the dinner shift." Danny grabbed his chef's jacket and stormed out. Then he stormed back in, realizing he had grown four feet. He angrily counted to 100 then stormed out again. Madeline bit her tongue to hide her amusement.

"You'll be back," Madeline yelled as he slammed the door. Madeline knew that running after him would only make things worse, so she would let him cool off. Madeline herself needed a distraction because she was still a little heartbroken from the trip. But just as Millie told Danny, Millie told her she didn't want Madeline to grieve for her either.

Madeline floated to the kitchen, grabbed a soda and the recently delivered package, and set herself down nestled in pillows on the bed. She very carefully unwrapped the box and found a handwritten letter and a book.

The letter said:

My Dearest Madeline,

I hope this letter finds you well. And that you were able to use the appraiser I suggested for the vase you bought in China. I'm so proud that you are considering opening a third gallery. I finally found this book; please study it before our first meeting. The less I have to teach you, the more time we have to drink wine and eat croissants. I miss you laughing with my wife as the husbands play chess.

Gros bisous

John Luc

January 5, 1806

*

"Hello," Danny said, chopping vegetables as Jane, Mack, and Steven came into the kitchen.

"Madds said you were back," Jane said. "But I thought you were going to take a few days off. No office, no kitchen duty."

"The good thing about owning a restaurant, you can make your own damn hours." Danny snapped, Mack gave Danny a dirty look, he apologized. "I'm sorry. It was a rough trip. I'm trying to compartmentalize, which I shouldn't. Good training but... emotionally draining."

"Did you see Henry?" Mack asked.

"And we met Millie," Danny said. "She was everything Henry described and more. Ida is the spitting image of her. which makes me feel like I lost both of them; again... Millie was very sick when we were there. It was hard watching Henry's heartbreak day after day, knowing... everything to come."

"I'm sorry," Jane said. "How long were you with Henry and Millie?"

"Six months..." Danny said.

"That would explain your 15 pounds and a few more gray hairs." Mack teased; Danny looked more upset than he should from Mack's ribbing.

"It seems I got all of Henry's bad trait's, none of his good," Danny told Mack; Mack would wait till they were alone to finish this conversation.

"I can't believe you guys were there six months," Jane said.

"We were there a few months longer than necessary for training," Danny said. "Both of us kept finding reasons to stay. It was so nice to be with Henry. And Madeline started taking care of everything and everyone. It's her nature. And I should send her roses cuz..." Danny sighed, still frustrated with his lovely wife but realizing he may have overreacted.

"Hi," Steven said, answering his phone.

"Shh, I need a favor," Madeline pleaded.

"Why? Where are you? Jane made cookies." Steven said. "Come over,"

"Nope. He's really mad." Madeline said.

"Are you really mad at your wife, Danny?" Steven asked, now putting Madeline on speaker. Danny sighed.

"I'm having lunch with Elizabeth next week." Madeline threatened, Steven picked up the phone again.

"What?" Steven asked. Madeline quickly explained, Steven remembered. "I think… there were three trunks marked JL? No one could open them, so we put them in storage. I will in the morning if you promise to be nice to Elizabeth… Pleasure doing business with you,"

"I'm not getting a week off from this pillar thing, am I?" Danny said.

"Nope," Steven said. "I think she had a moment of clarity and needs trunks from storage. Can I use your truck in the morning?" Danny nodded.

"Can you pick them up the day after tomorrow?" Danny asked. "My stubborn wife still owes me a day off, and I'm determined to get it even if we spend it fighting." Danny laughed, Steven agreed.

*

"So…" Danny said, setting Madeline on a table in the gallery as they waited for Steven to bring the trunks a few days later. Madeline giggled and played with his beard. "We are now on the same page, yes?" Madeline nodded flirtatiously. "As cute as you are, I am a lawyer, and I'm gonna need a verbal agreement with the all binding, never to be broken, pinky swear."

"Fine." Madeline sighed, rolling her eyes. "I will not try to kill the dragon by myself."

"And?" Danny asked.

"I will probably not blink you and Mack away if I sense imminent danger," Madeline said. Danny frowned again. "That's the best I can promise, Boudreaux."

"And…" Danny would work on her more about the dragon later…

"We won't try to get pregnant until I see the specialist in Boston." Madeline sounded a little sad. "I really wasn't going to try without talking to you first. You know that. But I do feel a little pressure to make sure the Guidry legacy continues."

"Henry told me," Danny said. "Getting pregnant might be hard on you, and if his legacy dies in your arms when I'm 400 years old, nothing will make him happier."

"I asked him not to tell you," Madeline admitted. "I knew you would worry.."

"Family trumps mentor," Danny said. "Plus, Millie told me the same thing. And the length a Guidry man would go to save his wife."

"Millie knew, huh?" Madeline asked.

"That Henry gave himself a magical vasectomy? Of course." Danny said.

"Millie is, was awesome." Madeline blinked away a tear. "Promise we will decide together. I do think Henry was wrong taking away Millie's choice.

"I actually do, too," Danny said. "But I do think we need to practice a lot so we'll be ready." They hugged. Madeline couldn't help feel his sadness and worry.

"Your turn." Madeline grinned, knowing they had finished her issues, at least for now. "How are you doing on the storm giant thing?"

"I..." Danny said. "I can, of course, see the benefit's in fighting the dragon. Henry thinks my max growth is 15 feet in battle. I need to train more in that size. Because I'm not a full storm giant, I cannot live in the water or clouds, which is not an issue. Why would I not lay with you in our bed every night?"

"But..." Danny said. "I hate admitting this, but apparently, I'm extremely vain; I do not like how the additional weight looks in my human form."

"I think," Madeline said. "You are absolutely gorgeous. But... if you want, we can try an illusion spell for when you are not in our home. No illusions spell in our home.... Ever. Unless I get freakishly ugly. There must be a reason the media portrays powerful old witches as hideous." Madeline laughed.

"No illusions spells in our home.... Ever." Danny grinned, pulling Madeline closer, getting ready to kiss her. Just then, the front door opened. "You're killing me... but let me go unload the trunks." They were expecting Steven. It was not.

"Hello, Madeline Guidry Boudreaux." Louis Delcroix said. Danny turned to him and sat by Madeline on the table. Madeline quickly reinforced the furniture with the touch of her hand. Danny grinned embarrassingly.

"How can we help you today?" Madeline asked.

"I just wanted to check in," Louis Delcroix said. "Congratulations on your marriage,"

"Thanks, I'm kinda smitten myself," Danny said. "We do have a busy day..."

"My editors asked me to do a fluff piece. It's not every day a famous New Orleans bachelor gets married to an unknown, kinda homely looking thing. "

"People have always told me I'm smarter than I look. Love potion, Vegas wedding. Fingers crossed the potion holds up." Madeline said, rubbing Danny's leg. Danny knew Madeline was forcing him to try to keep his cool, as Henry suggested. Danny seemed to uncontrollably grow when it was emotionally tied to her, which was a double-edged sword.

"I'm not sure how well your potion is working." Louis Delcroix said, starting to fish, "Danny has missed the two black-tie charity events of the fall. I thought that was a little odd. That he would not want to show you off. It would make me sad if he was embarrassed by you,"

"I'm working 24/7 in the restaurant. Although I did make significant donations to both, but I bet you knew that." Danny said, forcing himself to go into lawyer mode.

"And…" Louis Delcroix said. "This almost made me feel sorry for Madeline. I heard she was in the hospital about a month ago. She almost died. Your cronies were at her side, but you were nowhere to be found. That looked tacky, even for a first quickie marriage." Louis Delcroix looked delighted.

"I almost believed this marriage was a Vegas mistake, and Danny was just buying his time. Being an indifferent ass until his lawyers could get the marriage annulled with his big inheritance in tack." Louis Delcroix continued. "But here's the thing. I had a friend at your birthday party. They said you two are completely in love; you danced the night away. You could not take your eyes off of her."

"I doubled his love potion that night to keep up appearances. Like I said, I'm smart," Madeline winked.

"But I'm sort of wondering just how smart you are. I started to do some research…" Louis Delcroix said. "There's a legend that says when magic returned, a powerful witch would be reincarnated. She would marry a storm giant, and together, they would protect New Orleans for hundreds of years. I found a picture on a voodoo saint card. A few people swear you are a direct descendant… And I bet with a little makeup and a dress, you'd be tolerable in bed."

"Ok," Madeline said as she felt Danny starting to get up. "I'm going to ask you to leave right now. If Danny is a storm giant, which he isn't, wink, wink, and if he is in love with me, which he's not, he's about three seconds from throwing you out. And I mean literally picking you up and flinging you across the street into the full dumpster."

"I want to win a Pulitzer; I can portray you as a good couple or a bad couple. It really doesn't matter to me." Louis Delcroix said.

"Hey, I got the trunks. Can you help me, Danny?" Steven asked, yelling from the door before noticing Louis Delcroix. "Is there a problem here?"

"Nope." Louis Delcroix said. "I was just leaving. I'll be seeing you, Madeline."

"He needs to go," Danny said. "Until we need him."

"I can do a spell, making it very uncomfortable to be on our block," Madeline said, kissing Danny's cheek. "You did good keeping calm."

"I'll expect to be rewarded later." Danny teased, trying to hide how upset he was. Louis Delcroix had crossed the line from being a nuisance to being a threat to his wife.

"I actually found five trunks, Madds," Steven said, bringing in the last one. Jane came in with sandwiches as Mack and Danny were in an intense conversation outside the door. Madeline assumed it was about Louis Delcroix.

"You don't think it's your John Luc?" Jane grinned evilly as Mack and Danny came in, Danny in a pensive mood.

"Who is your John Luc?" Steven asked.

"A friend Madeline made two summers ago in Paris," Jane grinned. "So cute, so obsessed with Madeline."

"He kinda was..." Madeline blushed as she noticed Steven and Danny staring at her, very amused and curious. Madeline pointed at Steven. "You, nothing happened because we were still dating." Madeline then pointed at Danny. "And definitely not as cute as you. Can we just eat and open trunks?" she suggested. Giving Jane a strange look to be discussed later.

This time the trunks unlocked and popped open with one touch of Madeline's fingers. The group stepped back as all the trunks seemed to come alive, moving themselves to the back wall and unfolding into one huge wall unit made up of shelves and 100 drawers. The drawers looked like smaller file cabinets handcrafted from gorgeous wood.

Everyone was extremely curious as to what was in the magical wall unit. The first set of shelves had books, the second had beakers and metal frames. The third section had mortar and pestle sets. And a large, neatly display of rocks and gems.

The last section was drawers. All the drawers look to be the same size from outward appearances; opening them revealed a different story. Each drawer was the perfect size for it's particular item—a tiny drawer for a clear quartz, a larger drawer for keeping a spool of copper wire.

The 100 drawers were neatly labeled with all kinds of things, every label in Madeline's handwriting. Some stored normal spices like salt, oregano, sage, or basil. Some had unusual items like a hummingbird feather, a four-leaf clover, a rope, a honeycomb, or a vile of crocodile tears. A few items were just downright gross with odd contents, including vampire dust, a glass eye, bones, or a jar of fingernails.

"Oh my god, this is like the ultimate alchemist's kit." Steven was thrilled, Mack and Danny seemed indifferent. Jane and Madeline were doing a gross out dance.

"My wife, the most powerful witch in America, maybe the northern hemisphere, ladies and gentlemen," Danny announced, very amused.

"Thank you for coming to the freak show. Everyone out!" Madeline grinned, knowing most had kitchen or bar duties soon.

"Mack and I are going to do paperwork. Do you want to train tonight?" Danny asked.

"Yup." Madeline hesitated. "Are you sure you're ready to go back to the cabin, my love?"

"I miss them no matter where we are," Danny said. "We really do need to get back into our routine."

"I feel like this is a good time to share this interesting piece of trivia with you," Madeline said. before Danny left the gallery. "The only class I ever failed in my life... was chemistry."

"Why don't you make sure you have everything on John Luc's list. But Maybe not try any combinations." Danny smirked. "And we'll learn each potion together. Please, dear wife." He winked, pleaded, and left.

Madeline spent the next few hours comparing her stuff with the list in John Luc's book of necessary items, impressed that everything matched. She decided to go through each drawer one final time.

In the last column, Madeline found a drawer labeled "Louis Delcroix", in it was a pouch. The pouch had a tag with a note saying: "Potion: Line in the sand, for Louis Delcroix, spread on property's borders, not deadly, just itchy as hell." Again, in her own handwriting.

"Honey," Madeline rolled to Henry's office, finding Danny at her desk. "Look." She showed him the potion.

"I think this is more important than we know." Danny sighed. "So I called all of my friends who were at my birthday party. All of who, by the way, are now madly in love with you. But none of them ever heard of Louis Delcroix, so how did he know about my party and that we danced all night?" Danny seemed frustrated.

*

A few days later, Madeline stared at Danny from the other end of the table. He was teasing Charlie about something and had a twinkle in his eye. Danny caught her staring and grinned back. He finally looked relaxed, and they both appreciated a late-night dinner with their friends. Danny insisted on cooking.

"This is, hands down, the best bisque I've ever tasted." Jane raved to Danny.

"It was Millie's favorite, Henry taught me well. Or maybe I listened better." Danny admitted.

"Should I worry about my job?" Jane asked, a little kidding, a little serious. "Six months with Henry has turned you into an even better chef. Whether you admit it or not."

"Never. You have job security forever." Danny said. "I just wanna kill the dragon and spend time with my bride." He sighed.

"And do the books," Mack said. "Cuz I ain't doing the books." Everyone laughed.

"Elizabeth still wants you to teach," Steven said, now helping Jane clear the table.

"Maybe," Danny said. "It's tempting to try something new. Maybe after we are not on lockdown and Madds first love becomes the gallery."

"I think you, sir..." Madeline said. "Will be my favorite distraction for a very long time." Madeline glanced down at her phone. "Hey, my dad texted; he wanted to check if I got a package from him. I'm going to run home, check, and call him. I'll be back."

"Do you want bread pudding and a small glass of port?" Jane asked.

"Yes, please!" Madeline said.

"Why don't you blink home, wife?" Danny asked as Madeline rolled towards the door.

"Because it is a beautiful night," Madeline grinned, touching his back tenderly as she passed him.

Madeline hurried to the apartment, giggling about the package sitting in front of their door. She made the heavy box float to her kitchen counter.

"Hi, daddy," Madeline said on speakerphone as the box opened itself. "The chess set is gorgeous! Admit it, he is the son you always wanted... He's going to love it... Actually, the neighbor to our left is moving out; Danny might see what it would take to combine the two and have one bigger apartment... a bedroom would be nice... Next Sunday! It's just easier for us to fly in and out on the same day... I think it's gonna be a late night, but I know he will call you in the morning. Kiss mom. I love you, dad. "

Madeline carefully moved the chessboard to the center of their bed. She was so tempted to call Danny to come home to find his surprise but fought the urge. Even though Mack and Danny were always together, it was rare that they relaxed, either they were working or training.

Madeline slowly made her way back to the restaurant, enjoying the beautiful full moon. Saying hello to a passing neighbor. Staring at the fountain, hoping Kisseis could hold on just a bit longer. As she rolled to the restaurant. She was happy to see someone had convinced Charlie to sing as Mack and Jane began to slow dance. Steven and Danny were lost in conversation until Danny spotted Madeline coming. He grinned. Madeline was about to mouth, "I love you." When someone across the street called her by her full name.

"Madeline Guidry Boudreaux!" Louis Delcroix yelled.

Madeline was still looking at Danny lovingly as Louis Delcroix yelled her name. The next three seconds were a blur. Madeline was confused why Danny suddenly grew, now screaming and pointing. Madeline turned to Louis Delcroix as he tried to cross the street to approach her.

Louis Delcroix took one step towards Madeline and was blown back into the building behind him, catching the building on fire. The fire must have hit a gas line because, within milliseconds, the small building exploded. An explosion so strong that it threw Madeline into the restaurant while blowing out its large glass front exterior.

Madeline and Charlie were the only ones who didn't lose consciousness.

As soon as she could, Madeline floated back into her wheelchair, crying in pain as she forced herself to sit up. She had tiny cuts everywhere and a large gash across her forehead.

"Madeline!" Danny moaned, and she went to him. He was bleeding everywhere.

"Ok, Love," Madeline said. "We are going to blink to our apartment. And Charlie is going to get Clara to heal you."

"But Madeline, you're bleeding so much," Charlie said, trying but knew arguing was pointless. She then flew out of the restaurant like a bat out of hell.

"Ok." Madeline was able to blink Danny into their bed. "Charlie and Clara will be here in a jiffy, ok, my love?" Madeline kissed his forehead and blinked back to the restaurant before he could argue.

"Mack," Madeline said. he was the only one stirring, now able to sit up. "I'm going to blink you, Steven, and Jane one at a time to the hospital. You first so that you can watch over Jane and Steven, ok?"

"Madds, I don't think you should," Mack said. "Let us wait for an ambulance."

"They look bad, Macky. I have no choice. Please." Madeline pleaded. He looked at Steven and Jane, both moaning, and nodded. She was able to blink all three without any problem. Madeline wanted so badly to stay with Steven and Jane. Still, Mack finally put his foot down, so afraid that another avatar would find Madeline on unprotected grounds. Madeline watched as they rolled Steven into surgery. It broke her heart. Thankfully Jane just needed several stitches, and Mack pretty much walked it off.

"Go home, Madeline," Mack ordered, no longer playing. "I'll call you with the tiniest updates, I swear, but you've gotta go." They hugged, and she blinked home.

"Blinking hurts while bleeding," Madeline said. Flopping herself in a chair as Clara was finishing up with Danny.

"I gave him a sedative because he was determined to go find you," Clara said. "He will wake in an hour with a bad headache but fine otherwise."

"Thanks, Clara..." Madeline said.

"Your turn," Clara said.

"I'm fine, just a little light-headed, but I'm fine."

"Madeline, you're about ten minutes from bleeding out," Clara said. Pointing at a cut from Madeline's waist down to her ankle. Touching the gash across her forehead.

"Being paralyzed has its perks," Madeline said. Clara was not amused at all.

"Blink to the bed, Madeline," Clara ordered. "I'm going to ask you once." She laid by Danny; he instinctively reached for her, not fully waking. Madeline blinked away a tear as Clara worked on her.

"So…" Clara said. "I got you all stitched up. I suggest you both stay in bed for a few days. I have a bad feeling I'll be seeing you again. I owed Henry for saving me long ago. Now I'm here for you and Daniel. I won't like it. But I thought you ought to know."

"I'll walk you out," Charlie said.

"Thank you, Clara," Madeline said. She nodded and left.

"What the hell are you doing, Madeline?" Charlie asked, coming back in. Madeline softly moaned as she put on a sundress.

"I have to go talk to frank, board up the windows, go check on Steven, sweep up the glass, then figure out how the hell I messed up so badly," Madeline said. "I'd prefer you stay with my husband, but I'm going either way." Madeline moaned as she floated to kiss Danny, stroking his forehead. He smiled a bit… "Will you please call me when he wakes up?" Madeline asked and blinked away, not waiting for Charlie's answer.

"Please tell me that my wife is in the bathroom." Danny rolled over two hours later, finding Charlie sitting on a pillow by his head reading a trashy novel. "I think I remember vaguely Clara healing her and telling her to stay in bed for a few days."

"Have you met your spouse?" Charlie asked. "She may be a disobedient, stubborn wife, but she sort of a badass witch, already, taking care of business. She probably saved Steven. She talked to Frank, they decided it was a gas leak. And the last time I looked, she had boarded up all but one window. Do not yell at her, Daniel. She probably is going to blame herself for all of this, and when she runs out of things to do, Madeline's going to have a major breakdown.."

"I know that," Danny said, slowly getting out of bed. "But I did need a reminder." He softly smiled at Charlie while throwing on a t-shirt and shorts. "Everyone else?"

"Mack's fine… Jane will be fine." Charlie said. "Steven will be in the hospital for a few days. The flying glass clipped a major artery. I think Madeline has blinked in and out of his room a few times. You should probably let Madeline slide on that one too."

"Yup." Danny sighed, finishing tying his shoes.

"I guess asking you to come back to bed would be a waste of both of our time," Charlie asked. Now returning to her book, knowing Danny was finished listening to her sermon as he shut the door behind him.

Danny walked to the restaurant, dreading what he would find. He touched each boarded up window as he slowly walked past them. Danny sighed when he entered, the dining area was a mess, but it all looked cosmetic.

"Why, hello beautiful," Danny whispered. Finding Madeline out of her wheelchair, sitting in a corner on the floor behind the bar sobbing. Danny groaned a little as he sat down by her, gently pulling her onto his lap.

"This would be a very bad time to point out that you should be in bed, huh?" Madeline said, being dead serious. Danny smirked, deciding this would be her one free pass.

"I think," Danny said. "We should go home, catch a few hours of sleep. And tomorrow, we will figure out what happened. You look exhausted."

"I need to go tell Steven, good night. As much as I love you, it kills me to say, he and I are still best friends, and if I…." Madeline said.

"Then…" Danny whispered. "I'll go with you." Madeline squeezed his hand, and they blinked.

By the time they got there, Elizabeth was at Steven's side. She winked at them when they appeared. Steven told Elizabeth that Madeline knew some cool magic tricks for entering a room.

"Elizabeth, can I have a second with Madeline?" Steven asked. "She probably came back to confess her dying love for me and that her marriage to her handsome doting millionaire husband is just a fling," everyone laughed but Madeline.

"I actually want some coffee; I'll be back." Elizabeth winked at Steven and left.

"Will you make her stop blinking here? It's creepy when she's nice and worried." Steven asked Danny. They laughed.

"Want me to call your folks?" Madeline asked.

"Oh god, no," Steven said. "Madeline, whatever you are thinking, stop it. I know you. It was either a freak accident or an attack on you, neither of which is your fault, but you will spend the next three days trying to blame yourself. Go home, Madds, Please."

"Ok." Madeline kissed his cheek. And blinked home.

"Can I just cry myself to sleep in your arms?" Madeline asked as Danny covered them with Millie's blanket after they got in bed. Both achy and so tired.

"Yes, darling wife," Danny said. "But Steven was right. this is not your fault." Danny looked down and smiled; she was already out cold.

*

"Hey…" Danny quietly answered the phone a couple hours later. "No, I finally got her to sleep. I'm hoping she sleeps all day. I think we should close for the week. I'll take care of it. Yup… just pamper, Jane. Yup, I'll look now; why would I scream? Later Macky."

He quietly got out of bed. Madeline reached to stop him but was too tired, rolling back over. Danny poured himself a bowl of cereal, opened his laptop and clicked the link Mack sent… and screamed involuntarily, as Mack predicted.

*

A headline in today's paper: "Witch tries to kill reporter in a spell that goes boom." By Louis Delcroix

Although never publicized, locals have known Henry Guidry, a powerful magical user, had run this city for centuries and groomed his great-grandson, Daniel Boudreaux, to take his place. Government officials have always turned a blind eye because of Henry's numerous charities and his commitment to keeping the French Quarter crime-free.

As she is calling herself, Madeline Guidry Boudreaux moved into the apartment complex Henry owned seven months ago and has slowly taken over his family and dynasty. After Henry's untimely and questionable passing, in which Madeline was alone with him at the time of his death, Madeline has openly admitted to drugging the young and dashing Daniel Boudreaux and seducing him into marrying her in a quickie Vegas wedding.

Slowly, she has changed Henry's staff's dynamics by hiring her minions to work at the restaurant, including her "Ex" husband. Madeline also forced her sick mother-in-law to live in a tiny efficiency, next to her gigantic apartment, so that the evil witch would be able to keep the frail Ida under lock and key.

This seemingly sweet tyrant has even made Daniel quit his job and all other activities. The one social and brilliant lawyer has not been seen in his box seats at football games in months or at any charity events that he usually organizes and MC's. Locals say they even miss seeing him run through the park.

I have begged and pleaded for an interview with Madeline, hoping to be able to dismiss some of these wild tales of her rise to power, but time after time, her goons have thrown me out. The only one who would talk to me is Daniel's late father, Eugene Boudreaux, whose death is also under investigation. He implied that Madeline kept his son and wife away from him. He also implied that Madeline may have had some inappropriate relationship with the late Guidry, forcing him to leave his collection of books to her instead of Eugene's scholar library, where they obviously belonged.

I have tried to remain cordial and unbiased towards Madeline. Still, last night she tried to kill me as I was passing by the restaurant. During our accidental meeting on the street, I pleasantly told her hello. Madeline immediately became irritated. She then started ranting, raised her hand, and threw a fireball at me. Through the grace of God, the fiery flame missed me but destroyed a vacant building behind me. A flame so deadly it whipped around her, destroying Henry's 250-year-old business.

Madeline was later seen at the hospital crying at her ex's bedside, full of remorse, her husband nowhere to be found. I would not be surprised if they find Daniel's dead body in the destroyed restaurant today. The restaurant is probably now cursed. Madeline, the evil and vile witch, has single-handedly destroyed the legacy of Henry Guidry. What is she planning to do next?

I truly feel she is a danger to the city of New Orleans. We must find her, destroy her and break the spell she has over Daniel Boudreaux before taking his life as she did Henry Guidry, Eugene Boudreaux, and probably countless others.

*

"Madds?" Danny whispered. "I'm going to grab a coffee in the courtyard with Mack. Stay in bed. I love you." Danny tried to grin at her, but his anger was reaching a boiling point.

"Come back to bed," Madeline said sleepily. "You need to rest today too."

"I'll be back," Danny promised. Madeline rolled over and covered her head. Usually, this would have made Danny's heart melt, but he was about two seconds from coming unglued.

"Black coffee this morning, my brother," Mack was waiting for him by the fountain. "I have more news. That you are not going to like." Mack handed Danny a large cup.

"First, how are Jane and Steven?" Danny asked.

"Jane is sleeping on and off, probably will be good as new by tomorrow. Already worried about today's food deliveries and reservations." Mack said. "Steven is insisting they release him today. Elizabeth is going to try to push him to stay another night."

"Hey, Why are the gates locked?" Danny asked, taking a sip of coffee, noticing the gates to the apartment's courtyard were closed. They are usually only closed during hurricanes and mardi gras.

"Don't shoot the messenger," Mack took a large sip of coffee. "There's a mob in front of the restaurant; the men want to lynch Madeline. The women want to have sex with you to save your soul."

"Fantastic," Danny said. "You and Madds are going to have a field day with this one, Huh?"

"Yup. But seriously, What do you want to do?" Mack asked.

"The lawyer in me wants to sue the newspaper. I'm going to need more than an "Oops" on page 17. The storm giant just wants to break shit. But Louis Delcroix has written his last article, I promise you that. The only thing Madeline has done wrong is giving him the benefit of the doubt." Danny said. "I think we should go to the cabin until this blows over, and we figure out what to do about Louis Delcroix once and for all."

"I'll get Jane going and pack up the necessities. We'll drive out in a few hours." Mack said. "And Daniel, do not fly off the handle. This needs to be taken care of swiftly and with minimal casualties." Mack disappeared into Jane's apartment.

"Oh, Madds," Danny took a heavy sigh when he opened the door to their apartment. She was gone from their bed, her laptop by her pillow opened to Louis Delcroix's horrific article. He was relieved to hear the shower running. Danny walked to the door, surprised and a little worried that she had locked it. They never locked the bathroom door. He could hear her sobbing. "Sweetie, open the door."

"Nope," Madeline said. "My first instinct was to blink away, but I promised you I'd never blink to run away from you, so this is me hiding in the bathroom."

"Madds." Danny sighed, his back sliding down the wall, now sitting down by the locked bathroom door. "It was a ridiculous article, and after I know you're ok, I'm going into full pissed off lawyer mode. But I need to know you're ok."

"Have you ever thought…" Madeline asked. "That I am the… avatar?"

"When you drink out of the milk carton, a little," Danny said, thinking that Madeline was kidding. She was not.

"His article has a lot of truth," Madeline said through her tears. "This all started when I arrived. I tried to tell you I got Henry killed. I tried and tried, but you didn't want to see it."

"Madds." Danny sighed.

"We don't know anything about my birth parents. What if they are evil?"

"Please come out, Madeline." Danny pleaded once more.

"What if I'm a time bomb? Guys like you aren't even supposed to like girls like me. What if I voodooed you, and when I come out, I am programmed to kill you?"

"Are you?" Danny tried to hide his smirk because she sounded dead serious.

"I don't think so," Madeline said. "But if I'm an avatar, I'm probably a brilliant liar."

"I had enough; come out here, wife. Now. Or I am going to open the door by any means necessary." Danny said, trying not to yell.

"hi," Madeline blinked to the kitchen. She looked so sad, Danny found her irresistible.

"Ok, you're the avatar." Danny shrugged. "And let's say you're playing the long game. Maybe you even put a spell on me. But I don't think so. It's one thing if you only showed yourself to me, but Madds, you've touched my whole world with your kindness. Henry blessed our marriage in two lives. Ida now calls for you more than me. Mack worships you. And you do hundreds of things every day that make me fall more and more in love with you."

"I…" Madeline said. "That article has made me question everything."

"And I truly believe that's why he wrote it, to throw you off your game," Danny said. "I think the dragon and avatars are running scared because your powers are growing. I believe Louis Delcroix is an avatar. I think he would rather break you down emotionally than fight you. You have such a good heart you are going to doubt yourself until I prove you're wrong, which kind of is my thing.." Danny winked.

"We will work through this, but I want us to go to the cabin for a few days. Please. And I know you're not an avatar; an avatar would at least pretend to be more agreeable… less stubborn," Madeline smiled a little.

*

"Do you think she's ok?" Mack asked Danny as they stood on the porch at sunrise, their 3rd day at the cabin. Madeline was trying to meditate on the pier.

"Nope," Danny said. "To her, she watched Millie dying a few days ago. She emotionally had to bury Henry again. She truly believes she let Louis Delcroix destroy our reputations. Plus, now she thinks she has cursed me. So no, my wife is not ok. And I'd be an asshole if I expected her to be. And I did… because she's Madeline… I'm going for a very long run." Danny left the porch as Mack stared into the ocean, wishing Henry would come in with the tide, as he had done so many times.

Madeline wasn't proud of it, but she was sort of avoiding Danny, well everybody really. Jane wanted to talk, Danny wanted to talk, hell even Steven wanted to talk, but she was all talked out for the first time in her life.

"Hey, ya wanna blow stuff up?" Mack asked as Madeline returned to the porch after Danny ran the other way. Madeline sighed and nodded.

"Me too!" Charlie screamed, now appearing from the house.

"Why does that scare me, Charlie?" Mack teased as they slowly walked to the obstacle course.

"First run it a few times without firing on any targets," Mack ordered. Madeline nodded and began. Her first few runs were less than stellar, but after she got out of her head, Mack was absolutely shocked at how much training with Henry had improved her agility and speed. "Wow."

"And yet I watch yours, and Danny's restaurant and reputations shatter, so yay me." Madeline was angry.

"Try again, Madds, go faster. No thinking, only instinct." Despite his reputation, Mack didn't like being an indifferent jerk. But Mack thought maybe Madeline needed some tough love too. "Again. Backward this time."

"What?" Madeline was amused but did it, and did it well. Mack smiled to himself as Charlie did too.

"Now, shoot your lowest strength fireballs at all the odd marked targets." Mack challenged. Madeline hit the first seven targets perfectly, but the 8th target was a tall man's silhouette with a hat. It must have reminded Madeline of Louis Delcroix, making her fireball shoot out 50 times stronger than what it should have been, catching the whole backlot on fire. Shaking the ground. Lighting up the dome. Madeline was able to act quickly, putting out the rolling flames before they reached Charlie and Mack.

"Holy hell, that wasn't supposed to happen, was it?" Charlie asked Mack as they tried to keep up with Madeline as she cussed and muttered all the way home.

"Nope." Mack scratched his head.

"I can't wait till Danny really pisses her off." Charlie giggled. Mack hid a grin.

Madeline looked like a cartoon character as she raced back to the cabin, hair burnt, eyebrows singed. "Shut up, Daniel Boudreaux," Madeline said, passing Danny on the porch. Slamming the front door closed than their bedroom door, a few seconds later.

"So I have good news and bad news," Mack told Danny a few minutes after Madeline disappeared into the house. "She could take out Louis

Delcroix today, by herself. But I think there would be so much collateral damage because her emotions are woven into her powers. Which makes her great but very vulnerable. I'm guessing as she grows, this will be less of an issue. But for now, we will need to try to steer where the battles are so we can protect her, not only from avatars and dragons but from humans, too."

"I sure do hate your moments of clarity, Macky." Danny exhaled sadly. "Maybe the third pillar can teach us how to better isolate Louis Delcroix, so we don't have to take him out in front of an audience."

"We could try to lure him out here," Mack suggested.

"But we would have to break Henry's protection spell if we wanted to kill the avatar here," Danny said. "Madds and I want to build a house and fill it with kids, maybe. I need to do everything in my power to keep Henry's land sacred." Danny's fist pounded the porch rail. "Crap, I'm going to have to rush my wife into visiting another pillar."

"Give her a few days, let your wounds heal…" Mack said. "I'll do what I can from here, but it does seem like your best option."

"You know the restaurant will bounce back," Danny said.

"And you know I'd dig ditches for the rest of my life if we could just walk freely in town again," Mack said. "I miss you buying lunches and kicking your butt at racquetball. It's so satisfying." Mack joked, trying to distract his best friend, who looked broken.

"I'll cook a big lunch tomorrow; maybe she will smile. Then I'll crush her again and talk my wife into going to the next Pillar before I think we should." Danny said, frustrated.

"Nope," Madeline said, reappearing from inside. "I want to get this over with. We leave tonight," Madeline sounded cold and indifferent. Danny was concerned.

"I don't wanna be a jerk, Madds, but you probably ought to wait until you stop bleeding to visit your next pillar," Mack said matter-of-factly. He was looking at Madeline's leg, now bleeding again. "Don't do your arrogant

Boudreaux look; you're bleeding too; I'm going to get Clara. That ought to be a fun trip." Mack sighed.

*

"Do you think Clara really put a spell on this bed, and if we get up before the 72 hours are up, we will get zapped?" Madeline giggled after Clara left. She had to re-stitch them both and was not happy at all. Clara's bedside manner was especially unpleasant this time. Madeline was convinced she did not even bother to numb anything.

"I don't know, but I'm sure not going to be the one to find out," Danny grinned, rolling over to face Madeline in the cabin's master bedroom.

"Some brave storm giant you are." Madeline faced him and smiled; in all of her anger, she missed looking into his eyes. "I'm sorry." She brushed his cheek and kissed him.

"You can be angry or sad or mad or any combination, for as long as you need," Danny said. "But please do not shut me out. I know it's not fair, but after Ida... your silence scares me more than it should.."

"Ok." Madeline hugged him. "I'll try harder.."

"Wanna make up, now?" Danny raised his eyebrows.

"Wanna explain to Clara what happened if she has to come back to re-stitch you?" Madeline teased; Danny scooted away from her a little.

The two were fairly good for the next few days, although they did move to the couch during the afternoons and late into the evenings. Mack took away their internet privileges as the press was still having a field day.

As upset as Danny still was, he knew after they took care of Louis Delcroix, they could have a re-opening, he and Jane could smooze the forgiving city. Mack and Danny had actually talked about expanding the restaurant for a few months now. It seemed like a good time as any. They bribed Jane with a ridiculous budget for a new kitchen. She was giddy but insisted on keeping Henry's wood stove. Truthfully, everyone was a little excited but Madeline.

While Jane, Mack, and Danny planned the rebuild, Steven researched what Madeline would need on this trip as she tried to brush up on the book John Luc had sent her. Madeline was in no way as prepared as she would have liked, but they were out of time.

"Hey." Charlie knocked on their door late one night, the day before they were going to leave. Madeline had her nose in John Luc's book, and Danny was drawing sketches of the restaurant. "I need to talk to you both." Charlie closed the door behind her.

'What is it, Charlie?" Danny saw that she had been crying.

"I'm fine..." Charlie whispered. "It's hard being out here without Henry and Millie, even now. But they would have loved that the cabin is loud and filled with family again. And all this talk of Paris has been stirring memories up. Do you have John Luc's address?"

"I do," Madeline said.

"Good... Good..."

"Charlie, you're scaring me," Madeline said. "Is something going to happen to Danny? should I go by myself... you have to tell me this..."

"No..." Charlie said. "I'm sorry. You both will have a great trip; I wrote a letter and wanted you to deliver it. But I know I shouldn't, and you can't." she took out the letter, threw it up in the air, turned it into confetti, then the tiny shreds of paper disappeared before they touched the ground. "

"Charlie..." Danny worried.

"It shouldn't be this hard after all this time." Charlie chuckled to herself. "Behind John Luc's main house is an empty guest cabin; you should blink there. It's safe... and you can rest there until you regain your strength from the blink. I love you both, safe travels."

"Charlie!" Madeline called as her dear pixie left the room. Although both were curious, both had much work before their blink.

*

"Franklin." Mack and Danny screamed as Frank appeared at their door.

"I'm making breakfast," Danny said. "You know Jane and Steven?" Frank nodded. "Madeline is still sleeping. Can I make you an omelet?"

"Actually, I wanted to chew the fat with you and Macky outside for a second," Frank said. The three stepped outside. Danny offered to sit on the porch, but Frank steered them to the pier. Danny and Mack looked more concerned now.

"There's just not a good way to say this," Frank said. "I have a new boss, who no one has ever heard of... And he wants to make a case against Madeline for the attempted murder of Louis Delcroix and... you'll love this... the kidnapping and brainwashing of Daniel Boudreaux. I'm not going to find you for a few days." Frank sighed. "If there is a funny part, which there is, it would be after I find you, I have to take you to a witch doctor to determine if you are under Madeline's evil spell."

"Are we all under Madeline's spell?" Mack asked. "Because I'm sure I love her too." Mack was pissed now

"I just wanted to give you a heads up," Frank said. looking into the ocean. "Another piece of info, no one seems to know who Louis Delcroix is but my new boss. And for some reason, he took Delcroix's statement, that's usually my job. Y'all need to fix this. You know where my loyalties are, but I have to play the game."

"Yup," Danny said.

"For the record," Frank said. "As much fun as it would be to take you to a witch doctor, I'm pretty sure if anyone is under a spell, it's Madeline. She is too sweet for a cut-throat lawyer like you, Boudreaux... I'll be back with some bs warrant in three days." Frank left them on the pier, not looking back.

"Daniel," Mack said.

"I'm going for a run, Mack; ask Jane to finish breakfast, please." Danny's voice was shaky. "...I finally got her to sleep a full night..." Danny started to run.

"Yuck, you're sweaty." Madeline giggled as Danny woke her an hour later with a kiss.

"I want to leave now," Danny said.

"Like now, now?!?" Madeline sat up and rubbed her eyes. "Ok, husband." Madeline had a hundred reasons why she wasn't ready, but Danny's look was so urgent, she trusted him.

*

"Are you sure you are healed, Madds?" Jane asked.

"Yup," Madeline said. "I'm guessing we'll be there a month, tops... 15 minutes to you people." The group laughed.

"Are you really not going to explain yourself, Charlie?" Madeline asked.

"Ok," She flew to Madeline's ear and whispered a very strange request. Charlie then kissed her cheek and flew out of the cabin.

"Oh, Charlie..." Madeline softly sighed.

"Ready?" Danny hurried his wife as Mack stared at his best friend deciding to bite his tongue. Madeline blew a kiss to Jane, winked at Steven, entwined her fingers with Danny's, and blinked to Paris 1799.

Chapter 19

"Oh god, Madds, I'll apologize after I stop hurting..." Danny moaned from pain after he threw up on Madeline's feet. Before Madeline could say anything, she heard a high-pitched scream behind her. Madeline and Danny both turned to find the most gorgeous 6-foot blonde they have ever seen. More shocking, Madeline and Danny recognized her or at least thought they did.

"Am I hallucinating?" Still holding his head and stomach, Danny asked, that was the most painful blink for Danny yet. Henry had warned that although not deadly, the further back in time they blinked, the more painful it would be, especially for Danny. Madeline wanted to take care of him, but she was still in shock.

The couple assumed the recognition was mutual, it was not; the lady started screaming, even throwing a glass at Danny.

"Charlie? Charlie... Chenoa Enemene..." Madeline waved. "Hi."

"The swamp girl." The woman stopped screaming after taking one step closer and recognizing Madeline. Although she was still giving dirty looks to Danny ."Hi... I'm sorry. Usually, I am a much better host. Hey, you're the girl my Kisseis found. I was wondering if you'd show up again. Is there a reason you have arrived in the guest quarters instead of the main house?"

"Because of you... and I... then..." Madeline tried to explain without really explaining. "Hi... again... Chenoa Enemene... This is my husband, Danny. He usually looks less green... and occasionally, he speaks..."

"Have you come to visit me?" Charlie asked.

"Actually, I am looking for a gentleman named John Luc?" Madeline hesitated, still extremely confused. The woman looked exactly like Charlie, minus her wings. Charlie once had told Madeline she could never quite master the human form. Yet here she was, perfect. Maybe a little too perfect from the way Danny was trying not to stare.

"John Luc is my husband," Charlie said. "He should be on the terrace having lunch,"

"My husband and I have had a really long trip," Madeline explained. "Can we have a few minutes to get our bearings? We can even leave the property if..."

"Certainly not. I clearly remember you now." Charlie said. "And I assume your husband is not a pervert, and he has a reason for staring at me. I kind of find it endearing, although my husband won't. The main house is a quarter-mile north. Follow the gardens; you cannot miss it." Charlie nodded and left.

"That's not Charlie, Charlie? Our Charlie? It can't be? The one flying around in our room last night?" Danny hissed after they were alone. "A warning would have been nice."

"Handkerchief..." Madeline sighed, looking heartbroken. "She asked me to bring back one of his handkerchiefs dipped in his cologne; I thought she was kidding."

"You don't think Kisseis is here?" Danny asked, now feeling physically better, but concerned how hard this trip must have been for Charlie when they discussed it.

"No, it must be a few decades after Charlie brought Henry's father home from the dragon wars. I think Charlie mentioned she lived in France for a long time," Madeline said. "I asked her why she left, and she brushed it off by teasing she missed Henry's gumbo. I almost feel like we are intruding in her life."

"We'll just be here a few weeks... then we'll go home... and give our Charlie hell..." Danny said.

"And you can tell me why after talking to Franklin for eight minutes, you are running scared." Madeline softly accused. Danny bowed his head.

Madeline and Danny slowly walked towards the main house, too memorized by the beautiful grounds to think about their worries at home.

"Look…" Madeline said. She pointed, but Danny knew exactly what Madeline was staring at. In the center of the terrace was their fountain, the one in their courtyard. "I got chills."

"We can't mention Kisseis or the dragon." Danny reminded Madeline. She exhaled.

"Madeline, please come meet my love." Charlie waved to them. Danny squeezed her hand, encouraging Madeline to go ahead of him.

"Hello, John Luc." Madeline smiled as she and Danny arrived on the terrace.

"Welcome to our home." John Luc said, inviting them to join Charlie and him… John Luc was a soft-spoken gentleman, maybe in his early 50s. Very well built with graying hair and kind eyes. His arm around Charlie. "My wife is so happy to see you again."

"I am, too," Madeline said. It still felt weird to see Charlie as a human, never mind as a wife. "I'm sorry, this is my husband, Daniel Boudreaux."

"How long have you been married?" Charlie asked.

"Ah, that's a trick question." Danny grinned, Madeline giggled. "We've been together almost two years."

"Good answer, Boudreaux." Madeline teased. They hadn't quite figured out how to add time trips into anniversaries yet.

"How long have you been married?" Danny asked.

"35 years this June." John Luc said. Danny felt sad that he never knew this. "Do you have children?"

"Not yet," Danny said. "Hopefully, we will be blessed with them in a few years, but having Madeline to myself doesn't sound bad either." Madeline lovingly caressed his thigh, glad to hear he was still open to trying. "Do you have children?" Danny felt bad about asking but could not, not."

"I have an adopted daughter, but John Luc and I unfortunately never have been blessed," Charlie said, looking sad.

"The French men can have babies into their 90s. I'm still committed to trying for another 40 years, my dearest Charlie." It was obvious John Luc adored Charlie, and now Madeline adored John Luc. "So, Madeline, as much as my wife and I would love this to be a social visit, I have a feeling it is not."

"My mentor suggested I find you and ask you to teach me Alchemy," Madeline said.

"And who is your mentor?" John Luc asked.

"Henry Guidry," Madeline said. Danny bit his lip. Charlie looked at Danny with a curious glimmer of recognition.

"That's quite an endorsement." John Luc said.

"In full honesty, he is my great father-in-law, so he might be a little biased," Madeline said.

"He... is extremely biased about Madeline," Danny said. "But not about her incredible abilities." Madeline blinked away a wave of sadness.

"In full disclosure, I am a time lock and am learning to be a magic-user," Madeline said.

"You're wife understates her powers, yes?" John Luc asked.

"Yes." Danny smiled. "I'm working on that, too." John Luc laughed.

"May I ask what your gifts are?" John Luc asked.

"I'm..." Danny hesitated. "I'm about a 10th storm giant, and I know a little magic."

"My husband seems to be understating his powers, too." Madeline teased.

"I'm so intrigued; how could I possibly say no?" John Luc smiled. "Magic is welcomed in my home and on the property. Avoid using magic in the city. It is strictly against the law, and you will be hung if there are 2 or more witnesses, which there always are. While you are learning, this is your home. My servants are opening the west wing."

"This may be a bad idea," Danny said. "We are going to build our dream house soon. I can see Madeline getting ideas already.."

"Would you like to see my lab, Madeline?" John Luc asked.

"Yes, and I have almost finished the book," Madeline said as she and Danny followed John Luc through the gorgeous house. They passed through an enormous kitchen. Madeline had to encourage Danny to keep moving. Leaving the house, they walked 100 yards to another building. Madeline described it as 5,000 feet of sciency crap.

"Oh, you learned the primer book?" John Luc said. "You realize that there are 25 books in the series. Afterward, you will have a very good understanding of the basics of Alchemy, then the fun starts, yes?" John Luc asked.

"No..." Danny and Madeline whispered at the same time.

*

"Did I ever tell you I used to do questionable favors for Steven so he would do my lab reports?" Madeline whispered in the kitchen on their seventh night in Paris at some ungodly hour. Madeline was at the kitchen table, surrounded by books. Danny had awoken to an empty bed, again, and went to look for his wife. Now he sort of regretted his decision.

"What every husband wants to hear," Danny said, smirking, now sitting close to her. "I'm really hoping this has a point that does not involve your ex-boyfriend,"

"I just don't know if I can do this one. There's a reason, I'm a liberal arts major." Madeline said. "It crushed my mom's soul that I didn't even try for a hard science degree. But luckily, I married well." They kissed. "Seriously, I'm already drowning, and I think we are just at the elementary school stuff."

"Then I will help you more. I'll be your backup memory."

"Or..." Madeline suggested. "You can do this pillar, and I can... owe you. Anytime, anywhere, for like 100 years. The best offer you will ever get, Boudreaux."

"You do know I'm a lawyer, so I could make it stick." Danny grinned. "But…"

"No buts." Madeline pouted.

"You know that's not how this works…"

"Six years…" Madeline said. "John Luc said if I really want to learn Alchemy, it's a six-year program. Four years if I cram. Three years if I just don't sleep. Maybe I can do it in three? How can we be away from home for that long? I should try to do it in two… This is absurd. Why can't I tell him what we need, and he can just send home potions with us?"

"Like a drive-thru," Danny asked.

"Exactly." Madeline nodded.

"Jane said you get loopy when you're sleep-deprived." Danny grinned. "You know potions don't have a great shelf life. And what we need may change a hundred times before we use one.

"What if John Luc was on call when the battle starts?" Madeline was reaching for straws. "And I can blink back and forth."

"You would blink away from Mack or me in battle?" Danny asked.

"If it's saved me from four years of memorizing chemistry stuff, yup. You underestimate how shallow I truly am." Madeline smile… "No…"

"Henry said this is where we need to be, and I trust that. It should take five years. Study hard, have a few adventures here and there." Danny said. "We are going to disarm Louis Delcroix and kill the dragon. Then we'll both have work and the restaurant, and kids, and it will never be just us, again."

"Promise?" Madeline whispered, he crossed her heart. "You're not going to tell me why Frank upset you so much?"

"I will. I…"

"Hi…" Charlie said, appearing from another room. "I was going to warm a glass of milk."

"Let me." Danny insisted.

"Can I ask you something, Danny?" Charlie asked as she sat down at the table with Madeline.

"Yes, of course."

"Have I hurt you in some other time period? Because you seem so very uncomfortable around me." Charlie asked.

"No..." Danny said. "Of course not."

"Then before Madeline... did we... date? Maybe... You don't seem like my type, but..." Charlie asked.

"I'm going to put my head in the oven now," Danny screamed. Charlie and Madeline burst into laughter.

"You actually helped raised this brilliant man who we both completely adore," Madeline said. "We never knew about this part of your life, Charlie. We feel like we are intruding. And we are used to you... smaller. With wings... No offense."

"Ah, that makes sense. I never wanted to be human until I met John Luc. Aside from raising Kisseis, this has been the happiest time in my life." Charlie said. "I'm sure glad to be in the company of a Guidry again." Charlie patted Danny's hand. "If you are, in fact, related to Henry, you must be bored out of your mind."

"I'm fine," Danny said.

"Noooooooooooo, "Madeline mouthed to Charlie; they laughed

"Does he need a hobby, Madeline?" Charlie asked.

"Yes, dear sweet Charlie, yes." Madeline laughed....

"What does he like?" Charlie asked Madeline.

"And suddenly, we are home... I did not miss being referred to in the third person." Danny smirked.

"Cooking, exercising, lawyering, and me. Hopefully not in that order." Madeline said.

"Will you come into town with me tomorrow, Daniel? I have an idea." Charlie said.

*

"Hop in, Danny," Charlie said after she stepped into the horse-drawn carriage in front of her house the next morning, Danny hesitated. "Your wife storm giant proofed it this morning."

"Of course she did," Danny said lovingly. He now got into the carriage with absolutely no fear. Charlie nodded to the driver as they now traveled 10 miles to the city of Paris. Both unusually quiet. Thank goodness the scenery was breathtaking.

"This feels very complicated, our relationship." Charlie could not stand the silence anymore.

"You are... my greatest confidant in my time." Danny tried to explain. "I want to confess to my Charlie that I did a bad thing out of fear. Even though we were planning to visit John Luc, I pressured Madeline into leaving earlier than we should have. I think I sorta ran away from home. And I did not tell my wife. I should. She knows I did something, but she's trying to give me the benefit of the doubt. But Madeline has been through a lot lately. Like things that would break other people, she keeps going. I didn't want to crush her again."

"Madeline has the right to know," Charlie said. "But for now, she is safe. John Luc is already completely in love with her. Even though it's only our second meeting, I feel connected to her and you. I think I'd die to protect your wife already. What you did may have been out of love, not fear, to give her time to prepare for her next hurdle. For now, we can just let her be, without adding to her plate, Huh?"

"Vintage Charlie advice." Danny sighed and smiled a little. And for the first time in two weeks, Danny was able to see his second mother, Charlie. "Now, please tell me where we are going."

"Do you fence?" Charlie asked.

"I wanted to learn in college but between the restaurant and mom…" Danny caught himself. "No, mam, I do not know how to fence, but I would absolutely love to learn."

"Good answer!" Charlie said as they pulled into the city. "You are my nephew from the states. Your lovely wife is in a wheelchair because she was thrown off of a horse. Got it? They are expecting you. I'll be back in a few hours. If I go in, I have to talk to people."

"Thanks, Charlie." Danny winked at her and stepped out into the crowded streets of Paris. Danny grinned to himself as he stared into the largest fencing school in the city.

*

By the third year, Danny was teaching fencing, and he absolutely was loving their escape. Danny could walk down the Paris streets without worrying about avatars or dragons. The French men found him intelligent. The women found him charming, and the better his fencing got, the happier he became.

Every night he would go home to a beautiful estate, he would cook for a small group of friends or just John Luc, Charlie, and Madeline. After dinner, the friends would smoke cigars and drink wine. After everyone left, he would study for two hours with his wife then lay down with her.

As Danny had predicted, after Madeline got the basics of Alchemy, she did better than she would ever admit. On the other hand, Madeline gave Danny most of the credit; he worked with her at least two hours a night. He quizzed her and made her identify strange-looking liquids. He tested her different stirring techniques. Different potions needed different mixing from lightly stirred to shaken.

But by Madeline's third year, she was frustrated, lonely, and wanted to go home. John Luc was still one of the kindest men she had ever met. She grew closer to Charlie with every passing day. But somehow, in the shuffled, she and Danny had gotten out of sync. They had gotten into a few really big arguments. The worse was about a hypothetic pregnancy surprise. Danny went ballistic, and Madeline shut down. And he was too much in his head to see it.

She hated Paris. Danny had tried to get her more involved in his life in the city. But between her wheelchair and the color of her skin, the prejudice was unbearable. The evenings would end up in hurt feelings. One night Danny came home a little too late and a little too tipsy. He slept in another room. Madeline didn't come to find him, so he just stayed. She even felt a little relieved. He wouldn't see her changing body.

"Your 5 potions are perfect today." John Luc said.

"Thank you, John Luc." Madeline said, "I'm sorry it took me longer than it should. I'm not feeling well today."

"I see that," John Luc winked.

"Does Charlie… see that?" Madeline asked…

"Not yet. But soon, it will be obvious to a blind man." John Luc said. Madeline laughed and touched her belly.

"I'm sorry, it's me and not Charlie; I'm afraid this will make her sad," Madeline whispered.

"I think Charlie would absolutely be elated." John Luc said. "As would your Daniel."

"He will. Just not yet. A few years ago, I had a miscarriage.." Madeline had never said that out loud. "We were, dealing with a family member dying, and I was just a few weeks. I meant to tell him, but our world kept throwing bigger and bigger obstacles at us. Then it just felt mean to make him relive something from another lifetime. A few weeks ago, I asked if he would be happy if we accidentally got pregnant, and he exploded. And hasn't come to our bedroom since. He is hiding something, and this has brought it to the surface."

"Like an affair?" John Luc asked bluntly.

"No." Madeline giggled. "He has many faults, and he works through his stress by losing himself in work. But the bottom line is we are madly in love. I have to get through my first few weeks. After I'm sure we both are healthy, I'll tell him, then we'll figure it out. He will be thrilled. If you don't mind, I might go lay down."

"Can I go get the doctor?" John Luc asked.

"No…" then Madeline felt a strange pain. "Yes… Please hurry." Madeline shrieked from a bad cramp and blinked to her bed.

*

"Daniel, where have you been?" Charlie screamed as Danny stumbled in at midnight, three hours after she tried to find him.

"Shh, the avatars and dragon and police might find us. And I swore I saw Louis Delcroix last month. Here, In my fantasy world. I swear it was him. I wanted to tell Madeline, but I didn't know-how. A speechless lawyer, that's funny… Then I made up this crazy distraction… I thought it would be easier on Madeline if she thought I was screwing than if I saw Louis Delcroix… I need Macky. He would punch me and tell me to throw myself at Madeline's mercy. I should…" Danny giggled so drunk.

"Danny, shut up." Charlie snapped.

"Charlie," the doctor came into the kitchen, John Luc came from outside. "She was further along than she thought. There was nothing I could do. For a tiny thing, she lost a lot of blood. Please try to keep her still for a few days. She was inconsolable, so I gave her a sedative. She will be out cold till morning…"

"I'll walk you out." John Luc said.

"Shame. On. You. Her breasts were huge. Her belly rounded. I knew for two weeks. I was waiting for her to tell me. And she was probably waiting for you to fall in love with it…" Charlie hissed. "Do not go to her until you sober up. Or you are going to lose everything!"

"I'm sorry. Please don't leave me…" The next morning, Danny whispered as Madeline awoke to Danny holding her. "I think Louis Delcroix found us. And I spiraled. And the thought of him being in the same city as our hypothetical child was unacceptable. Still, the only thing worse is losing a child I never got to love." Danny sobbed for hours.

They mourned together for two weeks.

It took a month for Madeline to feel like herself again. Although Madeline did, Danny would never truly forgive himself for not being with his wife when they lost the baby. But they moved forward together. Danny still taught fencing because they both believed it was very important for his training, but now he always rushed home.

Madeline didn't ask but noticed Danny now limited himself to an occasional glass of wine. Probably something else Henry had tried to warn Danny about that he didn't understand until it almost cost him everything.

John Luc worked with the two from after lunch until late into the night, six days a week. On the 7th day, the four would go on day trips in the countryside. Madeline was still extremely homesick, but she didn't feel alone anymore. Slowly Danny and Madeline found themselves and each other again.

*

"Pop quiz." John Luc announced one afternoon. Danny looked excited. Madeline mocked him for being a nerd. "What are powdered potions?"

"Simplest forms of Alchemy," Madeline said. "For things like skin rashes, making hair grow, itching powder for annoying but harmless attacks. They are very good because they have a very long shelf life but are very limited in power."

"Healing potions?" John Luc asked.

"Six months to a year shelf life," Madeline said. "Unlike conventional medicines, they grow stronger and stronger. But when they reach their expiration date, that's it."

"What can more advanced potions do?" John Luc asked

"Body or structure modifications to growing things, including humans and plants," Madeline said. "Making people stronger, faster. Potions can change everything from the color of skin and hair, To even the sex of a person. For plants, potions can make them grow, tougher, weaker..."

"I could have fun with that," Danny said.

"Works both ways, Boudreaux." Madeline teased.

"Why is Alchemy very important to you?" John Luc asked.

"Because now I can turn my husband into a frog?" Madeline said. John Luc and Danny laughed. "It's important because it will help me recognize magic better, how it is being used, and how I can break it down."

"For the record, John Luc said. "Henry did not exaggerate about you at all." Madeline shyly smiled.

"John Luc, is Charlie out for the day?" Madeline asked.

"Yes." John Luc said. "She had a meeting, then lunch plans, then shopping."

"Go on, Madds." Danny encouraged Madeline.

"Madeline, you are like my sister now, yes?" John Luc asked. "I assume you have not given up four years of your life because you wanted to do beautiful tricks with your friends..." John Luc grinned.

"Although I can see Mack and Steven begging you to make strange potions for their pleasure," Danny said.

"It's good to be a witch." Madeline laughed then sighed. "I hesitate to beg for your help because Charlie is very much involved in the future. Telling her now would do nothing but bring her heartbreak and centuries of waiting."

"Is Charlie with you in the future?" John Luc quietly asked.

"Yes..." Danny said. "She helped raised my mother, then me."

"This pleases me more than you know." Tears streamed down John Luc's face. "Hopefully, I will have a very long life with her. But now, I will be able to go in peace when my time comes, knowing she will be truly in a loving community again. It's my greatest sorrow in life that our life spans are so different. If I was a better man, I would have walked away. Saving her grieving from my death, which is inevitable. But from the moment we met, she became my entire universe, I'm sure I'm just a footnote in the history of Charlie."

"She begged me to steal your cologne," Madeline said. He was forced to sit down. Overcome with emotions.

What can I do for the love of my life?" John Luc asked.

"You can..." Madeline sighed. "Tell me how to kill a dragon and its avatars so I can save a city, break the Guidry curse and bring Kisseis home to Charlie. That's pretty much it."

"And..." Danny whispered. "Stop a city from going on a witch hunt..." Danny looked down, ashamed to look at his wife. "Frank is pretty sure the dragon has a follower in the department; they are trying to build two cases against you. One for the attempted murder of Louis Delcroix. One for the kidnapping and brainwashing of Daniel Boudreaux." Danny bit his lip.

"It's why we suddenly left. It's why I forbid you to go home... How very storm giant of me... huh? You wanted to go home for a year. You said you needed a year. I thought you were just tired of my childish behavior. So I said no... If I had listened. " Danny sniffed.

"You were trying to protect me until you had a plan with a backup safety net... Hey, when have I ever listen to you, Daniel Boudreaux? We can't play that game, love. We can't." Madeline kissed his cheek; his guilt about their miscarriage was still so raw. "Can you help us kill a dragon, John Luc?"

"Let me think on it for a few days." John Luc said. "Please enjoy the rest of the week because you, my darling Madeline, are done; no matter how many students pass through here, you will be my most favorite and adored pet. This lab will be at your disposal as long as I'm alive. Please always plan to stay for dinner when you blink in, or Charlie will be so angry with both of us. Now I have to go do some research."

Chapter 20

"Why do you look so upset, Charlie?" Jane asked as they all waited on the porch for Madeline and Danny to return.

"It's only been 10 minutes," Steven added.

"Charlie, do you know how long they have been gone?" Mack asked; he knew she was hiding something...

"4..." Charlie offered.

"4 days?" Jane asked.

"4 weeks?" Steven suggested.

"Ok, 4 months, a little longer than Madeline had hoped, but it was Paris... with Danny... It must have been wonderful." Jane said.

"I only tell you because they are going to need a moment," Charlie warned. "Four years. And..."

"And what, Charlie?" Jane suddenly got very concerned.

"Madeline..." Charlie knew Madeline told Jane everything but did not want to overshare with Steven and Mack. "She just had a rough few years... Danny did too, but mostly Madeline."

"How do you know that, Charlie?" Steven asked.

"Because they were my houseguests," Charlie said. She did not offer anymore, and no one pressed. "Look, there they are!"

Charlie pointed at the pavilion in the distance. Two silhouettes appeared. The larger one immediately threw up. Then they sat for a while, longer than usual, Danny stroking her hair, kissing her forehead before Madeline floated into her waiting wheelchair.

"Hi," Charlie was the first to greet them when they arrived on the porch. In silence, Danny went to sit on the swing. Madeline pulled out a scarf from her pocket and handed it to her friend. Charlie smelled it and smiled sadly. "Out of all the things I know, I prayed and prayed this would somehow have a different ending. I wanted to warn you, but..."

"We will be blessed again," Madeline whispered. Everyone looked away but Jane, her eyes welled up with tears. Madeline sighed. "By the way, John Luc asked me to remind you that you were his everything." Charlie kissed both Madeline and Danny, then flew away.

"I have to get a few books from Henry's," Madeline said. everyone was still quiet. "Do you mind if I take Jane?"

"Ok… can you please blink to the office and back?" Danny wanted to say no but knew she needed a minute with Jane.

"And I should check on Ida," Madeline added.

"I'm hungry; we should get food, too," Jane added. She knew her best friend needed a girl's lunch; she ignored a dirty look from Mack. "Of course, not in the state, silly." Jane grinned at Mack thinking he would smile; he did not. Madeline blinked before Danny could express his objections.

"You didn't tell her, did you?" Mack asked after the girls left.

"I did…" Danny said. "But she thinks I can do my lawyer thing, and she can do a magic thing, and this will all go away."

"Daniel." Mack frowned.

"We went through a really rocky period." Danny said. "And the longer we were there, the problem that I made in our marriage seemed more overwhelming than Louis Delcroix. And when I finally got my head out of my ass, I couldn't say, thanks for taking me back, now you might go to jail for kidnapping me. Wanna fool around some more…"

"But y'all are ok now, right?" Mack asked. "Because I'm pretty sure Jane and I want custody of her in the divorce."

"Where is your loyalty?" Danny asked. "We are better. I love her more every day. It sounds like a cliché, but I do. And she has this ridiculously forgiving streak. But she is tired. And lost so much, especially this trip. She's so damn tired."

"Do you want to talk about what you lost…" Mack asked.

"I will," Danny said. "But right now, I need to talk about what I have and how I can keep that. I'm going to call Frank and ask him to come out in the morning. We can come up with a plan before he gets here, and hopefully, my wife will have a good few hours with Jane. She deserves a good day."

"Agreed," Mack said. "So, was it all bad? You are looking mighty buff, non-sexually, I mean."

"Fencing, five hours a day, six hours a week, four years," Danny said. Mack and Steven looked impressed. "And Madeline probably got an equivalent to a PhD in Alchemy."

"Out of all the crazy things I've learned this year," Steven said. "Madeline's a powerful witch is easier to accept than her really learning Alchemy... She almost didn't graduate because she kept putting off taking a science." they all laughed.

"Hey, you..." Mack answered the phone, "Don't be mad. Janie..." Mack got up and stepped off the porch. "They did what?" Mack looked at a picture Jane sent. "I know... I didn't want to scare you... I thought they would have gone by now? In blood? Oh, honey. I'm so sorry. I know... Where's Madds? Has she seen it... A shrine? It's a little funny... Ok. I'll tell him. Please get out of there. I really didn't think it would be this bad, Janie. Hurry back."

"What?" Danny asked. As Mack returned to the porch scratching his head.

"Bad or worse thing?" Mack asked.

"Worse," Danny said.

"Kill the witch," Mack said. "Is written on the windows. Madeline hasn't seen it. Jane is going to try to get her out of there without her seeing it."

"And..." Danny sighed.

"There's a makeshift shrine to you." Mack really tried not to laugh. "The women of the city are heartbroken that you are either dead or under Madeline's spell."

"We are going to have to talk to Frank today?" Danny exhaled and asked.

"Yup," Mack said. "I'll call him to come tonight."

"Steven…" Danny said. "A really bad storm is about to hit us. Macky is too dumb to leave, and Jane is probably too loyal. Madeline.. is Madeline. You can have a few weeks off. Paid, of course."

"Naw," Steven said. "What can I do?"

"We bring steaks and wine back to appease our males and Steven," Jane announced as they blinked back to the porch just before sunset. Jane carrying grocery bags, Madeline, books, and wine.

"Somehow, I know that was a dig at me, but I'm hungry, so I don't particularly care." Steven teased Jane.

"Hello. What was that for?' Danny grinned as Madeline kissed him long and tenderly upon returning, stroking his cheek...

"It's really bad out there," Madeline whispered. "It all clicked when I saw the threats written in blood. I'm sorry it scared you so much you could not tell me. Explain to me how to fix this, and this one time, I'll do exactly what you say." They kissed again. "But Mack and I are going to give you so much crap for your shrine. Including the bras and edible underwear."

"Please tell me you got pictures," Mack said.

"Of course I did," Madeline said. "Plus, the envelopes filled with love letters and glitter. We can pick out Danny's next wife before they burn me." Mack couldn't help but laugh; Steven and Danny did not. Madeline kissed Danny until he grinned again. "I'm going to help Jane make dinner and look over the books that John Luc told me to pull…"

"She must be scared to death if she is going to do exactly what you say," Steven said as the girls disappeared into the cabin. Mack smirked as Danny held his head.

*

"I'm sorry, that's the best I can do, Danny," Frank said as they finished dinner later that night. "It just would appear better if you and Madeline

Page | 345

came involuntarily. They really wanted you to come to the station. Still, I convinced them that the public would absolutely appreciate the care of the police if they accommodated one of their city's favorite sons. Plus, this unintentionally gives Louis Delcroix more media exposure and all that crap."

"Yup. I know. At least if it's done at the apartments, we can control part of the narrative." Danny scratched his chin.

"So... if this witch doctor decides I have put a love spell on Danny, I go to jail?" Madeline asked bluntly.

"Madds..." Danny sighed.

"And if I didn't, he might just say I did to please the dragon, so I'll still end up in jail?"

"Yes." Frank looked down. "Until I can prove my new boss is corrupt as hell."

"Hello?" there was suddenly a knock at the door. It was Charlie with a very old woman Madeline did not recognize.

"Aunt Geneva." Mack and Danny squealed and ran to hug her. Jane and Madeline stared at each other in amusement. Their bruiting men turned into little boys instantly.

"Did you bring pie?" Mack asked. Madeline and Jane almost choked on their wine from laughter.

"Yes, Malcolm," Geneva said. Geneva was a very large woman with dark skin. She looked to be the oldest human Madeline had ever seen. When she smiled, her face lit up the whole room. When she frowned, she was stern and scary.

"So. Many. Questions..." Jane hissed at Madeline.

"Frank, how's your boo?" Geneva asked.

"She's really good. I, however, am in denial. She threw out my treadmill. At first, I was happy because I thought she surprised me with a recliner. But nope, it was to make room for a crib for our first grandbaby, so..." Frank smiled. Geneva laughed.

"Your daughter will spit dat babe out, tell Diane no worries," Geneva said to Frank very matter-of-factly, then turned to Danny. "I'm sorry bout Henry, my Daniel. I wanted to be at his wake, but I had a horrible day that kept me in pain and in bed."

"He knew you were there in spirit, Aunt Geneva," Danny said.

"The bastard probably died for a bet; he always said I'd outlive him," Geneva said. Everyone laughed quietly. "Your mama's ok?"

"Yes, mam," Danny said. "She's... hanging in there."

"I should visit her more... I just don't get out often..." Geneva said.

"I will give her a big hug from you when I see her tomorrow," Danny said.

"Thank you," Geneva said. "So Danny, Votre amour?"

"Yes, mam!" Danny said.

"You don't think dat girl hexed you, and you're thinking with your little head?" Geneva asked dead serious, everyone else howled. Danny was mortified.

"If I die this very second, Please know I went so very happy," Mack said.

"Aunt Geneva," Danny said after regaining his composure and smacking Mack really hard. "This is my Madeline." Madeline and Jane had been hanging out in the kitchen. Madeline rolled towards her, now sensing that Geneva had many magical powers.

"Oh, my girl." Geneva sighed in amazement. "You are indeed the direct descendant, aren't you?" suddenly, Geneva's Cajun accent went away. Geneva enjoyed playing the crazy witch lady who lived in the swamp around strangers. It was part of her self protection. But the moment she saw Madeline...

"I don't know, mam," Madeline said shyly.

"We can discuss that later," Geneva said. "Have you put a love spell on my Daniel?"

"No, mam, I don't think so; I would think he'd behave better if I did," Madeline said. Aunt Geneva screamed with laughter.

"You married into Guidry blood. Not even your spells are that powerful. This cabin is bursting with magical energy, none of which is a love spell." Geneva sighed. Madeline hid a tear. "Frank, what time is the circus tomorrow?"

"Noon," Frank said.

"Can you get 5 of us upfront?" Geneva asked.

"I can try," Frank said.

"Walk me out, please," Geneva said as the very old woman struggled to get up. "Malcolm, you can get the pie in the car if you get off your butt and follow your heart for once in your life."

"Not as stinging as asking about my private parts, but she's still on point," Danny whispered to Mack, looking redeemed.

"Is it apple or cherry, Aunt Geneva? It might matter a lot..." Mack asked. Geneva laughed.

"Madeline, tomorrow will not be the best day, but you have had and will have far worse, try to get some sleep," Geneva said and disappeared into the awaiting car.

"I'm going to stay with Geneva tonight," Charlie said.

"Who the hell was that?" Jane asked after Frank said goodnight too. Shaking Danny's hand, whispering something Madeline couldn't hear.

"That was the head of the council of witches and best pie maker in the south with a Harvard law degree. I still call her for advice." Danny said. "Actually, all the kids were terrified of her. She and Ida were extremely close. We were too bratty and loved her pies too much to realize we should be scared of her too."

"And Madeline," Danny added. "As you do, without even trying, you won Geneva over. But I would like to question Mack on another issue, just for a second. So, Macky..."

"Shut up and eat your pie," Mack nodded to Danny. "Grown-up conversations can wait for another night. I propose we finish dessert and go for a long walk on the beach."

"I second that," Jane said.

"I think I might try to grab a coffee with Elizabeth tonight," Steven said. "Unless you…"

"Nope. All talked out." Madeline said.

"I'll check on the restaurant and the apartments, too," Steven said, squeezing Madeline's arm and kissing the top of her head. "We'll meet at 10?"

"Yup. 10," Madeline said.

*

"Is it ok that I'm here? I feel like this is kinda a private breakfast," Elizabeth said as they all gathered in Madeline and Danny's apartment.

"Naw, it's all good," Madeline said.

"Did you get any sleep last night?" Jane asked.

"Yup," Madeline said.

"Liar," Danny said.

"Maybe I would have if you weren't staring at me every time I rolled over." Madeline teased. "It was a bit stalker-y," Danny could not help but grin.

"So I revised my will," Madeline said.

"Madds," Danny whispered.

"Just indulge me…" Madeline said. "I couldn't protect my friends in the explosion, I invited Louis Delcroix into my gallery time after time. We should be knee-deep in diapers and spit-up instead of… I…"

"Madds…" Jane cried.

"Just…" Madeline forced a smile. "Ok, I want to leave Charlie my shares of the restaurant… Henry would approve. And it would keep a balance. Otherwise, Mack would lose all food decisions, and Jane would lose all the restaurant's votes. Tell me I'm wrong." Mack and Danny bowed their heads, knowing she was right.

"Steven gets all my books." Madeline continued. "I do ask that you keep them in Henry's office. I think if books had souls, they would say they belong there. And you should learn alchemy. You'll like it. And I know this is a big ask, and I know he has Mack, but…"

"Yup," Steven said. "It's not an ask anymore."

"Mack…" Madeline teased. "You know in your heart, it probably should be Jane and Danny and you and me."

"Probably…" Mack lovingly grinned, blinking away a tear.

"If…" Madeline hesitated. "If the worse happens, you need to talk him down. He still has the restaurant… and his practice… and Ida."

"But…" Mack exhaled… "Who will talk me down?" Mack shrugged. "I'm going to check on Frank; this is bullshit." The rest followed Mack out.

"In my top drawer…"

"I'm not doing this, Madeline," Danny said, trying not to yell.

"I enchanted all your socks." Madeline ignored his plead, "They will help you control your weight. And in a few years, when you start dating someone that Jane and Charlie pick out for you… you can. You know…"

"I'm pretty sure at this moment in time the whole world can see, you do not have a love spell on me," Danny screamed without screaming. "We are going to go out there just like we rehearsed. It will clean up everything. The city will apologize. We'll start the remodel, and while that's going on, I'm taking all of us to Hawaii for three weeks."

"Then what?" Madeline screamed back, in case they were fighting.

"I dunno." Danny shrugged. "I kinda lost my train of thought with you in a bikini in Hawaii." He reached to touch her when there was a knock on the door.

"It's time," Frank said.

"I have the exact same goal since the first time we talked all night." Danny choked. "Marry the girl, have a few kids, live happily ever after. And you know I'm very goal orientated."

"You wanted eight." Madeline reminded him.

"That was before I knew you would be with me just cuz," Danny teased. They stared at each other in silence for a very long time before Frank knocked on the door again.

*

Madeline was a little taken back as they walked into their courtyard that now looked like a set up for some kind of performance. There was a small stage. And about 75 seats, 25 more than comfortably fitted.

Frank escorted the two on the stage, making them sit on opposite ends. Madeline had to keep reminding herself to breathe. She wished she was still touching Danny, knowing if they were holding hands, she could so easily blink them to a desert island.

But Danny, of course, knew Madeline would have thought of this, so he made her promise not to, at least not yet. Danny knew there was a high probability that they could win back public opinion today with a little help. In the worst-case scenario, they would disappear to a desert island. At this point, between Danny's resources and Madeline's magic, it didn't seem like a bad option at all.

Madeline stared at the crowd as they entered now. Drag queen Charlie entered first, helping Geneva on her walker. They sat in the front row right in front of Madeline. Geneva winked. Charlie blew a kiss. Madeline recognized the other three ladies sitting with them from Henry's wake but did not recall their names or relationships to him. Mack, Steven, Jane, and Elizabeth were standing on Jane's balcony. Mack looked prepared to defend his turf as he and Danny stared at each other.

As the courtyard filled up, Madeline got more and more nervous. But she knew Frank purposely arranged the seating so she would see friendly faces in the crowd. She appreciated that more than Frank would ever know.

Madeline guessed a quarter of the crowd were police. A quarter were supporters of magic, a quarter were haters, and a quarter made up Danny's fan club. As Madeline gave him the evil eye, he knew what wild thoughts his wife was imagining.

After the chairs filled, the rest of the audience flowed into the streets. Madeline noticed many were in long flowing white gowns just like Geneva was wearing and felt a calmness from looking at them.

"I'm Franklin Trahan; I'm head of special investigations." Frank started, stepping onto the stage. "Daniel Boudreaux and Madeline Guidry Boudreaux have come here today voluntarily. We are trying to put together a case against Mrs. Boudreaux, including the kidnapping and brainwashing of one Daniel Boudreaux." Out of the corner of Madeline's eye, she saw Jane punch Steven, probably for a snide comment only Madeline would appreciate.

"We have hired an independent witch doctor, a Dale Roberts from Alabama, to help us determine if Daniel Boudreaux is indeed under a witch's spell." Frank hesitated. "If he is, Madeline Guidry Boudreaux will immediately be placed under arrest." Madeline winked at Danny, trying to distract him from allowing his anger to turn him.

Frank walked off the stage and stood in a corner where he had a clear view of everyone and wore an earpiece linked to Mack incase Mack spotted something Frank missed. Frank would have felt better if he had had the chance to meet Roberts beforehand, but his boss assured him that this was unnecessary.

Geneva smiled to herself as Dale Roberts made the crowd wait 11 minutes to appear. The classic stalling technique to intimidate and gain the upper hand. They warned Madeline this would happen, but it did not make the seconds pass any faster.

"Good afternoon," Dale Roberts said. He was a tall, bulky man with a booming voice. He wore a long black gown and a hat. Geneva assumed he ordered them on Amazon as she saw an untucked tag in the back of his neck. "Let us bow our heads for a moment of silence and pray that our ancestors guide us in finding the truth today. Freeing Daniel Boudreaux from any curses." All the civilians bowed their heads. But none of the women in white dresses, including Geneva, did.

Dale Roberts did not bow his head either. He kept shifting his eyes from Geneva to the crowd to the two men in the very back of the courtyard; one was Frank's new boss, the other was Louis Delcroix. Mack watched them like hawks because Danny could not.

"Will you Danny and Madeline hold hands?" Dale Roberts asked nervously. They did, and Danny smiled at her. Madeline was too focused on trying not to freak out to smile back.

"Excuse me," Geneva interrupted, Charlie helping her up. "Don't let that girl hold da boy's hand; it makes dat spell stronger. If she's a lot mad, he could go boom."

"I know what I'm doing." Dale Roberts said, his voice cracking a little, sticking to his performance, but signaling to Danny to release Madeline's hand. Danny did not.

Dale Roberts reached in his pocket and poured a potion around their feet. After four years of alchemy, Madeline easily recognized the potion was pure Himalayan pink salt, with absolutely no magic attached to it. Madeline was tired of being scared, and now she was just annoyed. But she promised to behave. Roberts continued his little dance for a few more minutes, then sent Madeline back to her corner.

"I proclaim that Daniel Boudreaux is..." Dale Roberts tried to finish his sentence, but his next words were muted. He tried again. "I proclaim that Daniel Boudreaux is..." again, his next words were silenced. He stared at Louis Delcroix and Frank's boss, then the first row of women. "I proclaim that Daniel Boudreaux is... free from any love spells. He takes her hand with completely free will and an open heart." 75% of the crowd cheered and rejoiced.

"Everyone hang on, while we are all here..." Geneva said as Roberts was trying to rush off the stage. "Madeline, do you see Louis Delcroix in the area?" Louis Delcroix now tried rushing out of the courtyard, but he was blocked by the women in white.

"I do," Madeline said.

"Did you try to kill him?" Geneva asked.

"No," Madeline said.

"Did you kill Eugene Boudreaux?" Geneva asked.

"No," Madeline said.

"And... I have to ask..." Geneva stalled for a second. "Did you kill Henry Guidry?"

"No," Madeline whispered. Danny blinked away a tear, hoping she finally believed it.

"That doesn't prove anything; you are probably one of her goonies." Louis Delcroix yelled.

"Henry sent me to law school, Harvard, class of 45. Just to save you from googling." Geneva said. "If this little girl put any kind of hexed on Daniel or touched a single hair on Henry Guidry. I can assure you that our community would have already taken care of her internally. Probably me, personally. Seems like a good way to use the few spells I have in me left."

"But..." Louis Delcroix said.

"Because I'm still a practicing lawyer..." Geneva said. "I feel required to tell you that, My friend, Mary, to the left of me, placed a truth spell on the stage..."

Before Geneva finished her speech, Louis Delcroix disappeared into the crowd, followed closely by Dale Roberts.

"I guess that concludes this circus." Frank announced, "Thank you to the Boudreaux's for their cooperation. If you do not reside here, please leave. This courtyard is now for tenants only."

"Hey, Danny." Rich approached him as he was hugging Madeline. Rich was the editor and chief of the newspaper. "We, of course, fired Louis Delcroix."

"That's a nice first step," Danny said.

"And we will, of course, print an apology to you and your lovely wife." Rich offered.

"On the front page, top fold," Danny said. "And a large article in the Sunday section next month featuring our chef the day before we re-open." Richard nodded and walked away, knowing Danny could have asked for so much more.

"Thank you, Aunt Geneva." Danny dropped to the ground to be face to face with her." Madeline nodded frantically, still overcome with emotion, unable to speak as the courtyard slowly cleared out.

"I feel bad that it was at Madeline's expense, but that was the most fun I had in many moons," Geneva said.

"I asked the nurse to take mom to the zoo today; they should be back in an hour," Danny said. "Will you stay? There's nothing I'd love more than to cook dinner for my girls."

"You can rest in our apartment for a while; we would be honored to have you," Madeline said.

"And… we can argue Louisiana vs. Smith?" Geneva asked Danny. He kissed her cheek.

"Did you read the appeal? Complete rhetoric." Danny said.

"You're jealous. You miss it?" Geneva asked.

"So much…" Danny admitted. This made Madeline sad. But for the moment, Danny seemed less worried. He seemed happy to be home. Happy to have dinner with Geneva, Madeline, Charlie, and his mom.

Madeline was relieved that the restaurant and Danny's reputation would make a full recovery. And that all her friends were healthy. And she really did try to enjoy the day. Madeline smiled during the celebratory dinner, surrounded by the people she loved most. But could not shake the feeling that the worse for her was yet to come, and that was unimaginable.

Chapter 21

"I'm so tired; rub my feet," Jane said, flopping herself onto Henry's couch in the office. Madeline was stretched out too.

"They keep telling you to hire a full-time sous chef," Madeline said.

"I'd much rather complain and have you rub my feet in the middle of the day," Jane said. "Maybe when Danny goes back to law. I like the challenge because I know Henry ran the kitchen for decades by himself."

"We recently doubled the seating and have been completely booked for the last month," Madeline said. "Besides now, we have more important stuff to do. Are you excited?"

"I am," Jane said. Madeline rolled her eyes. "I am as excited as you are happy. Danny thinks you... seem sad. All the time."

"I think Elizabeth wants to move in together." Steven barged in and flopped himself in the chair.

"How do you know that?" Jane asked.

"Cuz, she said..." Steven sighed. "Hey honey, let's move in together."

"And you said he didn't understand women and was emotionally stunted." Jane snickered at Madeline. "You haven't been home in two weeks; just do it. Mack needs the closet space."

"Right after you pick out a date." Steven pointed at Jane.

"He wants a big wedding," Jane said.

"You did too... once..." Madeline said.

"And..." Jane said. "We all know how that ended. I want to get married by Millie's roses. Just us."

"So tell him," Madeline said. "I think he suggested a big wedding because he thought you wanted one. Tell him you want a garden wedding." Madeline pointed at Jane, then turning to Steven, "You tell Elizabeth you'll move in..."

"Your turn," Jane said. "How shall we fix our most beloved witch?"

"Between us, I feel like I'm doing the best I can right now," Madeline admitted. "Hawaii was fantastic. The restaurant Is back on track. I'm researching and training every day. My husband still likes me, which is kinda cool.... but..."

"But what, honey?" Jane asked.

" I feel like we keep taking two steps forwards and three steps back. Louis Delcroix is still out there." Madeline said. "We still have two more pillars to visit. We are learning so much from each trip, but I'm emotionally drained. I keep losing parts of myself. And between us, as morbid as it sounds... the more I think about it, I think I'm supposed to sacrifice myself to kill the dragon. What if I have to turn myself into a powerful bomb? If it saves the world, my folks, you guys, and Danny, I think I can make peace with my fate..."

"But then I kiss him, or we talk about trips we want to take or our future. Even something as dumb as buying furniture. It takes everything in me not to fall to pieces. And he's standing behind me frowning his sexy frown, huh?"

"Yup," Steven said. "Frowning for sure. I don't know about the sexy part,"

"For a giant, you are awfully quiet on your feet," Madeline said.

"It's the socks." Danny grinned, pushing Madeline up so he could sit behind her and hugged her waist.

"Hello," there was a knock on the door, it was Geneva with Charlie behind her. Madeline sat up as Jane did the same.

"Aunt Geneva, what a wonderful surprise," Danny said.

"I had a doctor's appointment downtown, and I was feeling unusually good, so I'd thought I'd come to see Ida and you," Geneva said. "Ida didn't recognize me today."

"I'm sorry," Danny said. "She has been foggier lately; she goes through phases."

"May I bring you a late lunch?" Jane asked.

"No, thank you, child," Geneva said. "But I'm sure glad Malcolm used his 5 words this month to ask you to marry him." Everyone laughed.

"He's up to 10 words now, I'm very proud," Danny said. Jane and Steven excused themselves as Charlie helped Geneva into a chair.

"Madeline," Geneva asked. "Can I have one of Henry's secretly world-famous cigars? My nurse at home frowns upon them, but a girl has needs." Madeline grinned, going towards the room. Charlie declined, but Danny wanted one too, Madeline would share his.

"So," Geneva said. "As you can see, I'm on my last leg. But I wanted to give you this personally."

"Ms. Geneva, I'm learning alchemy. Is there anything I can do for you?" Madeline asked.

"One, call me Aunt Geneva," She said. "Or it will hurt my feelings. And if it was 25 years ago, I'd trade my left arm to have you work on me. But at this point. My body is too far gone. But you are just as lovely as Henry described."

"Not even something for the pain," Madeline offered again.

"Well..." Geneva sighed. "I am in a world of hurt... I'd sure appreciate you trying. Oh, I almost forgot, two, the delivery. This envelope is from Henry. I've been holding on to it since Ida turned three. He was very specific when I could give it to you."

"Thank you," Madeline said, hugging the envelope then putting it on her desk... "I'm sure it will keep me up all night. But for now, let's go in my potion area."

-

*

"Is your husband actually sleeping?" Charlie teased as Madeline appeared wrapped in a blanket in the courtyard in the middle of the night.

"Only took a month of 15 hour days..." Madeline said. "You look beautiful tonight, Charlie."

"The rain woke me," Charlie said. "I thought I heard Kisseis. Then I started thinking of John Luc, and I guess I turned into his wife as a reflex. Go figure."

"There's something I've been dying to ask you," Madeline admitted. "Last year, when we met, you told me that you were bad at magic and your drag queen alter was the best you could do..."

"John Luc helped me perfect my human form," Charlie said. "And I feel like I'm cheating when..." she shrugged.

"Surely, he would want you to be happy," Madeline said.

"Than he should have discovered a potion that would have made him lived longer." Charlie sighed, a little bitter.

"Elizabeth is looking for someone to teach alchemy," Madeline said. "You could ask to teach it in the gallery... I could give you a refresher course."

"Aren't you, Dear Abby, lately? Trying to send everyone in the right direction?" Charlie asked. "Have you interviewed Danny's future wife yet?"

"I know you're kidding, but that's a good idea," Madeline said. "Being a storm giant's wife... has certain issues."

"Stop." Charlie laughed.

"Will I ever be happy again, Charlie?" Madeline's tone turned sad.

"Yes. I promise." Charlie whispered.

"How about you?" Madeline asked.

"I had 70 years of wedded bliss. My kid is alive, I think. I get to watch a new generation in Henry's restaurant. It's enough." Charlie said.

"Is it?" Madeline asked.

"But maybe..." Charlie hesitated. "I'll talk to Elizabeth. Would you help me create a curriculum and catch me up? I remember the basics, I think. I should. I spent thousands of hours in his lab."

"Steven has been bugging me about showing him a few things, too," Madeline said. "Maybe in the afternoons? It probably will be good for me too."

"Yup," Charlie said. "Have you looked at what Henry sent you yet?"

"Nope," Madeline said. "I'm scared to read it. I'm scared of everything, Charlie. What kind of witch can I be?'

"Better than a careless powerful witch..." Charlie said. "So much better."

"Will you read the letter to me?" Madeline asked. She floated to lean against Charlie, wrapping them both in her quilt that Charlie recognized, one of the ones Millie had made.

"Sure." Charlie choked a little as she began...

"My dearest Madeline." Henry wrote. "When you chose me as your mentor, I was given one of the greatest gifts in my life. I would much prefer to be physically there so that I can help guide you. But I guess this will have to do."

"It saddens me to know you have hit one of the lowest points in your life. Your smile hides your fears, your laughter hides your longing temptation to give up. A lesser human would."

"But I do beg you to continue. I could give you the guilt trip of saving the world from the evil dragon, but it's much more personal to me. You deserve galleries and babies, and my Daniel deserves a happily ever after. And you can't just half-ass it. Half ass'ing it is the only thing that will assure your untimely death. And the only thing that will truly break Danny. So stop it."

"You have to continue to the next pillar. It will be physically exhausting, I'm not going to lie. But your heart will finally mend from Paris. I promise you that on everything I love."

"Please hug Ida for me. Thank you for loving her as you do. Although it will be short, get to know Geneva. She is a wealth of knowledge. No, your Masters in Alchemy will not save her, nor could it have saved Millie or even me. So stop thinking about it... See, I know stuff too."

"Thank you, sweet Charlie, for reading this. My love and complete adoration to you both. Safe travels Madeline, I'm afraid the next pillar is going to hurt."

"Wife!" Danny peaked out the door, rubbing one eye. Charlie gave Madeline the letter, kissed her cheek, popped back into a pixie, and flew back to her apartment.

"Coming, my love," Madeline said. "I think... We should go ahead and talk to an architect about tearing down the vacant apartment wall next to ours. We should start planning for the future.."

"He's coming at 4 Monday." Danny grinned sleepily.

*

"That's amazing," Mack said.

"Almost paid for the remodel in two months," Danny said, throwing a ball in Henry's office to Mack sitting across from him. "You really don't want to learn the books? Incase..."

"Nope," Mack said.

"You're an idiot,"

"So I've been told," Mack said. "Steven, is that you?" He was walking past Henry's office when Mack summoned him.

"Hey," Steven said. Mack invited him to sit.

"Do you know anyone who might wanna bartend during the week?" Mack asked. "You can take over the scheduling."

"I guess this is us talking about it," Danny said.

"There's nothing to talk about til I pass the tests," Mack said.

"Please tell me you have discussed this with your fiancé." Danny sighed.

"There's nothing to talk about til I pass the tests,"

"We are both going to be divorced by 35, just from sheer stupidity, aren't we?" Danny asked.

"Naw." Mack said. "They seem to embrace our stupidity, or you'd be separated by now."

"That's probably true," Danny admitted. "Frank wants to retire in five years, and he wants to groom Mack to take over his job."

"Is that what you want to do?" Steven asked.

"Yup," Mack said. "That was always the plan; bartending was going to pay for it. Then I got comfortable, then I met a girl... then Henry..."

"I think Jane would want you to be happy," Steven said.

"Hey..." Charlie flew in. "Why do you all look so damn guilty?"

"Little Macky is in the hot seat this week..." Danny pointed and grinned.

"I don't want to know." Charlie sighed. "How's your wife, Daniel?"

"She's..." Danny said. "She's trying harder. Which should make me feel better, but it actually has the opposite effect."

"Where is she today, anyway?" Charlie asked.

"Madeline..." Danny hesitated. "She has been working on a... potion... to take to prevent us from getting pregnant again until we are ready. Ya know after we kill the avatars and dragon... I guess my mighty sperm is too strong for human birth control," Danny tried to laugh, but no one else did. "Madeline wanted John Luc to triple check it and didn't want to make you sad knowing she would see him today."

"Naw..." Charlie said. "Other than me, she was his favorite person. Which is sort of why I'm here."

"What is it, Charlie?" Danny asked.

"You know how Madeline has you three, Kushemi, Henry, and John Luc. And probably almost everybody wrapped around her pinky after one, sometimes two conversations with her?"

"Yup," Danny said.

"Her next pillar..." Charlie said. "Is difficult."

"Difficult?" Danny asked. "Charlie, you said this trip would heal us…"

"Listen, usually I'd tell Madeline this," Charlie said. "But she needs to go uninfluenced and with an open heart. You, however, need to prepare yourself."

"Wow, I do not like this conversation." Danny raised his voice. "You need to tell me everything right now, or we won't go."

"Daniel!" Charlie said.

"You didn't even warn me about…" Danny threw the ball, breaking a frame on Madeline's desk. He sighed, walk towards the broken glass and magically fixed the frame. "I apologize, sweet Charlie, please tell me what I need to do for my wife." Charlie nodded and began.

*

"Danny… Love… not here…" Madeline giggled a little, eyes closed, too exhausted to roll over. "Stop… ouch. Daniel… What the hell, husband? That freaking hurts…" Madeline turned her head and opened her eyes.

Dread washed over her as she saw Danny lying next to her, still passed out cold from the furthest blink they have ever shared. Madeline rolled on her back and found a very old man standing over her. Poking her really hard with a bamboo stick.

Madeline closed her eyes again, still very weak from their blink. When she reopened them, Danny was now standing by her head, 10 feet tall. Growling at Yoritoshi. The two stared at each other for what seemed like forever. Then Yoritoshi took one step back from Madeline, slapped Danny across the face with his bamboo stick. By the time Danny could react, Yoritoshi was across the field.

After Danny watched the old man enter his house about 300 yards from them, Danny dropped to lay on his back, closer to his wife, holding her hand, now laughing.

"What is wrong with you?" Madeline asked, turning to look at him. "Sit up, honey, you're bleeding. Let me heal you." He sat up in the grassy field, his wife gently stroking his cheek.

"I owe Charlie $500," Danny smirked. Madeline grew annoyed, not understanding why Danny was smiling. "She bet I wouldn't last 24 hours here without going all storm gianty... Ouch!" Madeline's last healing stroke was less than tender.

"Who do you think that guy was?" Madeline asked.

"Probably the caretaker of this farm. We might be trespassing. We can figure it out tomorrow. Look, there is our cabin; let's go in there and catch our breath." Danny picked up Madeline and placed her in a cart.

"How do you know that?" Madeline asked. "Daniel..."

"Charlie prepped me for this blink..." Danny confessed.

"Why?" Madeline was almost afraid to ask.

"Just trust me," Danny said as they entered their new, very small, one-room shack. Madeline scratched her head, very unimpressed.

"Charlie described this as our honeymoon," Madeline said. "She has a very odd sense of humor, sometimes."

"I don't know, Madds," Danny said. "A honeymoon... A million miles from nowhere. No avatars. No dragons. Just us, sounds kinda perfect to me. Why don't we.... Stay in tonight. Unpack our trunks. Surely we could find something to do..." Madeline could not resist his smile and floated to hug him. Danny felt a little guilty about what was coming the next few months but for now...

*

"Wow..." Danny yelled. "This is really bad coffee." sitting up from the blanket they had slept on.

"Tomorrow, you can figure it out, husband." Madeline rolled back into the hut from outside, where they had started a fire to cook.

"I really love you. You are the most beautiful creature on earth." Danny said. He tells Madeline this about a dozen times a day and usually says it from the heart. But this sounded very suspicious, like a plea, trying to ease into something he regrets, a bribe or, worst of all, a pep talk.

"You've been fed and serviced... There is nothing in your amazon cart at home; I checked before we left. What have you done, Boudreaux?" Madeline teased.

"I'm a storm giant; I require much feeding and much servicing." Danny grinned. Stalling a little, he knowing they had to talk shop now. "So, what did Charlie and/or Henry tell you about this pillar?"

"His name is Yoritoshi," Madeline said. "He is the pillar of martial arts. I personally think this is a setup. You just wanted to learn to sword fight." Madeline accused. "Why do I need to learn this?"

"Nope, not a setup. But I shall keep that in mind for future trips." Danny said. "I have always wanted to be a cowboy in the wild west..."

"I would like to stay in our time for a year, or 20." Madeline tried not to sound sad. Danny pulled her closer, kissing her. "Yoritoshi, pillar of the sword, learn things, go home. That's about all I know."

"I think," Danny said. "We met him yesterday... and he may or may not be thrilled to see us."

"We'll apologize for landing in his field; you use your charm, I'll win him over with my poor little girl in wheelchair act..." Madeline smiled. Danny wished he could take a picture of her happy face. For she might never smile when talking about Yoritoshi ever again. "Let me get in my chair, and we'll float over."

"Madds," Danny sighed, "Charlie said he hates magic, so maybe I should carry you over... just for today..." Danny bowed his head waiting for the screams.

"He hates magic?" Madeline asked.

"And... females, that are... strong.... With opinions." Danny sighed.

"You should have told me last night," Madeline said. "I could have prepared better. Or have baked cookies with a "like me" potion. All of my pillars have found me irresistible. He will too. Stop smiling. I'm going to float over there and politely ask him to teach us."

"Madds, do not…" Danny said to an empty hut. "Blink… there… please…" Danny decided to watch Yoritoshi and Madeline's first interaction from a distance. "I will stay calm… Charlie was probably just messing with me. She over exaggerates all the time." Danny reminded himself.

Madeline blinked to Yoritoshi's door. He was not there when Madeline was still at the hut with Danny, but in the instant that it took her to blink to his door, he had appeared, seemingly waiting for her. Danny felt something and instantly began running to her, growing simultaneously.

Danny screamed as he watched Madeline blink to appear right in front of Yoritoshi. He made his bamboo stick appear out of nowhere and smacked Madeline on her neck in one swift movement. She immediately fell to the ground. Passed out cold.

Danny completely lost his temper, again. as Charlie predicted. He charged at Yoritoshi but came to a dead stop about a foot in front of him. As if there was an invisible forcefield around Yoritoshi. Before Danny could do anything, Yoritoshi took his bamboo stick and smacked both of Danny's legs, plus a bonus strike on his arm. Yoritoshi then turned, went back into his small house, and shut the door without saying a word.

Madeline woke about an hour later in their hut to Danny's pacing. She slowly sat up as he rushed to her side, sitting behind her as she rubbed her neck.

"After you rest, we can blink home," Danny said.

"What?" Madeline asked, very surprised.

"You heard me," Danny said in his callus lawyer storm giant voice, the one Madeline hated.

"Why?" Madeline asked.

"Because he tried to kill us twice," Danny said.

"Oh, silly boy," Madeline said. "I'm pretty sure that if he was trying to kill us, we would be dead."

"How can you not be going ballistic?" Danny asked. Almost shocked at her calmness. "Do you have a concussion?"

"I think," Madeline said. "He might be the most powerful pillar of them all. But Charlie obviously told you that..."

"Yes," Danny admitted. "She warned that he would be hardcore, and I needed to let you find your way with him. But he hit you, Madds, that's unacceptable."

"Henry knew," Madeline whispered. "And he sent us here anyways. That screams volumes of how important Yoritoshi must be. Henry specifically said this trip would physically hurt. I think we are where we are supposed to be. Besides you, Henry would be the last person on earth to put me in harm's way unless there were no other options, you know this."

"I didn't even see his attacks coming," Danny admitted. "How is that even possible?" Danny's anger slowly turned to tactical questions and curiosity. "I was the best fencer in Paris for two years, and I was completely blindsided by Yoritoshi. We are going to have to go back and try to play nice, aren't we?"

"I think so..." Madeline said.

"Charlie has a scroll; I'm supposed to give it to him. It should explain our predicament and make him more accommodating." Danny said. "You would have known that if you didn't go there half-cocked..." he smirked.

"You could have told me last night," Madeline accused. He smiled shyly.

"I got distracted last night. I think..." Danny said. "We should rest today... and try again tomorrow. One deadly blow a day on our honeymoon seems enough..." he made Madeline float to him.

*

"Charlie was very specific on this part," Danny said as they finished breakfast the next morning. "She said, I need to go to Yoritoshi's door, present the scroll while bowing on both knees. He might play hard to get for a few minutes. Then my winning smile will charm him. And he will train us."

"Don't you think I should do it?" Madeline asked.

"Charlie said it had to be me," Danny said. "I go make peace, clean the hut, woman." Madeline patted his butt as he left the hut with the scroll. "I probably shouldn't say that to the most powerful witch in America, huh?" he teased, walking backward into the fields stupidly grinning at his wife. She giggled.

As Danny walked closer and closer to Yoritoshi's hut, Madeline sensed the more serious Danny became. she laughed a tiny bit as Danny messed with his hair as he approached Yoritoshi's. Danny looked back at Madeline one more time for moral support, put on his game face, and knocked.

Being a time lock, Madeline knew it took Yoritoshi exactly 12 minutes and 51 seconds to answer the door. When Yoritoshi opened the door, Danny was on both knees, head bent over touching his thighs, holding the scroll straight out with both hands.

Yoritoshi took one look at Danny, let out a heavy sigh, and slammed the door in his face. Charlie warned Danny that this would happen and to not move from his knelt position because it was a sign of respect. Promising that Yoritoshi would return to read the scroll sooner or later.

Charlie was right. Although it was later, much, much later. After Madeline got bored of watching Danny staring at a closed-door, she returned to their hut. The least Madeline could do while Danny was on his quest was finish unpacking. Charlie had suggested to Madeline that she ship a few things to make her hut feel homier. This was the least Charlie could do, knowing how long they would be there and what a bastard Yoritoshi was.

Madeline closed the door and began. The first thing she blinked in was a wood-burning stove, then a bunch of Danny's books, then the chess set dad gave them. The blanket Millie made. A small suitcase of Madeline's potions and books. A simple table with one chair. And a wooden tub. After she arranged everything, she sighed. Definitely not as good as Charlie's estate in France or the ridiculous suite Danny got them in Hawaii, but it was kinda cute. And as long as they were together, maybe that was all they needed.

As the minutes turn to hours, Madeline would stare at Danny, still across the field. Still, on bended knees, Madeline felt her patience wearing very thin. By the 10th hour, Madeline had decided that Yoritoshi had 30 minutes left before she was going over there to shove the scroll somewhere Yoritoshi would definitely be aware of. She would have done this nine hours ago and on every half an hour since, but Danny made her promise not to. By the 10th hour, all diplomatic offerings were off for Madeline

On the 11th hour, as Madeline was storming out of the hut, Yoritoshi finally opened the door, let out a long, annoying sigh. Madeline swears she heard it from their hut. He grabbed the scroll out of Danny's hand, opened and read it, sighed again, then the paper turned to ash and flew away.

Yoritoshi circled Danny a few times as if examining his body structure. Poking him with the bamboo stick, yet again.

"I'll train you, not your crippled slave girl." Yoritoshi said. "No magic on my land. Learn to speak Japanese immediately; this is the last time you may use a translation spell to understand me. Be at my door at 6 am every day. if you are late, don't bother coming back." Yoritoshi went back into his hut, shutting the door.

Danny's body was completely locked up by now. He crawled through the fields until he felt it was safe for Madeline to come to help him back to their hut. He moaned with every step. Madeline hid her tears for his pain. And did not talk to him until he was ready to speak.

In silence, she helped him into the wooden tub, already filled with the hottest water she knew he could stand. Danny closed his eyes as Madeline gently washed him. He would tell Madeline Yoritoshi's demands... after he soaked in the therapeutic waters. Still in so much pain yet mesmerized by her beauty and devotion...

"Madds?" Danny called out after sitting up from their bed in the middle of the night... The soaking, massage, and few hours of sleep almost made him feel human again. "Where the hell are you, wife?" Danny mumbled, fidgeting with his time lock ring, knowing immediately that she had blinked somewhere.

"No yelling for 15 minutes, Daniel," Madeline appeared in the hut holding a small trunk, then laid down immediately, hurting a little from the fast blink. "Stop staring at me. Charlie said if I did it from our hut after sundown, I could blink home as many times as I wanted." Even with her eyes still closed, she felt his judgey disapproving look. "Forgive me, and you get shrimp." He grinned, leaving her side to unpack the trunk. She giggled.

Madeline woke 20 minutes later, feeling recovered from her quick blink home. Danny had already unpacked the trunk. And set the table. Besides food, there was a book and a few more Alchemy supplies.

"I really thought I'd be back before you woke up," Madeline said.

"You are so lucky you are gorgeous, and you brought shrimp." Danny teased. "I would prefer if we blinked home together, maybe once every other week, just for supplies."

"I am sorry," Madeline said. "You seemed ok with me blinking back and forth to John Luc's lately."

"From Henry's to someone we completely trust is different," Danny said. "John Luc even gave you an office that you can blink into any time without having to worry if anyone else is in the lab."

"Ok..." Madeline said. "But I did bring you something important. It's a magical learn Japanese book. Learn to speak fluently in two hours. Money-back guaranteed. Works for 90% of magic users. Sight effects range from craving sushi to only being able to speak Japanese for 24 hours."

"We really do watch too many late-night infomercials on the magic network, don't we?"

"Yup," Madeline said.

"You're really upset, huh?" Danny asked.

"Yup," Madeline said.

"Thank you for the book. love." Danny said. "I'll learn Japanese tonight and start training with Yoritoshi tomorrow, and I'll teach you what I learned at night. You can be pissed at me, but if we learn everything without you having to deal with him, I'm all for it. In a few weeks we do not see any progress, we'll reevaluate. He can't be the only guy with a big sword around here." Danny tried to make Madeline laugh. She tried to nod with enthusiasm, but she was frustrated. Again.

Chapter 22

"Don't get up," Danny whispered the next morning as he got out of bed before sunrise. Feeling Madeline stretching, "Today, you should write in your journal and study the research John Luc sent."

"That's freaky," Madeline said sleepily. "Now you are fluently bossy in Japanese." Danny playfully swatted her over the blanket and left, not realizing he was speaking to his wife in a foreign language. It was a bit disconcerting, but maybe it would help with Yoritoshi. For the record, it did not.

Danny got to Yoritoshi's porch 15 minutes before six to avoid any question of his commitment. Yoritoshi appeared at 8. Danny had never really considered just running away with Madeline, New Orleans be damn, until this very moment.

"Fill them up with water, quickly," Yoritoshi growled when he finally stepped onto his porch, pointed at the staff with two huge barrels on each end.

"Where is the water source?" Danny asked. Not trying to be smug. After all, Danny was an overachiever, finishing the book in an hour. Surely that earned him some brownie points.

"Your accent is worse than the sound of a pig having intercourse. Just don't speak to me, ever." Yoritoshi said, he stretched out his arm, his bamboo stick appeared, using it to point to the stairs behind his hut, leading up to the mountain. Before Danny could ask anything, Yoritoshi disappeared into his hut.

Danny was about to lose his temper, but then he spotted his wife outside their hut, trying to sweep out a dirt floor. He smiled to himself a little, then put the staff on his back while trying to balance the two empty barrels hanging down his sides and began the trek.

It was 293 steps to the plateau's top, where there was a beautiful meadow and a clear stream. Actually, steps might be a wrong description. The steep vertical pathway was made up of 293 slippery rounded stones.

Danny cussed every step going up. Cussed each one twice, going down with the 200 pounds of water.

If Danny wasn't worried about Yoritoshi watching him, he would have kissed the ground when he returned to the hut with the two filled water barrels. Surprisingly, Yoritoshi was on his porch sipping tea, waiting for him.

"Hand water the garden with this cup," Yoritoshi said. "Each plant needs exactly one cup poured around the roots," Yoritoshi disappeared again. Danny did as he was told, fantasizing that Yoritoshi was really Henry playing a gag on him. At some point, Henry would yell, "Gotcha." He. Did. Not.

Danny smiled as he watered the last plant. As he slowly stood up, Yoritoshi appeared a few feet in front of him. "Defend yourself," Yoritoshi yelled, throwing Danny a sword then making his own appear from thin air.

Danny did not block a single attack. In a minute, Danny had gashes everywhere, 3 on his thigh, 4 on his chest, two across his face, too many on his arms to count, and of course the final neck strike, leaving Danny unconscious.

The last thing Danny saw was Yoritoshi standing over him, sighing. Then Yoritoshi walked back to his hut and disappeared. Madeline, of course, witnessed the whole thing. She was livid. But was smart enough to wait til Yoritoshi was gone to blink to Danny. or so she thought.

By the time Madeline blinked to Danny, Yoritoshi had reappeared and was waiting for her. He used his sword to flip her out of her wheelchair, she fell on top of Danny. Yoritoshi took the chair into his hut and softly closed the door. Danny woke up about 20 minutes later and, in silence, carried Madeline back to their hut.

*

"What do you think you are doing?" Madeline hissed.

"I am getting in our bed to go to sleep," Danny said, a little confused that this act needed an explanation.

"No," Madeline said, already in the bed.

"Yup." Danny got under the blanket, now facing her as she stared at the ceiling.

"We are fighting," Madeline said coldly.

"Actually, you are fighting; I stopped an hour ago," Danny said, trying not to smirk.

"Get out of my bed, Boudreaux." Madeline hissed again and covered her head.

"Nope," Danny said, touching her waist. "Hey. We promised each other that unless we were physically distant, we would not not share a bed." Danny sighed, remembering how awful not sharing a bed with her in Paris was.

"Danny, that was different," Madeline whispered, trying not to soften. "You're defending Yoritoshi." She accused.

"I..." Danny just wanted to go to sleep. Maybe fool around a little... but his wife was still so mad. "I just said that some people would find Yoritoshi's actions justified because he did say absolutely no magic on his land."

"He... Took... My... Wheelchair... Daniel Boudreaux!" Madeline sat straight up and screamed, then laid back down, pulling the covers over her head. Danny tried really hard not to smile, knowing his wife could turn him into a frog.

"Do you think the avatars and dragon are going to let you stay in your wheelchair? Even if they throw you off for a second... What if that is the second they need to get the upper hand." Danny asked.

"That's not the point," Madeline said.

"I think it is," Danny said.

"Just get my wheelchair back," Madeline demanded. "Then I'll be all in love again and stuff." Now Madeline was more annoyed than mad... Danny was probably right from a strategic standpoint. "If I end up holding you in the middle of the night, it's because it's a reflex and because this is a tiny bed." Danny grinned as Madeline snuggled against him.

*

"Master Yoritoshi," Danny bowed to him, the second morning. Today Yoritoshi came out of his house a little earlier, but Danny had been waiting since 5:45, just in case. "Is there anything I can do to earn back my wife's wheelchair?"

"Complete your three tasks today." Yoritoshi sighed loudly. "Or have her crawl across the field to me and ask for it."

"What are the three tasks that I need to complete today, sir?" Danny asked. Not even being able to fathom a conversation with Madeline that involved Yoritoshi and crawling to him.

Danny completed the first task, although it took a bit longer than he had hoped. Yoritoshi had a large pile of stones he wanted Danny to take to the stream and place on a nearby grave. Danny was curious about who was buried there, but he knew better than to ask, although it made him sad that the grave seemed small.

Danny's second task was to bring the two barrels up the mountain filled with stones back down to Yoritoshi's hut, now filled with water. Every muscle in Danny's body hurt. And he was fairly certain that he had twisted his ankle. He thought it was strange, but he was actually looking forward to watering the plants. It was a simple but very controlled act. The only time his mind was silent. Danny suddenly wondered when was the last time Madeline meditated.

Again Yoritoshi appeared out of nowhere as he watered the plants and ordered Danny to defend himself. Again this ended with Danny marked with gashes everywhere and passed out. Madeline watched this from their hut, this time floating inside when her heart couldn't take her not trying to help her husband. When Danny returned to the hut 30 minutes later, bloody and bruised, she had his bath waiting with healing potions ready.

Madeline was still extremely annoyed with Danny but knew he was just trying to figure out this pillar so they could get home. And she needed to suck it up and help her husband.

After Madeline's potions and a nap, Danny was feeling good but restless.

"Your turn, my love," Madeline told Danny as they were relaxing in the moonlight. They were playing chess, but Danny's mind was somewhere else. Madeline knew this because she was actually winning.

"I think…" Danny said. "Yoritoshi is using some time manipulation or time compression when he is attacking me."

"Unless it's a spell, that's impossible," Madeline said. "Or he is a time lock? You don't think he is a time lock?"

"I don't know," Danny said.

"You know something…" Madeline said. "Danny, What!?!?"

"I need you to…" Danny rubbed his face, obviously overcome with emotions. "I need you to get close to him when he is attacking me so you can tell me what he is doing…. And that means… how can I even think of asking my wife…"

"You didn't. I volunteered." Madeline lifted his bowed head and kissed him. And they spent the rest of the night making a plan.

"Go…" Madeline whispered just before sunrise. Danny looked defeated but nodded, kissed her, and left their hut, headed for Yoritoshi's.

Before he left, Danny had encouraged her to try to meditate this morning. Even though Madeline didn't feel like it, she knew it would probably help with her task today. Still wrapped in Millie's quilt, Madeline floated to the dying fire outside and sat on a tree stump, warming her hands around a cup of pretty decent coffee. She watched Danny for a few minutes as he waited for Yoritoshi. Finishing her coffee, she put out the campfire and began her meditation.

After two hours, Madeline's cleared mind returned to her troubled soul. Although not as deep as Kushemi taught, she felt pretty refreshed. More focused than she had been in months. Madeline promised herself to do Kushemi's mind exercise every morning as long as they were here, feeling very guilty that she had lapsed.

"This is going to be fun," Madeline told herself. "I'm blinking in dinner tonight. He owes me." Madeline sighed, watching her husband as he began watering the plants. She took one more deep cleansing breath, floated to the ground, and started crawling into Yoritoshi's field.

It took Madeline 23 minutes to reach the part of the field Danny had told her to crawl to. She surprisingly felt better than she expected, minus the bugs crawling across her stomach. There was no way she would tell Mack about this; he might design a new obstacle course for her. Danny winked at Madeline, now only a few yards from him, as he continued to water Yoritoshi's plants.

"Defend yourself." Yoritoshi appeared from out of nowhere, in front of Danny. Yoritoshi immediately spotted Madeline but figured she was servicing her husband. As long as he continued watering, that was acceptable. Yoritoshi threw Danny his sword. Within five seconds, history repeated itself. Danny had gashes everywhere, twice as many as the day before. Yoritoshi looked directly at Madeline then walked back to his hut.

"Daniel!" Madeline whispered. Putting herself under his bleeding head. Fighting every urge to heal him right there or blinking them home. But she knew better, sensing Yoritoshi was watching them. She gently stroke Danny's forehead, tears of sadness for her husband's pain filled her eyes, yet she was intrigued. Very intrigued.

*

"This is the worse Ground Hog Day movie version ever," Madeline said. Bathing and healing her husband on the 90th night in futile Japan.

"I don't know, I'm kind of liking these quiet nights, Madds." Danny grinned, grabbing Madeline as she finished healing him. She laughed. Then he hugged her and sighed, "We have to take the next step."

"I know," Madeline said.

"You have figured so much out, just by watching him a few times," Danny said.

"But there's a difference between a theory and practical application," Madeline said, setting the table as Danny dished out the curry he had made. "We think. Yoritoshi is compressing his attacks. This means instead of taking 10 seconds for 5 strikes, he can perform them all in one second."

"The practical applications are mind-boggling," Danny said.

"And..." Madeline said. "I don't sense that it's rooted in magic, so I think it has to be a learned action, probably taught by a time lock."

"Bet not as cute as my personal time lock." Danny winked. "Come on, You've been practicing for a week."

"I'm not comfortable with the process because it even hurts me; I am not sure how you'll react. but I think..." Madeline said. "You can learn how. You just have to learn to recognize how to control your breathing so closely; it can slow time around you, but..."

"The pain can't be as bad as 45 daily gashes." Danny shrugged, "I really think you are ready to teach me."

After dinner, Madeline made Danny sit on the ground, cross-legged in front of her, intertwining their hands and began. She took a long, cleansing breath, he followed. Then she focused, guiding him deeper and deeper into a controlled state, where the mind and breathing co-existed and... Danny threw up. All over her. Violently and seamlessly, an endless stream of puke. He didn't even apologize until he bathe her.

"You can practice outside from now on, please, husband." Danny bowed his head in embarrassment but saw a glimmer, however faint, of how to defend himself against Yoritoshi.

*

"I'm suddenly questioning the compassion and encouragement of the mother of my future children," Danny smirked, later that month.

"I'm just saying that If they are dumb enough to get themselves beat up every day and choose to throw up all night, they belong to you." Madeline teased.

"One more time," Danny said in a child's voice.

"Stretch!" Madeline demanded.

"What?" Danny asked.

"If you can stretch without wrenching in pain from your stomach hurting, we will," Madeline said. He could not, pretended to pout, and went to bed.

Every night for the last month, Danny had been practicing time compressing. For the first two weeks, he was making absolutely no progress. And Madeline had almost convinced him to let it go. She was actually worried he might cause permanent damage to his stomach muscle with his violent vomiting.

By the third week, he had learned to compress a second of time, which made him more determined than ever. Motion sickness or not. Danny had this formula that he came up with. He tried to explain it to Madeline, something about physics and maximum strikes needed. But her eyes glazed over.

Bottom line, if Danny could learn to compress five seconds of time at will, this would be a huge advantage in battle without feeling any impairment. Madeline never told him she was up to 20 seconds.

"Drink this," Madeline ordered one night. "John Luc approved. Don't get mad. It was an emergency." Danny scowled at her but was curious about what she had concocted. "Now you are under my spell. Boudreaux." Madeline pretended to laugh evilly.

"I think we have established that was sealed the first time I saw you," Danny said.

"Now, try again," Madeline said. Danny dropped to the floor and tried to time compress. He made a strange face when he began. Madeline covered her mouth, trying not to giggle; it was adorable. Which Danny would hate knowing. But the end result was amazing. He said he still felt the motion sickness but could suppress the vomiting, and, even better, he compressed his time for two seconds.

"This is absurd," Madeline mumbled to herself from outside their hut, watching Danny start his daily climb to get water. Although she had to admit, the view was spectacular; he looked very rugged, now almost appearing to be jogging up the steps.

Aside from Danny's newest obsession, time compression, the nights were awesomely romantic and fun and easy. But besides that, Madeline was unbelievably bored. The days dragged on and on. It was the same routine. Get up at five, after breakfast, Danny would head to Yoritoshi's.

Madeline would meditate, write in her time lock journal, and make healing potions. Then had three or four hours of nothingness until Danny crawled home bloody and bruised. She was so bored, Madeline actually looked forwards to this time of day so she could try new potions on him.

Madeline knew she had hit rock bottom as she now crawled across the fields daily just to tell Danny "hi." It wasn't even a sexy "hi" or a meaningful "hi.". It was something to do. Danny let her because one, it was unbelievably cute, and two, whether she knew it or not, her time improved every day. So it helped her upper strength and body motion. If Danny called it a workout, Madeline would have stopped, just on principle.

Madeline tried so hard to be good. But one day, she just snapped. She was sitting about a foot away from Danny as he was watering the last row of plants. Madeline was twirling a stick she had found while begging Danny that they should blink together somewhere fun tonight. He almost agreed when...

"Defend yourself." Yoritoshi appeared and yelled at Danny, and began attacking, gashes on Danny suddenly appearing as if from thin air. Yoritoshi was going for his famous neck strike. Madeline was not planning to... but a bored time lock witch is sometimes a very bad thing. Madeline compressed time and easily blocked Yoritoshi's final strike.

She was so proud of herself as she was coming out of her time compressing, she let down her guard. Yoritoshi wacked Danny first, extra hard for not controlling his wife, then Madeline. Just because.

Madeline woke 20 minutes later. Her wheelchair beside her. Maybe a peace offering from Yoritoshi. And a very bloody, angry storm giant standing over her. At this point, she would have preferred the company of Yoritoshi rather than her frowning husband.

"Oh, quit pouting," Madeline said. Danny was quiet during his healing process and dinner. Although he was proud of Madeline for her defensive strike against Yoritoshi, a warning would have been nice. But that wasn't why he was upset.

Danny loved that his wife was spontaneous and often acted without thinking. He may have been jealous because he had lost this ability when Abigail died. In marriage, her whimsiness was sometimes a little frustrating. Still, mostly it had a ridiculously fun outcome. making another memory that Danny cherished. But in battle, her spontaneity could be a liability which scared him. He worried that a quick knee jerk reaction could get her killed.

Madeline floated to sit on his lap by the fire. She softly kissed his neck as he sighed with his eyes closed, his anger leaving him. "Hey." Danny pouted as Madeline suddenly left his lap, nudging him to open his eyes. In the distance, they spotted Yoritoshi waiting for Danny.

"Defend yourself," Yoritoshi said, throwing a bamboo stick at Danny. "With everything you have learned so far." Danny smiled to himself and began. With time compressing and focus, he blocked most of the strikes Yoritoshi threw at him, including the final neck blow. Danny then bowed respectfully at Yoritoshi.

"Tomorrow, we'll start training at sunrise," Yoritoshi said. "Will you consider still watering my plants? You have moved past that, but it does help your strength and focus. And saves my knees. I must confess."

"Yes, teacher," Danny said very respectfully.

"And…" Yoritoshi sighed, scratching his head as if trying to talk himself out of it but could not. "Danny's wife can train too. But no magic during training. No girl drama. She may not speak to me. No crying. I hate crying." And Yoritoshi disappeared into the fields.

For as long as Madeline lived, she would always gush about her pillars, most of them anyway. She would describe Kushemi as her favorite professor that became her dear friend. John Luc became her older brilliant brother, and Henry would always remain her north star. But to Madeline, Yoritoshi was a bastard, although lovable on rare occasions that she could count on one hand. More aggravating, Danny later wrote in his memoirs that Yoritoshi was his mentor.

Unlike the other Pillars, who sort of let Madeline have her way, Yoritoshi had rules. So many rules. The first time she broke one during the day, he slapped her across all of her knuckles with a bamboo stick. The 2nd time she broke a rule, she got sent to the porch. Madeline hated that.

Although not fond of watching his wife get hurt, Danny just had a different thought process. Here are the rules, here are the consequences. To be honest, from an objective view, Yoritoshi was one of the fairest, most virtuous men Madeline had ever met... She guessed she just liked being spoiled. Not exactly proud of that fact, but...

Every day for months, she watched Yoritoshi trained Danny. They would look so graceful, like in a choreographed dance, and Madeline would be so jealous. Her training felt the very opposite of that; it was clumsy and messy and stiff.

Yoritoshi and Danny didn't see Madeline this way at all. Although Yoritoshi never admitted it to her, he saw a great warrior growing right in front of his eyes, and it was amazing. He knew to bring out her greatness, he would either have to coddle her or be an asshole, and Yoritoshi enjoyed being an asshole.

To Yoritoshi, the first few months were about breaking Madeline of bad or ridiculous habits, like how Madeline insisted on wearing a kimono with nothing underneath. Because one, it was so hot, and two, Danny liked helping her dress that way.

She stopped when Yoritoshi sliced every button and tie in one smooth strike, leaving her naked. Madeline cried and ran home. Danny wasn't thrilled that another man had undressed her. But understood Yoritoshi was trying to teach her, that a clever opponent would use any means to throw her off her game.

The second lesson Yoritoshi tried to teach Madeline was that she needed to be armed and able to jump into an attacked stance at any second. Yoritoshi was very respectful of their hut, but everywhere else was fair game. Yoritoshi would sneak up on her everywhere any time of the day. If she wasn't ready to attack, he would flip Madeline out of her wheelchair, swiftly and painfully. To add insult to injury, he always chuckled when he walked away. This infuriated Madeline every single time, but she always carried a sword or knife somewhere on her wheelchair for hundreds of years from then on.

Danny swore that she was making progress but month after month of coming home bloody and bruised was almost too much for her. Danny was now the nurse, running scolding baths for her, healing Madeline nightly with her own potions. Madeline could not understand why Yoritoshi would not let her use magic and always made her fight from the ground.

One day she snapped. Yoritoshi had thrown her out of her wheelchair, into a pile of manure. He had ripped her favorite kimono yet again, and it was now storming, raining in sheets. He was coming at her with a bamboo stick, aiming for her neck. And Madeline decided right then and there she would shoot a fireball at him. Just a small one. Madeline could heal him easily. He would have to beg a little. She grinned.

Danny saw it in Madeline's eyes. He screamed "No." but she pretended it was too late. For the record, it was not. Danny and Madeline would never forget what happened next. They had never seen anything like it, nor did they know it was possible.

Yoritoshi dropped the bamboo stick, pulled out his steel sword. Danny had never seen him use it. For an instant, Danny was afraid Yoritoshi was going to kill Madeline. Still, for some reason, Danny knew in his soul he would not.

Yoritoshi made a look of annoyance as the fireball raced towards his nose. He sighed, raised up his sword, and sliced through Madeline's spell.

"magic is lazy, sloppy, and attack spells can be broke. But if magic is used correctly with physical fighting, you will be truly powerful and unstoppable. Remember that, Madeline." Yoritoshi said and walked towards his hut. It was one of the only times he ever called her by name.

*

Although it was physically exhausting, their first 5 years in Futile Japan flew by. The days were filled with training. The nights, Danny and Madeline grew more and more in love, more committed to each other and to killing the dragon so that they could have their lives back...

Always mindful of their problems in Paris, Danny allowed Madeline to blink to Henry's office twice a month to reconnect to her real life and friends. Danny occasionally went, but the 400-year blink was especially hard on him. Danny described it as the world's longest and worse brain freeze.

One morning in early spring during their 5th year, something happened. Yoritoshi was sipping tea on his porch. Danny had filled up his barrels at the stream and was halfway down the path. Madeline was meditating by the fire.

Yoritoshi suddenly screamed her name in a terrified voice Madeline had never heard. Danny immediately dropped the water and raced down the mountain while summoning his sword.

As Madeline looked up, three men were coming towards her. The closest, lifting his kimono, leering at the cute girl. Madeline was scared, not for the three guys approaching her but for the 11 other bandits now in the fields walking towards Yoritoshi.

"I'm a peasant girl. My husband works the fields; please leave us." Madeline pleaded, unprepared to kill. The closest one reached for her kimono, trying to rip it.

"Kill them, Madeline. Now!" Danny ordered, screaming in his loudest voice as he now joined Yoritoshi in a sudden, bloody battle. Yoritoshi had killed five by the time Danny reached him. Danny killed the other four coming at them.

Madeline didn't want to, but in a second, she killed the three surrounding her. Then raced towards the fields, killing the last two that were ready to ambush Danny.

The whole battle lasted maybe five minutes. Yoritoshi returned to his porch, visually shaken. Madeline and Danny followed after Danny kissed her entire face tenderly and checked her for wounds.

"You'd think there would not be such a large bounty on an ancient man of 120 years old," Yoritoshi said ironically. "Danny, take your wife somewhere for the day. I'll clean up. We'll resume training in the morning... and Madeline, you did well, and you didn't even rely on magic. But you did hesitate. I will break you of this before we part ways." He almost smiled at her but walked into his hut and closed the door.

The attack only fueled Yoritoshi to train them harder. Their last two years in Japan were brutal. For the first time in 13 years, Danny did not have to force Madeline to stick to her eight hour sleep cycle. Madeline now only blinked home when they needed supplies. Too tired for anything else.

Yoritoshi was getting down to the heart of the matter. Working with time compression, attacking and slicing magic spells, and teaching the couple to fight together, in sync.

Madeline's time compressing was ridiculously strong. And her sword fighting was nothing to laugh at but was far less superior than Danny's. This was exactly what Yoritoshi had hoped for because, combined with her other talents, she was amazing.

Danny was a bit frustrated. He never reached five full seconds in time compression at will. But Yoritoshi believed his accuracy with the sword made up for it. Watching Danny and Madeline fight together was a thing of beauty to Yoritoshi.

Yoritoshi felt his only failure was he didn't think Madeline would ever have a true warrior's mindset. Attack first, do whatever it takes to be the last one standing. Assume that if someone is attacking you, they intend to kill you. There was no question that Madeline would kill to protect Danny or even Yoritoshi, as she proved. He just could not understand why Madeline valued her life less than theirs. Yoritoshi's one consolation was that Danny would always be by her side, hopefully, and he... he had the mind of a warrior.

In the seven years that they lived there, Madeline was sad that she never really got to know Yoritoshi. After the first year, he and Danny would have tea a few afternoons a week and talk about sword and fight techniques. But Yoritoshi never opened up, or so Madeline believed. Danny was amused that his wife never caught Yoritoshi's eyes sparkle every time she mastered a new strike or attacked an impossible block. It must have been a guy thing.

"Danny's wife," Yoritoshi said one night, coming to them as they were relaxing by the fire. That's what he called her most of the time. The name eventually grew on her. "This is my favorite knife. Now it is yours. Tell the pixie she was right about you." Yoritoshi faced Danny, Danny stood up and bowed. Yoritoshi placed both of his hands on Danny's shoulders, sighed. And went back to his hut.

"We could stay here one more night, for sentimental reasons..." Danny teased. "Or we could go home to our perfectly firm mattress that I have missed almost more than my kitchen." Surprisingly. Even to them, they stayed in their hut one more night.

Chapter 23

"Ouch." Danny held his head as they landed perfectly on Henry's couch.

"Lay down," Madeline whispered. Patting his thigh. "I'll be back." She grinned knowing he would wake in 20 minutes feeling a whole lot better. She went to her desk to grab her phone and rolled into the kitchen, a little confused that no one was there. It was about an hour before the staff came in, but Jane usually made breakfast for everyone, even on her days off.

Madeline poured herself a coffee and turned on her phone to call Jane. She had seven messages from Mack and 12 missed calls from Steven in the last 25 minutes. Madeline started shaking.

"Hi?" Madeline called Steven. "Where? How bad? I'm coming...." She hung up and blinked to the hospital.

"Where is she?" Madeline asked, trying not to scream, rolling into the waiting room. Mack and Steven were crying. As soon as they saw her, the guys rushed to Madeline, pushing her outside to the garden, away from the crowded waiting room.

"She was at the farmers market at 6," Mack said, scratching his forehead, trying so hard to keep it together. "I was supposed to go with her. But we had stayed up late talking. We set a date. And she gave me her blessing to start with Frank next week... I was happy. And I just wanted 10 more minutes of sleep. She was going to run to the farmer's market then meet me for breakfast..." Mack said. He couldn't finish, now collapsing to the ground, openly weeping.

"Jane was attacked," Steven whispered, voice shaking. "Claw marks on her cheek. Tore off her left breast, and her leg was sliced open to the bone. If she doesn't bleed out, they will have to, at the very least, amputate a leg."

"What time was she attacked, Mack?" Madeline asked. Steven covered his face.

"6:15ish," Mack whispered.

"Madds…" Steven cried, still able to read her mind. "You will get yourself killed with the time lock laws."

"If it saves her," Madeline said. "I can die with that."

"I would go with you," Mack said." I would help you kill the avatar. And I'd die with you… but we'd just be replacing one tragedy with two. She would hate us, Madds."

"Again, If it saves her," Madeline said. "I can die with that. And if she still has you, you can make her forgive me. Please, Mack, Please!"

"Hello?" Steven answered his phone. "Yes, she is. I will do that. Oh shit… hang on. She just blinked away… Jane is in surgery. Yes, avatar, same wounds as Henry. It's really bad, Danny. Mack is shaking his head adamantly for you not to come. All updates, I swear. Will you let me know if Madeline shows up? Danny, she looked unhinged."

"Daniel." Mack cried very angrily but fell into his best friend's arms as Danny showed up at the hospital 20 minutes later, without his wife.

*

Madeline knew she was breaking a time lock law, but she just didn't care. She blinked back to 6:10 and watched Jane from a distance. It would be so easy to kill the avatar now, especially after her time compressing with Yoritoshi. If her death at that moment guaranteed that the world, especially her world, would be safe from the dragon, she would have killed joyfully. But Madeline had a moment of clarity, realizing it didn't work that way. Afraid her one action would cause a ripple effect. She wiped away a tear, blew a kiss to Jane and blinked away.

"We…" the doctor told Mack an hour later. "We just can't stop the bleeding. She's in a lot of pain. I do believe she still can hear you. I don't usually advise this, but if I was you, I'd tell her it was ok to let go." The doctor patted Mack on the shoulder and walked away.

Mack leaned on both Steven and Danny as they walked towards Jane's hospital room. Steven tried to open the door, but it would not budge. Then Danny tried. No luck, then they looked in the window. They should not have been surprised, but they were.

Madeline was floating above Jane, sprinkling potion everywhere. Steven, Danny, and Mack could literally see Jane's body glowing where the potion touched her skin. Madeline did this for hours. Then the door unlocked, the guys rushed in, Jane opened her eyes to Madeline passed out cold lying next to her, and there they slept for days. The door only opened to the three men.

Danny was still unhappy that Madeline blinked away from the hospital when she found out about Jane without talking to him, but he tried to understand. Danny didn't realize how much Madeline had done in those few absent minutes. First, she went to blinked back to try to save Jane but then decided to go to Henry's.

Before Madeline and Danny left Henry and Millie's from their six-month stay, Henry and Madeline shared a secret. Not even Danny knew. Henry knew Charlie would eventually have to erase Madeline from his memory, as not to influence Henry's interactions with Ida or Danny. Until then, Henry figured out a safe way that Madeline could always blink to him to ask time lock questions.

Madeline realized she had no objectivity when it came to Jane, and she needed Henry's knowledge and rational thought process. Madeline blinked to his office in the 50s; they agreed on that time frame. Henry always had food waiting for her. It was almost eerie his sense of timing. Madeline hoped that he could tell her how she could kill the avatar before it attacked Jane.

Madeline tried to convince herself that because she was in futile Japan the second that the attack happened, there was a loophole or a cheat. Henry looked at it from all angles but said there was no way to save Jane without destroying her own timeline and made her swear on Danny's life she would not try. Madeline sighed, kissed his cheek, and blinked away.

In all the years that they were married, this was one of the few secrets Madeline had kept for a while from Danny. Henry and Madeline had agreed it would be too hard on Danny. Knowing Henry was still somewhere and he could not see him every day. It was hard on Madeline, too, as his great daughter-in-law, but she still needed his guidance as a time lock.

After Henry's final say, Madeline blinked to John Luc's. She had never made a potion to try to save a life before. He helped without question. And after that, Madeline blinked directly to Jane's room.

Mack and Danny were so grateful that Madeline healed Jane. Although she didn't think that was an accurate description of what she did. Stopping Jane from bleeding out was the most powerful spell and potion Madeline had ever cast. No one knew it took the help of two pillars to do it. But the bottom line was even with the potion, Jane faced a lifetime of possible surgeries and chronic pain.

*

"Your husband says I should walk you home and make sure you go to sleep," Mack said after closing the restaurant, finding Madeline sitting in the dark in Henry's office. Elizabeth and Steven followed.

Danny insisted on staying with Jane in the hospital that night. It had been a week since the attack. Charlie and Madeline had placed a protection spell on the hospital immediately after Madeline recovered from healing Jane. So it was relatively safe for Danny to be there. However, if it was anyone else, Madeline might have argued, but it was Jane.

"Or…" Madeline suggested. "We could drink and have cigars."

"You really are too good for Danny." Mack teased. Pouring drinks for everyone.

"I really am," Madeline said. "How are ya, Macky?"

"I am frustrated," Mack took a long drink. "I know I shouldn't be. And I'm probably going to hell, but I just want to shake her. This should be the easiest decision she has ever made. Please talk to her, Madeline."

"I cannot," Madeline whispered. "I've told her a hundred times how much I hate being in a wheelchair. She even had to talk me…" Madeline sniffed.

"When…. Madeline?" Steven asked.

"Damn, you're arrogant," Madeline said. Elizabeth and Mack smirked; Steven and Madeline had a silent argument. "Look, I was a freshman, I was offered a part-time writing job, but it was on the third floor of a converted house that I couldn't get up to. And a guy I really like got drunk and told me he'd never date a chick in a chair. It was my perfect storm, but Jane talked me down. I cannot advise her to amputate a leg. I feel like I'm the reason she has to make this impossible choice."

"There's not a choice," Mack yelled loudly. "Healthy, pain-free life with me. How could she think I could love her less?"

"Nothing happened, and boy did they regret it..." Madeline said. "But... When we were away, I was almost violated. And it did cross my mind; if I was, Danny would never be able to touch me. Ever again. We both have ridiculous thoughts sometimes. It's a thing. You need to convince her."

"I know," Mack said. "For the record, she is angry but not at you."'

"I really needed to hear that, Macky." Madeline sniffed. "For the record, I think she should amputate. It would be healthier and less painful in the long run. She has job security and a hot guy."   Madeline kissed Mack. "I think I'm gonna sneak into the hospital and tell Jane and my husband goodnight and see if he wants to make out in a broom closet." They laughed as she rolled out of Henry's office.

*

"It's 3 AM!" Charlie said. "This better be good." Madeline had called her two days after Danny had spent the night with Jane at the hospital.

"We have decided to go on to my final pillar," Madeline said.

"Are you sure?" Charlie asked. "You still look exhausted."

"I am," Madeline said, trying not to break down yet again. "I am hoping that if we finish this, I could at least train here while we figure out the next step. That way, when we get back, Danny can really take over the restaurant for a few months, and Mack can focus on Jane."

"Is that what you want, Daniel?" Charlie asked.

"We need to finish this." Danny sighed. "I've been married to my wife almost 13 years, and... we haven't built a house or allowed ourselves to dream about careers and babies in such along time. But I tried to compartmentalize that each pillar was an adventure. And as bizarre as it was, the nights in Japan were magical for me."

"But Jane was my last reality check. What happened to Jane slapped me back into urgency mode, we are preparing for war, and everyone we love is a target. Madeline's love is the only thing that has kept me sane. But I feel myself cracking. Like after Abigail died. And I'm pretty sure if we lost Jane, I would have gone to a dark place where not even my wife could save me, again."

"I will always find and save you, husband.." Madeline said to Danny, then turned to Charlie. "We have decided. We are going to try to be back by breakfast. I usually tell Steven and Jane before I go, but... they worry, they say they don't, but they lie. And they have too much on their plates right now..."

"Madeline..." Charlie felt her sorrow. "Daniel..."

"We'll hopefully be back before anyone notices we are gone," Danny said.

"We wanted you to know Charlie," Madeline said.

"Ok, my loves." Charlie grew into a beautiful human and held them. "Believe it or not, one day you'll miss this chaos, knee-deep in a real, messy, hectic life. Do you know where you are going?"

"Nope," but I'm sure you do, Chenoa Enemene?" Madeline teased.

"Still, not how it works..." Charlie laughed.

"This is the pillar I know the least about..." Madeline said. "I have a year, coordinates, and a very strange name... I'll get Danny settled and come back for supplies. And Charlie, if I don't come back for some reason, can you adopt Jane? She's stubborn. She's going to spin out for a while before getting back on track. Mack's gonna need reassurances too."

"I will. They are my family now. Without a doubt." Charlie said. Danny took Madeline's hand and blinked away.

*

"Wow, that was only like a seven on the painful blinks scale," Danny said shortly after they landed. Madeline was already in her wheelchair; the scenery was picturesque. They arrived on a little clearing next to a large lake, mountains in the distance—thick forests 100 yards from them. Danny stood up and stretched.

"I think…" Madeline said. "We should have waited til…"

"Madds," Danny said.

"Please don't cut me off." Madeline was pissy.

"No, Love. Look!" Danny pointed at the tree in amazement. A creature stepped out of its trunks.

"Yr uffern ydych chi'n ei wneud yn fy llannerch." Nymiff sternly said. Madeline assumes it was a woman judging from her husband's dumbfounded look. Nymiff stood 6'5. Fiery red hair flowing to her thighs, covered in leaves, a crown of flowers on her head.

"She's speaking Welch," Danny whispered. Madeline looked at him, puzzled. "You truly underestimate what a lonely nerd I was." Madeline quickly cast an understanding spell.

"I am Nymiff Coed; you are in my woods; explain yourself. How have you entered my forest undetected?" Nymiff asked.

"I'm Madeline. I am a witch and a time lock. I request your help."

"Is he your slave?" Nymiff asked.

"Yes…" Madeline said as he growled. "He is also my husband… Daniel Guidry Boudreaux."

"How may I help you?" Nymiff asked.

"My mentor Henry Guidry told me you might be able to teach me archery, concentration, and focus?"

"Guidry, Guidry…" Nymiff said. "Oh my. Are you related to a Vodrich Guidry?"

"Yes, mam," Danny said.

"I fought beside him in the European Dragon Wars," Nymiff said. "What a horrible time. But what a mighty warrior."

"We have reason to believe that a dragon, Vodrich's son, Brogant fought, has been imprisoned for centuries. Now is breaking free, seeking revenge on my family. " Danny said.

"There are now dragon worshippers in the form of avatars," Madeline added. "Regretfully, it took Henry's, Brogant's grandson, life, last year. And the attacks are growing more and more frequent. The last, a few days ago on one in our small circle."

"And..." Nymiff asked. "You are the chosen one?"

"I was mentioned by name in a dragon's rant," Madeline said. "I am now a Guidry. By both marriage and loyalty to Henry. So even if I'm not, this is my fight now."

"My rules are simple," Nymiff said to Madeline. "You'll shoot 1000 arrows a day, six days a week. On the 7th day, you'll do something to give back to nature... You live off the land. You'll respect the trees. No magic outside of your shelter. No blinking back to your time until we are done."

"The first time you call lightning in my forest, I'll ask you to leave; the second time, I will kill you in your sleep," Nymiff now looked sternly at Danny, leading the two to their shelter a few hours after they had arrived. Danny wanted to explain that he was a runt and could not call lightning if he tried. But sensed it was a moot point. Nymiff's harsh warnings upset Madeline more than Danny. Again, he understood the rules.

"It's a tent!" Danny sighed, looking at their first night's accommodations.

"We have always found a way to enjoy... where we land." Madeline smiled.

"Indeed..." Danny said, touching his wife's neck. "However, tempted I am to take advantage of your good mood. You must be a little disappointed."

"I felt better when I knew I had the option to blink to Jane," Madeline confessed. "I know we will only be gone a few hours to them, but I already feel guilty and sad. I think we need to buckle down. Do twice as much as Nymiff expects and get the hell out of here in a few weeks."

"It might take longer, Madds," Danny said. "I wish she would stop giving me dirty looks. She hates me."

"Unless she beats you bloody for seven years, I think you can suck it up, Boudreaux!" Madeline slapped his back.

"You do know he adored you," Danny said.

"You adore me. Yoritoshi tolerated me because I entertained him." Madeline said.

"I do. Adore you." Danny said. "I wonder why I annoy Nymiff. Usually, I take longer to annoy."

"Not really." Madeline teased. "Come on, wood nymph, storm giant... lightning, rain, wind... not exactly a match made in heaven. You'll grow on her."

The only reason Madeline slept that first night was that she was still exhausted from their trip to Japan. Really besides passing out from the healing potion she placed on Jane, she hadn't slept in a week. Danny watched her dream. She was so pretty.

He was worried, thinking that this might be the worse pillar trip. Danny, himself, was still sort of a social loner. In lawyer mode, he could smooze, but truthfully, wherever he was, if Madeline was with him, he was home. But Madeline needed her parents and Jane, even Steven, and now Charlie and Mack. She missed their daily interactions.

Danny would follow his wife's lead. Get in, study quickly and go home. He could not imagine anything that would keep them here a second longer than necessary.

*

Nymiff woke with the sunrise, so the couple followed. She was quieter and a tiny bit more social than Yoritoshi. Madeline invited her to breakfast; she did and joined them almost every morning from then on.

Nymiff mainly talked about archery and how it worked well as a weapon, but it was just a tool for teaching concentration.

Occasionally Nymiff would talk about her children who had moved away and her lifelong mate who had recently died. She asked Madeline a few questions about her background. Nymiff answered any questions Danny had about archery but avoided any other exchanges. Never ever sitting close to Danny unless Madeline was in between them. This would have driven Madeline crazy, but Danny really made an effort to respect Nymiff's boundaries.

The first week was relatively slow. Danny went for runs around the lake as Nymiff taught Madeline how to talk to the trees. This irritated Madeline because they had a hundred things to do at home. Talking to the trees was not one of them. But Nymiff believed if one prayed to nature, her goddess would supply you with lumber for shelters, bows, and everything needed for a balanced life.

In the afternoons, they would go to the archery field. Nymiff would leave Madeline 20 arrows, and after she shot 100 that day, Madeline was finished. Danny would try to retrieve the arrows and pretend he wasn't bored out of his mind, since he couldn't practice magic and feared any weapons training would freak Nymiff out.

In the late afternoons, Nymiff would teach Madeline how to make arrows by asking the trees to supply the wood. Madeline would have to go to a tree, politely ask for a piece of wood to make an arrow, sometimes even feeling the tree grin as it set the bark at her feet. Madeline thought this was the coolest thing ever.

As the days went on, Madeline enjoyed archery but was still very focused on getting home. After she learned to make bows and taught herself as much as possible with Danny kibitzing, Nymiff started to train with her. that was when the real work began. It was not enough that Madeline could hit targets; Nymiff wanted her to hit the bullseye every time, no matter the distraction.

Nymiff was still very skeptical of Madeline's storm giant. Still, he seemed devoted to her. So she recruited him to distract Madeline. Danny enjoyed that. Madeline did not. Nymiff had forgotten how laughter sounded in her forest.

"Ok," Nymiff said, about three months after they got there, while Madeline was making arrows, yet again. "Here is a longbow; you may train with your wife. Stay in human form; if you change, I will need you to leave the forest. I just will." Nymiff said. Not looking directly at him.

*

"It's ok, come share the fire." Nymiff called to Danny. She was sitting by the fire, Madeline was trying to get to sleep early. Her hands blistered from shooting bows, her back hurting from sleeping on the grounds, all of her healing potions at home. Part of the luggage she was going to bring back on her second trip. The one that Nymiff forbade.

"Thank you," Danny whispered. He sat the furthest he could away from her that was still around the fire. "With respect, is there any way I can build a tiny cabin for Madeline? Her back is hurting her. She never complains about pain, but I can tell from how she pushes her chair. And by the length of her arrow pull."

"My husband used to notice everything too," Nymiff said. "It was annoying. I could never get away with anything...." She looked towards the sky for a long time. "The trees will never ever sacrifice themselves for a house or even a bow for your kind. We do not like storm giants. It's why the trees lean away from you as you walk amongst them."

"Vodrich Guidry was an honorable storm giant," Nymiff explained. "I sense you are too. But I think your family line is a rarity. The other storm giants we have encountered have been cruel. And my trees will never forgive your kind, nor will I tell them to. They only let you co-exist here because of Madeline."

"I can live in peace with you. But my trees, oh, they love Madeline just slightly more than they hate you... Tomorrow ask your wife to ask the great oak by the lake for a cabin; he is particularly fond of her. I'll be curious what he builds her. Good night Madeline's slave." Nymiff grinned ever so slightly and disappeared, blending into the dark forest.

By week's end the trees had built Madeline a cabin. It was a little bigger than the one in Japan, and somehow, it had the most comfortable bed Danny and Madeline would ever share. The odd thing was only Madeline could open the door. It always stuck for Danny unless Madeline said it was ok for him to come in.

*

"Please, Madds?" Danny begged.

"Nope," Madeline said. "We cannot keep a house plant alive. We pay a gardener to care for Millie's roses and one shrub in front of the apartments. We are just not those people."

"Please," Danny insisted, laying on the ground playing with a tiny creature. Madeline tried to remain strong but his giggling was beginning to suck her in.

"What is it?" Madeline floated to the ground. Nymiff was now easing up on her magic rules, although the blinking home was still a big no-no.

"She is," Danny said. "A Fairy Dragon. They grow to the size of a cat. Frida's fur will have one of the rainbow's bright shiny colors, with butterfly wings and a dragon's body. They are a bit mischievous but completely harmless. Henry used to tell Abigail and me about them. We always wanted one."

"That was a low blow, Boudreaux." Madeline sighed. "Miss Frida will be an outdoor pet, you'll release her before we go home."

"Yup," Danny said. Madeline made a mental note that he did not make eye contact when he agreed. Madeline knew this would eventually bite her in the ass, but her husband looked so darn cute sprawled out on the floor, playing with a dragon the size of a chick.

As often as it does, weeks turned to months, and months turn to years. Madeline was torn; she wanted to go home so bad, Jane was never far from her thoughts, but she was still learning so much from Nymiff.

By the 5th year, Madeline's archery skills had greatly improved. Nymiff would never be a great teacher, but Danny and Madeline felt it was a wood nymph lost in translations thing. Nymiff clumsily taught both Danny and Madeline how to concentrate while they were time compressing. This one thing was worth five years away.

*

"Stop, Daniel." Madeline rolled over. She thought she had a bad cold and annoyingly woke to find Danny creepily staring at her. Tracing her chest and stomach ever so lightly. It was the end of their 5th year with Nymiff. They were planning to leave soon. "I'll feel better tomorrow. My sides ache. Go to sleep." Madeline closed her eyes but still felt Danny breathing on her neck.

"Wife?" Danny said. Madeline grunted, wanting him to go to sleep. She expected him to push against her until she giggled, but he had a question from left field that she was not ready to answer. "How long was our birth control good for?"

"12 years guaranteed, 13 without strong swimmers." Madeline tried to close her eyes again. But they immediately popped back open; she rolled over and punched Danny.

"No…" Madeline whispered. "I have a cold."

"Your sides ache; you have an ever so slight pooch. Your boobs are larger." Danny smirked proudly.

"We can't be." Madeline cried. "For hundreds of reasons… Why aren't you freaking out?"

"Because I want this child. As much as the last two." Danny said. "Millie knew, but she… anyways… I love you, and I know you were protecting me. You always do. And before we get into a debate of how we can and what it will look like, I wanted you to know I want this. With you. now." He kissed her belly. She started crying.

"I might miscarry…" Madeline whispered.

"You might not," Danny said. "Ok?" Madeline nodded. Burying her head into his chest. They stayed up all night talking about what to do.

"Can we just go home?" Madeline asked.

"I think…" Danny hesitated, "We should stay here, and you should try to rest as much as possible."

"Ok," Madeline whispered. She knew if Danny asked her to have a baby in the middle of nowhere instead of going home, he had reasons. She assumed Charlie told him something. And looking in his eyes, there was no doubt he wanted this kid.

The plan was Madeline would stay in bed just for the first trimester. Luckily Nymiff had a little training in delivering human babies and fell in love with Madeline's as soon as she had a bump. Madeline tried to get out more during the 4th month, but she was so achy Danny put her back in bed immediately.

The 5th month was the only time Madeline felt human; she even enjoyed being pregnant for a few weeks. After the constant morning sickness, before the weight gain, which caused so much pain. Nymiff would find Danny sobbing by the lake. Unable to make his wife comfortable. She softened to him. No longer seeing him as a storm giant, just a man crying for his wife.

"Nymiff," Madeline called to her one night, during her eighth month, so huge she could no longer sit up for more than a few minutes at a time. "Danny won't be able to but save his child first, before me… They can live in London. He can be happy there. Please…"

Nymiff laughed to herself. Danny begged her to save his wife first that morning. Nymiff prayed Madeline would labor soon. The largeness of her belly concerned her. They were practically force-feeding Madeline her entire pregnancy, so her fullness was not from food.

"I'm never ever doing this again," Madeline screamed, in active labor, two weeks after they thought they were due. Danny kissed her hand. She was in labor 36 hours and lost so much blood Nymiff told Danny to tell her goodbye during the 33rd hour.

After the birth, Madeline slept for 24 hours, and Danny cried for just as long. "Look, mama's awake… Let's go see mama." Danny whispered softly as Madeline struggled to sit up. "Peter Henry and Millie are starving, mom." Madeline grinned. Healthy twins and an alive wife. Danny had his perfect family.

*

Danny secretly loved the next three years in the forest with Nymiff and his family. He knew when they got home, he would have 60 hour work weeks for a while. Plus training. The only thing that made this thought bearable was that the children could have a room by Madeline's office. He could see the twins on breaks and at meals. It was one thing Madeline and Danny had figured out. Only a hundred things more, but at least one problem solved.

Although Madeline blocked it out, Danny knew it was a year, maybe even two, before her body recovered from the pregnancy. Peter Henry was the clone of his father, cautious and thoughtful from day one. Millie was much more spirited and seemed to have strong opinions on everything. Both very healthy although Millie noticeably smaller than her brother. The couple decided that they would wait a few years to blink home. Madeline was certain it was safe but thought it would be easier if the kids were at least three.

"He really is a good man," Nymiff told Madeline as the two sat by the fire the night before the family was planning to go home. Madeline wanted to celebrate the twin's 4th birthdays at their restaurant. The two women laughed as Danny chased Frida in the moonlight as the twins sat on his feet, giggling until they almost passed out.

"Thank you for bringing the forest back to life again," Nymiff said. "The trees are happy. They stopped growing for a while after my husband was killed."

"May I ask what happened to him?" Madeline whispered...

"There was a village across the lake," Nymiff said. "We had many human friends there. One day the village was attacked by five storm giants. My husband went to try to help. He never came back,"

"I'm so sorry, Nymiff," Madeline said.

"Ever since then, I have been terrified of storm giants." Nymiff sniffed then grinned at the twins, who were now jumping on Danny's stomach as Frida licked his face; Danny caught Madeline staring at him and blew her a kiss.

"I'm sorry, I know I am not a very good teacher," Nymiff confessed.

"I can shoot 50 bullseyes with birds flying around my head. That's pretty impressive. And maybe I'll take care of Danny's grandmother's roses with the kids from now on." Madeline took Nymiff's hand, and they sat in silence, each in gratitude of each other. For many reasons, but mostly for two.

"Mama?" Millie ran to Madeline. Madeline feared she was being coached as she saw Danny and Peter Henry watching from afar.

"Yes, my love?" Madeline said. As Millie climbed on Madeline's wheelchair, squeezed her mom's face, and hugged her.

"Can we take Frida home, Please, mama?" Millie asked. "Daddy says yes if you say yes too! And he says she could live in grandma's garden."

"Did he?" Madeline gave Danny a dirty look. But knew she was outnumbered.

Chapter 24

"Mama, daddy's dead, Mama, Mama..." Millie shrieked after they blinked back to their apartment.

"Don't you ever listen?" Peter Henry teased. "Shh! Daddy has to sleep after blinks." He climbed on Danny behind his sister, both now bouncing on Danny. They wanted to help him wake up.

"Are you ok, munchkins?" Madeline asked. They nodded excitedly, showing no pain from the trip. Madeline smirked.

"Again, Mama, again, best ride ever." Millie proclaimed.

"Where's Frida?" Peter Henry sat up and let the little dragon out of Madeline's backpack. The little boy hugged Madeline extra tight. Peter Henry looked excited, but Millie was very concerned, still sitting on her daddy, waiting for him to wake up.

Although the twins seemed perky and unphased, poor Frida crawled out of Madeline's backpack like death warmed over. Eyes crossed, looking like a drunk sailor. Frida hissed at Madeline, knowing she caused this, then the little fairy dragon passed out at the twin's feet.

"Mama?" Millie asked.

"Yes, love," Madeline said.

"I don't like this place." Millie looked around at her new surroundings and pouted. "The walls don't smile at me, the ground is hard. And that thing make noises." She laid her head on Danny's shoulder.

"Daddy explained everything." Peter Henry said. "That's the frigator; it holds daddy's most favorite thing ever, ice cream!"

"I wanna go outside!" Millie pouted.

"I want Ice cream..." Peter Henry joined the protest. Madeline was 90% sure Danny now indeed had recovered from the blink and was keeping his eyes closed just because he could.

"Ok, you... despite what dad says, ice cream is a dessert or a special treat, and you... tomorrow, we'll go to our cabin, and you can run free, wild nature girl. But for now, We are going to play the quiet game!" Madeline said as there was a knock. "I have to answer the door. nurse your daddy."

"hey," Madeline answered the door.

"Let me in, you freak," Steven said.

"Hi..." Madeline said, sticking her head out of the door.

"Are you going to the hospital?" Steven asked.

"Yup," Madeline said.

"Can we blink there?" Steven asked.

"Danny is in the shower and is grumpy," Madeline said. "Can we meet you there in an hour?"

"Yay! Daddy's not dead," Millie screamed, giggling.

"What's that?" Steven asked.

"Tv," Madeline said. "Hey, can you bang on Charlie's door and tell her I need to ask her a thing."

"Madds, you're acting very weird," Steven said. "Are you guys fighting?"

"No... We will explain soon. But we need to take care of Jane first. Then I want to tell Jane my news second." Madeline sniffed. "I'll see ya in an hour. Please bang on Charlie's door and tell her I need help. Right now... Wait, one more thing, give me your coffee. If you ever loved me, you will give me your coffee." She shoved an arm out the door. Steven took another sip then handed the cup to her.

"You didn't kill your husband, and now you need Charlie to bury his body or anything, right?" Steven said, backing away slowly. Madeline never even opened the door more than an inch. Slamming it right away as Steven walked off.

"Hi," Madeline whispered as Danny was coming to.

"So, I had this crazy dream that we found two wild children in the woods," Danny teased Madeline. The twins climbed back on his lap. Millie looked relieved sucking her two middle fingers, "So, thing one and thing two. Mom and I have a few very important errands to run. Auntie Charlie is gonna watch you guys. We told you all about her, remember?"

"No," Peter Henry said. "I want mama."

"We will be back then we'll show you our restaurant and mom's office. And we'll buy you beds. This week will be all about introducing you to your home, you are going to love it." Danny said. The twins nodded sadly.

"Hello. I've been waiting for you." Charlie came in, grinning from ear to ear. "You must be Millie, and you must be Peter Henry." They giggled. She got it backward. "I'm going to walk your folks out and find out everything we cannot do, so we can do them." Peter Henry cheered. Millie continued sucking her fingers.

"How are you, my loves?" Charlie asked, a few minutes later, right outside the door.

"I think that trip should have come with a warning label," Danny said.

"At least that my husband would fall in love with a dragon. And use his children to take her home." Madeline said. "God, my parents..." reality hit Madeline, "I have to tell my folks. That my blood twins are adopted. Then Ida, then the staff... mother of the year... and... avatars... we can't do this..."

"We can. Remember, one hurdle at a time, love." Danny said. "So, we are going to run to check on Jane..."

"You have to tell them," Charlie warned.

"Hey, Jane, while you were in ICU, we were gone for 8 years and had twins cool, huh?" Madeline said. "I want her to focus on her decision before we share our news. They are already almost four, what's another year..." they both gave Madeline dirty looks.

"You look so happy, Daniel." Charlie kissed him. "You look happy but tired, my love." Charlie hugged Madeline.

"I haven't slept in four years…" Madeline teased. "They never sleep, not even in my womb." Danny made his wife float to him and hugged her.

"Do you know anyone who might want to be their nanny?" Danny asked. "They, of course, can't leave the block. Except when we are training, we will usually be one or two rooms away. But it would be easier if we had an extra set of eyes."

"I will. " Charlie said, without hesitation. Madeline burst into tears, so relieved. If Danny or herself could not be with them, Charlie was the next best thing, "And congratulations, they are perfect." Charlie disappeared into their apartment.

*

"Morning," Danny said as he and Madeline went into Jane's room. Steven, Elizabeth, and Mack were already there. "How ya doing, chef?"

"I'm ok," Jane said. "You guys kinda look… different…"

"We haven't worked out in a few weeks." Danny grinned. "Anyways, it's all good; we are getting back to training soon." Madeline looked embarrassed; she had already lost a lot of the pregnancy weight, but it was so much, she had a ways to go. And Danny ate everything she wouldn't or couldn't during her pregnancy… so they were both kind of roundish. But getting back in shape was on the to-do list. Mack stared silently at Danny.

"So…" Jane said. "I've decided about the leg. They'll do it on Friday. I'll be out for two months. That's all I want to say about it. Can you handle the kitchen till I get back?"

"Yes chef," Danny said. "I was thinking, I will make a weekday one-dish lunch, and the full dinner menu. That way, we don't have to hire a tempt to help. All in favor?" everyone agreed it was a good solution, and Jane looked relieved. Which was what Danny was hoping.

"Do you have anything to share with the class, Madeline?" Danny asked.

"Nope," Madeline said.

"Mama!" Millie suddenly appeared in Madeline's lap. The twins were not time locks, but they could blink to each other or their parents at will. Which was both good and bad. It was less of a problem in the woods.

"Well," Jane asked, almost giggling, "Who are you?"

"Millie Jane Boudreaux." Millie shyly said, then buried her head in Madeline's chest. Jane stared at Madeline in amazement.

"We found her this morning outside our door, Cool huh?" Madeline said.

"Mama!" Millie looked confused and upset.

"I'm kidding." Madeline kissed her face till she giggled. "Are you suppose to blink without asking?"

"No, mam," Millie said.

"Blink home and apologize to auntie Charlie," Madeline whispered.

"But now I have to kiss daddy," Millie said and blinked into Danny's arms. He tried to be mad, but Danny was so in love with his daughter.

"Hey," Danny said. "That's Miss Elizabeth, and Uncle Steven and Auntie Jane, and that funny-looking man is Uncle Mack."

"Your brother?" Millie asked, remembering that's what Danny told her. Mack teared up, and Millie went to him.

"Might as well get the other one." Danny smiled.

"There's another?" Mack asked.

"Your friend here seems to make gigantic babies, in pairs." Madeline teased, then blinked to get Peter Henry.

After the introductions were finished, the twins were sent home. Danny made it very clear that they were to stay with Charlie for the rest of the afternoon. They were smart enough to know Danny wasn't playing anymore.

"The cuteness factor threw me off..." Mack said after the children went home. "But you should have told me you were leaving. Daniel."

"I know," Danny said. "We wanted to finish the last pillar. So we could stay home for a while. About a week before we were planning to leave, we found out we were pregnant."

"Did you do ok with the pregnancy and delivery, Honey?" Jane asked.

"Easy peasy," Madeline said. Everyone sensed she was lying. But compared to what Jane was going through, it didn't seem to matter. After visiting Jane, Danny's next stop was to Madeline's lab to make a new batch of birth control potions. Madeline thought he was kidding that this was the second thing they had to do when they got home. He was not.

If the decision was left to him, Danny would have said the twins completed their family and would have gotten a vasectomy that day. But Madeline wanted another 5-year potion, in case they changed their minds. Danny agreed to please his wife, but this time he would keep better track of the expiration date.. Ever since the twins were born, Madeline had more spinal pain. She never mentioned it, but he noticed.

The couple stayed as long as they could at the hospital, grateful to be with the only people who could know the truth about Peter Henry and Millie. They were not happy about it, but decided to tell everyone else that they became the twin's guardian from a cousin of Danny's who passed away, living in England. Even though they were clones of their parents in almost every way. This tore Madeline up, but Millie and Peter Henry thought it was the funniest thing ever when they were old enough to understand.

-

*

"Steven." Someone called him from the bar a few days after Danny and Madeline returned with the twins. Danny was prepping for the dinner shift. Madeline was doing the books. Peter Henry was exploring her office while Millie was in a high chair in the kitchen with Danny.

"Mr. Jourdain..." Steven said. "How are you, sir?" Steven was bent behind the bar, doing inventory, and was surprised to see him.

"I'm fine," Peter said. "I have to fill in for a guest lecturer at some conference in the morning; I'd thought I'd see Jane before... and my daughter and son-in-law. Are they around?"

"Yes, Danny is in the kitchen." Steven showed Peter to the back.

"Hello, Daniel," Peter said. Danny looked up and nervously smiled. Normally he loved seeing his father-in-law. They talked a few times a week and played chess via email. The two really did enjoy each other's company. But this time, Danny felt skittish.

"And who is this little girl?" Peter asked, trying to sound stern. Millie giggled and sucked her two middle fingers, and Peter melted.

"Sir. Madeline!" Danny screamed. "Madeline!"

"What!?!" Madeline yelled. "Your son is trying to read Henry's diary... I'm pretty sure he's a genius." Madeline rolled into the kitchen with the little boy on her lap.

"Daddy!" Madeline said. Half excited, half-filled with dread. Peter hugged her tight. "What are you doing here?"

"Oh, I couldn't stop thinking about Jane, and I was asked to fill in at a conference. Is there anything new with you, Madeline?" Peter asked as Millie climbed out of her high chair onto Madeline's lap.

"I did get a haircut. Do you like it?"

"Best look ever!" Peter said as the twins reached for his hands.

"Danny's cousin from England suddenly passed away, and he had twins..." Madeline said quickly as she had rehearsed, then gulped, she hated lying to her father, but it was safer. "We were going to wait a few weeks after Jane's surgery and after they were acclimated. Then bring them home to meet you and mom.."

"Is that true, son?" Peter asked Danny.

"Would you like a bowl of gumbo, dad?" Danny changed the subject.

"Coward." Madeline mouthed to Danny.

"The truth is… Danny has a mistress and she just dropped them off. But they are so cute, I'm going to try to love them…" Madeline said. Danny looked mortified. Peter was amused. Madeline could never lie to her dad, not even as a kid. And the more she tried, the wilder the stories got. It was a game between them.

"Have I ever showed you the picture I have of Madeline in my wallet?" Peter asked Danny, pulling out the picture. They both got choked up a bit. It was of Madeline as a little girl. If Millie had the outfit, no one would be able to tell the picture wasn't of Millie.

"Third try, daughter. Make it good." Peter teased his daughter, now taking Millie and Peter Henry into his arms.

"Hello?" they were interrupted.

"Aunt Geneva," Danny said, putting a mixing bowl down to hug her. Peter had his back turned, lost in love and conversations with his new grandchildren.

"Another damn doctor's appointment." Aunt Geneva said. "I heard about Jane. How is she?"

"You know, it will be hard…" Danny said.

"How's Mack?" Aunt Geneva asked.

"Oh, Mack is Mack," Danny said. "He's going to get Jane through it… then…" Danny chose his words carefully. "Then we will rectify a situation that should have been corrected a year ago."

"Will you send him my love and strength?" Aunt Geneva said. "On my next good day, I'll make him a pie. And he won't even have to share with you this time. So, Danny, I heard a rumor that I know cannot be true."

"Aunt Geneva, can I explain when I call you tonight?" Danny raised his eyebrows at the man that still had his backed turned to them.

"Sure." Aunt Geneva said, "I was also going to ask if Madeline could make me more potion. It really helped, love.."

"I'd be honored to," Madeline said.

"Geneva?" Peter turned and asked after Millie started crying, now wanting Danny.

"Peter?" Aunt Geneva said in both delight and disbelief.

"Ok, twins, Auntie Charlie is in the garden, go play, then maybe your daddy can cook dinner for all of us," Madeline said. Peter Henry ran to Charlie waiting by the door; Millie lingered holding Madeline's leg until Peter Henry called for her.

"You are looking as beautiful as ever, Geneva," Peter said.

"I'd correct you, but I needed that," Geneva said.

"May I buy you a cup of coffee?" Peter asked.

"Or… something stronger?" Geneva suggested.

"I'll be back, daughter," Peter said. "I can't wait to hear your third and final answer," Peter said. Kissing Madeline on the head, then helping Geneva to the dining room.

"Hey, spy on my dad, and I'll give you Saturday night off." Madeline texted Steven as soon as he left the kitchen.

"What are you doing?" Danny hissed, seeing Madeline's text.

"My dad is hiding something," Madeline said. "How does he know Geneva?"

"Ok, one, your dad grew up 45 minutes from here. It is not that far-fetched." Danny said. "And you just told your father that I had a mistress and kind of disowned your children in that lie, so I wouldn't point fingers at this moment," Danny teased.

"On a side note, that might make a better story; I'm raising your mistresses' children. You can keep your bad boy status. Women will stop giving me dirty looks." Madeline was amused. Her husband was not.

"You really need more sleep," Danny said. "When Jane starts rehab, we should go away for one night." Danny kissed her.

"We can't… besides, your children. They'll find us. They always find us." Madeline smirked.

"Madeline," Danny whispered as she tried to peak out at her father and Geneva. "Seriously, what do you want to tell your dad?"

"Are you really that uncomfortable with having a mistress?" Madeline teased. Danny tried not to smirk. "I don't know. Can we say we have a friend who is a time lock, and we were away?"

"We could," Danny said. "I'd prefer we didn't," Danny said, now sitting down. "I think we can tell him part of it. That you are a time lock. We were on vacation when we got pregnant, and were worried about blinking with infants."

"Ok," Madeline said.

"Good." Danny made Madeline float to the island to face him. He grinned and went in for a kiss when Peter Henry blinked, standing on the counter.

"See. They. Are. Everywhere." Madeline laughed. "I'm going to make a potion before Geneva leaves." She kissed him, tickled Peter Henry and blinked to her gallery.

*

"Here you go, Aunt Geneva," Madeline rolled into the dining room with a paper bag 15 minutes later. "May I join you?"

"Thank you, child," Geneva said. "I am pleasantly surprised to know you are Peter Jourdain's daughter."

"How do you know my dad?" Madeline bluntly asked, dying of curiosity.

"Daughter, one conversation at a time. We are still discussing how I became a grandfather of two-three year olds in a week?"

"You can tell him, Madeline." Geneva said. "He will understand."

"It has to be better than Danny has a mistress..." Peter said.

"Excuse me..." Steven interrupted. "Mack just called. Jane's having a bad day. He wondered if you and I could bring her dinner and he would do closing with Danny. I think they both need a distraction."

"Yup." Madeline sighed. "I'm sorry, dad."

"I actually have nowhere to be until the morning," Peter said. "I would love nothing better than to play with my son-in-law's mistresses children." Peter teased Madeline. "Let me know if Jane feels better later. I'd loved to see her this trip."

"I'll call you, dad." Madeline hugged Peter. "Aunt Geneva, please call me when you run out again. Day or night. One of us is always awake. Make Danny take a break and properly introduce you to the twins."

"I wasn't planning to leave until he did..." Geneva said. " Plus, I think I'll try to stay until I can at least hug Malcolm."

"Madds," Steven yelled from the kitchen. "Our dinners are ready; Mack really sounded bad; let's go." She squeezed Geneva's hand, patted her dad's shoulders, rolled into the kitchen, and blinked to the hospital.

*

"The kids wanted to tell everyone good night," Charlie said, following the twins into Henry's office a few hours later.

"Where's my mama?" Millie whined, trying not to cry. She hopped in Danny's lap. Peter Henry sat close to him too.

"Mom is hanging out with Jane tonight, but I'll bet she will wake you up with kisses in the morning," Danny said.

"Will you be here tomorrow, Grandad?" Peter Henry asked Peter.

"I'll try. I was supposed to go home tomorrow afternoon." Peter said. "Your grandma is going to be so jealous that I met you before her. But I'm going to see if I can take the latest flight home so maybe I can take you to the zoo. Your mama loved the monkeys,"

"NO. Absolutely not." Danny didn't mean to scream, but he did. The twins cried, Peter looked a little hurt, and Mack stared at Danny. "Hey, daddy is grumpy and tired. And so jealous. You can't go to the zoo without me. I'd cry and cry. In a few weeks, we'll go to Houston, and all of us will go to the zoo. Ok?"

"Let's go to bed, you two," Charlie said. The twins hugged everyone, although Millie didn't want to hug Danny at first. He had never raised his voice before, and it scared her. Danny made silly faces at his daughter until Millie smiled again. And Peter Henry just wanted to know exactly how many days until the zoo trip.

"I apologize, dad," Danny said. after they knew the kids were gone. "Where should I start?" After debating with himself, Danny decided to tell his father-in-law everything, just watered down a bit. Madeline was too close to her dad, whereas Danny was close enough. And he appreciated Peter's very high IQ, logical brain.

The short version was, Danny's family is being targeted. He stressed that the twins were safe as long as they were on Henry's block. And that he and Mack were training to take care of the situation.

"You know about your daughter, don't you?" Danny asked, realizing nothing that he said shocked Peter. "Why haven't you told her?"

"Because she had Henry to guide her," Peter said. "And I just wanted to be her daddy for as long as I could. The first time Millie calls you dad instead of daddy, it will crush you." Peter laughed. "And I knew when I told, she would feel even more responsible and worry about us every second of every day."

"Did you know Henry?" Danny asked.

"One of my biggest regrets," Peter said. "I was so looking forwards to getting to know him. I knew of him through Geneva."

"My wife is just baffled how you know Geneva," Danny said.

"We lived next door to her," Peter said. "I was very close to her grandson. She taught us a bit of magic before it was cool. William was the brightest guy I have ever known. We were inseparable till college, but we kept in touch. We loved studying different battles and how they were won. Generals and their strategies. We have been playing chess in one form or another for 40 years. He was so brilliant at it; he became a pillar," Danny and Mack stared at each other.

"He passed away nine years ago in a suspicious car accident. He left me all his books and historical reference material. William was Geneva's last living relative, so I try to see her when I can. Recently she has been after me to become a pillar. I never saw the need. Until now..." before he could continue, they were interrupted.

"Hey," Frank said, coming into Henry's office. "I hear congratulations are in order."

"Thanks. We feel very blessed." Danny said. "Do you want a bite of something?"

"Naw," Frank said. "How's Jane?"

"Not good," Mack said. "Not good at all. The surgery is the day after tomorrow. She wants to get it over with."

"You guys will get through this," Frank said. "Hey, is Madeline around? I wanted to ask her a quick question."

"Should I be jealous?" Danny said.

"If I was like five years younger and unmarried, probably..." Frank said.

"Five? Really Franklin?" Mack smirked...

"Frank." Madeline smiled as she rolled in, going straight to her dad. "Have you met my father, Peter?" they shook hands. "Jane sent me home, but Steven is staying tonight. I was going to check on everyone then go back maybe." Madeline hugged her father and kissed her husband.

"I actually wanted to talk to you for a minute, Madeline," Frank said. "Will you keep me updated on Jane, Mack?"

"Yup," Mack said.

"I need coffee," Madeline said. "Come with me, Frank," Danny and Mack stared at each other as Madeline rolled away.

"So," Frank said, grabbing the coffee cups as Madeline got cream from the refrigerator. "We have Louis Delcroix in custody."

"You're kidding?" Madeline said. "On what?"

"Arson..." Frank said. "Witnesses say it looked like he was performing a ritual that went bad. There's more. He wants Geneva as his lawyer. And he's asking for you. he says if we let him out, he has information that will save your family. He mentioned the twins, by name. I figured Mack had too much on his plate, and Danny would lose his shit."

"I wanted a few days to catch my breath, get the twins settled, and Jane to rehab before dealing with this… but obviously, it won't wait," Madeline said. "I don't think we should get Geneva involved."

"Agreed," Frank said.

"I think I might pay him a visit tomorrow," Madeline said. "If I can place a protection spell on myself…"

"We want coffee," Danny said; Mack and Peter followed.

"Danny, she won't run away with me yet." Frank pretended to be heartbroken. "Nice meeting you, Peter. I'll see you guys soon." And left through the back door.

"What did Franklin want, Madeline?" Danny said in a stern voice.

"Just stuff about Jane; he didn't want to upset Mack," Madeline said. "I was hoping we could have lunch before you left, Dad?"

"Actually, I talked to your mom," Peter said. "I forgot she was going to see your aunt in California for two weeks. I'd thought I'd stay through Monday."

"The kids would love that. And so would we." Danny said. Madeline nervously nodded. "There's a vacant furnished apartment in the complex that you can stay in."

"I'm going to check on the kids. And unlock the apartment." Madeline rolled away.

"Do you know my daughter crinkles her nose when she's trying to hide something bad," Peter asked.

"Yup," Danny said. "It's how most of our biggest fights start."

*

"Don't be mad husband, I woke you with kisses and hugs today." Madeline smiled the next morning as the twins were finishing up their breakfast.

"Why were you in your potion room all night?" Danny was fishing.

"I couldn't sleep," Madeline said. "And I feel like I've been on maternity leave for five years. I need to get back to training and alchemy while taking care of Jane and you and the kids. It's a lot. And I don't know why my dad is staying the whole weekend."

"It's not like his daughter gave him two brand new grandchildren or his second one is in the hospital. What a freak. I should throw him out." Danny teased.

"Did you find out how he knows Geneva?" Madeline asked.

"I did," Danny said.

"And…" Madeline asked.

"I'll tell you when you tell me what Frank actually wanted," Danny said.

"He was updating me on Jane's case,"

"Wow," Danny said. "If this badass witch thing doesn't work out, you should become a lawyer."

"I learned from the best," Madeline said. "Hey munchkins, I'm going to see Auntie Jane. I'll be back, and we'll have lunch with granddad in the garden, ok?" Millie pouted a little. Peter Henry was eating pancakes and didn't care. She kissed them then blinked away.

*

"Why, hello, gorgeous," Mack told Millie as he and Steven came into the kitchen. The little girl grinned.

"What are you guys doing here?" Danny asked.

"Jane has pre-opt stuff until one," Mack said.

"Did Madeline know this?" Danny asked.

"Yup. She practically had to force-feed Jane breakfast this morning before the doctors sent us home." Mack said.

"Damnit, Madeline," Danny muttered under his breath.

"I tried to take Jane and Madeline golfing once; it did not end well." Peter teased Mack about an hour later as they were sitting in the kitchen watching Danny prep for lunch.

"Danny... Daniel, your father-in-law, asked if you played golf." Mack said.

"I'm sorry, I'm feeling frazzled today. Yes, I do." Danny kept looking at the clock, growing angrier and angrier.

"Who are you mad at, daddy?" Peter Henry accused from his grandad's lap.

"I'm having a bad day, and I'm missing sharing the kitchen with Auntie Jane," Danny told his son.

"Mama." Peter Henry grinned as Madeline rolled back into the kitchen 37 minutes later, as Danny noted.

"Where's your sister?" Madeline asked.

"Watering grandma's roses with Auntie Charlie." Peter Henry said.

"Hey, your mama needs a huge hug," Madeline said, snuggling her little boy, hiding a tear. He climbed all over her. they both giggled. "Dad, can you take Peter Henry to join Millie?" Madeline asked.

"I would actually like to talk to you for a while, Madeline," Peter said.

"I go all by myself," Peter Henry hopped off Madeline's wheelchair and ran towards the garden, as Charlie opened the door. He giggled.

"Where have you been, sweetheart?" Peter asked. "Your husband seemed really worried about you." Danny could not look at his wife, not wanting to explode in front of his father-in-law.

"With Frank. He has someone in custody that might know who attacked Jane." Madeline whispered.

"Sorry, dad." Danny slammed down a pot, left the kitchen, and marched towards Henry's office. Madeline followed a few steps behind. The floor shook a little; he was in angry storm giant mode.

"Please tell me you didn't have coffee with Louis Delcroix in a jail cell...." Danny hissed after they were both behind closed doors..

"It was tea..." Madeline said, trying to be cute.

"Damnit," Danny said, even madder.

"Look, Boudreaux," Madeline said, now not playing. "Louis Delcroix wanted to see one of us, and I'd figured you'd break him in half when he asked about your gorgeous twins with hazel eyes." Danny grew two feet just thinking about it.

"Did he?" Danny asked.

"Yes," Madeline whispered, horrified. Danny softened a little.

"What does he want?" Danny asked. Leaning against Henry's desk.

"He pissed off the other four avatars with the witch hunt debacle. Now he is scared that they will bring him to the dragon," Madeline explained. "He'll give us the other avatars and their locations if we hide him. I told him to give me two names, and if they check out..."

"As a witch, you're kind of amazing..." Danny sighed. 'But I really wished you would have told me. What were you thinking, Madds, love, out there, unprotected?"

"I had a protection potion on me," Madeline said. "And a truth spell. He attacked Jane and the restaurant and killed Eugene... And, honey, he killed Fr. Karl. But not Treeva, and not Henry."

"I was thinking I needed to know. I was thinking I wanted Jane to be able to sleep. I need this to be over. Jane needs to be ok if I leave my kids without a mother; that was what I was thinking, husband..."

"You need to let me be mad for the rest of the day. I really need to know where you are 24/7. And it might be a caveman storm giant thing, but this is me." Danny said. "I love you so much." He kissed her forehead.

"Ok…." Madeline pouted but knew how unbelievably mad he must have been.

"Oh, by the way, we have one more pillar this weekend," Danny said.

"No more pillars," Madeline cried.

"You'll like this one," Danny promised.

"Don't go, love." Madeline pleaded.

"I have to finish lunch," Danny sighed, still a little distant. Madeline understood but hated when they fought. She shut her office door and laid her head on Henry's desk, sad, frustrated, and so angry. After Madeline wallowed in self-pity for as long as she could, she pulled out the piece of paper Louis Delcroix gave her and studied the two names. They looked so familiar.

"Steven, where are the job applications from last week?" Madeline asked a few minutes later, rolling out of Henry's office. Steven was helping Danny plate as Peter had his nose in his laptop. Steven pointed to the stack of papers on the desk in the corner.

"Did you interview a Tommy Whitman and a Hanna Evans?" Madeline asked.

"Yes," Steven said, trying to remember. "Tommy couldn't make a dry martini, and Hanna was very inquisitive about Mack and Danny. You're welcome."

"Why are you asking, Madds?" Danny asked. She pulled their applications from the stack, laid them between Danny and Steven, and showed them Louis Delcroix's note. All three sighed.

"We just have to get Jane through surgery, then I might have to make a deal with the devil." Madeline whispered..

"Mama, I sleepy." Millie ran to Madeline from playing outside. "I want us to go home to Nymiff now."

"Millie, we've talked about this remember? This is our home," Madeline said.

"Daddy's always mad and never plays with us, and you are sad all the time, mama." Millie sniffed...

"Come here, thing one." Danny dropped to the floor. Millie sucked her fingers and climbed on him. "Jane is like mama's sister. You'd be so sad if Peter Henry was sick, right?" Millie shrugged. "And I'm going to make sure every afternoon until you're like 90; we play in the garden."

"With mama, too?" Millie asked, now giggling as Danny blew her a raspberry.

"Yes, with your gorgeous, brilliant, wise, mama." Danny grinned at Madeline and winked.

"And Frida?" Millie asked,

"Yes, and Peter Henry, too" Danny said.

"Sometimes. Peter Henry can be only sometimes." Millie giggled and ran to the playroom.

"Do we really have to do another pillar, husband?" Madeline quietly asked hoping that they were talking again. "I worry we might be gone 20 years and have triplets with huge heads, who won't sleep either."

"We won't even have to leave the kitchen," Danny said.

"I don't understand," Madeline said. Then her father looked up from his laptop and smiled.

"Hi." Madeline's phone rang before she could question her father.

"It's me," Jane said on the line.

"How was the pre-opt stuff?" Madeline asked; Danny, Steven, and Mack casually eavesdropped.

"Ok. How was lunch?" Jane asked.

"It was extra packed today. I think there are a bunch of conferences in town. Your partner in crime made an excellent Jambalaya and key lime pie. Do you want a plate?" Madeline said.

"Naw," Jane said. "How was the meet?"

"Fine." Madeline lied.

"I need a distraction, tell me," Jane said. She was the only one that knew Madeline was planning to meet Louis Delcroix. The only reason Jane didn't tell Danny was she knew Frank would have her back, and he did.

"Can I tell you tonight?" Madeline asked.

"Surrounded by men, aren't you?"

"Yup," Madeline said.

"Was it awful?" Jane asked.

"Pretty much, I kept my temper but barely. He knew stuff he shouldn't." Madeline whispered. Danny noted.

"How mad is your husband?" Jane asked.

"Pretty damn mad… probably closer to a deal-breaker than I should have pushed it." Madeline looked down and sniffed a little.

"Hey, I have a favor." Now Jane was crying. After Jane explained, Madeline cried a little harder.

"I think that's a bad idea, Janie," Madeline sighed. "But, at least we'll both get dumped on the same day," Madeline said, hoping that was a joke. "Ok, I'll send Steven now, and I'll come after I put the kids to bed; I love you." Madeline hung up and took a long breath.

"Steven, can you bring Jane a plate? She says she's not hungry, but I don't believe her." Madeline said.

"I'm there," Steven said.

"Macky, why don't we go work out for a few hours... You need it... and I am so out of shape." Madeline said.

"I can't Madds, I should either be with Jane or stocking the bar," Mack said.

"Gee, I wish you were half owner of this restaurant and had minions…" Madeline teased. "Oh, wait."

"She suggested it, huh?" Mack said.

"She's buttering you up so you won't get mad when she requests that... only I stay with her tonight. You're the first eyes she wants to see after the surgery. Jane and I plan to wallow all night. Probably not smart, but It's a thing we do before really hard days. You are her everything, Macky, but she just needs this."

"Ok..." Mack sighed, looking very hurt.

"let's go work out; I have many new tricks to share." Madeline teased. "Gotta show you what I can do with an arrow and a sword." Mack felt bad, but he was tempted and tried to hide a grin.

"We'll be back, dad," Madeline said.

"I think I might go with Steven to see Jane," Peter said. Steven carried a take-out box and held the kitchen door open for Peter.

"Wanna come? You have three hours before dinner shift." Madeline asked shyly.

"I would like that very much, wife." Danny said. "And you keep forgetting, no deal breakers, Madds," Danny agreed and kissed her softly.

For the first time in ages Danny, Mack, and Madeline, blinked to Henry's land for a few hours. Mack was blown away by their latest trick, time compression plus concentration.

Even though it broke Mack's heart, Jane only wanted Madeline with her that night and before surgery. Madeline wanted to lecture Jane about trusting her significant other but thought maybe it wasn't the best time.

The next day was one of Jane's worse and, therefore, one of Madeline's too, but the group was waiting when Jane rolled back to her room. And Jane knew she would survive rehab with the unconditional love and support of Mack.

Chapter 25

"Do not leave this couch, wife," Danny ordered a few minutes after they blinked back from 1980s Venice.

"Don't you feel a little guilty," Madeline asked.

"We got a fabulous meal, I got a little loving, and you got 10 hours sleep," Danny said. "Kids didn't even miss us. I have absolutely no regrets." Danny whispered as Madeline leaned against him.

"Why did you let me sleep for 10 hours?" Madeline pouted. "We could have done some sightseeing; you'd love St. Mark's Square."

"You needed it," Danny said. "If we must travel to swanky hotels for you to sleep, I'm ok with that. We can take the kids for a few days when Jane gets back."

"Daddy." Peter Henry ran into Madeline's office. "Where were you for 12 hours?"

"You have got to work on your timing, son," Danny said as Peter Henry jumped on the couch. Madeline sat up, playfully pushing her husband away.

"They know all." Madeline teased. "Where's your sister?"

"Trying to train Frida to bite me." Peter Henry snickered. "I'm not worried; Millie is meaner, so Frida likes me more. She's gonna get bit." Danny rolled his eyes.

"Your pet," Madeline said. "Your problem." Danny and Peter Henry giggled.

"What can we do today?" Peter Henry asked.

"Today and tomorrow are our busiest days, plus mommy and daddy have to do more studying," Danny said. "But we've decided to close the restaurant on Mondays and Tuesdays until Auntie Jane comes back. And we'll do something fun the whole day, day after tomorrow."

"Ok. I'll go tell Millie." Peter Henry hugged his parents and ran to the playroom. "Hi, granddad!" Peter Henry screamed in passing.

"Hi, dad." Madeline got up and hugged Peter. "I would make my husband cook you breakfast, but we are supposed to be meeting with someone in a minute." Danny looked at the door and made it close.

"Wanna hear me out or jump directly to questions?" Peter asked his daughter, knowing her very well. Madeline looked at Danny; he nodded, reassuring her.

"Henry wanted you to have a little extra help before facing your battles," Peter said.

"Are you a pillar?" Madeline asked. Surprised, but for some reason not shocked.

"Yes and no." Peter scratched his head. "First, I know Geneva through her grandson, William. He was a pillar. I didn't know this until he passed away nine years ago. His death was very hard on Geneva, so we've sort of reconnected. In the 10 boxes William left me, I found a very detailed letter Henry wrote him. It touched me how much Henry respected and loved you, daughter."

"Do you know, I'm… special?" Madeline asked.

"Now that's a loaded question, Madeline." Peter and Danny teased. "I knew you were special from the moment I held you. I suspected you were meant for greater things a few years back. And when you brought Danny home, all the pieces fell in place."

"Does mom know?" Madeline asked.

"No," Peter said. "She wasn't raised around magic. It makes her very nervous."

"So I can't tell her my kids are mine?" Madeline said sadly.

"She'll come around," Peter promised. "The second she hears Peter Henry's laughter and sees Millie's pout, you can tell her you have three heads, and she won't care. I swear."

"What did my granddad want you to teach us?" Danny asked.

"He was concerned, Madeline would go into battle to protect her family on a heated whim without a plan," Peter said.

"Surely not," Danny smirked

"William and I have studied every major battle ever recorded," Peter said. "We have been playing chess since we were eight. I love you, Madeline, but you're not a planner, and you often act before you think. And you cannot do that here. I think Danny is a planner, but I see the way he looks at you. Even when he is so mad, he cannot speak. But I have no doubt, he'd blindly follow you into a burning building, even on your worst days."

"How much do you know, dad?" Danny asked.

"Dragon controls five avatars," Peter said. "I've studied every book on dragons that I could find in the last few years. As a father and now a grandfather, my first instinct is to send you somewhere safe. New Orleans be damned."

"John Luc..." Madeline sniffed. "I was going to send Danny and the kids there. He was my alchemist mentor. Charlie was married to him. They have a very good life; the twins could flourish there with their dad. This isn't a spur-of-the-moment decision. I've thought about it every single night since they were born."

"Madds," Danny whispered.

"Henry predicted that would be your plan," Peter said. Danny laughed loudly, Madeline covered her face.

"Here's my offer," Peter said. "Let me try to help make your plan, with 3 backup proposals. I don't think your husband would leave you... even to go with the children."

"No," Danny said. "I'd take them to John Luc's without hesitation, to save them, to make sure they had a good life. But I'd die with Madeline. It's not what she wants to hear, but it's the truth."

"If all scenarios end with both of your..." Peter couldn't finish... "Your mom and I will take the twins and..."

"Yes," Danny said. Madeline nodded, unable to speak.

"But, we are no where near that, ok?" Peter said. "First, Henry described your powers and what you have learned so far. But I need details and demonstrations, so I'll have a better idea." And so they did. Peter was at a loss for words when they first blinked to the cabin.

"That was wilder than anything I imagined," Peter said as they blinked back to Henry's office two hours later. Mack was on the phone with a vendor. Steven was writing a paper for his ethics in magic class.

"I'm going to check on the twins," Madeline said. "You and Danny make a plan. Just tell me what order to blow stuff up. I will actually follow instructions this one time," Madeline promised, kissing her father and husband, then rolled away.

"It's not going to be that easy, is it?" Danny asked, sitting on the couch.

"So, I have to ask a rather personal question," Peter said.

"She is about 80% speed and 70% agility from her peak training. I'm 85% overall. Maybe..." Danny said, knowing exactly what Peter needed to know, "She is still impressive. But after Japan she was in unbelievable shape, but pregnancy and delivery were very tough on Madeline's body. And because I put her on bed rest, I started skipping my runs. And it snowballed. Madeline planned to start working out, hoping to help her back and weight, when Jane started rehab. But I worry there aren't enough hours in the day for hardcore training. And the avatars are getting more aggressive."

"I have to ask Dad," Danny said. "Knowing full well, she would never forgive me, but is there any scenario where Madeline doesn't have to face the dragon? I would, if it saves my family, I will go on a suicide mission without a second thought."

"Selfishly, and I'm not proud of this, but I've thought of that," Peter admitted.

"I'd go too. I'd kill the avatars and the dragon with Daniel." Mack said. "If Jane had Madeline and the twins and the restaurant, they'd be ok."

"Me too," Steven said.

"I need you to stay, run the restaurant, and in 20 or 30 years, you can marry Madeline with my blessing." Danny told Steven half kidding, half not.

"Would I sacrifice you three to save my daughter, Jane, and the twins?" Peter asked. "I probably would. But I truly believe I'd just be sending you to your execution. Madeline's powers and training combined with Danny's are the only things that could defeat the dragon. And until the dragon is dead, my grandchildren are in danger. And that's unacceptable to me."

"What are you thinking, dad?" Danny asked.

"You and Madeline need to go somewhere and focus on training. I need to study your talents and skills and know them like the back of my hand so that we can strategize," Peter said.

"Like another pillar trip? Or staying on our land?" Danny asked.

"I would absolutely love to train on Henry's land and stay at the cabin," Peter said. "But I think, if we do this right, it will take more than a few days or weeks. And if time is of the essence..."

"Pillar trip..." Danny sighed. "Without getting into it, besides the twins, each trip has emotionally broken her. I think she will refuse, because now with Millie and Peter Henry, it's twice as complicated."

"If we take them, they will grow up, making it harder for them to fit in when we get back." Danny continued. "If we leave them, in their minds and by the clock, we are gone 15 minutes. But in their hearts, they will not understand why we left them for months. Or even years... if I had to, I could; I would hate every second I'm away... But to me, it's like soldiers going to war or a navy guy deployed in a submarine for a 6-month pack. But Madeline won't leave the twins. We snuck away last night, and she barely survived the guilt."

"Hi." Millie appeared on Danny's lap and gave him a loud, silly kiss. "Daddy, star shape cheese sandwich, Please..."

"My child speaks!" Danny tickled Millie and put her on his shoulders. "Dad, we'll do anything you think we need; one of us may be kicking and screaming all the way, but..."

"Daddy!" Millie squealed. "Stop talking about me!"

"You? I meant your Mama!" Danny said. Millie laughed because it sounded funny. Everyone else laughed because it was true.

*

"They are, essentially sending me to a fat farm." Madeline hissed. "And not even a nice one, like in Malibu... my husband could afford it. But they are sending me to the middle of nowhere. Why?" Jane laughed from her bed as Danny and Mack tried not to. "It's not my fault I gave birth to gigantic storm giant babies who left all their fat in me."

"Is that how you really see it?" Danny asked, amused.

"Yup," Madeline said. "And I'm a little pissed off that you seem excited. You and your daughter are giddy."

"I'm sorry. I have fallen off the 60-hour week work wagon. I miss playing with my kids without watching the clock." Danny admitted.

"Do you really not want to go, Madds?" Jane asked.

"I don't know," Madeline said. "I thought we were done with pillars. I knew we still had a lot to deal with. I guess I was naive when I thought we could do it all from here. and I wanted to get the kids settled."

"Dad says it might take three years," Danny said. "They really haven't met anyone besides our close-knit group. I think if we have to go, this is the ideal time."

"We are going to screw them up." Madeline sighed.

"Charlie said they will remember this as a wonderful adventure with their parents and granddad," Danny said.

"No one dies?" Madeline asked.

"Nope," Danny promised.

"We won't have any unplanned surprises?" Madeline asked.

"Nope," Danny grinned. "Although we do have to keep practicing for later."

"So, what's the plan?" Mack asked.

"My dad wants us to go back to the 1800s, buy 10,000 acres in Colorado, build a cabin with the kids, come back for my dad, so he can join us, and we can train. See fat farm."

"Stop saying that, Madeline." Danny teased. "We can bring everything for the kids, do a protection spell on the land."

"Peter Henry wants his books; Millie just wants to know if she can sleep outside again," Madeline said. "So essentially, this is a vacation for them."

"Come on, Madds," Danny said.

"When are you leaving?" Jane asked.

"Monday morning," Madeline said. "Steven is doing land research, and we have a lot more to pack with the kids."

"Are you worried about anything else?" Mack asked.

"I'm not thrilled about blinking with my dad 250 years back," Madeline admitted. "I might try to make him a potion to help with nausea."

"Ok, I'll try to come back tomorrow," Madeline said an hour as they finished a late lunch.

"Madds," Jane said, trying not to cry. "You cannot spend every moment here."

"I'm a freaking time lock; you bet I can," Madeline said.

"A very tired time lock, at the moment," Danny said. stroking her back. "I do think this trip will re-energize you."

I'll be fine for a day. And I would like to start planning my wedding when you get back." Jane announced.

"Here I am," Mack smirked.

"Silly man, this wedding is for us," Madeline said as she held Jane's hand. The men laughed. Madeline kissed Jane's cheek, not ready to leave again. Still, she knew this was her only option without putting everyone she loved in even more danger.

-

*

"You got the coordinates?" Steven asked.

"Yup," Danny said. "It's kinda cool that you found the deed to our land."

"It has been in a trust for 200 years in both of your names," Steven said. "The weirdest part is, I tried to see it on google earth; it's blurry. The land around it is crystal clear, but you can actually see your property lines. Everything insides the border is smudged."

"Like a protection spell?" Danny asked.

"Yup," Steven said.

"It's good to be married to a witch." Danny smiled.

"Ok, Madeline," Peter said. "Go to your land, build a cabin with your family then come back for me. I'll be waiting."

"You do know I married money; he could buy us a mansion in Aspen today. We could be drinking cognacs by a fire tonight," Madeline suggested.

"No, daughter, although we should do that next Christmas," Peter smiled.

"Done," Danny said.

"Build a cabin with your husband; it's good physical labor with a bit of problem-solving," Peter said. "And Madeline, your husband and children have been told you are not to use any magic while building the cabin." Millie and Danny grinned. Peter Henry shrugged.

"Ok," Madeline said, rolling her eyes at Steven, he laughed and blew the kids a kiss. "I'll be back, dad." Millie put her head on Danny's shoulders, sucking her fingers.

"Mama, you were trying to leave without Frida!" Peter Henry yelled as he climbed onto her lap. Frida hopped on too, hissing at her, knowing the hell that was coming. Danny and Madeline held hands and blinked.

*

"Is everyone ok? Millie? Peter Henry?" Madeline asked as they landed in Colorado. Danny was stretched out in the grass, already moving a little. Millie was giggling. Peter Henry looked cautiously curious. And Frida immediately threw up on Madeline's leg without any signs of remorse.

"Mama, I'm going to tell the trees hello," Millie said.

"Wait," Madeline said. Millie was vibrating in place. "Take your brother and Frida and stay within my line of sight, or you will be in so much trouble. I'm dead serious, Millie Jane."

"Yes, mam." The twins both giggled and ran around their parents. Frida hissed at Madeline, licked Danny, then followed the twins everywhere.

"Your pet hates me so much," Madeline said, floating to the ground to sit closer to Danny.

"But boy does she love those twins..." Danny said.

"So," Madeline said. "I know you've been putting off this conversation, but Peter Henry weighs at least twice as much as Millie."

"I know," Danny whispered. "I wanted to get everyone settled before I talked to him..."

"It doesn't have to be a bad thing, love," Madeline said, stroking his face.

"I know that logically," Danny said. "I never realized how much I hated my life before I met you. And a large part of it was trying to hide my storm giant side."

"I think we need to celebrate his strengths and growths," Madeline said.

"The other thing is, I don't think Millie has any storm giant in her; I worry she might feel left out," Danny said.

"Oh, I think she has other gifts," Madeline said, pointing at their daughter. They both smiled.

"What in the world is she doing?" Danny sat up, pulling his wife into his arms, staring at his little girl in amazement. It just occurred to both of them that Millie had been in an intense conversation with the biggest tree in the clearing for seven minutes. They studied her expressions. Ranging from concern to laughter and agreement.

"Mama, I have to ask you a few questions for the forest," Millie said, running to them, looking very serious. Peter Henry flopped on top of Danny.

"Yes, mam, ask away," Madeline said, resisting the urge to kiss her daughter from head to toe.

"Will you be the woods' caretaker?" Millie asked.

"Yes," Madeline said; Millie began running back and forth, each time lovingly petting both her Mama as well as the tree.

"Will you promise not to cut any of the trees down?" Millie asked.

"I cannot promise that, Millie," Madeline said. "We have to build a few buildings. We need wood for cooking and warmth. And daddy and I need a large area to practice our magic. But I will always ask the woods for permission like Nymiff taught us." Millie sighed as if she was stuck in the middle and ran to the tree.

"The trees will give you wood as you need it." Millie ran back to her Mama with this offer. "But mama..." Millie whispered in Madeline's ear. Madeline tried to hide her smile as her daughter told her something horrifying.

"Come storm giant, you look mean," Madeline said. making Danny get up. "Let's go state our intentions to the woods."

"Yes, wife." Danny stood up. Still a bit skeptical about this talking to nature, but knowing he did see some amazing things when they lived with Nymiff. They bowed at the tree that Millie was talking to. And by the time they returned to the children, there was a wood stack for a small fire. It broke Madeline's heart a little how happy the kids looked at this moment.

The trees made the family a temporary shelter that night. Over the decades, the couple would build a beautiful compound with many houses on the land. Still, Millie would always be happiest in the little shelter that somehow stood for centuries.

Madeline hated to admit it, but Colorado was a very good time in their lives. As instructed, the family-focused on building their permanent house for the first year. Millie explained to the trees that it was very important that her parents got a lot of exercise. Hence, the trees only donated lumber on the other side of the lake.

This tickled Danny, not his wife, who cursed every load they had to drag around the lake. But the curse jar did help pay for college. There was also a jar for every time Madeline tried to use magic while building their house. That paid for the twin's first car.

They did a few other big projects that were ongoing. Danny homeschooled the kids. Peter Henry loved it; Millie tolerated it if they studied outside. The girls planted a huge garden. And Peter Henry and his mom put protection spells on every inch of the land, weaving between the trees.

Madeline forced herself to use a manual wheelchair to do everything, even a few runs a week with Danny. She enjoyed his company and their talks and how it was rebuilding her strength. But in all the years she rolled with him, she never understood the act of running, or rolling, as enjoyable.

Danny requested a very good steak when Madeline blinked home to pick up her dad. The steak did much better than the surprise ice cream and dad. It took Peter a couple of hours to recover from the blink, and they agreed once they returned to New Orleans, no more traveling back in time for him.

Peter was such a young-looking 50-year old that they probably should have done more research on blinking with older humans. But once he felt better, Peter was glad to be there with his daughter and her family.

Peter was very impressed with the cabin that the couple had built. Danny enjoyed building it and was already drawing house plans to build together on Henry's property when they got home. Madeline was not as enthusiastic, teasing it could be a Danny and Mack project.

Besides building the house and their other chores, Danny and Madeline were back in tip-top shape by the second year. They built a huge obstacle course in the back of the property, and the kids loved watching them practice. Madeline was a bit concerned about how much Millie enjoyed watching mom blow stuff up.

Peter Henry enjoyed the occasional race with his sister. Which he always won by minutes, despite his parent's nudges to go easier on Millie. But honestly, Peter Henry would rather be inside reading a book. On the opposite end of the spectrum, Danny usually had to carry his daughter kicking and screaming when it was time to come in just before sunset. Millie would be so upset if she didn't have time to hug the trees goodnight.

After the kids went to bed, Peter and Danny would discuss strategies of battling the avatars and the dragon. And played at least two games of chess. One, because they thoroughly enjoyed the game, and two, it helped them think and share ideas.

Madeline agreed to kill the dragon by any means necessary. She, however, did not wish to kill the avatars if it could be avoided. She wanted to gather them up, place them somewhere. Thinking that after the dragon was killed and the links to the avatars were severed, the dragon worshippers could face their crimes in a court of law. This cause Danny many sleepless nights with an internal conflict between the storm giant and the lawyer.

"Madeline!" Danny whispered loudly one night and rushed to her as not to wake the children. Madeline was lying on the couch reading one of her time lock books as Danny and Peter played chess. All of a sudden, Madeline started bawling and laughing uncontrollably. At first, it scared the men to death. Madeline never ever broke down near the twins, even if they were asleep.

"Look!" Madeline wiped away a tear but still visibly shaken. "I've read through this book a hundred times. I know every spell by heart. I have never seen this one before. I think it is from… I'll be back." Madeline blinked away. Before Danny could calm down, she appeared again.

"Madeline," Danny scolded, "Where did you go, and why do you smell like cigars?"

"That's not important." Madeline said, still crying, "Look at this spell. Look." It was: how a time lock kills a dragon in 5 steps. Without learning from the pillars, this spell was utterly impossible. With Madeline and Danny's knowledge, it was doable, dare they believed, easy.

Danny poured himself a single glass of port that night. They cautiously had reasons for a toast. And it was the first night since the twins were conceived, Madeline let herself believe she might actually be able to watch them grow up.

In all honesty, although Madeline would never admit it, she would have loved to stay another year. Still, the 3rd winter was brutally cold, and everyone but herself got something ranging from a bad cold to probably bad pneumonia, all in the same two weeks.

Peter Henry was the best patient; he just wanted books and food. Millie wanted to be held 24/7. It went downhill from there. Madeline's potions helped, but she did not like how long it took her dad to recover.

*

"Honey, please stop crying." Danny pleaded with Millie as they started packing up to go home.

"I.. love… it… here… and I… don't want… mama to blow up Frida with a… fireball…" Millie cried, stuttering and jumping into Danny's arms. "I forgot to let her out last night; it's not her fault she pee'd on mama's new rug." The young seven-year-old came unglued.

"Millie, your mama is not going to blow up Frida, I promise!" Danny said, trying to hide his amusement. Very glad his wife didn't think of it first.

"She said so." Peter Henry said, for once defending his sister. "Mama told grandad last night after she thought we were in bed. After she kills the dragon, she deserves a month in Hawaii alone with her husband," Millie nodded.

"And where were you two, thing one and thing two?" Danny asked.

"Hiding in the kitchen. Mama said no snacking in bed, so we thought it'd be ok in the kitchen." Millie explained.

"One, you were eavesdropping, so you owe mom an apology," Danny said. "And two. Mom was not talking about Frida."

"You promise?" Millie pouted.

"I do," Danny said. Millie was satisfied. Peter Henry was not.

"Is mama going to kill a dragon?" Peter Henry asked. He waited until Millie ran outside to hug Madeline. "I'm older and much more mature than Millie. Mama tells you that a zillion times. So you can tell me."

"One, family talk on eavesdropping tonight; two, you are three minutes older!" Danny said, pretending to be exasperated. "Remember I told you there were both good and bad kinds of creatures in the world?" Peter Henry nodded thoughtfully. "We just want to be prepared in case a nasty creature surprises us. It's like taking karate for protection, for magic users." Danny said. Peter Henry seemed satisfied but a little worried about his Mama.

Chapter 26

"What the hell is happening in my office?" Madeline teased and floated to sit by Jane on the couch a few days after the family returned from Colorado. "I'm pretty sure world leaders have met in here," Jane laughed at Madeline. The twins were sitting on Madeline's desk, coloring and bickering. Danny, Mack, and Steven were sprawled out on the floor talking about sports, playing with Frida.

"Are you glad to be back?" Jane asked.

"No." Madeline sighed, smiling a tiny bit. "Millie misses Colorado. Peter Henry misses his granddad. Danny misses not sharing a bed with children. He woke to Millie's foot in his ear. And they all seem to blame me for everything. Fun times. "

"But the contractors are starting the remodel today, so we should be a three-bedroom family in a few weeks. In Colorado, the twins shared a bed in their own area. Still, they have never slept in separate rooms ever, so I think that might be more traumatic to them than dragons and time travel. How are you, Janie?"

"I get fitted for my leg tomorrow." Jane said, "I am a bit concerned about standing 12 hours a day."

"What kind of jerk makes you work 12 hours a day?" Madeline teased as Danny joined them.

"I told you, Jane if we have to gut the kitchen and build everything to your specifications, we will," Danny said.

"We did the major remodel three months ago!" Jane said.

"I don't care. Not even a little." Danny shrugged.

"Or. You could finally teach me how to cook, and I can be the third chef." Madeline offered.

"No." Danny and Jane shouted, a little too loudly, smirking at each other.

"Auntie Charlie," the twins shouted as Charlie came in. She flew over to them and kissed each of their noses.

"Ooo, look, your mom is mad at me. I better go make nice." Charlie said.

"She can't stay mad if you give her a raspberry on her cheek," Millie suggested.

"When you stop being cute, you are going to be in trouble all the time," Peter Henry muttered, still coloring.

"Not as long as I have my daddy." Millie stuck out her tongue at her brother. The adults tried to hide their amusement.

"Madeline," Charlie said.

"Charlie." Madeline gave her a dirty look.

"I just went to mass; that makes twice this week. Fr. Karl would call me a lapsed catholic." Charlie said. "Your property spells are becoming more and more annoying. Do they give you printouts of who leaves the block?"

"Not yet, but maybe by the time the kids learn to drive." Madeline grinned. "Just let me sprinkle you with a protection spell before you go. Please." Madeline said, knowing if she said anything else, it would upset Charlie. The pixie gave a non-committal nod.

"Hello Jane, you are looking better," Frank said, coming into the office.

"Will you put my fiancé to work next week? Please. He is hovering." Jane asked.

"Sorry, the program starts in three," Frank said.

"The one you run, and Mack is the only student?" Jane teased.

"Two weeks, my compromise," Mack said, standing up from the floor. Jane rolled her eyes and agreed to avoid another fight.

"kids, this is your Uncle franklin," Danny said. The twins smiled.

"Ok, twins, let's go outside for a while," Charlie said.

"That means they are going to talk about the dragon," Millie told Peter Henry.

"And the avatars." Peter Henry added as they ran to Charlie.

"Your. Children." Madeline teased Danny, he sighed.

"Not to be nosey, but…" Frank said.

"We were gone three years," Danny said. "They just turned seven. Peter Henry is showing signs of being more of a storm giant than I did at his age."

"It's startling, that's all," Frank said. "He is the spitting image of you when you were 12."

"Ida keeps calling him Danny," Danny said. "Peter Henry says it's fine. We've told the twins that grandma is sick, and they are so sweet, they try to understand. But it has to hurt Peter Henry's feelings a little.

"Because Millie looks so much like Madeline, Ida seems to acknowledge that she is her daughter. But not mine? I don't know. But the twins seem to adore her, and she seems to enjoy them. I do worry she's going to bring up Abigail, and it will upset them." Madeline cuddled with Danny.

"What are you telling people?" Frank asked.

"They are our magical children," Madeline said. "Our friends know the truth. Strangers can translate that into anything they want as long as they leave the twins alone. We hated saying they are adopted when they clearly aren't."

"Was it a good trip?" Frank asked.

"Family wise, the best," Madeline said. "But more importantly, we figured out how to kill the dragon. There is a little prep, and Danny and I will need to be in sync with clear and focused minds, but I really think it's possible."

"I hate rushing you," Frank said. "But the word on the street is more people are worshipping the dragon. The avatars are good protection when the dragon reappears to claim everything that the Guidry's have taken from her."

"Bet ya are glad you married me now," Danny said. Madeline winked at him.

"There have been four attempts on Louis Delcroix's life in the last week," Frank said. "I'm certain he's only still alive because Madeline put a potion around his jail cell."

"We need to go ahead and find the other avatars," Madeline said. "I have two of their names. They have been in our restaurant. If we can find them, I'd like Geneva with me if we do truth spells. I don't think I can be impartial."

"Here is where Madeline and I go round and round," Danny said. "Madeline wants the avatars to have their day in court, as do I... but I know it will take the judicial system at least 50 years to catch up to magic users. Their needs and proofs of guilt are different. Most magical users won't leave DNA, but there should be a standard truth spell that can be recognized as evidence. "

"And we don't want to put you in between a rock and a hard place, Frank," Madeline said.

"What do you want to do, Madeline?" Frank asked.

"I think," Madeline said. "I want to gather up the avatars, put them in jail, and let the council of witches and lawyers sort it out.

"Madeline!" Charlie screamed. "Peter Henry fell off the swing. He's fine, but he says mama fixes his boo-boos." Madeline touched frank's arm and blinked to her son.

"Do you agree with your wife, Daniel?" Frank asked.

"In theory, yes," Danny said. "In practical and weighing the dragon's vendetta against everyone I love, no."

"Madeline still thinks the avatars are human and can be saved," Jane said. "I was attacked by a monster. I did not see Louis Delcroix's face at all. If taking my leg is the last evil thing he does, I'd say let him rot in jail, but..."

"Daddy." Peter Henry appeared on the couch by his father. The little boy was clearly upset.

"What happened, son?" Danny hugged him. Peter Henry whispered his side of the story. "It's daddy's fault. I should have checked the swing set.

It probably had a rusty chain. And Millie shouldn't have teased you about your weight."

"I don't wanna be a storm giant, daddy." Peter Henry sniffed.

"I know," Danny said. "We will figure it out. Mom made special things to help me. I bet she will make them for you too."

"Millie's crying; mama must be scolding her. I'm going to watch. Mom's super mad. Millie's not going to sweet-talk her way out of this one. ha!" Peter Henry decided this would make him feel better. Jane, Mack, Steven, and Frank hid their smiles as Danny hung his head in defeat.

"Hey, one of my C.I.'s texted me," Frank said after Peter Henry ran to the playroom. "There's supposedly a big dragon worshipping ceremony this weekend with blood sacrifices."

"I'll go." Madeline reappeared on the couch. Danny hung his head again with an even louder sigh. "What if all of the avatars are there?"

"Or, what if it's a setup, Madds?" Danny asked.

*

"Leon..." Danny said. "I admit, I am tempted, but my chef is out for at least two months, my partner is starting a new job. My wife is now the restaurant's business manager, not her dream job that I lured her here with, and we are homeschooling the kids. I'm pretty sure she would shoot me or something far worse."

"You'll have to explain how you have twins seven-year-olds. Did you take a DNA test?" Leon asked. "I'm asking as your lawyer."

"I can assure you. They are definitely mine. Do you really care?" Danny asked as he was finishing up his unexpected business breakfast.

"Not really," Leon said honestly. "I see the wheels are spinning."

"Autonomous department?" Danny asked.

"Completely," Leon said. "First in the country. You'll only report to me. Start with five lawyers, all the bells and whistles. I'm not crazy about your suggesting having an office on this block, it's a little out of the way from the courts and police station, but if you sign a 10-year contract, I'll do it."

"I'll need six months to get my ducks in a row if I agree," Danny said.

"Four, while overseeing building and setting up the office," Leon said. "I need your answer by Monday. I really don't want to interview anyone else."

"Hello, Leon," Mack said. Mack and Steven entered the kitchen, where the two men were finishing up their conversation.

"Mack." Leon nodded, "I'll look forwards to your call, Danny. I'll send you the name of an architect if you want to play with the idea of building next door." Leon left, passing Steven.

"What was that?" Mack asked.

"Trouble." Danny sighed. "A temptation I should not be considering. How did Jane sleep last night."

"She didn't." Mack shrugged.

"Elizabeth, what are you doing here?" Steven asked. As Madeline and Elizabeth came into the kitchen from Henry's office.

"Hi honey," Elizabeth said. "I was bending Madeline's ear about something." She kissed Steven.

"Look how terrified he is," Madeline teased and pointed at Steven. "It's adorable!"

"Anyways…" Elizabeth said. "I have to get going. Will you think about it?"

"I will." Madeline nodded, very flattered.

"The president says he will bend over backward to have you in any capacity you would consider from guest lecturer to professor on the tenure track," Elizabeth said.

"You know I can't til the dragon is dealt with," Madeline said. "And Jane is comfortable being back."

"Yup. I hated adding to your plate, but he wanted me to offer it to you, personally. And I said I would. " Elizabeth said. "Between us, I'm pretty sure the offer will be good for years."

"I want to take it because it's making your boyfriend cringe," Madeline said. Elizabeth laughed. "if I survive the next month, we can talk seriously about it. And I could teach while getting my masters?" Madeline asked.

"Yup," Elizabeth said as they hugged, Steven offered to walk Elizabeth out.

"What was that?" Danny asked after Elizabeth left.

"A job offer." Madeline sighed, "A very tempting job offer."

"What did Leon ?" Madeline asked.

"A job offer." Danny sighed, "A very tempting job offer."

"Should we talk?" Madeline asked.

"Daddy, come to my tea party." Millie pleaded from her playroom.

"And like that, the temptation is gone," Danny said, taking off his apron.

"liar." Madeline accused as he kissed and walked by her.

"Did you tell him?" Mack asked.

"Of course, I told him last night," Madeline said. "After 25 years together, I tell my husband everything."

"You were scared that the twins would rat you out." Steven teased.

"So scared. They are devious little humans..." Madeline smirked. "I'm considering putting some kind of hide when blink spell on myself, but except for when it's beneficial for him, Danny would be so pissed." The guys laughed.

"Frank said I could go to the dragon ceremony too," Mack said.

"Maybe Danny will be less mad if you are there," Madeline said. "He wanted to go, but unless it's a two-person needed spell, I would prefer one of us was with the kids when the other is battling evil. Wow, what a bizarre thing to say…"

"What's the plan?" Mack asked.

"Go to the dragon ceremony," Madeline said. "Find the avatars. I still would prefer to send them to jail, but Danny, Frank, my dad, and Henry have all convinced me that I need to strip them of their powers and fling them back in time."

"Henry?" Mack asked. "When did you talk to Henry?"

"When mama thinks daddy's asleep, mama goes to see grandpa Henry." Peter Henry announced as he climbed on Madeline. "Mama, I don't want you to go fight the avatars by yourself."

"Hey," Madeline whispered. "One, again, eavesdropping. Two. Do you know how hard it is for you to be away from grandad Peter and how you miss him?" Peter Henry nodded. "Sometimes, I need guidance from Henry. And daddy misses him so much that it would make him, well, actually both, so sad if they only had minutes with each other. Do you understand?"

"Yes, I do." Danny crouched down by his son. Peter Henry nodded.

"I'm sorry," Madeline whispered to Danny. "We try to keep on topic. He misses you so much… but as my mentor…"

"He sent you the spell for the dragon…" Danny said. "I'm pretty sure he was the only one in the world who could talk you down from trying to save Jane and… I'm happy you have him." Danny sighed and smiled at his son. "So if grandpa Henry says mom can take care of the avatars, I have no doubt. I just wanted to go with mom because she's kind of amazing to watch, ok?"

"Ok." Peter Henry gave his mom a kiss. "But can I watch you both kill the dragon?"

"No!" Madeline and Danny both shouted. Peter Henry giggled and left the kitchen.

*

"Please, mama?" Millie cried as she sat on Henry's desk with her arms crossed.

"Nope, maybe we can go a few hours tomorrow," Madeline said.

"And we can start building our girl's only treehouse?" Millie asked.

"Do you want a treehouse that daddy could not come into?" Madeline asked; Millie shrugged. "What if Peter Henry and daddy built a treehouse only for boys?"

"That's silly, mama." Millie giggled, pushing Madeline's face away as Madeline gave her big loud kisses.

"I only told you because you asked me to tell you whenever I blinked off the block until you felt safe in your new home," Madeline said. Millie nodded. "I have to go meditate at my spot for three hours. It helps me focus. Like how daddy runs. Then I have an errand with Uncle Mack. Then I'll tuck you in tonight."

"I can meditate with you," Millie explained.

"For three whole hours? In complete silence and stillness? No wiggles?" Madeline asked. "If you can sit here for 20 minutes, quiet and still, I'll take you." Millie sighed, looked at the clock, played with her mama's fingers for a minute, let out a heavy sigh, jumped off the desk, and ran to her playroom. Madeline laughed, wiping away an unexpected tear.

"Hi," Danny whispered, shutting the door behind him.

"I did the paychecks early. All deliveries are set for next week." Madeline said very formally.

"Madds..." Danny sighed.

"'Can we not do this?" Madeline begged. "It was easier to be a badass witch when I didn't promise tomorrows to little kids."

"I know," Danny said.

"I should be able to capture these two avatars in my sleep," Madeline said. "But if there is a freak accident."

"Madds…" Danny whispered.

"Bottom left drawer." Madeline continued without looking at her husband. "Henry and I wrote a backup spell for you and Mack to kill the dragon if that's your last and only option. It's much harder and more complicated, and you'll need to train Mack how to time compress, but if anyone can do it, it's you both. Henry also left a training guide, so you'll know when you both are strong and in sync enough."

"Can we just…" Danny asked.

"That's how we got twins." Madeline teased. "I have to go, my love. I'll be back. I promised Millie I'd tuck her in tonight. I love you so damn much, Boudreaux." Madeline blinked before he could stop her.

*

"Gentlemen," Madeline said, blinking to Frank's unmarked car. Mack and Frank had been outside the hall for an hour, watching the people go into the Dragon service. They counted 57 worshippers, figuring most were curious, a few were searching for salvation. Even fewer true believers, but that was still too many for Madeline's taste. "Protections spells for both of you." Madeline blew golden dust on them. They knew better than to argue.

"What are you thinking?" Frank asked.

"The good news is," Madeline said. "The avatars will be easy to spot. The bad news is the avatars will just as easily recognize me. I will find them, break their links to the dragon, and send them back in time. Please stop looking at me, Mack! If I can't disarm an avatar after 25 years of training, I really suck." Mack and Frank tried to hide their smirks.

They knew the avatars would be on stage. Mack and Frank decided they would go on either sides of the building, and Madeline would enter from the hall's back.

The service was already going when the three entered in through different doors. Tommy Whitman was on the stage. Madeline recognized him from Steven's research. He was in a long hooded red gown dancing around a cauldron of something boiling, spewing something about the seven powers of the dragon.

"Madeline Guidry Boudreaux." Whitman hissed the second Madeline appeared in the back approaching the middle aisle. "The dragon thought his vendetta would end with Daniel Guidry Boudreaux, but now we will have two more little ones to sacrifice. You can watch Mama Madeline."

Until this moment, Madeline worried if she would be able to send a human back in time without their day in court. Whitman made it easy. He said the one thing that made him unredeemable.

Madeline shot Tommy Whitman with a spell that broke his avatar link to the dragon. She blinked at him, took his hand, and blinked a second time. Madeline went back in time as far as she could, left him in an empty field, and returned to the hall in less than a second, feeling a little dizzy. But Madeline knew she had more work and needed to focus.

"Madeline, behind the curtain." A voice she didn't recognize screamed. The curtain fell to the ground, and Hanna Evans appeared, arms out, summoning a glowing fireball. What happened next surprised everyone, especially Madeline.

 While Madeline was still trying to get her bearings, Frida suddenly appeared. The small dragon flew up into Hanna Evans' face, made a squeaky roar, and blew a large grayish ball of hallucinogenic gas in her nose. Suddenly Hanna's whole demeanor changed. She got a funny look on her face, then sat down and began to uncontrollably giggle.

"You're the cutest, funniest dragon ever!" Hanna could not stop laughing. She turned to look at Madeline. "And you... you don't look mean at all for someone who scares the dragon. And by the way, how yummy looking is your husband? Y'all make pretty babies... Ooh, pretty colored walls."

After Madeline realized what was happening, she regained her focus. Madeline quickly severed the avatar's link, then blinked Hanna back in time with Tommy Whitman. By the time she returned again, Frida was gone.

Madeline quickly cast a freeze time spell on everyone in the hall except Mack and Frank. After the two left the building, Madeline made everyone forget the last five minutes. Mack and Frank took care of all the cameras and security videos. After the clean up and a shared sigh of relief, the two men hugged her before the three-parted, Madeline still a little shaken.

"Mama!" Peter Henry and Millie squealed as Madeline blinked to their apartment, the twins were just getting in bed. Frida was on a pillow. The little dragon hissed, then winked at Madeline.

"Shh! Mama's sleeping. She said she wanted to cuddle for a few minutes before she went back to the restaurant but fell asleep. Silly mama." Peter Henry told Danny when he came to check on them a few minutes later. Danny's big grin hid his tears, and he finally could breathe again.

*

"We cannot have this discussion in bed; it's unfair," Danny said as Madeline giggled from their cabin. "Let me get this straight, you want to run the restaurant and gallery while getting your masters and teaching a class while homeschooling the kids and making more babies. And you will not consider hiring an assistant?"

"My reward for killing the dragon..." Madeline grinned, kissing his chest. "You're reward are opening a law office specializing in cases involving magic... and me!"

"I only want the latter," Danny whispered. "If you can tell me you don't have chronic back pain since giving birth, we can have as many kids as you want." He knew that was a safe offer.

"I need to find a better potion for my back. I have not taken the time." Madeline sighed. Danny was in too good a mood to argue how idiotic that statement sounded. "And... You should tell Leon, yes."

"What I should do is give up law and commit to running the restaurant, full time," Danny said. "It's not a bad gig." Madeline was not sure who he was trying harder to convince, her or himself.

"You like being able to see the kids all day," Madeline said. "You have fun with Jane and Mack. But you love the law."

"No. I love you and the kids. I enjoy the law because it's challenging and structured. Truthfully, I do enjoy it more than cooking. And a tiny part of me wants to accept the offer from Leon. I think I can push back starting the groundwork to eight months." Danny said.

"And I have been toying with a schedule that would work for all of us. Maybe I can work from 7 to 5? And unless it's life and death, we both have to commit to spending every evening with the kids. All of this pending on Jane and... We could even have... scheduled lunches." he raised his eyebrows, Madeline laughed.... He moaned when his cell rang.

"This better be good, Malcolm," Danny said. "I am trying to get to second base with the pretty girl. She is sure making me work for it... What? But Madeline put a... is he dead? Stay where you are; we'll grab you and blink home. Yup." Madeline was dressed by the time Danny hung up. He looked perplexed and concerned. "Louis Delcroix was found dead in his cell."

*

"Ok, thing one and thing two," Madeline whispered, feeling bad about waking them up in the middle of the night. Frida sat up at the end of the bed. But Danny needed to talk to Charlie in Henry's office and wanted the kids near them tonight.

"Where were you?" Millie asked. Rubbing her eyes as Frida licked the still sleeping Peter Henry.

"I told you, daddy, and I go for runs at the cabin late at night," Madeline said. Millie looked sleepy and confused.

"What's wrong mama," Peter Henry asked, now awake.

"Your daddy..." Madeline tried to smile. "Has gone crazy and has decided to make Sundaes for everyone! And everyone yelled at daddy, we can't have sundaes without Millie and Peter Henry."

"Yay!" Millie screamed and jumped on Madeline's lap. Peter Henry looked worried as Frida nudge him to sit by his sister. Madeline winked at Frida, she hopped on the back of the wheelchair, and the four blinked to Henry's office.

"Sweets for my sweets," Danny said as the twins appeared.

"Not to criticize, but I think my Sundae needs more cherries," Steven said. "Will you help me, kiddos?"

"Yup." Millie ran to the kitchen.

"No, I wanna stay with mama." Peter Henry pouted, surprising everyone. Peter Henry inherited Danny's sweet tooth and never turned down a dessert in his life. Frida whispered something in his ear. Peter Henry sighed and stomped to the kitchen.

"Am I the only one who didn't know Danny's pet dragon talks and kinda kicks butt?" Madeline asked. Everyone nodded as Madeline pretended to bang her head on the desk.

"Did you get Frank home?" Mack asked.

"Yup," Madeline said, rubbing her face.

"Did he show you the security footage?" Mack asked.

"Yup." Madeline looked frustrated. "He was hit by a fireball that appeared out of nowhere. I was nervous about the spell and potion I used on Louis Delcroix's jail cell, so I made Henry and John Luc double-check my work. Both said it was 99% effective from any evil. If I was wrong about this… what else an I wrong about? I was starting to plan my happily ever after." she covered her face and started bawling. Danny closed the office door.

*

"This is one of the owners and chefs, Daniel Boudreaux," Steven said, walking in the kitchen with a young woman named Christy. Danny said hello. "Christy will be the hostess in training this weekend."

"Thanks for starting immediately," Danny said. "I hope you don't scare easily. Saturday is our busiest day." Christy smiled at Danny.

"And this is our head chef, Jane. Who is supposed to be on leave." Steven said.

"They said I could sit and chop," Jane smiled as Madeline rolled in with Peter Henry on her lap

"And this is Madeline, our business manager." Steven introduced Madeline. She shook Christy's hand.

"Is Millie still sleeping?" Danny asked.

"Yup, but she did say earlier that her tummy was better. I think it's a bug mixed with her late-night Sundae. " Madeline told Danny. "Charlie is going to try to keep her in bed, for today."

"Good luck with that," Danny said.

"Mama says I can be her assistant today, and I get a dollar an hour." Peter Henry said.

"No fair, that's how much I make." Danny teased.

"Come and have coffee with me later," Madeline told Jane. "Nice meeting you, Christy. Let me know if you need anything." Danny made a silly face at Peter Henry as Madeline rolled to Henry's office.

"It's nice that you hire people with disabilities," Christy said, watching Madeline.

"She's actually a partner here. and my best friend…" Steven said. "She is also married to Danny."

"I'm sorry. She's … and he's…" Christy whispered. And was mortified.

"Let's go learn the reservation software," Steven said hurrying her out of the kitchen.

"Shut up." Danny hissed after they left, Jane laughed.

"Yay, that was the first time you hissed at me since I lost my leg. Now, if I can only train Mack." Danny brought her some more onions to dice and kissed her forehead.

"How's your wife?" Jane asked.

"She has been really good for a long time." Danny said.. "But Louis Delcroix's death has made her question everything..." Danny began to chop faster in frustration.

*

"Hi." A man told Christy two hours later, the restaurant was packed.

"it's an hour wait. Can I have a name?" Christy asked, still trying to figure out the seating chart as a line was forming in front of her hostess's podium.

"I'm here to see Madeline; I'm her linen vendor." The stranger said. Christy looked confused. "Madeline Boudreaux, I think she's the business manager... in a wheelchair."

"Oh yes." It finally clicked for Christy. "Through the kitchen to the hallway, I think her office is the first door to the left. Or is that the playroom? I'm sorry, I'm brand new. You'll see it."

"Why thank you." the stranger said. "Thank you very much."

"Daddy." Peter Henry screamed four minutes later. So loud it was heard clearly over the busy kitchen, he was crying. Peter Henry was not a crier. Mack even heard him from the bar, rushed to Danny, who dropped a large bowl of flour then ran towards Henry's office.

Danny was stunned at what he, Mack, and Steven saw when they rushed into the office. In the middle of the room was a frozen fireball. Danny easily made it disappear. Peter Henry was crying, standing behind Madeline's desk, nine feet tall. Danny ran to him, growing in size, so he could hold his son.

"Mama's gone." Peter Henry was hysterical.

"Nope." Madeline blinked back, a little dizzy and in a lot of pain, but she had to show Peter Henry she was ok.

"Let's go sit on the couch," Danny told Peter Henry as they both slowly returned to human size.

"Hey, I'm so sorry I scared you!" Madeline said. "I'm ok," Peter Henry hugged her neck. "I'm a little jealous; I hate how short I am. I think you might be taller than daddy. How cool would that be?" Peter Henry nodded. "Do you want to go watch tv with Millie and Charlie? We will bring you both a late lunch." He nodded again. Then Madeline blinked him to the apartments and was gone 10 minutes.

"Who's cooking?" Madeline asked after she blinked back to her desk. Mack and Danny were waiting for her.

"Jane," Danny hesitated. "She's trying a levitation spell I taught her." Madeline looked worried.

"Don't, Madds, it's the first time she has smiled since the accident." Mack sighed. "Steven is watching her."

"That should end in bloodshed," Madeline smirked.

"What the hell happened, Madds?" Danny asked, shutting the door.

"I don't know." Madeline scratched her forehead. "He walked in, shot a fireball. But for some reason, I could not destroy it. It's the simplest defense spell I know. When that failed I froze the fireball and blinked to the avatar... He resisted my first pull. He went on the second try, but I have never felt like that before. It felt like I was dragging him all the way through. My back physically hurts. My head is killing me. I think he was using some kind of a defensive spell. How did he even have powers in Henry's office?"

"Lay down, wife." Danny pointed, and Madeline floated to the couch.

"Millie wants you to come home to see her," Madeline said, closing her eyes, trying not to moan from the pain.. "And please check on Peter Henry. He is trying so hard not to cry. But he has to be scared and confused. Then go help Jane, or she will work until closing."

"After my head stops pounding, I might try to meditate and see if I can figure out what I did wrong," Madeline said, trying not to but moaning a little. "Can I lay against you for a second? Then you can go... This is the worst headache I ever had." Danny gladly held his wife as he stared at Mack with worry and horrible dread.

Chapter 27

"Mama & daddy are fighting." Peter Henry announced as Mack and Jane came in for breakfast.

"No, we are not." Danny annoyingly sighed.

"I'm going to close last month's books," Madeline said. "Then I'm doing two blinks, then I have to measure the windows of the gallery. Then I'll have lunch with my favorite children". Peter Henry seemed indifferent.

"Can I blink with you, mama?" Millie asked.

"It's not fun blinks," Madeline said. "Why don't you try to convince Uncle Mack and Aunt Janie to come with us to the cabin tomorrow?" Millie agreed. Madeline kissed the twins and rolled to the office, shutting her door.

"See, mama only closes the door when she is mad or when mama and daddy are taking a nap." Peter Henry told his sister; Jane, Charlie, and Mack laughed. Danny remained pensive.

Madeline's first blink was to John Luc's. Although she didn't admit it, and her head felt 75% better, her back was horrible. Not as painful as it was in labor with the twins but pretty darn close. Danny had wanted her to stay in bed that morning, but she blew him off, hence the silent treatment at breakfast.

John Luc didn't like how strong a potion it took for him to see some relief in Madeline's eye and suggested she had physically torn something and the only cure was... Madeline kissed his cheek and blinked away before he finished ordering her on bed rest.

Madeline's second jump was to Henry's. She grinned as he had a glass of port waiting for her. Henry was livid that an avatar was in his office with his grandchild. Although he hid a tiny smile when Madeline told him how much Peter Henry grew. Henry said he would do more research, but it seemed like the worst-case scenario, that the less number of active avatars there were, the stronger they became.

And Madeline may have to consider killing the last one instead of blinking them back in time. Even if the link was severed, Henry could not promise her safety while blinking an avatar that strong. Henry wanted her to promise to tell Danny everything he said. She disappeared before he finished; the last thing Madeline heard was growling.

Madeline smiled when she returned to find her husband waiting for her on the office's sofa; without saying a word, she stretched out, head in his lap. He rubbed her back as she tried not to cry in pain.

"How were your visits?" Danny asked.

"When my three men tell me I should rest a few days, I think maybe I should," Madeline admitted. Danny hid his vindication dance, knowing it could set his wife back from sheer stubbornness. "Hour left with the books, then I'll measure my windows, then I'll take it easy for 48 hours," Madeline pleaded her case.

"That's the best I'm getting, huh?" Danny asked. "I'd be pushing my luck if I offered to do the books and got Steven to measure the windows, huh?" Madeline grinned as they kissed until the twins ran into the office and jumped on the couch.

"Mama, can you let Frida out when you're staring at your windows?" Peter Henry asked about an hour later as Madeline grabbed her measuring tape.

"Yup, and one day you will explain to me why I have to let a magical dragon out," Madeline said; Peter Henry shrugged. Frida hissed, hopping on the back of Madeline's wheelchair.

"Why can't we play outside, Mama?" Millie whined.

"Tomorrow, 48 hours on grandpa Henry's land, my flower child," Madeline said, kissing her daughter's face. Millie grew less mad but never smiled. She truly wanted to be outside all the time with her daddy.

"I see you silently judging me, Frida," Madeline said as she measured the windows. "Why do you never talk to me?"

"Never saw a need." The little pet dragon said.

"How did you learn English?" Madeline asked.

"The kids." Frlda said.

"Why do you pee on my rugs?" Madeline asked.

"Because I can," Frlda said. Madeline cracked up.

"You are really good to the twins. I do thank you, but please stop peeing inside." Madeline begged.

"If you stop taking me on adventures. That time traveling hurts like a..." Frlda said. Madeline laughed. It was a fair statement. "I don't think you should cross the street, Madeline."

"One second, I need to visualized the window's..."

As Madeline's wheels left the protected block, Frida screamed. Madeline turned around. A lady with a gun was inches away from her. She immediately compressed time, but so did the female avatar, which stunned Madeline. Frida flew at the avatar, knocking the gun from her hand. Madeline threw a fireball at her, but the avatar disappeared before the fireball reached its target.

*

"Madds? Why is the door locked?" Danny asked about an hour later after the lunch rush. He, Steven, and Mack were coming into the office to relax for a while.

"I must have accidentally locked it," Madeline said, sounding very odd. "Can you come back in 30 minutes, honey?"

"Is Jane in there?" Mack asked.

"Yup," Jane yelled.

"And Charlie, if anyone cares," Charlie said. Madeline and Jane giggled loudly.

"Come on, open up," Danny said, half kidding, half annoyed. The door opened by itself.

"Are you guys day smoking?" Steven accused.

"And drinking!" Jane said. Mack frowned.

"We have reason to drink and smoke." Jane giggled, slightly tipsy. "I lost a leg. Charlie is sniffing Madeline because Madds smells like John Luc and Madeline..." Madeline threw a pillow at Jane.

"And Madeline, what?" Danny asked.

"I just wanted one hour before my gorgeous husband got that look," Madeline said.

"You mean that look?" Jane pointed.

"You know, I swear he has had that look since he was like three." Charlie laughed.

"Peter Henry has that look; it's very unsettling... he's like an old soul in a boy's body," Madeline smirked.

"Ladies, focus!" Mack said. "Did something happen?"

"Nope." Madeline took a sip of Jane's beer. Danny raised his eyebrows. "I wanted 30 more minutes before we got into a fight."

"You always underestimate me, Madeline," Danny said. "You always think I'm going to fly off the handle."

"So if I told you." Madeline hesitated. "I went outside... without putting on my armor... and rolled off our block for like three seconds; you would not be mad?" Madeline grinned; Danny hung his head and sighed.

"I think you missed the headline," Charlie said.

"Madeline, no more cutesy games," Danny whispered, which was far worse than yelling for him, and Madeline knew it.

"While I was on the street, the last avatar tried to shoot me," Madeline said.

"So... you waited... an hour to tell me? Jesus, Madeline."" Danny said loudly. "Do. Not. Follow. Me. And do not leave this restaurant, or I'm done. I'd rather be divorced than a widow."

"He's just terrified, Madds," Mack said and left the room.

"Two days ago, we were talking about making more babies." Madeline hid her face in her hands, sobbing.

"Hi daddy," Madeline exhaled 10 minutes later and answered her phone, trying to control her voice. "Millie is better. Did she call you? You bought your grandchildren a phone, so that's on you." Madeline laughed but was still crying. "What? No, I have not. I will right now. No, I'm tired. Ok. I love you."

Madeline rolled to her desk and laptop. Her father had sent her an article about the head of the dragon church in France. It talked about the dragon's rebirth this year and featured its human leader with a picture. The article also said their annual convention would be this week in New Orleans.

"Do you think that's her?" Charlie asked.

"It looks like her body," Madeline said. "I only saw her for a millisecond before it turned into the dragon's face. I could probably see it clearer if I go in a meditated state."

"If you can confirm she was the one who attacked you, I can find her," Charlie said.

"No, Charlie," Madeline said.

"I got a kid at stake, too," Charlie whispered. "Her magical energy will be ridiculous. If she's in the Quarter, there will be a spotlight on her. Then you and Danny can take care of the last avatar easily."

"He is coming back, right?" Madeline asked.

"He always does," Charlie whispered. Madeline sniffed.

"Will you wear armor and a protection spell?" Madeline asked.

"Sure, ya little hypocrite." Charlie teased.

*

"Mama, Daddy, made finger sandwiches," Millie screamed with glee as Madeline rolled into the playroom. Danny was sitting at the kid's table with them.

"Yuck, whose fingers are they?" Madeline asked as Millie fed her a bite; Millie giggled. Danny was still stewing. Peter Henry was enjoying lunch too much to speak.

"Hang on." Madeline swallowed to answer her phone. "Hey, Frank... That's bizarre... two minutes? It was the same on our security video, snowy static when I was... Mack just pulled it. It had to be well planned... Yes. Other ways seemed the easiest... Charlie is insisting. Probably tomorrow...Mack will keep you updated. Thanks, Sir.."

"Mama," Millie asked. "What time are we going to the cabin tomorrow?"

"I'm sorry, ladybug, something urgent came up, and I don't think I can go tomorrow," Madeline said. "I have some important stuff to do with Auntie Charlie."

"But you promised we would start my treehouse. I hate you!" Millie unexpectedly screamed and blinked to Danny.

"Hey!" Danny said. "No, mam. Apologize to your mother now." Millie folded her arms, ran to her napping mat, and very dramatically threw herself down... Danny hid a smirk; it was a very storm giant bratty move. Madeline was too upset by the whole day to appreciate the irony.

"I'm going to my potion room," Madeline told her husband, then turned to her daughter. "I hope you feel better, Millie Jane. I'm doing the best that I can. We will hopefully have hundreds of days at the cabin. Tomorrow just might not be one of them." Madeline stared at Danny for a long time then rolled away.

"I'm going too!" Peter Henry said. And ran out of the room.

*

"Please, mama." The little boy begged, bouncing on the counter a few minutes later.

"Please, Madds?" Steven, who had joined them, was now encouraging Peter Henry. "It will make you happy."

"I doubt it," Madeline whispered to Steven. "But for my son and his favorite playmate." Madeline grinned at Peter Henry, grabbed a few things from her alchemy drawers, leaned against the counter where her son was sitting, and let him mixed the concoction.

"Remember, stir 38 times clockwise," Madeline instructed. "Then go sit on the floor. With your eyedropper, place a little of the potion in front of you, and as the bubble floats up, say what you want the bubble to form." Peter Henry smiled and began.

"I'll do a flower for you." Peter Henry said. Madeline smiled as the bubble turned into a rose and slowly floated towards the ceiling before popping. "What do you want, Uncle Steven?"

"How about a kite?" Steven asked and cheered when he did.

"Are you feeling better?" Steven whispered. Peter Henry was now distracted.

"Nope," Madeline said. "Not even a tiny bit, but I have to focus on getting the last avatar. I just... wanted to have lunch with Charlie and Jane because I knew once Danny realized about the last one, it would consume us 24/7 until it was finished. One way or another."

"And my back hurts so much. I'm worried it will distract me when I'm time compressing. Even a millisecond would make a difference. And my husband and daughter aren't talking to me. What if I get killed right now? An avatar could shoot me with a fireball this very second. Would I be ok with Danny never having sex again out of guilt for being an ass the last time he talked to me? Sure. But Millie. She remembers everything..."

"Wow... How much did you drink? Major spiraling..." Steven smirked.

"Hi, daddy." Peter Henry shouted as Danny came into the gallery holding Millie in his arms. "What do you want me to conjure?"

"A big bubble." Danny teased, Peter Henry rolled his eyes.

"Mama?" Millie whispered as Danny sat her in front of Madeline on the counter. "I'm sorry. I just really wanted to start on our treehouse tomorrow."

"I know," Madeline said. "And I'm sorry I broke a promise, but it's really important, ok? But the next time you yell at me, you are going to be grounded." Millie nodded, kissed her mother's nose, and ran to play with Peter Henry.

"That Millie girl sure has a bad temper; I wonder where she gets it from?" Danny grinned bashfully. Madeline was not ready to flirt. "Mack updated me on everything. Charlie wants to locate the avatar?"

"Yup," Madeline said. Not looking at Danny, knowing she would either yell at him or melt in his arms. She had time for neither. "I was going to unpack the armor and put an extra protection spell on all of them."

"Tomorrow Charlie is hoping to locate the avatar, then we can decide what to do. or you can decide and text me." Madeline didn't mean to sound that snarky, but she had reached her emotional and pain threshold for the day.

"I am going to blink the trunk back to my office, ice my back, then start protection spells," Madeline said. "Peter Henry, please rinse out the beaker when you're done." Madeline blinked before Danny or Steven could say anything.

"She's really pissed." Danny sighed.

"She's..." Steven said, trying to look for a better description but pissed seemed the most accurate. "So pissed. But you know she just wanted to feel normal for an hour more with Jane before the shit hit the fan."

"I know," Danny said. "It scares me to death that one of the most powerful and well-studied witches in the world almost got shot two feet from the curb. We practiced a hundred scenarios, and that was so unexpected."

*

"This is kind of sexy," Charlie said, flying around Henry's office the next day. "It really is incredible. As a woman who once wore French King's Armor. The mobility is amazing, and it's so light."

"All of it cost more than a house; Henry designed it, Danny found the material and had them made," Madeline said, laying flat on her couch. "Enough of this crap; laying down makes it hurt more when I get up." Madeline groaned as she sat back up and floated to her wheelchair.

"You're supposed to lay still for an hour. That was like three minutes." Charlie said.

"Save the world, my marriage, my relationship with my daughter, then I'll save my back," Madeline said.

"Have you tried your armor on?" Charlie asked.

"No," Madeline said, covering her face. "I think that would make it too real... I never was hoping to die but before we had kids saving the world with Danny seemed like an adventure. And if I died, there was a tragic romantic sad righteous ending. I had a great love I never imagined I would ... Jane had Mack. My folks would survive."

"But it feels different going into battle with kids, knowing they wouldn't care about the sacrifice; they would just be sad that I am not here to tuck them in. damnit, Charlie, what have I done?" Madeline banged on her desk as Danny, Steven and Mack came in. Jane was at rehab.

"All the more reason to put it on, Danny might be into leather. Boom marriage fixed, nine months later Millie gets her little sister she asks for, daughter problem fixed. And you might not get killed if that avatar is cocky enough to try to shoot you again. Win-Win," Charlie said, everyone laughed.

"I do think Millie just really really wants someone to boss around. But it would crush her not being daddy's little girl." Madeline said. "Ok, so. You really want to do this, Charlie?"

"We think the last avatar is from France and their convention is this week.; we can call a few hotels. Offer dinners for leads." Mack said.

"That would take too long; the avatar probably knows Madeline isn't at full strength. We need to attack first and without mercy. If the avatar was in the middle of the street with a gun, she has lost any redemption." Danny said. Leaning against Henry's desk. Everyone agreed, even Madeline.

"So, you are going to fly around the quarter looking for an avatar?" Madeline asked, not completely sold on this plan.

"The avatar will give off a magical energy that I can sense. It will be much more glaring now because of her strength." Charlie said. "If we find out where they are staying, and exactly how many members are there. Danny and your dad can plan the safest, most efficient attack. Steven put a webcam on me."

"I'm sorry this is hard on you, Madds, but it's almost liberating for me," Charlie said. "I haven't flown around the city in a year. It will be like breathing again. Steven will watch my every move, and if I need help, you'll blink.."

"You bet!" Madeline said because that's what Charlie needed her to say. Charlie kissed everyone on their cheeks and flew away without another word.

"So, we sit here and wait?" Madeline asked. Mack and Steven were watching Charlie on the notebook on the round table beside Henry's desk. Danny was pretending to look for a book on the shelf. "Y'all want drinks? I'm going to check on the kids too."

"Coffee, please," Steven said.

"Me too," Mack said.

"Coffee, love?" Madeline asked. Danny nodded and winked. They hadn't really made up but agreed to a truce. Both feeling justified for their anger, but sorry for their overreactions.

"How's it going in here, kiddos?" Madeline peaked into the playroom. Peter Henry was reading; Millie was painting Frida's toenails.

"I'm finished with my homework, Mama," Peter Henry said.

"I'm about to start mine," Millie said. Madeline smirked.

"Do you two want a glass of milk?" Madeline asked. They both nodded.

"Mama," Peter Henry showed up in the kitchen while Madeline was pouring drinks. "Where's Auntie Charlie? Is she looking for the last avatar? Is that why she was crying when she said she was going on an errand? Don't worry, Millie didn't notice."

"Oh, Peter Henry, you're too smart for your own good," Madeline said, hugging him. "She promised me she would be back. And I have known her for centuries and don't tell her, but she is almost always right. she said daddy would be the love of my life. And we would have brilliant children... So she'll be back."

"Madds! Come here, Please." Danny yelled. Madeline handed Peter Henry two glasses of milk and playfully swatted him on the behind. Then grab the tray of coffee, floating them into the office in front of her.

"She flew around the quarter three times and landed at the hotel two blocks from here," Mack said as Madeline rushed in; she rolled by Steven at the table. Danny stood behind her, hands on her shoulder. "They aren't hiding; there was a 'Welcome Church of the Dragon' in the lobby, opening services, midnight' sign."

"Isn't Olivia the manager there?" Danny asked.

"Franklin can call and ask for a guest list; I'll text him," Mack said. Danny smirked.

"Weird vibe that I must know at a later date. Who's Olivia? Oh... was that Macky's first..." Madeline teased Mack. "Wait, why is Charlie hanging out? She found the hotel."

"Nice job, Charlie," Danny said on the two-way mic. "Now come home, please. That was the deal."

"Let me find the avatar's room," Charlie whispered. "Then I'm home.... I heard the church rented the entire 4th floor. I'll just sneak up." Mack and Steven began to give each other dirty looks. Madeline concentrated on

Charlie as if trying to will her to come home. Danny's fist pounded the table in anger.

"Room 405," Charlie whispered. "I have never felt such strong magical energy except from Danny and Madeline."

"Please come home, Charlie." Danny sounded like a scared little boy. "Charlie. Don't."

"Charlie, stop screwing around," Madeline whispered. Almost overcome with a horrible feeling.

"I…" Charlie was about to say something when the door to room 405 violently opened. "Oh, crap…"

"Why, hello, you little bitch, I've been waiting to send you straight to hell so you'd be reunited with your precious Kisseis." And a loud, fiery boom was the last thing they heard before the webcam went dead.

Mack covered his face. Steven slammed the laptop closed and cursed. Madeline stared at her husband for what felt like seconds waiting for his blessing; tears ran down his face then he nodded…

Madeline blinked to Charlie. The first thing she did was freeze time; Charlie was unconscious, wings completely burnt off. 2nd and 3rd degree burns on every inch of her body that was not protected by armor. Madeline wanted to hunt down and kill the avatar right then, but she knew Charlie had minutes if that long. She gently put Charlie in her lap. Charlie woke long enough to scream and passed out again.

"Ok, I'm going to put you in a magical coma for a while," Madeline said, knowing Charlie would not survive the blink otherwise.

"Clara?" Danny answered his phone 40 minutes later. He had been pacing since Madeline had left, feeling very anxious but sensed his wife was ok. He just wished he had confirmation. "Yes… yes… ok. Is she going to survive?" Danny exhaled loudly. "And Madeline?" Danny pinched the bridge of his nose. "No, Thank you, Clara. After she is released, we definitely will. Do you know how long the surgery will be… Ok."

"Charlie is in surgery," Danny said. "Madeline had to go in with her because she somehow kept Charlie alive with a spell for 30 minutes. And the doctors want to make sure Charlie can breathe on her own for an hour before Madeline leaves her side."

"I'll head that way," Steven said. "And I'll make your wife blink back after she recuperates."

"Thanks!" Danny said. "Tell her... Tell them both that I. "

"They know," Steven said. And left.

*

"Hey, Miss Pouty Face," Danny said about an hour later as Millie climbed on him.

"Where's mama?" Millie asked. "She has been gone a really long time."

"Go get Peter Henry," Danny said. "I want to talk to both of you,"

"Peter Henry!" Millie screamed from Danny's lap. Danny frowned at Millie; she smiled, knowing she was clever. Peter Henry ran in, jumping to sit by his sister.

"Look, two little monkeys jumping on my sofa," Madeline said, rolling into the office. Danny stared at her in amazement and relief.

"Daddy, why are you crying?" Millie asked.

"Because your mama is so gosh darn beautiful that sometimes it makes me cry when I don't tell her how much I love, appreciate, and trust her."

"Yuck! But ok." Peter Henry said. Millie giggled.

"I think," Madeline said, floating to the sofa to hug the twins and kiss Danny. "We should be really bad tonight and order pizza! I do believe I hear Auntie Jane and Uncle Mack in the kitchen. Take everyone's order, then dad will call it in."

"Hi," Danny whispered. Pulling Madeline closer as the twins ran to the kitchen.

"Hi," Madeline said. "Very nice apology, counselor."

"Maybe, new rule, never go to bed angry?" Danny said.

"Then we would be up for days at a time," Madeline said.

"This is true," Danny admitted. "I heard you did really good today."

"Charlie will be in an induced coma for at least a day, in a magic capsule as they call it. In the new wing of the hospital, so her burns can heal. That doesn't feel like a win. Clara is one of the department heads." Madeline blinked away tears. Danny held her tight.

"Clara said you saved her life," Danny said.

"I hope it's a life she wants," Madeline said. "For a while, Charlie was in and out of consciousness. She said the avatar implied Kisseis was dead. After surgery, she whispered she didn't know if she wanted to live without Kisseis. I should have gone with her to the hotel... Even Peter Henry sensed she was saying goodbye. Oh, honey, What are we going to tell the kids?"

"That Charlie had a family emergency and will be back in a few days," Danny said.

"The problem with having magical geniuses is that they will figure it out," Madeline said. "I think we should say she had an accident."

"Ok," Danny said. "We'll tell them at dinner. How are you, really?"

"I am frustrated," Madeline said. "And I am angry. We've trained for over 20 years for this. I want this chapter in our lives to be finished. Right now, I need to go meditate a bit, or I'll come unglued, and I don't know if I'll recover. On the bright side, I think I twisted my back the other way, so it's better. I'm going to hide in the gallery for a while... Call me when the pizza is here?"

"Yes, my love," Danny said, sighing as Madeline kissed him long and tenderly.

*

"Best day ever!" Millie screamed as the four blinked from the cabin back to the restaurant.

"Y'all want a snack?" Danny asked. Millie shook her head, Peter Henry nodded.

"Why are you studying in the kitchen?" Madeline asked Steven, who usually worked in Henry's office.

"You'll see," Steven said.

"Should I be scared?" Madeline asked.

"Nope. But I told her she should." Steven smirked.

"Oh crap, you're kidding?" Madeline groaned, half angry, half delighted.

"Yay, Auntie Charlie is home!" Millie screamed and started running. Madeline stopped her.

"How did she know?" Steven asked.

"I told you. my seven-year-old is running this asylum." Madeline said. Steven and Danny laughed. Millie smiled proudly, although not completely sure why. "Stop, Millie Jane! Remember we told you Auntie Charlie was in an accident? And she might look like a mummy with all her bandages? Let me go check on her, then you guys can come in." Millie pouted but nodded.

Madeline had mixed emotions finding Charlie on a pillow on the sofa. Frida laying at her feet. Madeline noticed Charlie was trying really hard to keep her eyes closed. Madeline would probably not yell at her if she thought Charlie was asleep.

"You have got to be kidding me." Madeline hissed, "It hasn't been 24 hours,"

"Technically, it's been 27," Charlie argued. "I feel good."

"You're probably higher than a kite," Madeline said.

"Hence, I feel mighty good," Charlie laughed, then groaned. "I missed the kids... I wanted to see Daniel... I wanted to check on you. Besides, you can whip me up some better drugs than any hospital."

"I did learn from the best!" Madeline said.

"He'd be so pleased to know Danny's armor saved my breasts and my..." Charlie giggled. "Damn, I am high."

"The kids and hubby want to see you," Madeline said. "I'll go make some potion. Selfishly I'm glad you're home. But I ain't dealing with Clara."

"That's fair," Charlie said. Then got quiet. "Madds, you know time is not on our side."

"I know," Madeline whispered. "I went on a mini-date with my husband this morning. I gave the kids a great day at the cabin. I'll decide tonight."

"Let me talk you through it," Charlie said. "Does Danny know?"

"Nope. I'm sure he suspects..." Madeline said. "I can't bring myself to think about it, much less talk... This will change me fundamentally. What if I don't like me... what if he can't get past it?"

"Would you still love him if he did anything to save the kids?" Charlie asked.

"Yup, of course," Madeline said.

"Mama, I wanna see Auntie Charlie," Millie demanded from the door. Charlie giggled as much as Millie did.

"Gentle!" Madeline said. "I'm going to make a potion, Millie will you read a story to our patient?" Millie grinned and ran to get a book.

"Madds," Charlie said. "This will be one of the worse things you will ever do, but somehow it will make you even stronger, even more empathetic, even more beloved. Danny will question a million things, but never this one. and if it weighs in, I know, for a fact, the last avatar killed Henry, and without Danny's armor, I'd be dead."

"I'll go get the potion..." Madeline sniffed, and Charlie began to pray.

*

"Please, open the door, my love." Danny cried. Now sitting by the sealed office door. "You're really scaring me. Madeline! Madeline! Are you there?" he knew she was. She had been crying for hours, only stopping to throw up.

"Wow, you look like crap," Mack said. staring at Danny from the kitchen. "Are you guys fighting?"

"No," Danny said. "I don't think so. We put the kids to bed, Charlie between them. Everyone seemed happy. I still felt bad about our fight, so we indulged ourselves with a bottle of wine in the courtyard. Then she wanted 30 minutes of reading in the office, so I decided to snuggle with the kids until she came home. guess I fell asleep."

"I got up about 4..." Danny said. "And came over. Henry's office door was locked. More than the little lock, we figured out how to pick when we were 12. It's like she placed a spell on it. And hasn't said two words. She has thrown up nine times."

"Do you think the avatar is holding her hostage?" Mack asked.

"No. I'd sense her energy," Danny said.

"Do you think she's... If she's throwing up..." Mack asked. "You did say you didn't want any more kids."

"No." Danny said. "I said I was scared of her being pregnant again. If I thought her back could take it, I'd have 10 more kids with her., She had a really rough pregnancy with the twins, and honestly, it was the scariest thing I've been through. But she knows if she was, I'd melt. I'd want to be mad and worried and upset, but I'd melt. That's not it."

"Hang on," Mack said, answering his phone. "Franklin. Not yet. I was getting going... What... When... Do you need help? I already dropped Jane off at rehab. I'm headed your way. Yup. He's right here; I'll be damned. five minutes."

"The avatar/head of dragon church dropped dead at midnight service, looks like a heart attack." Mack said. "It's pretty cut and dry. There will be an autopsy. Frank's going to do interviews. I'm headed that way. This is good news, huh? Daniel?"

"Yup..." Danny hesitated. "Keep me in the loop." Mack nodded and left.

"Madds... Please open this door." Danny whispered, feeling her leaning against the other side. "Even after 24 years, every time I see you, my heart skips a beat. I don't ever see that changing... I need to see you. Please let me..." The door opened. Madeline had floated to the sofa, curled up in a ball, still crying.

"I remembered a spell." Madeline began. "A spell so hideous that I had tried to forget... Last night I was watching the church of the dragon's midnight services. Did you know they were aired?"

"No..." Danny whispered, touching her legs.

"She was boasting what she had done for the dragon." Madeline began crying again. Danny let her, wanting so bad to take her in his arms and rock her, but he knew that was not what Madeline needed. "She boasted about killing Henry Guidry. But I was still calm."

"Then..." Madeline said loudly. "She said the dragon wanted more Guidry blood. And it would happen tomorrow. That she would make Daniel Guidry, the last adult storm giant male, watch his children, bookworm Peter Henry, and the spirited Millie, die. She described and spoke the names of our children." Madeline began to shake...

"And then, the avatar continued that his witchy wife, Madeline Guidry Boudreaux, would be raped by many followers and be brought to the dragon herself. Leaving you alone, sterile, and within an inch of death. I kept hearing her voice.... Saying their names. As if she knew our children."

"Madeline," Danny whispered.

"I thought the spell would be harder," Madeline said. "Or I'd stumble on the words, or I'd stop in the middle. But I said every god damn word without hesitation. It was a long spell I only glanced at once. But it flowed out of my mouth, I touched her face on the tv screen, and she just dropped dead. What kind of monster can do that?" Madeline threw up on Danny. He didn't care.

"After I stop throwing up," Madeline said. "I'm going to kiss the kids goodbye and turn myself in..."

Danny scratched his head. He knew exactly what he wanted to say. But that would push her right over the edge, so what he said was, "Let's go clean you up; you can take a nap. Then Franklin can take you in." Madeline nodded, too broken to notice the patronizing tone in his voice.

"Ok, I'm going to give you a little sleeping potion," Danny said. After giving her a shower in the half bath in Henry's office. She nodded and laid on the couch, back towards him. It broke his heart that she hadn't spoken since her confession. And this was going against every fiber in him, not shaking her, not throwing her a freaking parade. "I'll be in the kitchen Madeline, I love you."

"Mack, plan B," Danny said on his call. "No, I haven't.. wow, my wife actually made the sermon less horrific than it was? geez…. Ok… I'm leaving the employees' checks for a month. I want to leave tonight. Tell Steven he and Elizabeth are welcome but it's not mandatory. Six. Madeline ought to be ready to blink by then. She's emotional and not thinking. Macky, it's almost over." Danny broke down and openly wept.

*

"Millie Jane, why are you sucking your fingers, my beautiful girl? It took you two years to stop, love?" Madeline asked; waking two hours later with her daughter lying on her, she silently shrugged. Peter Henry was sitting at the other end on the couch, his feet pressing against hers, reading a book.

"She thinks you were lost last night and that you didn't want to come home to us," Peter Henry whispered, staring at Madeline. "We'll stop arguing so much, mama." Millie nodded too.

"I…" Madeline was at a loss for words. "I had a really bad tummy ache last night and fell asleep on my couch. I'm sorry. I'll try not to do that again."

"Do you feel better now?" Peter Henry asked.

"Truthfully, not yet, it was a really bad tummy ache…"

"I won't leave your side until you feel better," Millie whispered, then immediately stuck her fingers in her mouth again.

"Where's Daddy?" Madeline asked.

"He's closing the restaurant." Peter Henry said. "He said we are blowing this pop stand because you and Jane and Charlie need fresh mountain air, and he and Mack need to blow stuff up."

"And we need to make you feel better so you would go with us willingly." Millie declared.

"You weren't supposed to say that!" Peter Henry said.

"Daddy told me to be cute; ever wonder why he never tells you to be cute?" Millie asked. Madeline hid her face, half still hurting, half laughing.

"Of course I'll go," Madeline said, trying to hide her pain. Madeline was now thinking with a clearer head. She could not turn herself in until she killed the dragon because her babies were still in danger.

Chapter 28

"Thank you for traveling Madeline's Air," she said, finishing her last blink. It took four trips; Danny, Frida and the kids, Jane and Mack, Charlie, Ida and her nurse Amy, and Steven and Elizabeth. Because there was no time travel, it was an easy trip for everyone, even Frida.

"Mama, look at how much the house has grown!" Millie said. To her, the family was there a week ago. In reality, the house was 200 years old. "Can I..."

"Same rules, kiddo," Danny said. "If we cannot see you from the deck, you have gone too far."

"Can Grandma Ida come with me? I want to introduce her to the trees." Millie asked.

"I'd love to go too," Amy said. Danny mouthed thank you, kissing Millie on her head.

"Come on, Peter Henry," Millie whined.

"I wanna hang out with mama." Peter Henry said.

"I have to open the house up. Boring stuff." Madeline said. "Go play with your sister. I feel better." He didn't believe his mom, but Danny encouraged him to go. Madeline's heart felt a little joy as she heard the twins laughing.

"My word, this is gorgeous," Elizabeth said as the rest of the group entered the house. The first floor was a chef's kitchen opened to the great room. The master's and the kid's rooms were on the other side of the huge fireplace. There was now a second story with four other bedrooms.

"Hello, Master Danny; we are so excited to have you all home." A fairy dragon greeted them in the great room. Two other dragons followed, taking everyone's luggage.

"A colony of fairy dragons lives here?" Danny asked, very shocked.

"Yes, sir," the dragon said. "The trees said you wouldn't mind. We have earned our keep, and we, of course, are clean and housebroken. There are five of us."

"No, No. I think it's wonderful!" Danny said.

"I'm afraid the chipmunks have moved into Miss Millie's room. Shall I relocate them?"

"My daughter's heart would break if you did." Danny smiled. "Have the groceries come?" The small dragon nodded, pointing to the full pantry.

"I'm going to make sure everyone has fresh towels," Madeline said.

"Madds," Steven said. "Come have a drink with us while we watch Danny and Jane cook dinner."

"Naw, I'm going to check on the rooms, then lay down for a bit. But the sunset is spectacular from the deck." Madeline said and floated up the stairs.

"Bump in the road," Charlie whispered in Danny's ear as he sat her on a pillow on the kitchen's bar. Danny exhaled slowly...

*

The whole house woke to Madeline screaming at 3 am.

"She's not here. She's not in her bedroom. Where is my daughter?" Madeline rolled frantically through the house, Danny was sleeping in a recliner. He had tried to go into their bedroom earlier, but Madeline had locked herself away in their suite since before dinner. "They took Millie because I killed the last avatar." Danny had never seen her so unhinged.

"Madds, calm down," Danny said.

"I. killed. Your. Daughter. Don't you see? By killing the avatars." Madeline screamed, now waking everyone. "Please kill me. If you sacrifice me, the dragon might be satisfied. End this before they get Peter Henry too." She kept babbling, now inconsolable.

"Madds. Stop." Danny held her until she stopped shaking. "Can you sense Millie? Close your eyes and find her." Madeline nodded. "Can you take my hand and blink to her?" it took Madeline a few minutes to understand what Danny was saying, to stop her heart from beating out of her chest. But Danny held her until she did.

"Mama, daddy... You found me." Millie cheered and giggled, after her parents blinked to her. "Technically, I'm touching the house, and you can see me from the deck if you look up..." Madeline cried and laughed, still feeling out of sorts. Danny hung his head in defeat, knowing his daughter would be the death of him. And it had nothing to do with magic.

"The trees made me a bed on the roof, isn't it lovely? Come sleep with me, pleasssssssseeeeeeeeeeeee." The couple climbed into her bed without saying a word. The chipmunks lying by the young girl's head scattered. Millie fell asleep smiling.

*

"Good morning," Ida said as Madeline rolled onto the deck, very surprised to find her mother-in-law wrapped in a blanket sipping tea.

"Good morning, mom, you look..." Madeline stumbled on her words.

"Sane? Present?" Ida smirked.

"Let me go get Daniel," Madeline said.

"No, please don't," Ida whispered. Madeline stopped rolling. "It will give him hope... It's so beautiful out here, so quiet that I can almost hear my voice over Abigail and Henry's screams in my head."

"We could live here," Madeline said.

"Your lives are back in New Orleans." Ida said. "May I ask you something bizarre?"

"Yes," Madeline said.

"Frida... is real, right?" Ida said.

"Yes." Madeline couldn't help but laugh loudly. "And apparently, she has been talking to the children all their lives and is sorta a badass. How did I miss that?"

"Saving the world, raising the twins, dealing with my perfect although maybe slightly stubborn son, it happens," Ida said. "And, from what I'd heard. The dragon who greeted us is Frida's mate. And Frida is now a granny which does not delight her."

"I cannot tease her, can I?" Madeline asked.

"She would pee on every inch of your carpet," Ida laughed. Madeline hid a tear. Danny had always told her that his mother had a great laugh; she had never heard it before. "I think the magic and the dragons on this land dilute the fog in my head, but it feels thicker as the day goes on."

"Let me say this while I can..." Ida laughed to herself then sniffed away a tear. "It's not fair to ask, but be stronger than me, Madeline. Even if you kill the dragon, if you lose your heart in the process, my son loses the one thing that saved him. Please stay strong. We all love you so much." Ida made Madeline looked directly at her, softly kissing her daughter-in-law's forehead. They stayed locked in an embrace for a long time.

"Anyways..." Ida sighed. "Can I wake up the kids and enjoy them. Just for a little while?" Madeline nodded, too broken to speak as Ida disappeared into the house. Then, Madeline spotted Danny running towards her, coming around the lake, Peter Henry by his side.

"We have another runner in our midst," Danny said as he and his son stepped onto the deck.

"Daddy said you had a nightmare last night." Peter Henry said, hopping into Madeline's lap. "Tonight, I'll read a story to you so you can fall asleep happy." Peter Henry said. "Now I'm going to get a bowl of ice cream; daddy said if I ran two miles, I could have one." Madeline gave them dirty looks, both shrugged; Peter Henry ran inside before Madeline could overrule Danny's decision.

"Ice cream for breakfast?" Madeline sighed. Danny sat in the lounger and made his wife come to him, wrapping his arms around her.

"He was upset, Madds," Danny whispered. "I wanted to wait a few days to let you sort it out, but you are freaking out your unfreakable best friends, and you're scaring our kids."

"I know," Madeline said.

"I have to say my peace," Danny said. Madeline tried to float back to her wheelchair, but he continued to hold her. "What do you think would have happened yesterday when I found out what the avatar said? I already got 25 emails and text references to it, so don't even ask how I'd find out."

"I dunno," Madeline whispered.

"After 25 years, you don't know?" Danny asked.

"You and Mack would have flown off the handle," Madeline said. "Probably getting both of you killed. Logically I understand what I did; it might have even been the only way…. But I took a life. It was so damn easy."

"Looking at you right now, I see it was the hardest, most painful thing you've ever done. I see it in your eyes.." Danny said. "Do you regret what happened in Japan?"

"Yes," Madeline said. "But I have no doubt that after they raped me, they would have killed you and Kushemi."

"I don't see the difference," Danny said.

"I should have done it another way, made her look into my eyes, so I'd know…" Madeline sobbed.

"I'm really trying to be empathetic, Madds, I am." Danny sighed. "But to me, this was the best possible outcome; I think the city of New Orleans should throw you a parade. You may mourn; I will hold you through every nightmare."

"But you aren't going to jail for trying to save the world," Danny said. "And because I know you need an unbiased person to tell you… Geneva reviewed the sermon. She's 1000% sure the avatar would have come for our kids. They would not have been able to defend themselves, Madeline; think about that. And if you still need redemption, the council of witches will absolve you on the record."

"I've decided you are right…" Madeline said. "I need to be here for my kids… We are going to kill the dragon… then I'm going to tie my powers." Madeline floated back to her wheelchair. "I've gotta check on Ida."

*

"Happy birthday mom," Danny barely got the words out a couple of days later.

"Your birthday should be every day, Ida; Danny never cooks me a breakfast buffet." Mack accused as everyone got plates and enjoyed an early meal on the deck. Millie was climbing a tree. Peter Henry was playing chess with a dragon.

Geneva, who Madeline picked up earlier that morning, was talking to Ida and Charlie sitting around the fire pit. All three were laughing. Ida was still a little lost, but this was the most interactive Ida has been, probably since Abigail died, which was very emotional for Danny and Mack.

"We could have a double wedding," Jane said. Jane, Steven, and Madeline were crowded around the bacon tray.

"Told you, he's freaking out. The eight-month itch." Madeline told Jane. "If anything, he's predictable."

"Hey! Sometimes being your persons sucks." Steven said. "I'm not freaking out, she had to get back to teach Monday, and I can finish my thesis outline here."

"If you break up with her, you're out; she's in." Jane shrugged.

"We can always find men to worship us," Madeline said. "Good, brilliant, gorgeous girlfriends are harder to find; I stand by Jane's statement."

"Speaking of freaking out…" Steven said as he and Jane turned to Madeline.

"I thought we were judging Jane next; I have officially lost interest in this conversation," Madeline smirked.

"You can't really give up your powers…" Steven said.

"I can," Madeline whispered. "Danny never wanted our lives to revolve around magic when we got together. I'll still be a damn good alchemist. He doesn't love to show off, but Danny is probably a higher wizard than me, minus the time lock thing."

"What about your kids?" Jane asked.

"They aren't that magical," Madeline said, as Millie was now dancing with a dragon on the roof and Peter Henry was swimming happily in the icy lake…

"I hate to bother you, Madeline," Geneva said. "But my back hurts like hell today."

"Let's blink to my bedroom, Aunt Geneva." Madeline took her arm.

"Should we tell her?" Steven smirked.

"No," Jane said. "She's trying, but she's still holding on by a thread. It will click."

"I hope so; I really do like my fresh bagels from New York Tuesday mornings," Steven said.

"Hey," Danny came over. "Can I see you in the office?" Steven nodded. Mack followed them.

"Break up with Elizabeth, no more fresh bagels for you!" Jane yelled at Steven.

"Do you need to talk?" Danny teased as Mack closed the door behind them.

"Nope. Your women are quite enough." Steven said.

"Dad sent the names of three guides in Mexico he thinks can be helpful. Can you check them out?" Danny asked. "I was going to let Charlie help, but…"

"I'm on it…" Steven said. Sitting down at the desk, staring at the maps on the wall.

"Did you tell her your plan?" Mack asked.

"No," Danny said. "I don't know what I'm scared of more, a huge fight or a shrugged."

"What's the tentative plan?" Steven asked.

"She blinks me to Mexico…" Danny said. "After I find the dragon. She blinks back… We always said when the time came, we would both go with Charlie. Charlie might have been able to sense Kisseis. But now everything has changed. Charlie is recovering. Madeline can't be away from the kids for a week or longer; we can't search in any other time frame in case the dragon is moving."

"I'll go with you," Mack said.

"No, Jane needs you here," Danny said.

"I'll go," Steven said. "I've studied all the maps. I speak Spanish. This could be my Indiana Jones moment."

"Day after tomorrow?" Danny said. "I want a day with my wife and kids."

*

"Stop licking me, Frida!" Danny screamed the next day as the twins giggled in delight. Danny was lying in the grass in front of the deck. Near the fountain that they had never finished running the water lines to. The kids were chasing each other around their father.

Danny kept looking at his wife, who would not look back. Madeline was still angry, sad, and frustrated, but she knew she had to pull herself together knowing she only had a few days to get everyone to safety before meeting Kisseis.

"Mama Madeline, mama Madeline" suddenly, the little dragons came running from all directions of the woods, racing towards her. All screaming at the same time in high pitch broken English that Madeline could not understand.

"Danny, take the kids in the house, now. Now damnit." Madeline felt something coming. Danny did not question her. He grew into a storm giant immediately, scooping them up. Millie screamed, and Peter Henry kicked. They wanted Madeline. They did not understand why Danny would leave her. The small dragons now flew into the house, following the kids.

"Madeline, I tried to follow our plan but the dragon escaped before I could tell mom. I thought I would have more time to warn you…" suddenly the dry fountain came to life. It was Kisseis.

"Go into the house, Kisseis. Your mother is waiting for you." She screamed as the bright sun faded behind a large shadow of the dragon. Madeline wished she had meditated this morning. She had so many jumbled thoughts in her head, but she knew she had to focus on the dragon. Madeline floated upwards, quickly and as far away from the house as she could.

"Don't worry, your mate and children will see you in hell very soon." The dragon roared; breathing a fireball so huge that Madeline's clothes were melting before the ball was fully formed.

Madeline stopped time just as her wheelchair's tires melted. Closing her eyes, she slowed her heart rate, compressing time as she was taught, clearing her mind from all distractions, whispering her husband's name, in case it was the last time.

And with her last conscious breath, she spoke the deadly spell and closed her eyes. Waiting to die, knowing the kids were in the house, knowing the death of the dragon freed Danny. The dragon plummeted into the empty field nearby, as Madeline fell to the ground too. Danny caught her and soaked her burning body in the lake.

*

"Wow, you're huge," Danny said, coming into the kitchen finding Jane eating breakfast and looking at resumes. "When your belly prevents you from reaching the stove, you might wanna consider maternity leave.

"Ha. Ha. Can you do interviews at three?" Jane asked.

"Nope. But I trust you." Danny said. "Mack wants to make you an honest woman before…"

"Steven is still in Europe," Jane said. "And… it's not a good time. I told him I'd go down to the courthouse if it means that much to him."

"Scream if you need help," Danny said. "I'll be in the office."

"Hello, Leon," Danny said from Henry's desk as Leon came in a few minutes later.

"Why didn't you hire Melody. She was devastated."

"Because she wasn't wearing panties and made that very clear," Danny sighed. "You said I could do all the hiring."

"I just thought… you'd appreciate a distraction." Leon smiled.

"The lawyers are moving in a week from Thursday. I'm a month earlier than I promised. You should be thrilled." Danny said.

"I am," Leon said. "Will you look at this case? It might be the right fit for your office's coming out." Leon smiled, handed Danny a stack of files, and left. Danny got up, poured himself a whisky, smelled it, and put it down as he heard the twins coming.

"Hello, Thing 1 and Thing 2," Danny smiled.

"They wanted to tell you hi before our morning assignments," Their new tutor said.

"Good morning Millie Jane and Peter Henry, loves of my life," Danny said. "I sure miss hearing your voices." Danny sniffed. Millie had stopped talking completely after the dragon attack; Peter Henry spoke only when necessary or for his sister. "Your mama would want you to giggle and laugh and sing…"

"Then she should tell us." Peter Henry said and ran to their room. Millie put her fingers in her mouth then followed.

"I agree," Danny whispered after Peter Henry was out of earshot. Danny took one sip of the whisky, poured the rest back into the decanter, and began looking at the files Leon had left. It was easier than missing his wife.

"Hello, Daniel." Charlie appeared two hours later as Danny was doing research for Leon.

"I asked you not to set foot on my property; please get the hell out," Danny screamed as loud as he could without letting the kids hear him.

"Can I see the twins, Daniel? I miss them." Charlie said.

"And they miss their mama, so I guess we all are screwed. I will ask you one more time. Get out." Danny hissed.

"Daniel." Charlie began to cry.

"Did you not know or did you not care? When you said you would do anything to get Kisseis back, did you know Madeline would be collateral damage?"

"She knew, she knew everything … she just thought she had another few days to prepare," Charlie whispered. "It was the only way to save you and the kids."

"It's why she was going to let me go to Mexico… To send me away. Then she was going to send the kids to Houston. I found a note she had started writing to me. Kisseis was planning to lure the dragon to her. You, as my godmother, should have told me." Danny was sobbing, his tears diluting his anger. "Why won't she wake up Charlie? I need her to wake up. The doctors woke her a month ago from her induced coma; all her burns are healed. She needs to wake up."

"I…" Charlie was about to say something when they heard the twins start screaming; Danny and Charlie raced to their room. Danny fell to his knees.

"Hello, husband." Madeline grinned as the kids climbed all over her. Danny kept nodding, unable to speak for minutes.

"Mama mama." Millie screamed frantically, "Daddy took us to the zoo and the square doughnut cafe and the museum and …"

"What was your favorite place, Peter Henry?" Madeline asked as now Millie was sitting on her shoulders. Peter Henry was standing in front of Madeline. Madeline hid a tear, shocked at how much he had grown.

"Here, with you." Peter Henry climbed on Madeline and kissed her cheek.

"Mama's probably still tired," Danny, overwhelmed could barely get the words out. "Let me get her back to the apartment, I'll come to get you, we'll take an afternoon nap together, then I'm buying everyone dinner!" The twins nodded. Madeline blew them kisses and blinked.

"It's ok," Madeline whispered in their apartment, trying to kiss all of Danny's tears away. But they kept coming. "Hey, we need to go see Ida."

"Wait…" Danny said. "I'm not done crying."

"It's important. And you'll cry more." Madeline said. They hugged for a very long time. Then Danny and Madeline walked hand in hand to Ida's apartment.

"Madeline." Ida was in a rocking chair as the couple came in. "You know…"

"She's alive," Madeline whispered. Ida smiled and burst into tears.

Made in the USA
Columbia, SC
04 October 2022

68522843R00267